I0664183

CONCEPT YUS

S E T   W A G N E R

Published by GRAVADANS PUBLISHING
ISBN: **0995740402**
ISBN 13: **9780995740402**
Cover art: YOULL ILLUSTRATION
Cover design: LOOSE CHANGE STUDIO

PART ONE

CHAPTER 1

I was at the Special Sector gate ten minutes early. I thought this would give me enough time to make my appointment, but the exaggerated formalities before I was allowed to enter took longer than I expected. Then I learned that Enzo Genetti, the chief of the sector and the person on whose behalf I was supposedly invited here, didn't even know about our meeting. While his secretary looked for him, or for some other unknown reason, I was kept waiting at the gate.

It was nearly noon when I finally arrived at Genetti's office. I knocked, took the raspy exclamation from within as an invitation, and walked in. Behind a huge desk boasting only a telephone sat a dry old man, around seventy, in a baggy laboratory jacket with rolled-up sleeves.

"So you're Terence Simon!" he said accusingly, his nearsighted eyes flashing. Clearly unhappy with my appearance, he glared at me as I sat down across from him. After staring a few seconds longer, he suddenly blurted out, "You're young. You don't look more than thirty!"

He shook his head reproachfully.

"Mmm, yes—obviously Franklin underestimated."

"Professor, it would be best not to question my chief's judgment," I suggested coldly. "If you really need the cooperation of the International Bureau of Investigation, let's not waste time with unnecessary chitchat."

But the white-haired scientist had already turned away and was looking somewhere to the side, slowly rubbing his finger against his unshaved cheek. That quiet, but intrusive, scraping sound emphasized the silence between us, increasing my anxiety. All morning a premonition of imminent danger had haunted me, which increased rapidly as I shifted in the uncomfortable chair, waiting for Genetti to turn back and explain why I was here.

"I'm listening to you," I finally said, encouraging him.

"Good!" he said intimidatingly. "Then listen well. About a year ago, we were given an opportunity to establish a colony on another planet. The first and only one—for now. You would be wise to take careful note of this, Simon! So, in complete secrecy, our sector was established for the specific purpose of preparing and organizing that colonization."

"Established by whom?" I asked.

"The Center for Space Exploration, naturally," Genetti replied, not very convincingly, and continued quickly. "Preparations are nearly complete. According to the plan, colonization was scheduled to begin in two months." Narrowing his eyes, Genetti leaned toward me and added sadly, "But that is no longer possible. Now its initiation depends on you. And please understand this: the sooner, the better! Mmm…yes…the sooner."

As his voice faltered, I sensed his unease and again took the initiative. "Please be more specific, Professor. How can the IBI be of use to you?"

Genetti peeled a soiled Band-Aid off his right thumb and stared closely at an almost imperceptible scratch. "Two scientists at the base are dead," he murmured.

"I see." I automatically added, "Under what circumstances?"

"I don't know. All I know is that they died at the same time, one hundred ninety-seven days after they landed on the planet."

"Was it homicide? Or an accident?"

"Unfortunately, it's possible it wasn't homicide." Genetti examined his hands.

"'Unfortunately'? How should I interpret that, Professor?"

He raised his eyebrows, feigning surprise. "Isn't it clear to you what such an accident would mean? Postponing colonization for fact-finding commissions and investigations, maybe even a public scandal, would compromise the whole project—not just this sector but the center itself!"

I shrugged my shoulders. The prestige of the center didn't concern me much. I opened my mouth to say that, but Genetti stopped me with an abrupt gesture.

"An unfortunate incident like this could mean something worse, Simon. Something much more frightening."

Rising, he began pacing back and forth, rubbing his chin and grimacing, sighing loudly and throwing me meaningful glances. If he wanted to pressure me with such obviously contrived and theatrical gestures, he would never succeed. On the other hand, his circuitous talk and abrupt shifts had already pushed my patience close to the limit.

"And what would that something be, Professor?" I inquired, still politely.

"What would it be!" he exclaimed. "Yes, I'll tell you. Conflict with the Yusians—that's what!" Observing the surprised expression on my face with satisfaction, he concluded, "Well, how do you feel about that, Inspector Simon?"

When I didn't respond, Genetti fell or, to be more precise, collapsed into his chair.

"The problem, Simon, is that the planet we intend to colonize belongs to the Yusians. They had just given us permission to settle it. It's very close to Yus."

"To where!" I couldn't believe my ears. "Close to Yus?"

"Yes, it's in the Ridon and Shidexa system. That's the reason for—" He shuddered and worriedly looked around. "But the details aren't important. What matters is that the colonization must take place as soon as possible."

"Even if the unfortunate incident was caused by conditions on the planet?"

"Maybe…yes…no, no! Only an unpredictable anomaly could have caused the incident—nothing else seems likely! The data is unambiguous: according to all life indices, Eyrena is almost like Earth."

"Almost?"

"Yes, since in many respects, conditions there are better than on Earth: rich vegetation, a more temperate climate, and more oxygen. In short, picture Earth, but without people, and then you will understand what Eyrena is like."

"Who is the source of this data? The Yusians?"

"Yes, they provided both a general overview of the planet and specific details. And I *repeat*," Genetti emphasized with growing irritation, "conditions there are *ideal*."

"Or ideal for dying," I noted. "How many people are still at the base?"

"Five—three men and two women."

"What shape are they in?"

"They're in perfect physical condition."

"And psychological?"

"They are very stable, Simon. As you might guess, they were not chosen randomly. I assume their psychological condition is still good. While the incident probably upset them, it would hardly have thrown them off balance."

"'I assume,' 'probably,' 'hardly'—your expressions are very indefinite, Professor."

"I'm afraid you're right. We haven't received detailed information from them. The distance and these disruptions—"

"How long have they been on Eyrena? How often have you been in contact with them?" I really needed more precise information.

The professor was obviously under great strain. Our meeting was no doubt being monitored and recorded, which forced him to respond not only to me but also to the hidden microphones and cameras planted around us. That came with the territory for the head of a "Special Sector."

"Today is the—one hundred ninety-ninth day—of their stay," he said, pausing between his words and rocking dangerously on the back legs of his chair. "And we have had seven transmissions. The last one was yesterday. That is when we learned of the accident."

"Really? And what's the average amount of information you receive during one transmission?"

"About a megabyte."

"Very strange, Professor!" I stopped trying to hide my indignation. "Just how do you intend to accomplish this colonization? This planet is no one knows how many light-years from Earth, so we would be completely dependent on the Yusians. Given that fact, who in their right minds would volunteer to travel to Eyrena, even if it is as hospitable as you claim? And if there are volunteers, do you really have the right to send them?"

While I was talking, Genetti had unexpectedly become livelier. He was nodding energetically, even approvingly, but that just increased my irritation. Why was he agreeing with me? Wasn't he one of the creators of this insane project?

"To launch a handful of volunteers without providing them with at least moral support," I continued, "to send them such a distance, and to leave them completely dependent upon the kindness of the Yusians—that's a crime! A vile betrayal."

"Spare me your personal feelings, Simon!" His voice sounded surprisingly sharp. "I'm trying to answer your questions, and that effort is more than enough for me."

He leaned back and slightly narrowed his eyes. His lips briefly seemed to form a thin, guilty smile, but I could have been wrong. I resumed the conversation, trying to avoid any hint of emotion.

"What's your plan for the first phase of the colonization?"

"On the appointed day, a ship will leave for Eyrena carrying only the colonists. Everything they need to sustain themselves will be sent from Yus."

"Who will be the first colonists?"

"Mostly volunteers, plus certain others—convicted criminals and the terminally ill."

"Do the Yusians know that?"

"Yes."

"And they agree?"

"Yes."

"And the friends and relatives of the convicts and the terminally ill—do they know?"

"They will be informed."

"And you think they will give their permission?"

"They won't be asked. Well, except for the closest relatives of the mentally ill, of course," Genetti explained with sudden enthusiasm. "And the convicts will go to Eyrena voluntarily, since they will be freed there. We should have little trouble convincing the terminally ill that it is also in their best interests; you have no idea what healing powers the Yusians are said to possess!"

"And are you aware of the other rumors about the Yusians?" I asked acidly.

He thought that over but finally dismissed it with a wave of his hand. "Rumors, merely rumors! I know of no confirmed incident where a Yusian has ever done—well, what they have been accused of doing. Of course, no Yusian has ever demonstrated healing powers either. But think about why that might be so: you know how limited our contacts have been with them. Under other conditions, however, why not? We can't be sure, right? So do we have the right to discourage the terminally ill from joining the colonists? They believe. Believe! Do you understand—"

I cut him off. "And what about the second phase of colonization?"

"There is no second phase. As soon as the ship arrives, a closed system will be formed: the Yus-Eyrena system."

"How will this happen?"

Leaning his elbows on the desk, he cracked his knuckles loudly and replied, "After the colonization, all communication between this system and Earth will be suspended for thirty years."

I hid my consternation, though it wasn't easy. "But why?" I asked quietly. "What purpose could that serve?"

"Those were the explicit conditions of our agreement, without which the Yusians would have refused to sign. And as to what our purpose is, even a child could understand that."

"Yes, but I didn't mean your purpose, Professor. I meant the Yusian—"

"Which makes your question even more meaningless," he snapped. "You know very well that their purposes have never been understandable to any human."

"So what you're saying is that you've entered into this agreement *on faith*, is that it?"

Genetti didn't answer me, but he didn't have to. Clearly, he had not been a party to either the negotiations or the so-called agreement. Someone at a much higher level had chosen to take this huge risk. But who? And why had the two of us been brought together here—this old man and me, two pawns in that someone's dangerous, maybe corrupt, game?

"Please show me yesterday's transmission, Professor."

"There's no need. I can quote the relevant part for you: 'Andrew Fowler and Hans Stein: dead. Date: March the twenty-sixth. Reasons: unknown.' That's it."

"Hmm. Are the people at the base working together with the Yusians?"

Genetti blinked, frightened. "With the Yusians?"

"Yes. What are the relations between your people and them?"

Perfect," he announced after a brief estimation, "because they've never met. The Yusians have a base about fifteen kilometers from ours, but so far they haven't paid us a single visit. Nor have we visited them, as you probably guessed yourself. Nor have we!" He grabbed his head and laughed—a short, loud, artificial laugh.

"But they must have established contact."

"No contact! Everyone minds his or her own business, and that's it!"

"What work did Fowler and Stein do?"

"Those at the base have many assigned tasks, Simon. With such a small group, that is necessary," Genetti responded evasively.

But that nonanswer gave me a pretty good idea: they were laying the foundations for an espionage network at the base on Eyrena, while, of course, they were also preparing to establish the colony. And the Yusians established their base not only to assist colonization but also to prevent our lingering beyond that period. Ah, but it would be good to get under their skin! And to get them out from under ours, even if only for thirty years. But at what price? Again I had to ask myself what devil would agree to such a cost of human lives?

"Professor, who chose the experts for this mission?"

"I don't know," he mumbled. "At a certain point in our preparations here, we informed those in charge at the center how many people we needed and what their skills should be. In a month they arrived—the exact personnel we had requested, without backups. After another month of training, they left for Eyrena."

"During their training you formed some opinion about their qualifications, didn't you?"

"No, I never even met them. As head of the sector, my duties are more theoretical and administrative."

"OK, but what do you expect of me? As I understand it, only you can give me the information I need, and it seems that you can tell me almost nothing."

"Ah, as you put it yourself, 'almost.' At least I have given you the general picture—as much as that's possible."

He reached for the telephone and picked up the receiver, held it in his hand for a while, and then put it back in its cradle. Then he went to the door and somehow opened it with his back, without taking his eyes off me. A trembling smile, like a nervous tic, appeared on his lips. After a few seconds, a middle-aged, poker-faced woman walked briskly into the office. Genetti led her to a huge cabinet near the window, unlocked it, and moved aside. From where I sat, I could see that it contained a massive, fireproof safe. When the woman bent to unlock it, I noticed the unmistakable bulge of a revolver beneath her simple, loose-fitting suit jacket. Function obviously outweighed fashion even for women in this business. She entered the triple code that opened the safe before silently leaving us.

Genetti took out a small black briefcase. "This is for you," he nearly shouted, moving toward the desk. "I'm leaving you the key too, and later you'll receive the code for the case inside. I assume it contains the files of those—at the base. Probably other papers as well."

He gripped the handle of the briefcase so tightly that his knuckles turned white. His eyes wandered wildly above my head; little drops of sweat glistened on his forehead. Something was clearly wrong, but I couldn't quite understand what.

"Thank you, Professor." I tried to include a warning note in my voice. "I hope these documents will help me complete my assignment."

Trembling as if with a chill, he pushed the briefcase across the desk, took an uncertain step backward, and then sat down heavily and pressed his temples with his hands. Whatever was causing his distress, I felt it would be best for both of us if he tried to pull himself together, so I quickly asked another question.

"When can you give me a copy of the official agreement?"

"I have no such copy." He spoke so quietly that I could bare-ly hear him.

"Oh, please, Professor! How can you *not* have a copy? I thought your work was governed by its specific requirements. Or did I misunderstand you?"

Genetti regarded me with a weary hostility as I continued to badger him.

"Surely, signing the agreement committed us to particular obligations that needed to be fulfilled—and fulfilled diligently. I mean, we're talking about Yusians, not some charitable organization. Isn't that so, Professor Genetti? Yet now you tell me that the sector charged with carrying out those obligations has no idea what they are? Your sector must be very 'Special' indeed!"

"Enough! Everything is quite—normal. It's just that we have separate groups, and the work of each is strictly classified. Each receives its assignment from the directorate"

"Aha! And you, the chief of this Special Sector, don't know what these groups directly under your authority are doing? Excuse me, but what are you coordinating then—maybe the domino tournaments between them or the performances of their musical groups?"

"This is taking us nowhere, young man!" Genetti exploded, reinforcing his exclamation with a few incomprehensible Italian expressions.

He was right. We *were* getting nowhere.

I tried again, very calmly. "Fine. Just tell me exactly why I'm here."

He sighed heavily, as if the hardest part of our conversation was yet to come—and unavoidable. As we sat in silence, I seemed to sense an underlying tone of menace in the concatenation of city sounds that floated into the office.

Finally Genetti roused himself enough to continue, "You must solve this crime, Simon, no matter what it takes. Do you understand me?"

"Are you hoping that I will twist the truth to do your feckless sector a favor? To make it easier for you to accomplish this pitiful project, conceived by a gang of mad cowards? That, no matter what it takes, I too will do my part to satisfy the whims of the Yusians?"

Almost fatherly concern seemed to flicker in his tired, dark eyes.

"Not just for those reasons, Simon," he said gently, "not just for that. On Eyrena you will have a chance to understand the situation better than I can, better than anyone on Earth could. Just don't rush your decisions! It's easier for some people to sacrifice themselves than to judge if that makes sense, and such people sometimes cause harm that even the worst bastard or coward would be incapable of inflicting."

As I listened to him, I could see the journey that awaited me with merciless clarity: in an isolated chamber on a monstrous Yusian starship, I would be locked in, looked at with inhuman curiosity, left alone.

"You have to understand me, Simon—you have to!" Genetti doggedly tried to hold my gaze. "Do you think that during this year I haven't asked myself the same questions you are asking now? And other questions you will ask yourself later? And questions you would probably never ask yourself? Oh, thousands of times! But even if I have found the answer to some of them, so what? I—

"But why are we talking about me?" He waved his hand in a gesture of grief and self-humiliation. "We're just wasting time."

He slowly moved to the window and stood there looking out before turning to me again. His huge laboratory suit drooped in ugly wrinkles over his frail body, the unbuttoned collar revealing thin, angular collarbones. His shabby shoes looked enormous under his scrawny ankles. I only now realized what a small and brittle old man he actually was.

"Eyrena!"

I strained to understand his whispers.

"What if it's our only chance? You understand me, don't you? Don't you? Those—creatures! Maybe they will finally leave us alone, and we—"

He didn't have the strength to continue. Or perhaps he had found the strength to stop. His white head dropped as if he were awaiting sentencing.

I stood up. The awareness that I was going to go away from this man, probably forever, without telling him anything positive, bothered me. But all I could offer was, "I'll do my best to complete the investigation quickly, Professor."

As I took the key to the briefcase, his face suddenly turned deadly pale. I stared at him, and he gave me an almost imperceptible nod, crossing his trembling hands in front of his chest. What did he mean by that!

I put the key in my jacket pocket and casually reached for the briefcase. As I grasped the handle, yes, I felt an oblong piece of foil, glued to its underside.

"If I have any additional questions, I'll find a way to reach you," I concluded, while unobtrusively removing the foil with a twist of my thumb and placing it between my pointer and middle fingers.

"You will hardly have time to do that," Genetti said hoarsely, "since the starship conveying you to Eyrena will be launched from the Erdland site at five p.m. today." Then he gasped for air, his terrified eyes staring at my fingers.

"Today! At five! That's the limit! And what if I hadn't accepted your proposal?"

As I had hoped, this last stupid question revived him like smelling salts. He answered contentiously, "I'm not offering you a trip on a gondola, Inspector! And I certainly haven't asked you to accept anything!"

Then he stopped, looked at me cunningly and smiled.

"Well, go, Simon—go! I wish you a speedy return. And good luck!"

He stepped back and hid his hands behind his back, confused—a handshake, of course, would reveal our secret. I tried to thank him with a nod as I picked up the suitcase and walked toward the door, but I don't think he understood what I meant.

CHAPTER 2

Leaning against the wall just across from the professor's office were two husky Neanderthals, complete with sloping foreheads and jutting jaws. As soon as I walked out the door, they attached themselves to me.

"Sorry, but you'll have to come with us," one of them muttered politely. He had an impeccable face and scarred knuckles, cause for sober reflection.

I inquired, also politely, "Where?"

"There," the other answered noncommittally. He had thick muscles, broad shoulders, keen eyes, and an unreadable expression on his face.

I looked around. Not a soul in the long corridor. Yes, there was certainly a sudden interest in my eternally priceless self. I had become a ticking time bomb of compromising information, so someone was making sure I didn't go off before I was safely ensconced in the Yusian starship. After that, there would be no reason to worry—since there could be no greater isolation on this side of the grave.

So far, so good. But where was "there"? These people were not amateurs, and the Genetti interview had its flaws. If their monitoring had picked up on those, I could expect a quick and thorough search.

With that last thought, the piece of foil seemed to burn my fingers. I had to do something quickly. I could claim a misunderstanding later, if necessary. I casually shifted the briefcase to my left hand and was about to step forward when the two, as if on cue, closed in and pinned me between their shoulders. I could feel their muscles tense, but their expressions remained serene. I took the hint and, rather than create a scene, forced myself to relax. In fact, why hurry?

I hesitated for only a few seconds but long enough to make my new companions uneasy, so I nodded, and we moved down the empty corridor like a single unit. Soon we changed directions from the way I had entered, crossing the elevator landing and passing through a carefully hidden exit. Then, still shoulder to shoulder, we descended a narrow, spiral staircase. When we reached the ground floor, my companions checked their watches almost simultaneously and then grew visibly calmer. I relaxed too: if our handling of the foil had been detected, the retaliation measures couldn't be this elaborate, not with these needless delays and their preoccupation with the exact time. Clearly they haven't discovered anything so far, but what was Genetti trying to tell me? It must be something extremely important to take such a crazy risk.

Across from the staircase were two dark bulletproof doors, side by side. We stood near the one on the right, and the built-in monitor flashed "Synchronizing B5–D3." With a slight nod, my companions directed me to the left door. As we approached, it quietly opened, releasing an unrecognizable pungent odor, but the room was empty. We crossed through to another door and started down a labyrinth of low, brightly lit corridors. We still moved three abreast, evenly, which I guess pleased whoever was observing us, but I was finding the whole journey more and more torturous.

An alarm clock was going off in my head, telling me to end this charade, when events entered a new and thus slightly more hopeful phase. After they checked their watches again, we picked up our pace significantly until we encountered a massive metal gate. My companion with the battered knuckles worked the control panel, and the barrier slowly opened. We stepped out of the building into a back parking lot just as an ambulance pulled up and stopped in front of us. The driver, a white-coated misanthrope, waited until we were settled in the side seats before skillfully maneuvering out of the lot and speeding off.

Meanwhile, the two Neanderthals also donned white coats. Then out of their pockets appeared surgical bonnets, which they jammed on their heads to complete their flimsy attempt to pass for hospital attendants.

"Very elaborate, boys!" I complimented them, momentarily impressed by their efforts.

The "boys," of course, simply stared at me without blinking, their faces as blank as the tinted window behind them. The bonnets didn't look good on them.

When we exited the sector premises, the driver turned on the siren. As the ambulance rushed through the foggy, unfamiliar city, I hoped—but did not expect—to be taken directly to the launch site. Instead, we jumped on the south freeway. As the haze lifted, the lights of a low-slung sports car glittered in front of us, while the dark-blue Toyota I had glimpsed earlier behind us now grew clearer and closer. We shifted to the far-left lane, despite the light traffic and our moderate speed. A black BMW replaced the Toyota. The sports car stopped. We passed it and zipped forward as if unleashed, or maybe as if we were being chased.

After passing the first motel, we exited and turned down an empty back road, followed by the BMW. A disturbing rattle came from the medicine cabinet next to me, and the stretcher on the floor rocked clumsily, flipping its carefully folded sheet onto the feet of one of my companions. He kicked it back, anxiously touched his bonnet, and sank again into gloomy apathy.

A few minutes passed, dull enough to make my eyes blur before they glimpsed the wings of an iron gate. The ambulance slowed to a crawl as we drove down the narrow paved drive. The boys both perked up—obviously the moment of our separation was approaching. My uncertainties prevented me from sharing their joy. Wherever we were going, the fact that they didn't hide the road from me was hardly a manifestation of trust.

We stopped in front of a modest building with a sign above the main entrance: "Milera Private Clinic." Though nothing was any clearer than before, by now I was ready to destroy that piece of foil without even reading it first. Six people met us outside as we exited the ambulance. Two devoted their attention to me, while one went back to the BMW that had followed us in. After a few words were exchanged, the car turned around and drove back down the drive. The last three had joined the ambulance driver and the boys, who now seemed quite nervous. Obviously events had not gone as anticipated.

I entered the clinic with my two new companions. In the lobby, the younger one quickly reached for my briefcase. I pretended I didn't see him until he peevishly whispered, "Give it to me!"

Seeing no way to avoid the inevitable, I turned as if to hand him the briefcase. When he reached for the handle, I kicked him in the knee. As his leg collapsed, I kicked him in the neck. As the briefcase fell to the tile floor, he tried to regain his balance. His partner instinctively caught him under the armpits but a moment later dropped him and made a rapid, almost successful, attempt to smash my nose. Wrestling one another, we fell to the floor. A fat man now approached us at a loud trot. Soon he was moving in circles around us, looking for a convenient moment to show his abilities. Finally he kicked my ear. When he lifted his leg a second time, I managed to grab it. I pulled him down sharply, attached the foil to the sole of his shoe and rolled to the side as he fell. A scream convinced me that he had flattened our "sparring partner." As I started to rise, the first one showed me that he had recovered: his fist hit my head with the force of a mace. I put off my getting up for a while.

I was dragged up the stairs, my ear buzzing like an over-heated electrical coil. I wasn't feeling well. Psychologically either, but not that bad. After all, there was a possibility the old man could escape discovery. Actually my attempt to hide the foil wasn't very clever, but with a little luck. When they don't find anything on me, these guys will ransack the ambulance and its crew, the lobby, even their own clothes. But they might not check the soles of their shoes right away, and under the weight of the fat man, that foil should be rubbed out in no time.

We entered a luxuriously equipped changing room, where a flight suit lay ready for me. Obviously the airport was nearby, but I wasn't exactly anxious to get there. Two of my guards pulled out chairs and sat down, waiting for me to undress, their eyes glued to my hands. The third guard, the one so interested in my briefcase in the lobby, now tackled it. He limped over to a corner table, unlocked the briefcase with his own key, and turning to watch me, proceeded to open the lid slowly, with two fingers. Despite his apparent impassivity, his eyes eagerly anticipated a reaction from me, but he was to be disappointed. I merely pulled a clean towel off the shelf next to me, put it across my shoulders, and kept watching him.

Finally he flipped the lid back, donned a pair of plastic gloves, and carefully started cutting something inside with a razor blade. I recognized the rustling sound of unfolding cellophane as he pulled out a flat metal case. Then, from under the table, he produced a similar briefcase, only gray. He transferred the metal case into it and, with a flourish, pushed the new briefcase toward me. I crossed to him, picked it up, and headed for the bathroom, not without noticing that the black briefcase now contained nothing but the ripped cellophane wrapping.

Between the changing room and the showers was a narrow, oblong hall, ideally suited for, thus confirming my belief that I would be subjected to, a thorough laser examination. As I passed through it, I fervently wished that all such searches would be as futile. I then put the new briefcase far from the showers and went under one of them. For some time I diligently alternated the warm and cold water, which is supposed to ease the swelling of bruises, clumsily wrapped the towel around me, and then returned to the changing room.

It was empty. The black briefcase, as well as all of my personal belongings of course, was gone. Like it or not, I was forced to don the flight suit. As soon as I was dressed, one of my guards reappeared at the door. Carefully scrutinizing me, he crossed the room toward me, followed by two people in PSD uniforms and another man, a civilian. Without exchanging a word, we left the room together. And what could we have had to say to each other indeed?

CHAPTER 3

I was led into a spacious room with drawn blinds and soft, luminescent lighting. A short, plump Chinese man stood next to the door, gently smiling at me. I recognized him instantly: that wide, fleshy nose; those deep-set, sly eyes; and the thin lips, always stretched into a smile. In short, before me was Vey A. Zung himself, heartily extending his chubby, well-groomed hand to me. I took it listlessly, and after a long handshake accompanied by many friendly nods, he waved hospitably toward the table in the middle of the room.

As we sauntered over, the plainclothesmen took their places and stood at attention, while the other two from PSD marched on either side of us and pointed to one of the huge leather armchairs with icy politeness. Zung waited for me to sit down before, fastidiously adjusting his trouser legs and sitting across from me in a chair specially equipped with multicolored buttons. After his security team carefully checked out the room, making sure there was no apparent danger, they marched out in a straight row through the slightly opened door. While I was watching them, I felt an oppressive, exploring stare, filled with tangible malevolence, crawl over me. Yet when I turned around, my famous host was glowing with sympathy and responsiveness.

"A cup of coffee?" he offered. When I accepted, he was obviously surprised. Nevertheless, he pressed a button and started smiling again. No matter how silly it was, I smiled back. What else could I do?

Soon a young man, his face as wide and flat as a griddle, peeked in the room. He squeezed inside, balancing an exquisitely embossed silver salver, and inched his way toward us. As he began to serve the coffee, Zung patted him on his bent back.

"This is my nephew!" he announced with pride. "He not only makes perfect coffee but also has many other skills."

The nephew straightened up, flipping his straight bangs back from his forehead. He tried to appear unmoved by this praise, but when he couldn't muffle his spontaneous chuckle, he grabbed the empty tray and ran out of the room.

Once we were alone, Zung decided it was time to get down to business. "I know the head of your bureau well, and I trust his choice completely."

The first part was true, but I knew that the rest was a lie.

We exchanged friendly looks. Zung continued, "You have already talked to Professor—hmm, hmm?"

"Yes."

"Enzo Genetti."

"Yes."

"So everything is clear to you?"

"I would be exaggerating to say that, Mr. Zung."

"I'm not referring to that terrible double tragedy—"

"Nor am I."

A slight shadow of displeasure crossed his face: the special chairman of the Security Council wasn't accustomed to being interrupted.

"What was your name again, young man?" he asked politely but intimidatingly.

"Simon. Terence Simon."

"Ah, yes. Monsieur Simon. No, Terence! Allow me to call you Terence. You could be my son."

Now that struck me as absurd. "Of course, Mr. Zung!" I said with a youthful affability. I was very nervous, and every minute spent with him increased my tension. It's common knowledge that no one is eager to meet him.

"Let me put your mind at ease, Terence!" Zung sipped his coffee, quietly smacking his lips. "Your assignment is not as difficult as it seems. Except for the inconveniences of the trip, the investigation itself should be a piece of cake—even prosaic."

He shook his head as if overcome momentarily with grief and then settled more comfortably into his chair before beginning his *pitch*. "This is what happened on Eyrena, Terence. A scientific competitiveness gradually grew between Fowler and Stein, two talented and ambitious scientists. At first they tried to hide it, even from themselves. Their noble characters resisted such an assault on their dignity, such a contradiction of scientific ethics, but—"

Zung raised his finger enthusiastically, as if he were coming to the moral of his story.

"But the antagonism grew stronger, penetrating deep into their hearts. It was poisoning them! The desire to dominate, to conquer this new, virgin world, turned out to be stronger than their moral scruples.

"Still, their quarrel would probably never have led to murder if the young and strikingly beautiful Linda Ridgeway had not been working at the base. Fowler and Stein were scientists, but they were also men, and both men fell madly in love with this charming colleague. First rivals in work and then rivals in love. As the saying goes, 'the stronger the passion, the sadder its end.' Unfortunately! That's the story." Zung spread out his short hands, sadly smiling.

"Aha! I see," I said with barefaced irony. "It *is* rather poetic."

"Isn't it!"

"But if this is so obviously the situation, Mr. Zung, why must I even make the journey to Eyrena?"

"Well, dear Terence"—he sighed—"all of us are slaves to formalities. When the colonization, including the deaths of Fowler and Stein, is revealed to the public, we will need to be able to refer to an official investigation."

"And you think the public will believe this science/love triangle as the motive for two murders?"

My words inspired hilarious laughter. "Fortunately, ordinary people are not as suspicious as those in your profession, Terence. And your bureau has a good reputation."

"Well, yes, as does the Center for Space Exploration. The difference is that we would not agree to serve the initiatives of others, especially such an initiative as the colonization of Eyrena, nor would we allow our investigations to be influenced by others. The IBI wouldn't risk being discredited, Mr. Zung."

He skillfully ignored my comments about the center and responded only to my final phrase. "To be discredited? What a strange notion! Do you find something unconvincing about our incident? Similar incidents occur on Earth every day. Why shouldn't they happen on Eyrena? A man is a man, no matter where you send him. It's naive to suppose that Fowler and Stein left their flaws behind them, right?"

I finished my coffee and added bluntly, "I imagine that others at the base will offer different versions of what happened there."

"Of course. It's their right to believe what they will."

"Yes, but when they return to Earth—"

"They won't return, Terence."

"Why!"

Zung crossed his legs and admired his diminutive, highly polished shoes before replying. "Because they will be the first of the colonists. Our goal is to send people to Eyrena, not to bring them back to Earth, right?"

"But when they arouse suspicions among the new arrivals, then—"

Again he cut me off. "That shouldn't concern you, Terence. You have enough worries."

"My biggest concern has always been to work in the light, Mr. Zung."

"But I'm not the sun, my friend!" he exclaimed, playfully pressing his palms together as if he were praying.

I began to understand why my boss always raves for days after visiting the venerable Mr. Zung. Still, I decided to forge ahead. "Do you suppose the Yusians had anything to do with the deaths of Fowler and Stein?"

His face grew sphinxlike. "So far, none of us has entered the world of their thoughts, Terence."

"But if they did have something to do with this," I persisted, "wouldn't your version about fatal passions surprise them, to say the least?"

"No, Terence. Just the opposite! It will convince them of our loyalty."

"'Loyalty'! What are you talking about?" I mumbled, confused.

"Yes, yes." Zung closed his eyes. "Loyalty. Exactly! At present, we have no other choice. We must be loyal."

I listened with shock and consternation. Have we sunk so low?

"It's possible that Fowler and Stein are accidental victims of some Yusian reactionary group," he posited in a monotone, "or that they had become—unsuitable—for some reason. Anything is possible. But whatever happened is their own business. We aren't foolish enough to try to pull someone else's chestnuts out of the fire!"

"Nor would you pull me out if I were in danger of being burned," I added.

Zung shook his finger at me. "Look how suspicious you are! You clearly graduated from Franklin's training. But anyway, that's not so bad. 'Distrust is half wisdom,' as the Romans said." He smiled, winked at me and then became stern. "Let's be serious, Terence! If there is any danger for you, it could hardly be from the Yusians. It's most likely they had nothing to do with the incident. But even if they are connected, so what? As long as you are in their starship, or on Eyrena, naturally they won't touch you, because that would amount to a clear confession that they were involved in the other two deaths! And most importantly, if Yusians are involved, no doubt they have already protected themselves from any danger of disclosure."

Even if he were talking about humans, his words made no sense, but in reference to Yusians they were absurd, as he understood perfectly. Meanwhile, the damn flight suit was becoming more and more uncomfortable—my ear was burning, and my face was much the worse for wear after being hit by his man. On top of that, I had to listen to his nonsense.

"We can be sure of two facts, Terence!" he abruptly changed the subject. "First, the Yusians insist on this colonization. And second, we are in no position to challenge them at the moment. But we can snoop around a little, right?"

"Perhaps," I replied, "but why are you telling me this? My specialty is investigating crimes, and *snooping* into Yusian business has always been your area of competence, as you have often insisted."

"True, but the situation has changed. There is no point in lying to you, Terence, Franklin has never paid attention to those parameters." Narrowing his eyes, he asserted, "The secret archives of the IBI are probably full of materials about Yusians."

"That may be," I offered, narrowing my eyes as well, "but I'm not familiar with any such materials. They weren't relevant to my investigations. And now, when I do need information, you have obstructed me. Is your main goal to prevent me from contacting Franklin?"

"Whatever my goal is, it's for your own good," Zung announced impudently. "You have to go to Eyrena—unprejudiced."

"So far we have exchanged only nonsense," I complained. "Now I want you to give me the full information you have on the Yusians."

"But, in fact, I don't have any information." His continued impudence shocked me. "I have gathered this and that, but it's only been heard, seen, described, and not understood. Can what is not understood be called information?"

"Don't exaggerate!" I said angrily. "Ever since the Yusians came, you have engaged our most authoritative academies and institutions, our most talented scientists, to analyze those facts you gathered, haven't you?"

"And what do you think they've offered me so far? Only some vague guesses and dubious hypotheses. So, in this regard, Terence, what I have has already been given to you."

Zung pointed to the briefcase at my side.

"But I'm leaving this afternoon. When am I going to study? Should I take aboard the Yusian starship—what I was given!"

"Of course. Why not?"

"Listen, Mr. Zung, let's be rational."

"We really don't have any information, Terence," he murmured, his voice suddenly weary. "So tell me, how can we 'be rational' in this case?"

Then he shrugged his shoulders and sighed with suppressed reproach. I realized my objections would have to wait: the special chairman of the Security Council was about to perform his next pantomime. He seemed to shrink before me—his arms, searching for support, helplessly flopped on the armrests of the chair. With a new sigh of suffering, he dropped his head and wearily closed his eyelids. Before my eyes emerged a man wrongfully tortured and subdued by terrible worries. At first I was annoyed by such a performance, until a thought gradually entered my mind: after ten years in his position, how else could he really feel?

"Ye-es, dear Terence, yes, such great responsibilities weigh heavily on my shoulders," he began. "Oh, what responsibilities! Decisions have to be made. Important decisions. Even crucial ones! And whether they are going to be the right ones will depend also on you. Don't ever limit yourself only to the investigation. Other things are even more important. So many years we have been living as if we were blind. This can't continue! It's true that, so far, the Yusians have demonstrated goodwill, but for how long? Psychologically, their superiority has already crippled us with a sense of our own inferiority. They created complexes in us from the day they arrived. Do you remember?"

"Yes, but—"

"But what? What 'but'!" he interrupted me, nearly shouting. "Do you realize the state that the human race is in by now? The worldwide crisis? Stagnation, moral and psychological collapse! And do you know that the Yusians still refuse to explain to me what purposes those diabolic constructions around their embassy serve? Yet they want us to give them lands to use forever so they can build *more* structures like that! What if they are some kind of weapon? What then? Can you imagine how I feel when I see us moving closer and closer to our destruction but can do nothing—and just have to smile at those monsters, to be polite to them and wonder what compromises I should offer to keep our relationship with them at least at its current level? At least, because it could get worse. And it will, if we don't finally take some measures. Drastic ones!"

Zung doubled his fists and pounded them on the table. He was breathing rapidly, his eyes burning with anger and hatred. "There is only one way out, Terence! The colonization! It will interrupt our relationship with them—will buy us time to recover, to make our own advances. Because among the colonists, besides criminals and the terminally ill, will be many talented and brave people. They will mingle with the Yusians, get to know them, and learn their vulnerabilities. And Eyrena will not be completely inaccessible for us. I, and after me my successors, will visit it every year."

"How?"

"The Yusian starship will take us there and back, from our moon. Thank God, we can at least get there on our own! So the isolation of Earth itself will remain intact, while we'll be able to watch over the interests of the colonists."

"And also receive the reports of those *talented* people you mentioned," I added. In fact, I was beginning to think his plan was very well designed.

"Exactly!" Zung confirmed passionately. "And one more huge benefit: according to the agreement, after the thirty years are over—when, I'm sure, we will also have our own flotilla of starships—Eyrena will be ours! Ours, can you imagine? A *new* Earth! With untouched resources and in a conveniently strategic position, close to Yus. Soon we'll be able to act from a position of strength, Terence! It's in our nature to succeed. We have the ambition, the readiness to fight, and the eagerness to win. And the Yusians?"

He threw back his head and laughed contemptuously. "They lack our human soul! Their only advantage is that they appeared a few millennia earlier. In spite of that, we *will* take the place we deserve. And that must be first place—nothing less would do!"

His optimism was contagious. I could imagine humanity starting to chant its triumphal hymns. Still, I had to ask, "Well, yes, but what if the causes for Fowler and Stein's deaths turn out to lie in the planet itself?"

"I already explained to you what the causes for their deaths were!" Zung replied abruptly. "And remember, the project will be realized. In any case!"

"Even if we have to pay the price of other victims, maybe hundreds of them, among the colonists?"

"Yes! So that billions of other people can live."

"But what is the sense of that? If Eyrena is unsuitable for us."

"We'll still have thirty years without Yusian interference. That's something."

I wearily disagreed. "No. I can't accept this way of thinking."

Zung exploded, "Listen, Terence, and understand! The Earth must have a different future; we cannot and will not go on this way. I intend to see to that, no matter the cost. No matter what! And as for you, it's in your best interest—"

I interrupted him right away, "I'm not used to ultimatums, Mr. Zung. If you expect to find in me your next obedient pawn, you will be disappointed. And I may well have supporters."

He crossed his arms and asked tauntingly, "Who? From whom will you gain this support, Terence? From the Yusians?"

"If they are benevolent, why not?"

"Because you're human, that's why! I know you will endure anything—everything!—rather than ask them for help. You know that too."

When I remained silent, Zung nodded at me, satisfied and somewhat disdainful. "Your assignment is clear, isn't it? Fulfill it, and you won't be sorry. Vey A. Zung takes care of his people."

He looked at his watch, and I, assuming that he wanted to finish the meeting, willingly rose from my armchair.

"Sit down, sit down!" His face was glowing with kindness. "We still have more time."

Soon the telephone rang, and Zung quickly picked up the receiver. I could guess what he was expecting. After listening to a monologue, he hung up and stared sadly for a long time at the opposite wall. Finally he purred, "Now, Terence, that we have agreed to work together, I can confide in you. It's better that you didn't read the note on the foil. It would only have confused you."

Too bad! His people were quick. The old professor was in trouble, and for nothing.

"Why do you think I didn't read it?" I tried to add a tone of irony.

Zung shrugged his shoulders condescendingly. "Genetti was a talented scientist," he reminisced, lost in thought, "but as a person—now, remembering him, I understand: he was very suspicious too."

The smile on his face belied the threat of murder haunting his eyes! Tilting his head, he looked at me with real curiosity while his finger casually pressed a button. Three people came in. When I rose, they surrounded me on three sides. Then Vey A. Zung approached and heartily shook my hand.

CHAPTER 4

I was not surprised to be taken to a secret airport near the "clinic." A Mirage, ready for takeoff, awaited me there. Once Zung's people made sure that I was safely aboard in the rear cabin, their car pulled away. Settling the briefcase on my lap, I then put on the communication helmet provided. Of course, nothing was being communicated to—or from—me. The pilot revved up the engines, and we took off.

Seized by the usual vertigo, I watched the ground recede until the plane sliced through the clouds and rose above them. As the world gave way to endless azure, reality expanded as well, acquiring a new, dual meaning. Not simply a measure, time was now eternity and a fiction, space not a road to elsewhere but infinity and an optical illusion, our movement not a direction but life itself—and its impossibility.

Gradually the passing scene shrank to invisibility, and the peace of resignation cradled me in its arms, until my nagging conscience quickly put an end to this relaxation. Never before had I flown without some control over where I was going and who was taking me there, without any orientation or even assurance of my final aim. What if we were not going to the Erdland launch site? Couldn't it be that, if I had a backup and he had been better at negotiating, Zung would certainly replace me? Then my destiny would probably be similar to Genetti's.

Genetti—I won't forget him. *If I survive, whether here or on Eyrena, I will remember him often, Mr. Zung. And I will remind you of him as well, at the first opportunity!*

My sense of time completely disrupted—first the flight seemed too long and then the landing much too soon. For a moment I couldn't believe our journey was ending, but our velocity downward quickly convinced me—and also taught me the value of our training sessions at the military air base.

The ocean emerged from its misty shroud, noiselessly roaring against our intrusion. Its waves swelled larger and higher, like hundreds of trembling manes of light, glimmering and darkening, stretching endlessly away from us. Then the plane veered sharply toward the turbulent gulf in the distance. As we skimmed just above its surface, my heartbeat matched the surf beating against the rocks, my staring eyes misted with the white steam coating the rocks to the sand line, dark from the rain, and I realized that the pilot had given me, his unknown companion, a gift. Yes, this was a man capable of great generosity. Never has anything struck me as so unbelievably beautiful as this bubbling, barren gulf below us—probably the last I would see on Earth.

Either my eyes simply refused to focus on anything else or the runway really did appear abruptly out of nowhere. We hurled headlong over it, then banked sharply, and were soon taxiing into a huge hangar. As we stopped, my communication helmet regained its voice: "Please enter the robocar that is coming for you."

I waited a few seconds for additional instructions. Receiving none, I picked up my briefcase and deplaned. I glanced through the window of the pilot's cabin but could see only a bent shoulder.

I climbed into the waiting robocar, and it set out. Heavy, armor-plated barriers lifted in front, freezing at a few centimeters above and then lowering behind the car with a thud. The cement track meandered downward, probably toward the very heart of the vast, underground complex. Again I had no idea where I was being taken and hadn't even noticed whether or not the complex was connected to the launch site. Such was the price of those sentimental moments I spent admiring the seascape at the end of the flight.

After turning into a side corridor, the robocar stopped. A stout, red-haired man in a military uniform warily approached me, gestured for me to follow him, and after a short walk, led me into a small, carefully arranged room.

"Please prepare yourself. Liftoff is in half an hour."

He closed the door behind him, and I was alone. So, it seemed that I had been cleared to travel. Suddenly this alternative, while preferable to the others I had contemplated, chilled me with its immediacy. How would I handle meeting the aliens? What would be their attitude toward me? What awaited me in their starship?

I started pacing the room. And why were they insisting that people settle on Eyrena? More generally, what has attracted them to us for all these years? They are searching for something. They want something that only we have! Maybe our flesh? Our brains?

A primal, almost savage panic rose in me. Yet somehow I also managed to remain detached, an observer ironically monitoring his own reactions and patiently waiting to see where they might lead. Walking over to the sofa, I stared blankly at its colorful upholstery until my eyes clouded over and a simple thought slowly and painfully emerged from the chaos in my head: *I should prepare myself for the liftoff.*

I opened the closet and discovered a new sports suit, a light-blue shirt, a pair of shoes, and underwear. In plain sight on one of the shelves lay a sphinx pistol with a holster and an unopened carton of bullets. In other words, I found everything I needed, including an electronic notepad and a watch supplied with a compass and various other devices.

I took off the flight suit and tried on my new clothes. Not surprisingly, my jacket was too tight, and the pants too loose. I was foolishly pleased that at least they were the right length— as if it mattered how I would look to the Yusians. Or even on Eyrena, after all, unless the breathtaking beauty Linda Ridgeway awakens a desire to impress her with my taste in clothes.

When the redhead returned, exactly on time, we climbed into the robocar, heading who knew where? Now the shelf behind us bore two bulky suitcases: my "personal" luggage. We entered a tunnel that led steeply upward, apparently to the above-ground exit. Exiting the robocar, we each took a suitcase, while I carried my briefcase as well. The escalator took us up to a small platform. As we crossed it, the door at the far end opened, and ahead of us spread an endless concrete expanse.

The rain had stopped, replaced by a damp, cool silence. A shiny new robot approached us and took the suitcases. A currently popular *retrofantastic* type with precisely human features, it wore the manufacturer's label, "ESSIKO," on its left shoulder. Then the redhead, relieved at having fulfilled his duties, wished me a prompt return and, stepping back, disappeared through the automatic door. At least *I* could no longer see *him*.

As I walked toward the Yusian starship, its unearthly blackness nearly blinded me, freezing the surrounding air into bright white outlines, and the slender connecting arcs of its fuselage glittered like lightning. Enormous, perfect, and absurd. And unshakeable! Its antigravity flaps fiercely grappled the ground; its stabilizers, which looked like suction pumps, dug in as if they were thirsty roots absorbing moisture.

The starship had landed between two of our launch pads and towered over the shuttles parked there. How tiny and vulnerable they seemed by comparison. These same shuttles, which had filled our hearts with pride as symbols of human progress until ten years ago, were nothing but feeble dwarfs next to the wizardry of the Yusians.

I started walking faster and then turned to glance over my shoulder at the robot. He was striding quietly and rhythmically behind me, my man of steel, silicone joints extending and contracting without a sound. Water drops glimmered on the angular shoulders: he must have waited for me in the rain. I slowed so he could catch up, and we continued on together.

Soon I could clearly distinguish the Yusians near the starship. They were lying in heaps on the concrete surface, their bodies jerking spasmodically. Their limbs would sometimes shorten and shrink until scarcely visible and at other times stretch to amazing lengths, slapping and bubbling in the puddles left by the rain. When I stopped, one of them rose and rushed toward me. For a moment I thought that we would crash and fought my impulse to jump aside.

He stopped short a meter away. His squared torso, split by deep horizontal clefts, towered above my head. Waves of heat rhythmically blasted from his body—maybe his breath? I was shaken with disgust. Only when my fingers began to tingle did I realize how tightly I had been clutching the handle of my briefcase. I transferred it to my other hand, just to have something to do, and then tried to appear relaxed as I waited for his next move.

Still trembling, the Yusian was rearranging himself, accompanied by an intermittent wheezing. Finally seeming satisfied with his appearance, he then pulled down the skin on his forehead and bit into it with his left aperture. Two huge milky lidless ovals slowly surfaced and stared at me. I starting feeling dizzy, almost paralyzed, and my head grew so heavy that I needed all my energy just to hold it up.

The Yusian, probably sensing my condition, bent backward and covered the eyes with his limbs. The effect produced was more bearable, and I began to regain my equilibrium. I knew that, according to established protocol, I was supposed to stand on his right side when I was ready to have a conversation. When I did so, the Yusian adjusted himself again, and his torso clefts slowly opened. I understood that he was about to talk.

"Will bodily connection with Eyrena be yours?" it asked me in intricate English.

"Yes," I croaked.

My short answer had a very strange effect on the creature: his body stretched upward, the whites of his eyes were swallowed by an amazing expansion of black pupils, and his voice intensified into a scream, "Our awaiting is stopping! Leave to go!"

We started walking toward the starship. The other Yusians had already gathered in front of its opening. They were swaying unpredictably, emitting continuous rumbling noises and moving closer and closer together, doing their best in order to express—who knows what?

We passed them and entered an elevator. Noiselessly we ascended to a room with many trembling ellipses at the edges. The Yusian moved toward the nearest one, crossed it, and was engulfed in rays of dense violet light. I followed uneasily, while the robot following me carried with ease both the suitcases and his serene electronic soul.

We found ourselves in a narrow gallery with high, curved brackets along the sides, from which spouted, as if from fountains, unbearably bright blue sparks that spread all around us without dying out. Almost blinded, I continued to follow the Yusian, trying to keep my distance from him—and from it all.

The gelatinous floor shivered and squelched under my feet as I constantly sank up to my ankles. I tried taking enormously wide steps but staggered and instinctively grabbed one of the idiotic brackets. Before I could open my fingers, it split up the middle and slipped, or more precisely flew, out from both sides of my clenched fist. Then the bulging ends thinned again and lengthened toward each other, reuniting forcefully but silently. I had the queasy feeling that I had touched something living: flexible, cool, and able to react. As far as I could see, my hand was unharmed, though it felt drier than the other one. The Yusian stopped, apparently to wait for me. It dawned on me that, if he thought I was having problems, he might want to support me himself, so I made a supreme effort to walk normally.

I was pleasantly surprised when we entered a spacious living room that looked entirely human and, most importantly, had ordinary illumination. The room was luxuriously furnished with a thick Persian rug, huge mahogany bookshelves filled with carefully arranged books, sumptuously comfortable sofas and armchairs, a cellaret, and an audio and video system.

"Will stay alive here without worries," the Yusian said.

"But how did you manage to arrange all this in such a short time?" I asked, pleased to hear my cordial, conversational tone of voice. "The decision to send me on this journey was made only last night."

Or maybe the decision wasn't made last night? I asked myself.

"Always we model anticipations in advance!" the Yusian sang enthusiastically, swaying to the rhythm of his words. "Will accomplish that what our persistence."

"Persistence" indeed! *And what might this persistence amount to?* When I met his manic gaze, my entire body shivered with disgust. I had no desire to answer him, nor did I know what to say. Nodding evasively, I waited for the Yusian to begin, hoping he would tell me what I needed to know and then leave me on my own, as far as that was possible on a starship.

"This robot be with you," the Yusian started again. "You ask for him travel advises only among agreements of human agent, but we not avoiding him too."

"Yes, yes," I vaguely confirmed my "asking." "I am glad that the human has received your agreement too. Did he visit you today?"

"He visited us. As a voice," the Yusian replied. "If surroundings outside make comfortable, then can embark on it now. Afterward it produce Yusian conditions, and some space suit obtrude on you."

I refused to "embark on" anything, so I simply stopped speaking once again. The Yusian also remained quiet for a long time, but this didn't seem to bother him. He just stood there, not even looking at me—or anything else, for that matter. His eyes bounced around their shared socket like ping-pong balls.

"Differentiate yourself for while!" he unexpectedly broke the silence.

If I knew how to "differentiate" myself, I would probably have done so, just so he would leave me alone! His presence weighed on my nerves like a hydraulic press.

He finally stirred and approached one of the living room doors, freezing there as if trying to hear something. Instinctively I listened as well. At first I heard nothing but then detected a vague stamping, scratching, and finally—a dog whining! The Yusian opened the door. On the threshold stood a little black puppy, swaying unsteadily. When the huge inhuman figure bent above him, the puppy froze and, as if in slow motion, sank to the floor. I hurried over and took him in my arms. His little body trembled convulsively, his heart beating against my palms in his panic. I stood up and stared angrily at the Yusian.

"Is Jerry" was his only remark as he turned and exited out the door we had entered.

CHAPTER 5

Left standing in the middle of this imitation of an ordinary, earthly living room, I tried to calm the trembling puppy by tenderly repeating his name, "Jerry, Jerry, Jerry." Haunted by the memory of that grotesque inhuman creature bending above his little body, I could barely swallow my hatred and frustrated rage. I stared down at the feebly drooping head, not knowing what to do.

I pressed him tenderly to my chest and carried him to the sofa. Lowering my head to listen to his breathing, I was aware of nothing but this little fragile ball of life, thrust into my hands by the unfathomable whim of a Yusian mind.

Before long, Jerry pulled himself up, sat stiffly on my knees, and raised his dark velvet eyes to me. I smiled at him, and when he settled comfortably and curiously nuzzled my coat, I frankly laughed with relief. The sound of my own voice startled me, and I cast an embarrassed look around. The room was dead silent, both utterly ordinary and unbearably alien at the same time. Alien! My journey was beginning, toward two dead bodies at some base on a distant planet. My one hope was that I would at least arrive safely.

I looked at my watch: 4:27 p.m. Thirty-three minutes until liftoff. No doubt they were watching me, so I decided to demonstrate my composure by exploring my temporary residence.

When I set Jerry down on the carpet, he joyfully wagged his stub of a tail and snapped at one of my trouser legs a few times, already over his fright and ready to play. Not relaxed enough to join him, I casually continued my explorations while he lay by the sofa, obviously disappointed.

One door led to the kitchen—entirely automated, in perfect order, absolutely clean, and white. The only spot of color was a clumsy and pretentious still life hanging above the table. I immediately crossed to stare at it openmouthed, as if I were an art critic enthralled with a masterpiece. Picturing a vase of yellow carnations surrounded artistically with red fruits, this daub would look out of place anywhere, even more so on a Yusian starship, was my first thought. But then I sympathized with the artist—another human. To paint the carnations in such details required great patience. And the tablecloth with its miniscule patterns too—great patience, if no imagination. Yet, the flamboyant signature suggests that he must have been pleased with his work. So here I find myself, on a Yusian starship, identifying with him. How bizarre that only now, standing in front of an unsuccessful painting, do I realize that I love everything human, with an unimaginable love—as overpowering as suffocation, as deep as despair, and as blind as fanaticism!

I left the kitchen, hopefully as casually as I had entered, and next discovered a spacious bedroom, amiably furnished with light-blue silk wallpaper, a crystal chandelier, a king-sized bed, thick golden curtains, and a skillfully carved walnut wardrobe. Unquestionably the Yusians had gone to a great deal of trouble. "Let us immerse object in natural environment" was probably what they told each other.

When I returned to the living room, Jerry didn't budge. My gloomy mood must have infected him as well. As I sank into one of the armchairs, my attention was immediately drawn to a strange little object at the center of the otherwise-bare table. I should have noticed it before I left the room earlier. *Or wasn't it here then?*

I reached for it unwillingly, holding it gingerly between two fingers. It was warm—or *still* warm? And flexible, as if made of rubber. One side was fluffy and light brown, while the other was whitish. No, pale, like—like the color of human skin. Yes! This was a miniature effigy of a human head!

Placed on my palm, the effigy was as small as a marble. Examining it closely, I recognized my own image—complete in every detail, down to my reddish ear and the bruise beneath my eye. I gazed at it more closely: the cheeks and chin were brown with stubble, unshaven—as was I! The hair separated into thin fibers, even the eyebrows. When I pushed them carefully with my finger, the lips opened to show white teeth, as small as grains of sand.

There was no point in trying to guess what it meant: a mockery, a gift, some kind of a hint, or something else entirely incomprehensible to me. Even after I put it in the cellaret, its warm, soft touch seemed to linger on my fingers.

When I returned to the armchair, the curtain behind the sofa caught my attention. A heavy brocade. What would I see if I pulled it aside? Probably an imitation of a window and some landscape as phony as that painting in the kitchen. But what if the window were real and on the other side were Yusians in some of their disgusting positions—performing *inner transformations* or *splits*—and what if this apartment were part of their laboratory? Right now they could be observing me, preparing me for some inhuman experiment!

Time was flying; very soon the Earth would be far out of my reach.

The clock now read 4:43 p.m.—only seventeen minutes left. I turned to the robot. It was high time he gave me the promised *travel advises*. But he stood motionless and silent, his yellow eyes emitting a dull, indifferent glow.

"Hey, you, robot!" I shouted. "Isn't it time to begin preparing me for the flight?"

"There was no preparation planned," he replied rhythmically.

"What?" I was amazed. "No preflight program? No cameras to monitor the launch or other orientation?"

"This apartment is provided with everything you will need for your safety," he continued in a monotone. "We have launched already."

"Already!" The image of the concrete launch pad stuck in my mind—simple but human. Long gone now. We left the Earth just like that, without a tremor! How was this possible?

"If in jolt because of our new condition, don't need it more," a polite voice suggested from somewhere above.

I lost my temper.

"But this is ridiculous!" I objected, without having anything in mind.

"Opinion lacks meaning," the voice answered tenderly. "Best not occupy psychologically unhealthy position."

"Position?" They are watching me from above, bent and miserable in their luxurious armchair. I rose abruptly, which I shouldn't have done, and crossed my arms.

"Oh, don't worry about me, Yusian! I'm just fine."

"I not attach worry minimum to you even!" the words above my head continued rapturously. "Pleasing me to investigate you, my fixed primary task. A chance!"

"A chance?" Trying not to scream, I barely whispered, "Really? And during the entire trip you plan to—investigate me?"

"Yes! During every second. Until you become past."

The last expression, whatever it meant, did not ease my mind. "Very well, very well," I murmured.

"So you like to be chance for incoming conclusions?" the Yusian asked joyfully.

I had heard that they expressed themselves oddly in Earth languages. I also knew that the meaning of their words had little, if any, connection with their pompous, markedly benevolent tone. Despite that, I was momentarily convinced that I was talking to a silly child, which was sufficient motivation for me to blabber mockingly, "Mmm yes, I find it very likeable. Exceptionally likeable!"

After a short silence, the Yusian added, "Apprehending you effort yourself, but meet no result. I find beginning of my patience but do not have end. Judge me—must search it in you?"

A child? I think this "child" was threatening me! "I'm surprised you don't know where the end of your own patience is," I said slowly. "I, for instance, always know where mine ends."

"Where it ends now?"

"At the same place where your tolerance ends!" I hissed, obviously irritated.

And, of course, I immediately received my comeuppance: "Are efforting self again! But are under our stopping and more tolerable is to accept us."

Or in other words, *There is nowhere to run, buddy! You're showing off in vain.* And that was the truth. So why did I give him a reason to say it? Why!

"Your way of expressing yourself is hard for me to understand, Yusian." I tried to sound both polite and, at the same time, confused. "This tires me. I would prefer to stop our attempts to communicate."

It may have sounded pompous and negligent, but at least the creature could not say I was "efforting myself" again. He seemed to hesitate a moment before he sang, "All right. My presence will become unnoticeable. Yet must not finalize. Possibility to feel it again."

"Yes, yes," I indolently nodded and headed toward the bookcase, picking a book without even noticing its title, although I searched quite a while to "choose" it. Then I collapsed on the sofa to recover from my "jolt."

I had always known I lacked diplomatic skills, but this time I hit a new low. If I continued to antagonize my host, others would have to pay for my mistakes later. So this is what we have come to—permanently expecting punishment, measuring each word and deed according to only one indicator: whether or not the Yusians will like it. We have turned into wretched toadies.

Pretending to be absorbed in the book, I put my feet up on the table.

How we had longed for contact with other intelligent life! For so many years, we felt isolated and sent out messages. Well, the "brothers" came. And now our greatest desire is to rid ourselves of them. True, thus far they have never harmed us. Yet they hang above our heads like a sword of Damocles, don't they? And not one of us understands these creatures or their ultimate intentions toward us. But what good would such knowledge do us, since we are helpless to defend ourselves? All we can do is tremble, shaken by Yusophobia. It is gnawing our hearts, bemusing our brains. We are degenerating! The best human virtues are becoming stunted. So why should they be aggressive, since their mere presence has been enough to cripple us?

"Hey, Yusian!"

Yes?" immediately echoed in my ears.

"How long will the flight continue?"

"Who is this flight?"

How to communicate with this weirdo! "The trip to Eyrena."

"Time depends on you."

"So—approximately how long?"

"May be between nine hours and eleven days and nine hours and twenty-three days. Depends on adaptation. If you not oppose it."

I skipped his final remark without any comment. "You probably want to say nine days and between eleven and twenty-three hours?" I suggested.

"Why should say such unpacked facts?" The creature was puzzled.

I returned my attention to the book. What a discouraging exchange! Even if the trip did take twenty-three days, I would bear it somehow, I told myself. Then Jerry jumped up on the sofa, curling against me familiarly, while the robot continued to stand at attention by the exit door, his yellow, unblinking eyes fixed on us. What a motley crew we were, including especially our invisible Yusian host, who had joined us so insolently.

Never before had I dealt directly with robots, but I had heard only praise for this model. Examining him with interest,

I decided he resembled those little toy robots in store windows, only full size. Not big enough to create a sense of inferiority, though: no more than a meter and seventy centimeters. The psychologists from ESSIKO know their business—as does the entire company. And they could expect to have no rivals for a decade or two. Their creations are always brilliantly engineered and appear so pleasantly human that they calm the hearts of even their most virulent opponents.

"Siko, come here," I said kindly.

The robot approached me quickly and nimbly.

"Have you ever been to Eyrena?" I asked him when he stopped in front of me.

"No."

"Did the man who ordered you to accompany me tell you that you would be staying there?"

"He did."

"So he explained to you what you will be doing at the base, didn't he?"

"Yes. I will wait for new orders and will obey them."

"And who do you have to contact to receive those orders? What is his name?"

"I don't know." The robot answered, exactly as I expected.

But I was sure that Zung's people had filled him with information and instructions I wasn't supposed to know and that *somebody* at the base would find a way to get them.

"All right, Siko." I sighed. "Now go prepare tea for me. And feed the dog."

Siko turned and hurried toward the kitchen to fulfill my orders. Jerry, however, suspecting that he was trying to run away, leaped from the sofa and ran after him with a menacing growl, fiercely waving his ears. I watched him with a smile; having a dog traveling with me was a wonderful diversion. Besides, he didn't look troubled at all. Despite his reaction to the Yusian, he had clearly not been mistreated. Humans act similarly when they first meet with such creatures, don't they? Supposedly this is caused by a temporary "psychosensor overload."

Soon I heard Jerry crunching energetically from the kitchen, and Siko appeared with the tea. He served it with a plate of cookies, which shows he didn't lack initiative. I was really beginning to like him and couldn't blame him because he had been programmed to spy on me.

As I sipped hot, fragrant tea, I picked up the book again. Then I started thinking about the briefcase. The complicated precautions taken to protect its contents—the triple-coded safe, the switch to the gray briefcase, and the metal case (a money box?) inside wrapped in cellophane (for preventing fingerprints?)—all seemed illogical. But those precautions convinced me that the contents were meant only for humans, not for the Yusians. Otherwise they wouldn't have been entrusted to me.

Suddenly something stirred behind me. Lightly, just a puff. And again. My hair stood on end. I could feel a presence very close, just behind my back. Breathing down my neck. I calmed myself, refused to look back, and slowly sipped my tea before placing the cup carefully on its saucer. Feeling as if electricity ran down my spine, I slowly pulled back from the table. Whoever this was, whatever it was, it was still behind me, so close that I could hear it breathe. I turned my head one centimeter—two—yes! I detected motion out of the corner of my eye. The curtain behind the sofa was slightly swaying. The curtain at the "window." I clenched my fists and tightened my muscles, ready to confront it on the count of three. One—I took a deep breath.

What was that smell?

Clean air. That was all—simply ventilation. Damn! I could just see that freak laughing from above, laughing at how childish a thirty-year-old human could behave.

I walked around the room for a while before entering the bedroom, where I took off my jacket and tie and threw them on the bed. I began to understand Genetti and Zung, anyone who had been in close contact with the Yusians, much better. Although I was a trained investigator, after only an hour among them, a tiny voice inside me was already screaming, "Alien! Alien!" I kept expecting something terrible to happen, with no idea of what that something might be. I suspected them of maliciousness with no justification and saw menace or mockery all around me with no provocation—maybe. Simply because *they were not human?* No other reason. No matter how primitive it sounds, this fact could well become an insurmountable barrier for the human psyche.

I retrieved the briefcase from the living room, placed it on the nightstand, and opened it. "Later you'll receive the code for the case inside," Genetti had promised, but I was given no such code. Maybe it's planted in one of my suitcases? Another child's game: hide-and-seek. On a hunch, I checked the memory of my watch and discovered a seven-number code.

Bending over to block my actions from the Yusian surveillance equipment, I punched in the new code, and the case immediately opened. In other situations, this cloak-and-dagger secrecy would either amuse or irritate me. But at this moment, I lacked the strength for any reaction. I simply froze in that uncomfortable position—hunched over the nightstand, my knees bent—and stared at the open case.

It was empty.

CHAPTER 6

For two days and two nights, I acted as if I'd come on the Yusian starship for a vacation. Of course, those were not my true feelings, but I made an effort to keep up appearances. And that Yusian *investigating* me must have been really bored with recording how I played with Jerry, read, listened to music, ate, slept, or engaged Siko in long and meaningless dialogues. He certainly didn't succeed in receiving from me any chances of "incoming conclusions" except, perhaps, that I was yet another dumb human with a brain as big as a pea, or let's say, as big as that little effigy of my head that I had been given at liftoff.

Even worse, I had reached a similar conclusion about myself. What else could explain why I had believed Zung that there would be some documents in the case—especially after he prevented me from getting in touch with my bureau chief? Franklin, of course, could have provided me with information and instructions.

Now I had no other choice but to accept the current situation. Zung was light-years away, and I was floating in a gigantic black starship. Obviously my return to Earth was not a part of Zung's plans, nor would Franklin be able to help me from Earth. So I decided to help myself, by doing something useful—like spying on the Yusians. Exactly what I was advised to do by Mr. Zung, who had screwed me.

So, on the morning of the third day, I broke my long silence and asked my invisible Yusian if it would be possible for me to have a tour of the starship. He accepted my wish with what I took to be great amazement, if such a feeling, or any other *human* feeling, could be assigned to these creatures. As for our conversations after that, nothing was generally new in them. In other words, I offered only trivialities, while his replies, even if they had harbored exceptionally deep meanings, reached me only as depressing gobbledygook.

What I did manage to understand, somehow, was that in an hour I would have to leave my "physical apartness" and experience a "short left connection, whose end" would "swallow" me to "express" me in "concrete form" according to my "model." I mulled over this while I lay on the sofa, pretending to take a nap.

Seven minutes before the appointed time, the Yusian gave me more proof that neither he nor others like him were very strict in terms of punctuality.

"And here what is desired!" he roared, as if trying to shake the ceiling overhead. Only my willpower saved me from leaping off the sofa. Instead, I rose slowly and calmly left the room. I assumed that "short left connection" meant to turn into the left corridor. But since I expected the corridor to have walls, floor, and a ceiling as on Earth, I was surprised to discover otherwise. What I saw made me feel nostalgia for the squelching floor and the brackets shooting out blinding sparks of my earlier Yusian experience. I now found myself in front of something completely different, a series of closely aligned rings, some spinning clockwise and others counterclockwise. Since I clearly had to pass through them, I cautiously stepped on the first ring and then on the second. By the third one, I was pleased to find that they helped rather than hindered my balance, stabilizing it by transferring me lightly and imperceptibly from one to the other. Thus, in only a few seconds, I reached a barrier, round like the bottom of a cylinder but divided in the middle by a deep vertical cleft that didn't appear to be wide enough for me to squeeze through. But squeeze through I did somehow—or had it indeed *swallowed* me?

I emerged, again without understanding how, entirely naked in a well-lit space scarcely large enough to contain me, which immediately shrank even further, wrapping itself around me like a cocoon and filling with darkness. When I thought I would suffocate, it slowly returned to its former size, leaving a swarm of reddish grains on my skin. I could barely suppress the impulse to shake them off, especially after they began splitting and releasing tiny sticky threads that immediately started crawling all over my body.

For a minute or two, I looked as if all my capillaries had risen to the surface. Then the web of threads tightened and blended into a homogeneous, pliable membrane that fit me like a second skin. Next, something heavy poured down on me. I looked up just in time to see a muddy, mucous gush over my face.

"Now are together!" I heard the voice of the Yusian as if in a dream.

"With whom?" I managed to articulate through the membrane that covered my mouth and kept my eyes from blinking. "Together with whom?"

"Model space suit," came the laconic answer.

Again the cleft opened, this time to spit me out beyond the barrier into a wide, empty hall. Here the membrane in front of my nostrils and my mouth started to pulse lightly. Apparently the air was already Yusian, and the suit was supplying me with needful oxygen while keeping out gas that might harm or poison me.

The suit was unquestionably a brilliant product of bioengineering, and despite my initial antipathy, I had to admit to feeling quite comfortable in it now. I took a few cautious steps. I could sense that the gravitation was far greater than that on Earth, but the space suit compensated for the difference. So it had antigravitation features, and who knows what else? Yes, a wonderful creation! Would we ever be able to invent such marvels?

A slight rustling caught my attention. The Yusian was standing about twenty meters from me, but looking more like a variegated pattern in a huge kaleidoscope than like the creatures who had met me in front of the starship. Quite picturesque. I headed in his direction with great interest.

"Withhold yourself, human!" he unexpectedly yelled at me, before becoming entirely dark.

I stopped, bewildered, and the Yusian withdrew as many steps as I had taken toward him. He stood still for a few moments and then glided toward me—slowly, lightly, and gracefully. Even solemnly. It occurred to me that he might have chosen that wide, empty room to give me more time to admire him as he approached me. I had to admit it was a sight worth seeing, especially when his kaleidoscopic hues returned. Gone was the ugly muddy-brown cover, which my recent experience suggested had been merely his terrestrial space suit.

Here, however, seeing the Yusian in his natural mode—possibly the most *un*natural for my human perceptions—blew my mind. Not a living creature but some weird, colorful wave was approaching me, because his forms merged into each other with every move. He was not walking but overflowing in my direction, his limbs stretching and sliding along the mossy blue floor.

And his skin: a veil of stars lightly embracing the side clefts of his torso, glowing like a rainbow. Not homogeneous like our skin, it consisted of various zones—some larger, some smaller; some bulging out, others receding—separated by an exquisite pattern of narrow, asymmetrically branched channels. At that moment, the zones focused their bright rays directly upon me, and I was probably reflecting them back, a living mirror attesting to their multicolor magnificence.

But if I admired the way the Yusian solemnly overflowed in my direction, that admiration disappeared entirely the moment he stopped in front of me and moved aside his forehead membrane. Again I was weighed down by those huge floating eyes—their gelatinous, deadly white substance surrounding dilated pupils as deep and dark as craters sinking into his mind, churning up from those depths the vague motion of that same brain—staring at me.

I have no idea how long we stayed like that—maybe seconds, maybe minutes. This time he didn't try to mitigate the initial effect their eyes had on us. And because he knew perfectly well what I was experiencing, I supposed he was doing this on purpose: that here, in his own territory, he wanted to hurt me, to make me feel insignificant, dependent, and alone.

When that terrible stiffness caused by his gaze left my body, I stepped toward the creature, looked him up and down, and stretched my face into a smile that amazed even me how the mask of my space suit could stand it without cracking.

"Well, shall we begin our little tour?" I asked him very politely.

"Pass through you, without you having it," he answered me just as politely.

I laughed. But since the Yusian remained standing in front of me, and protocol approved silence only if we were moving in some direction, I had to add another comment. "I will be your guest for many more days, and during that time, we will certainly chat very often. Tell me, how do you want me to call you? What's your name?"

"If you want it, name—Chuks."

"So, you don't have a name?"

"Could have not name? I am with you, right?"

"Aha. And does the name 'Chuks' have a certain meaning in your language?"

"Yes, is marked. By first two stones hit one another: Chuks! Millions of times before, before." The Yusian moved back and sank until his upper limbs touched the floor.

"All right," I murmured. "I will call you Chuks."

The Yusian stood up. "Me too," he declared.

Oh my God! How could we ever communicate if we could not even explain to each other what our names were?

"No!" I shook my head. "My name is *not* Chuks. My name is *Terence*. Ter for short."

"So, remain unchanged toward me—or just nostalgia?"

"No matter how you take it, it would be true anyway."

"Yes, are equalized things." Chuks probably agreed.

Then he articulated some phrase that I took as an offer for me to follow him, and we headed toward the nearest wall. I assumed that we would stop in front of it, but Chuks kept moving until the wall split and folded around his body upon contact.

I passed through the "door" created that way and, after a few steps, turned back. The wall had already closed behind us.

"Deprived of toleration of intelligent touch, but given them urge to be together," Chuks explained.

"Are you saying that this wall is alive?" I wondered.

"Are creatures. But alive sometimes and almost."

Though I didn't understand this answer, I suddenly felt good. Here I was, walking side by side with a Yusian on an intergalactic starship, being treated as an equal. Maybe we *are* equals, despite their biotechnical wonders, their five planets, and their thousands of years of traveling through space. Well, yes! In the final reckoning, they are the ones who sought us out, aren't they? Would they do that if they considered us lower forms of life? Probably not. More likely, in some areas we excel them. There must be some! We just don't realize it yet. They do, however, and that's why...

I was getting carried away, developing my ideas and enriching them with logical conclusions that stimulated my confidence in humanity even more, until I finally started to accept the Yusians with condescending kindness. Since we were then passing a device that looked as if its only purpose was to spread clouds of dust around, I asked Chuks about it, just to be polite, "Tell me, Chuks, what is this—used for?" I casually waved my hand at the device.

"Used for example, because has many difficulties." Approaching it, he literally dived into the dust. From within its whirlwind, he added, "Misses original planet, so grant regular approval."

For some reason I thought he wouldn't hear me if I spoke normally, so I almost screamed, "Is it a plant?"

"Has been, but now a memory. Grows only in our visions," the hardly distinguishable silhouette of Chuks offered sotto voce.

Our tour continued with an unpleasant surprise. We had moved away from the "memory" plant, and I was absentmindedly observing how Chuks absorbed its pollen through his skin, when the floor around us quickly dropped away and we found ourselves some distance beneath its regular level. Then it closed over our heads, forming a semitransparent capsule, which carried us headlong downward. I tried to find out what surrounded us but could see only long luminous lines and feel that we were sinking rapidly. Nor was this an illusion. Then the capsule stopped softly, as if it had shock absorbers, and fell apart. Its remnants merged with the new floor beneath us, which resembled the back of an enormous panting reptile. Chuks confidently started walking on its heaving back, so I had no choice but to follow.

We soon stopped on a square platform that seemed to be suspended in midair. At its edge was probably a force field, which allowed Chuks to occupy a position that would have been impossible to maintain otherwise. I stepped back a little; this vantage point offered a good view, as if from a high balcony. I wish I had understood better the view beneath me. Something was spreading, some kind of room the size of a soccer field, but its outlines were too amorphous to determine its precise shape. The scarlet walls meandered randomly, uniting at the top to form a cupola dotted with dark greasy residue that constantly shifted position, somehow crawling and stretching. When these touched, they abruptly contracted into spheres, remaining in that position for a second or two before exploding, during which they erupted with yellowish bubbling foam.

The bottom of the room was rough, composed of a combination of substance and energy that sometimes sank and other times swelled and folded into smooth, shiny waves that mirrored its depths, where wide ribbons of fire leaped in a wild contest, tangling into complicated ornaments before slowly extinguishing in the gushing foam. In the center rose three towering pillars, as if formed of petrified darkness, through which veils like thick transparent glass undulated rhythmically while circulating a grayish fluid within.

From the direction of the meandering, or maybe wriggling, walls came sounds that dwindled swiftly and frighteningly, like death rattles, and then, after moments of silence tense with expectation, began their moaning anew, like the groaning of dying animals.

"Time down there!" Chuks's scream startled me.

I turned mechanically toward him, dumbstruck, as he hung above me, apparently so that I could hear him better.

"Time down there," he repeated, "and undoubtedly recalling Eyrena, since there we captured selves belong to it. Able regain them only through three near shadows of nothing."

I guessed that his "three near shadows" referred to the black pillars, and once again I stared at them. This creature had quite a vocabulary: "near shadows of nothing"! I shrugged my shoulders and started backing up. I didn't want to have to yell up at him all the time.

"What is our present velocity?" I asked him in a businesslike manner once we had settled in a quieter place.

"No, no!" Chuks heartily but worriedly objected. "Must not move. Is time! Only to wait for it—"

"But we are *traveling*, aren't we?" I interrupted him impatiently. "Otherwise, how will we ever reach Eyrena?"

"Traveling drastic distance away Earth, Ter. With motion we cross when everything ours already somebody else's. Why collide with natural limits?"

I made a thoughtful face, as if considering the reasonableness of his argument, finally concluding sharply, "Yes, that would not be in our best interests."

We left the seething flux of "time" as we had reached it, in yet another capsule. When it stopped and disintegrated, before my eyes appeared a new, equally incomprehensible vista, though not as exotic as the previous one.

Now we were standing at the foot of a pyramid-like structure with an open top from which, at regular intervals, arose clouds of thick white steam. The steam condensed into large drops on the low ceiling, from which grew long, flexible leech-like forms. They stretched toward the drops, swallowing them quickly, sometimes even quarreling over them, their actions accompanied by the slurping sounds of a herd of unrestrained greedy creatures. After all the drops had been devoured, they returned to the fleshy tissue of the ceiling, lurking there until the condensation of their next "meal."

After watching the creatures feed for a few cycles, I directed my attention toward the pyramid itself. The surface layer was composed entirely of shells as big as a human palm, which amazingly resembled mussels: the same shape, the same lustrous nacreous lining, and even the same small protuberance in the middle. While I was examining them, they entered their next cycle, because all of them opened at the same time and uncovered their soft rosy flesh exactly as common mussels do. The similarities were really incredible, fantastic! Or maybe it was even a *common phase* in the evolution of two distant planets?

"Are mussels," Chuks's remark brought me back to reality. "And made them ours. For now, only give us their cautiousness, but soon foresee more transformed future for them. Being used, being used."

He lifted his lower limb and pressed it toward the flesh of some of the mussels. When he pulled it back, they remained just as trustfully opened.

Beneath the disgusting membrane space suit, I broke into a cold sweat. *A common phase*—what an absurd idea! The Yusians had probably started their surreptitious campaign of conquest long ago. These mussels were hardly their first victory. Who knows how many other earthborn creatures have "transformed future" by them? And who knows whether they are preparing the same for us too. But, after all, Zung was right: they must have a weak spot. We only have to find it. We have to!

I said with feigned indifference, "I would like to see where you do your calculations. The control of such a starship is probably a very complex task."

"No, is not," Chuks confirmed, cheerfully leading me toward one of the tunnels to the right of the pyramid. "Is not, as calculations not be any help. Starship must be always in wholeness, as you or I. How calculating our personal control?"

"So this starship is actually a living organism?" I smiled at him skeptically, although I had heard other people say the same thing.

"Yes, it turns out," Chuks confirmed again and then added, "But human meaning very much aside from Yusian truth."

"Well, all right, I didn't express myself very precisely. I meant that the starship is like a gigantic biological robot or self-regulating biological machine. Whatever we call it, the important thing is that it *functions* according to the principles of a live organism.

Of course, it's not alive in the sense that it can reproduce itself. On the other hand, if necessary, maybe it can regenerate each of its parts, and this ability…is…characteristic of…of many living organisms." I had confused even myself, so I stopped speaking.

Chuks gladly picked up where I had left off. "Can be anything you wish to it, but not with all uses. Will meet you with it. Is near here."

While I was wondering who or what he had in mind, we came to the end of the tunnel and stopped in front of a porous vertical plane that thinned and then split at Chuks's touch. We entered a small rectangular white room.

"There is," Chuks announced, stopping next to a diminutive transparent sphere filled with silver spots that seemed to be roaming randomly.

"What is this?"

"Starship."

I felt a strong need to sit down, to hold my head, or at least to swear aloud, but I allowed myself only a deep sigh.

Chuks said, "Realize with trust is ordinary object."

"An artificial mind!" I exclaimed, delighted with my guess.

"No! Is ordinary object! But maintains strict requirements toward surrounding anything. When different substances and energies subordinate to it, pays back in details vital conditions needed for us."

Chuks crossed to what looked like a wall shelf with separate compartments, in which were placed tiles as small as playing cards.

"These signs so ship combines with chosen planet," he continued. "This sign of Earth until recently was affected. But inside is already sign of Eyrena, then will be this one." He tenderly touched some of the tiles.

When I looked more closely at the sphere, I noticed that there was also a tile in its center. I don't know why, but it all seemed to me absolutely ridiculous, as if a passenger seeing an airplane for the first time were being told by some joker that it flies only because inside is a blinking "No Smoking" sign!

"Not to confront from this place more, Ter," Chuks warned me. "Starting to effort self."

We left the room with the "starship" and again started roaming along the "substances and energies," toward which, as I already knew, it had "strict requirements." I felt demoralized and dispirited after this avalanche of inaccessible and incomprehensible sights and explanations.

Chuks, however, showed no intention of parting from me. He couldn't seem to get enough of my presence and wouldn't stop babbling on. I was dizzy from listening to him call incandescent balloons "climatizers" and announce that a zone dotted with simple spongy funnels provided "balance retention." Then he led me through a labyrinth of gloomy slippery pipes, which were, in his words, generating an "external insulation veil." And so on.

Would this damned tour ever be over? Then, when its end was finally near, I had to squeeze through a narrow lane between at least twenty more Yusians! They had gathered, presumably, to honor me. They were roaring something, and all of them gazed at me with their horrible eyes, clearly finding me quite an amusing attraction.

I made an effort to respond in kind and, I think, succeeded to a great extent, because this time their paralyzing gaze had little effect on me. I stopped, looked at them with no more than a passing glance of curiosity, asked Chuks a few questions, laughed a little, and waved my hand playfully. Zung would have been proud of me—I had followed his directives to the letter. I understood him better now and felt more and more sympathetic toward him. One or two more experiences like this, and I would probably become his most fanatic supporter.

By the time I sank into the familiar cleft, I could hardly stand on my feet. I was even numb to the relief of my space suit melting. I simply waited until the procedure ended and returned through the rotating rings, entirely naked again, as if in a trance. Since nobody bothered to give me back my clothes, I assumed that they didn't exist anymore. Were they cankered or absorbed by something? I didn't know.

I entered the apartment without even paying any attention to Jerry, who rejoiced at my return, and headed for the bathroom to take a shower—the memory of the cloying reddish threads clinging to my body still made my skin crawl.

When I finally reached the bedroom, the first thing I saw in the open closet was my gray suit, the same one I thought was destroyed. I also found my blue shirt, my shoes, my underwear, and my socks. I took them out and examined them carefully. Were they really the same ones or not? This question obsessed me, causing me to forget all about the starship, the tour, and even the Yusians. But why? Only a competent psychologist, or psychiatrist, could answer that.

Of course the clothes weren't the same ones, as I determined when it occurred to me to look for their labels. Where they had been I saw the entirely inappropriate stamps of "ESSIKO." Was that a mistake—or a hint that they intended to turn me into a robot?

I put on the clothes and returned to the living room to listen to music. I needed to take my mind off this unpleasant adventure. But even more unpleasant thoughts tortured me: my fears of what I would be facing on Eyrena.

PART TWO

CHAPTER 7

"Now in an event!" I heard the ecstatic voice of Chuks. "Your opposition only fourteen Earth days and now nine hours over."

Somehow I understood from his words that we had arrived on Eyrena, although the landing was as light as the liftoff. But this time I wasn't particularly impressed. I simply ordered the robot to collect my luggage and waited impatiently to leave the starship. Whatever next awaited me would be better than being surrounded by only Yusians!

After about ten minutes, Chuks walked in, wearing his terrestrial space suit. I hurriedly gathered the puppy in my arms, hoping to shield him at least partially from the initial "psychosensor overload." Unfortunately I couldn't protect myself, let alone Jerry, from that.

"From now on will desire summary," the Yusian said heartily when I came back to my senses.

"Are we leaving?" I asked.

"And summary always indolent," he continued, "by choosing only similarities to merge."

"But after all," I replied reluctantly, "finding similarities is the easiest way to reach logical conclusions."

"Not easy if not safe!" Chuks objected.

Our few previous conversations gave me no reason to assume that exchanging two or three seemingly shared phrases would lead to anything but more confusion. "Maybe you're right," I yet argued, "but there are many complex situations or, let's say, phenomena, that require us to summarize. It's going to be difficult, if not impossible, to understand the basic principles if we focus only on specific details."

"Can't find basic because already known," Chuks noted. "One for everything and is little. Who disregards will lose above-mentioned distinctive complexity."

"What could be better than the absence of complexity?" I smiled wryly.

"Better the slow approacher giving chance to react," Chuks answered my rhetorical question.

My growing impatience became unbearable claustrophobia. I wanted out—immediately. I had to escape! "We have to go, Chuks,"

"We have to go, Chuks," he repeated and finally headed for the door.

The gallery that had disappeared during the journey was back in place. I walked behind the Yusian, my feet sinking into the spongy floor, almost blinded by the constant sparks spouting from the brackets along the sides. The robot plodded mechanically behind me. Jerry was trembling violently, his head buried under my jacket. From time to time, his curiosity overcame his fear, and he peeked out—a good sign that his psychological condition was improving, as was mine. Good or bad, the way was familiar and, most importantly, led to the exit.

We entered the hall with the vibrating ellipses. Chuks kept moving, but I stopped and, as soon as my eyes adapted to the new lightning, looked around for the elevator we had used when we were here before. It was nowhere to be found, but a sluice slowly rising on the other side of the hall caught my attention.

Soon a pulsing elastic substance began flowing—or crawling—out, upon which floated a bluish-white object that I couldn't identify in any way. The substance expanded sideways until it resembled a shallow pond, while the object bobbed up and down like an oversized polyhedral buoy. When the "pond" suddenly swelled in the middle, the polyhedron slid down the newly formed slope. Inertia carried it beyond the substance, which quickly receded into the original opening, and the sluice closed.

"Should exploit readiness!" Chuks exclaimed, but I didn't budge. He waited for me, next to that extremely, even hideously, absurd object. If I had seen it on the monitor and couldn't judge its size, I would have guessed it to be a crushed cardboard box completely covered with small, uneven handwriting. But I hadn't seen it on a screen and could tell by its size alone—as big as a minibus!—that it certainly wasn't a box. Nor were those skewed blue and purple markings anyone's handwriting.

Although it seemed improbable, I finally realized the repugnant truth: I was actually looking at a Yusian vehicle. Had they no sense of shape!

As I approached it, even Jerry barked disapprovingly before again hiding his head under my jacket. Moving to the most prominent side of the vehicle, Chuks climbed in with a well-practiced maneuver. I followed, but nowhere near as skillfully. Then I remembered the robot and got out again.

"Come on, Siko!" I urged him nervously.

But he didn't move—just stood in the middle of the hall holding the two suitcases. His head was tilted backward on that unnaturally extended bony neck, his eyes, glowing like burning coals, firmly riveted on something above us. I traced their direction and discovered that they were locked on a long, narrow opening in the ceiling, through which a few Yusians, closely squeezed together, were looking at us.

"Come on, Siko!" I repeated, vague suspicions about him creeping into my mind. "Get in!"

The robot rocked back and forth, stopped for a moment to regain his equilibrium, and then moved rapidly toward me. We climbed into the vehicle, where Chuks was already crouched in a very particular, yet obviously totally comfortable, position. As for myself, I found all the surfaces disturbingly soft and sensitive to my touch. The lack of any windows intensified the impression that we were enclosed in a hollow, dark womb.

There were no seats, backrests, or even handles in the vehicle, and though the floor turned out to be surprisingly flat, I didn't like sitting directly on it. To make matters worse, Jerry wouldn't stop squirming in my arms, while the robot remained upright, looking like any movement would cause him to stagger and fall into my lap. The hot, humid air coming from the Yusian convinced me that his space suit ventilation system was working flawlessly, which did little to brighten my mood.

Chuks closed the entrance to the vehicle with an abrupt snap. Reaching above my head, he thrust a limb into the wall and scooped out a piece, which stretched as if it was made out of dough, broke it, and turned it into a ball.

"Robot to transfer right direction," Chuks said, handing me the ball.

I quickly shoved it into Siko's hands. He bent over and studied it in silence, as if he were casting a spell or working black magic. I would have burst out laughing if my sense of humor hadn't already petrified. When the robot returned the ball, I gave it to Chuks, who stuck it back into the wall. There the ball quickly transformed into a pulsating, glowing hexagon.

As I was wondering how this wonder of Yusian technology could even move, it took off, thus striking a crushing blow to my belief in aerodynamics: the need for minimum frontal drag and stabilization and the other battles, large and small, that our aircraft designers have fought and won against their sturdy foe, wind resistance.

Disappointed, I questioned Chuks, "Tell me how this—machine—overcomes air resistance."

"No resistance, because puts vacuum around self always," Chuks explained helpfully. "Some air for us, but rest repulsed so not to disturb structural readjustments."

"Where does it get the energy it needs to operate? How does it work?"

"Energy derived from vacuum, but machine operated by determination of ongoing readjustments." Chuks either imagined or pretended that he was answering me.

I looked down, absorbed by my thoughts, and my heart started racing wildly; the floor of our "aircraft" was thinning fast! It was melting—no more substantial than a dirty whitish fog dissipating beneath us. And through that fog, I could see the starship far below, squatting like a black beetle on a wide pink plain.

I snuck a glance at Chuks, who didn't seem at all worried. *No, it's not becoming thinner, just transparent!* I assured myself desperately, adding a few curses to increase my resolve. In my line of work, unpleasant experiences are commonplace, but at that moment, I refused to imagine a worst-case scenario. Bouncing along on a totally transparent rubbery substance with the ground kilometers away was sufficiently worrisome and undesirable.

We landed in about five minutes. I popped out, cradling Jerry in my arms, followed by the robot. Chuks remained in his wrinkled "aircraft." At first I stepped away to let him take off faster but then, after a short hesitation, went back and looked through the still-open entrance. The Yusian had changed positions, now flopped over to one side and looking even more repulsive and disproportional yet somehow less horrifying. His eyes looked white in the soft diffuse light, their pupils contracting and enlarging as if responding to an insistent inner rhythm. I unintentionally waved good-bye.

"Chuks, Chuks!" he exclaimed in a low voice. "Will remain on Eyrena so effective when you seek me."

Was this an offer for a new meeting? Or a hint of its inevitability?

"I wish you all the best, Chuks," I added insincerely and quickly walked away, stopping only where I felt safe, and then I turned around to watch the takeoff. The numerous notches on the "aircraft" deepened and opened like toothless blue mouths, grew round, and exhaled something—or more likely "nothing"—with such force that it created shimmering waves of haze all around. Liftoff looked even more rapid than it had felt from inside. Soon the machine was just a shapeless shrinking spot, then a dim dot, and then gone.

Only now did I fully realize where I was and experience the ambivalent emotions that any human would feel stepping for the first time on another planet. I looked around at a field of peculiar pale-pink grass. Above me stretched a strange, cloudless, pale-pink sky pierced like a wound by the crimson sun, without rays or corona, as if a rough, cruel hand had cut it out.

To one side loomed silhouettes of tall, thick-branched trees; the field in front of me ended abruptly in the distance, cut off by a darker-green strip flowing toward the hazy horizon. The air was totally still, but cool and clean, filled with unknown fragrances. And with silence—indescribable, complete silence, penetrating into all recesses of the brain, all cells of the body, absorbing even my heartbeats, and my breathing.

I broke the spell with a whisper, feeling that my words would be locked in that silence forever, like insects preserved in amber. "Are we supposed to wait here, Siko?"

"Yes."

"When are they going to come for us?"

"In about thirty-two minutes."

"Who told you about the place and time of the meeting?"

"A human told me."

"Who was that human? How and where did you receive the information?"

"A human with a password gave me the information using a radio connection on the Earth," said the robot.

His answer shattered my romantic mood. Before we left Earth? That's interesting! Especially if we consider how extremely rare and difficult connections with Eyrena were and that I left just a day after the message about Fowler and Stein's deaths.

I started fishing for more information, whatever that might be.

"Had you ever been in a Yusian starship before, Siko?"

"That's not possible."

"Why? Why is it not possible?" I asked, struck by a vague guess.

The robot waited a minute or two before answering, "I was created three hours before our departure."

"OK, but if you hadn't been on a starship before, how did you know we had departed?"

"By the change of the magnetic conditions that occurred at sixteen hundred twelve hours."

"And how did you know that the apartment was equipped with everything I would need for my safety?"

"I have indicators for reading basic life parameters and detected no deviations."

"And did you register any deviations later?"

"Only once."

"When did that happen, and what were the deviations?"

"Nine minutes after the takeoff, the content of nitrogen in the breathing mixture decreased, and the ionization increased. I didn't signal because neither would be harmful for you."

So it seemed that the deviations began when I first noticed the miniature likeness of my head. Did this mean that the effigy was created at exactly that time? Incidentally, I had brought it with me, hoping at some point to determine its meaning or at least to analyze its composition.

I continued the interrogation: "Have you been in contact with any of the Yusians on the starship?"

"No."

"So how did you find out what you were supposed to do in order to pilot the Yusian shuttle?"

"By drawing logical conclusions."

"Oh."

I was silent for a while, petting Jerry, preoccupied with my thoughts, before I spoke again.

"Besides the orders from that human with the password, did you receive orders from anyone else?"

"Yes."

"From whom!"

"From you," replied the robot.

"I see. By the way, how long did you wait for me at the launch site?"

"Two minutes."

Remembering the raindrops on his shoulders, I realized that he was lying.

"Do you have any other messages for me?"

"No."

Although it was nearly impossible that my boss had contacted this robot, which no doubt had been sent by Zung, I decided to try my emergency password. I pronounced it distinctly.

"I don't understand you," the robot said.

"OK."

I opened the larger suitcase, took out my bathrobe sash, and tied Jerry to the suitcase handle. Then I turned back to the robot. "You know the coordinates of the base, right?"

"Yes."

"Tell me what they are."

"Why?" Maybe the robot had guessed my intentions.

"Just tell me!"

This time he answered, though reluctantly. I saved them in my watch memory so that, in case those who were supposed to meet me didn't show up, I could reach the base on my own.

"Come with me!" I told the robot, heading in a direction opposite to the one they were supposed to come from.

He followed me. I didn't want him behind my back, so I waited for him to pass me. He was walking slowly on purpose, I was sure! As we distanced ourselves from him, Jerry started to whimper, afraid that I would leave him. I resisted the temptation to look back and offer some comforting words. I was concentrating on the back of the robot, keeping my right hand in my unbuttoned jacket. We walked about three hundred meters. The forest was still far away; I didn't have time to take him there.

"Stop!"

The robot stopped and turned to me. He looked intensely into my eyes, though not as fixedly as he had stared at the Yusians yet with a dim red glow that, I suspected, reflected some inner suffering and a deep, nonhuman insight.

I told him to turn around and took out my gun. Aiming at the sensor bump on the back of his head, I pulled the trigger. The massive, flawlessly made body quivered as if alive and then collapsed. I bent over, turned it on its left side, and released and lowered the molybdenum armor on the chest. It moved and stretched its arms toward me, but I was faster—removed the energy battery, isolated the reactivators to prevent an explosion, and cut the emergency switches in its backup system. I carefully disengaged the deactivated circuits, put them next to the body, and reinserted the battery. Then I stepped back.

At first nothing hinted that steadily increasing energy was moving through the robot's arteries, but soon its open chest started radiating a strange, almost mystical glow. That glow soon surrounded the arms, legs, shoulders, and even the pleasant face with its grotesquely simplified human features, a fatal aura wrapping the robot like a shroud. Only a moment later, the surrounding grass literally evaporated, leaving it at the center of a completely empty circle, isolated from the field. As its metal components heated to the melting point, I could hear cables hissing inside the body, the plates and condensers cracking. Then came the first rupture in its outer shell.

When only a peculiar, shapeless mass remained, I turned and walked away. This was one of those many moments when I regretted my choice of profession.

Jerry had climbed on the suitcase, both little front paws tucked close to his body. He looked miserably out of place: a small pet tied to a suitcase in the middle of some pink field who knows how many parsecs from Earth. I hurried toward him, calling, "Hey, Jerry!"

He jumped down from the suitcase, pulling it frantically toward me. I rushed to untie him; the sash was tight around his neck, almost choking him. But Jerry wasn't angry with me. He recovered quickly and began exploring the area immediately, free for maybe the first time. Yes, it was worth taking him with me. Still I felt vaguely remorseful because of him. Did I have the right to take him to the base, not knowing why or how he had ended up with the Yusians? No, I didn't, but to leave him with them just like that, because of unproven suspicions, seemed a worse betrayal. It was time to stop being afraid of those nonhumanoids!

I sat on one of the suitcases. The wide-open spaces gradually relaxed me, releasing my built-up tension, the continuous expectation of unwelcome surprises. Everything was peaceful, cool, and quiet. The starship was far away; I was waiting to meet humans. Humans! I whistled to Jerry, and he bounded toward me with admirable speed. He looked so good, hovering in the light grass and jumping elegantly, warm mahogany gleams dancing on his little black back. Every inch of his body radiated eagerness, thirst for play, attention, and petting.

I jumped to my feet and began running, pretending to be afraid. When he reached me, we started roughhousing until we were both out of breath and then lay together on the grass. I talked to him quietly, my fingers buried in his soft fur, while he gazed at me with utterly faithful dog eyes, gleaming with love and excitement. It felt good to be together, and we accepted each other completely, without the slightest doubt or hesitation.

CHAPTER 8

Twenty minutes later than the time predicted by the robot, the roar of an engine came from the north, disrupting the serene surroundings. As I rose, a small, open jeep approached me, a long-haired figure behind the wheel. Jerry got up too, growling with dissatisfaction and suspicion, while I stood with my hands in the pockets of my corduroy trousers as if I were bored. *If this is a woman*, I thought, *her late arrival makes perfect sense. Women wouldn't even be on time for the Last Judgment.*

And a woman it was. She slammed on the brakes and rested her elbows on the steering wheel. I watched to see if she would look around for the robot, but she didn't. She just sat there a few moments, surveying us with narrowed eyes, and then burst into a playful ringing laugh. I listened suspiciously but detected neither madness nor hysteria in her. It was just the normal laugh of a tactless young woman who obviously thought we looked ridiculous.

"It's a pleasant surprise to find you in such a good mood," I said wryly.

She stopped laughing, jumped with surprising ease—considering her tight skirt—over the jeep's door, leaned on it and, again tactlessly, started studying my face. I knew it must look ruddy in this damned sunlight, which embarrassed me a bit. Of course her face looked the same way, but on her the glow was flattering. All in all, a very pretty woman, even stunning: tall and slender, thick brownish hair, slightly elongated light-blue eyes, straight aristocratic nose, and full sensual lips. An ideal oval face, a knockout figure, and perfect posture.

"You must be Linda Ridgeway," I guessed.

"Wrong already, Inspector!" she said gaily. "I'm Elia Slade."

I shrugged and was preparing an appropriately cutting reply when I noticed that her attention had shifted.

"Where did you get *him*?" She gestured toward Jerry with obvious affection.

"I never abandon my friends," I said half-jokingly.

"Did you bring him from Earth?"

"As far as I know, dogs are born only there—for now."

Elia nodded seriously, paused thoughtfully, and then crossed to us and sat on the grass next to Jerry. But he wasn't thrilled by her closeness and showed it with his own lack of tact. He jumped backward, growled threateningly, and even bared his baby teeth with a snarl when she tenderly extended her hand.

"Well, well!" Elia exclaimed approvingly. "Not very friendly, is he?"

"Sometimes he's a little hot tempered," I said, smiling, "but—I'm sure your good influence will gradually calm him down."

"That's a compliment I could only get from a total stranger!" She stood up, adding, "Well, Terry, are we going or not?"

Her excessive familiarity not only surprised but also pleased me. Still, I decided it would be wiser not to encourage it. Taking the suitcases, I silently headed to the jeep and put them in the trunk before climbing in front. Jerry joined me, but only after plenty of coaxing, and I quickly closed the door behind him.

Meanwhile Elia, who had returned to the driver's seat, was needlessly straightening her hair and impatiently tapping on the gas pedal.

"Everybody ready?" She turned the key in the ignition without waiting for an answer.

I usually don't pay attention to people's clothing, but hers immediately confused me. Such extravagant elegance didn't match either the battered jeep or the whole situation she had lived in, not for a day or two but for seven months now. Her tight-fitting long skirt with interwoven gold threads boasted a side slit to midthigh. It was matched by golden spiked heels that struck me as extremely uncomfortable. Her creamy-pink blouse irresistibly caught my eye with its plunging neckline. To top it all off, bracelets and rings adorned her hands, and a necklace accentuated the plunge. Was this outfit just for my arrival?

"I'm still a little drunk," she blurted, gently massaging her forehead with her long, slender, aristocratic fingers, a statement that completely startled me.

"Is that so?" I tilted my head politely. "And what was the occasion?"

"There are always occasions here," she retorted sharply, "for everything."

I expected to hear some supporting examples, but Elia Slade just kept driving through the field. A slight smile of malicious joy suggested that she was waiting for me to ask impatient questions that she never planned to answer. I probably disappointed her by turning my attention to the surrounding scenery.

I had examined the grass before the jeep came into view but decided to check it out again, mainly just to fill the time. I leaned out the window and, after a few misses, managed to pull out some stalks. I separated one of them and twisted it absentmindedly in my fingers. It was covered with long soft hairs, which made it look light pink and fluffy, but after removing the hairs at the base, out of which they actually grew, I could see that the stem was dark and tubular, the two edges along its length leading to a sharply bent top.

I took out my penknife and cut the stem along its edges to reveal a hollow, smooth, and shiny interior.

"Yusians are extremely intelligent and noble creatures," Elia blurted out unexpectedly. "Or more correctly, they are what we imagine *we* are. I think that's why they disgust us."

"But—why are you telling me this?"

"Because of your curiosity." She pointed at the cut stem in my hand.

Puzzled, I looked at it again. When I saw it move, tickling my palm a little, I dropped it on the seat. There it kept moving, trying to grow back together. Elia picked it up and pitched it out the window.

"What did that mean?" I mumbled.

"I don't know. Maybe just an extreme vitality."

"Why 'maybe'? Don't you study them?"

"Of course, we study them. We study them all the time. We burn them, cook them, cut them, poison them. Not only them but also those trees over there—everything that we come across. You know the appropriate response to such situations, don't you? When you encounter something unknown, you put on a laboratory coat and a mask and—go!"

"Why don't you suggest better ways if you don't like that response?"

"The point is I don't know any," Elia admitted frankly.

The field ended, and the green strip I had seen before in the distance turned out to be the beginning of a vast terrain covered with fernlike plants as tall as a man. We drove down a narrow, steep road that cut through them. Interestingly, around the base of each plant grew a nest of light-pink fluff similar to the hairs covering the stems of that "extremely vital" grass.

As the road descended steeply, Elia turned off the engine. We rode in almost complete silence, the oncoming air fluttering our hair. I closed my eyes and imagined myself back on Earth at some quiet spot filled with familiar greenery.

Some time later, I commented, "I still don't understand why you were praising the Yusians."

"Never mind," Elia shrugged. "Just suppose it's the role I have taken here, and I will keep playing it regardless of your presence."

"What about applause? Do you get any recognition for your performance?"

"I'd consider the hiss of fools a surer sign of success." Frowning, Elia stared at the road ahead.

I didn't let her brood long, although her profile was as appealing as the full face view. "When did you learn of my arrival?"

"About"—she checked her little gold bracelet watch—"about an hour ago."

"So the Yusians gave you the message?"

"Yes, but it came from Earth."

"Are you trying to say—"

"Look, Terry," Elia interrupted me with annoyance, "it's easy. Our people prepared the message and asked the Yusians to give it to us when you reached Eyrena, along with the meeting's coordinates. That's it.

"Hey, Ehrlich! Ehrlich!" she shouted abruptly, waving her hand jubilantly.

I looked ahead of us just in time to see a tall bony man reluctantly emerging from the ferns by the side of the road. We stopped next to him. He also gave no sign that he expected to see a robot with me.

"Where are you heading this early?" Elia asked him briskly.

"*You* took the jeep, and *now* you ask me!" the man said, growling.

"But I had to meet the inspector, Ehrlich. I had to do it right. And you could have waited for us. Why this hurry? By the way"—Elia turned to me and continued solemnly—"Inspector Terence Simon, allow me to introduce to you our exobiologist, Ehrlich Reder!"

I climbed out of the jeep and crossed to him. Lowering his huge bag to the ground, he came to attention, tapped his heels, and nodded briskly. About forty years old, he had a long ascetic face with a high forehead and an arched nose that resembled a bird's beak. His thin lips stiffened into an artificial smile; unusually round and inexpressive eyes stared into mine as if they were looking at empty space.

"I am sorry I didn't *wait* for you, Inspector." Reder spoke with a husky voice and seemingly randomly emphasized some of his words. "I have been very busy *lately*."

"It's only *six or seven kilometers* to the base, Ehrlich." Elia echoed his pattern of emphasis, as if mocking him. "Come with us, and then you can have the jeep."

I calculated that Reder must have left for this place right after the message about my arrival came. And what was he carrying in the bag? I wanted to check but knew from experience that such a rough beginning would complicate my job further.

"Thank you, *Elia*," he responded, his voice ice cold. "I will continue *on foot*."

"Well, I'm sorry! I took this route only because I thought we would run into you, but I see now it was just a waste of time."

"Good-bye, Inspector! I'll *see* you around noon." Reder tapped his heels again, picked up the bag, and headed up the road.

Elia grinned behind his back. Once I returned to the jeep, she immediately slammed the gas pedal. The road was still descending, but she was no longer content to coast down.

"Ambushes, eh?" I asked casually.

"Well, yes! See how I'm helping you? You just arrived, and there you go, meeting the first suspect! In such a hurry with that big bag on his shoulder—"

"What was that about the jeep?" I interrupted her babble. "Don't you have any other means of transportation here?"

"Oh, we do! Plenty. But Ehrlich wouldn't use anything else, even in a fire or flood."

"Why?"

"The others are Yusian—that's why—and he violently detests anything Yusian. If you knew how he felt in the starship."

"I think I do understand," I replied. "But tell me, Elia, was everyone at the base when you left?"

"No. The mission commander has been at the research field since yesterday."

"And the other two?"

"My colleague was asleep. I guess the deputy chief won't be available either. He was very drunk. We were having drinks with him when we got the message."

"It's obvious you don't let your work schedule interfere with parties and sleeping," I added.

"It's night now, Terry. That ugly light up there is Shidexa. Ridon won't rise for more than four hours."

"Oh, I forgot you have two suns."

"It's not a big luxury!" Elia pursed her lips with surprising malice.

The fern fields ended as abruptly as had the grasslands. We entered an expanse of thick, leafless, cylindrical, deep-crimson plants. But for their rough, cracked husks, they would look exactly like pillars rising from the ground.

"Are there animals here?" I asked Elia.

"Unfortunately, we haven't come across even primitive, unicellular organisms that are not plant related. Nor is the flora very diverse; we're almost certain that only four kinds of plants grow on the planet. At least on land."

"And in the water?"

"The river and the lake next to the base are as dead as—"

"I meant seas and oceans."

"They will be studied by the future colonists," she replied, clearly irritated, and drove even faster.

We covered the remaining distance to the notorious base in silence. Hidden among monstrous trees with five trunks, its walls paneled with rough-hewn wood, the three-story building looked more like a hunting lodge than a research facility. A front terrace and french windows adorned the first floor, while the second and third floors boasted balconies with bronze railings that looked like stylized birds in flight. An old-fashioned new england weather vane, cock and all, perched on the orange slate roof. Above the main entrance hung a deer's head, with a huge rack of antlers!

"This, this"—I pointed with my finger because I had almost lost the ability to speak—"*this* was made by the Yusians?"

Elia shrugged impatiently, as if to say my question was unnecessary.

"Oh my God," I cried, losing my temper. "What are they doing here, mocking us?"

Elia shrugged again. She stopped the jeep, waited until Jerry and I climbed out, and then drove into the small garage decorated with intricate wood carvings. I gaped inanely after her.

"Welcome," I heard a rough voice behind me.

I turned around. A man in a light suit stood on the terrace, inhaling deeply on the butt of a cigarette vanishing between his fingers.

"Look at you, Phil! So you got your energy back!" Elia shouted from the garage. "Come on then, meet the inspector. I'm on the verge of total exhaustion! This is Philip Vernie, Terry. You can count on him for anything, as long as it doesn't really matter and has nothing to do with his work."

Vernie nervously flipped away his cigarette butt and crossed to me, extending his hand. We entered the building together, passed through a wood-paneled foyer, and climbed an elegantly curved staircase to the third floor. The thickly carpeted hall was lined on the right side by doors to apartments with balconies and on the left by windows offering views of the landscape, an unobstructed panorama of a stately forest rising up the hill behind the building.

When we stopped in front of a window, Vernie opened it and abruptly started to speak, randomly pointing at objects in the hollow. "Over there are the laboratories. We have only three. The medical building is across from here. The tennis court, swimming pool, and gym are on the side. As you can see, the Yusians decided that the sports complex should take up more space than the laboratories. As if to say, 'Pay more attention to your physique, boys and girls! You're not evolved enough for science yet.' And these are the garages. Pretty big, ha? They supplied us with all kinds of vehicles: cargo transports, aircraft. We can't complain, can we? And those arched buildings—maybe we can call them block buildings?—are for storage. In half of them we stored our own materials, but those are empty now. We used up everything! Those on the other side are still packed with all kinds of materials, but not from Earth, you know. But we don't go in there. Only robots go there. We have plenty! Long live ESSIKO company, right? Everything belongs to the company! But the laboratories, as you saw for yourself, are small. Other than that, they are perfectly equipped, but—"

Philip Vernie slammed the window shut and headed down the hall, a short, chubby man with stubby arms and legs, walking so clumsily I thought he might fall. His rumpled suit coat didn't fit him well. His curly brown hair was parted on the side, apparently with a wet comb.

"I am now the deputy commander of this base," he said, turning to me. "Larsen went to the research field. *Alone*, of course!" He gave me a mysterious wink and then continued, "So here you are now—while I am in charge! What a surprise, ha? I decided to put you in Fowler's apartment. It's not bad. The location, I mean. Here it is!" He gestured me through a wide open door. "As soon as Elia left to meet you, I ordered the robots to prepare it for you. Please! Make yourself at home!"

He made another expansive welcoming gesture, as though he were a hotel proprietor. When we entered the living room, he dove into the first armchair he saw and energetically rubbed his hands together. Jerry then appeared in the company of a robot, who was carrying my suitcases.

"Leave the suitcases in the bedroom and get lost!" Vernie shouted.

The robot rushed to carry out his order.

"This place is literally infested with robots," Vernie found it necessary to point out again. "When we need them, we can call them right away. But if we don't need them, why should they be in our way? Am I right?"

I nodded in agreement and at the same time considered the possible implications of what he said. Was he implying that he knew I had destroyed the robot assigned to me?

"But come to think of it," he added, "you're probably not used to them yet. Where on Earth can you have such luxury?"

"I'll get used to them," I said. "I think I'll get used to them quickly."

I waited to give him an opportunity to reply, but since he restrained himself, I started checking out the apartment. I soon recognized its similarities to the one in the starship—the same floor plan, even the same style of furniture. Apparently Yusians didn't have much imagination. I came back into the living room and asked, "Well? Are we going out?"

"No," he replied. "We can talk here. Fortunately the whole base is constructed solely of materials from Earth, so we managed to take precautions against eavesdropping in the lodge and at all other important places around the complex."

"Finally, something good."

"Well, yes! At least as far as antisurveillance is concerned, our technical equipment works perfectly. As you know, we have made great progress in that area, *especially* during the last ten years."

We exchanged a look of complicity.

"Hey, you're probably hungry," suggested Vernie, remembering to play the gracious host. "Let's go to the dining room."

I politely refused and sat across from him, hoping that we would get right down to business. But he jumped to his feet and rushed into the kitchen, muttering, "Just a moment."

He soon returned, carrying a tray containing three plates of sandwiches, two glasses, and a bottle of wine. He put the tray on the table in front of me, took one of the plates, and put it in front of Jerry.

"I love animals." Vernie reclaimed his previous spot with a sigh. "I like all kinds of animals but dogs most of all. And out of all dogs, I like cocker spaniels the best. This one is purebred, I guarantee it! Who gave him to you?"

"An acquaintance."

"I see. Looks like it was a close acquaintance."

"Probably."

"Exactly—'probably'! One can never be sure of anything. If you trust anyone too much—you're lost! Just like me. Because I trusted myself! I overestimated myself, and that's why I came here. Do you know how I looked before? Like you! I was still shorter than you, of course, but in every other way, I was like you: young, healthy, strong, and handsome. Oh! But now? Look at me. I ruined myself! Just look!"

It was true. His face was far from young and handsome. But as far as I was concerned, that last epithet never would have fit him anyway. His forehead bulged, his nose was flattened, and his mouth was too wide. Not qualifications for conventional masculine beauty. Nonetheless, this face had something attractive about it. Pleasing and somehow vulnerable at the same time. At least that was the impression created by his eyes—big and warm brown, with a surprisingly childish look despite the red lids and swollen skin around them.

"How old do you think I am?" he asked and, thank God, saved me from the trouble by answering himself, "Thirty-four! Yes, *just* thirty-four, but unfortunately you'd never know it now. She thinks I'm almost an old man!"

"Who is 'she'?"

"It's clear who—*Elia*." Vernie poured himself a glass of wine and, with a grimace of deep sadness, took a few sips.

Here's Zung's traditional love drama, I told myself, *the short, plain man and the splendid indifferent beauty*. Well, fine, I understood, but did the deputy base commander really have to begin with these totally inappropriate revelations?

"Yes." I shook my head. "I suppose it's hard to live this way, far from Earth, and no regular contact—"

"It's not just 'hard.' It's unbearable! The Earth is not just 'far' away—it's *galaxies* away. And we not only have 'no *regular* contact'—we have *no* contact at all!" Vernie specified zealously.

"No contact? What do you want to say?"

"I don't *want* to say it, Simon! I *am* saying it. We have no *direct* contact with Earth. We...well...you probably know better than I do how things are here."

It would be tiring and useless to pretend I was thoroughly well informed, but to acknowledge openly that I didn't know the main facts of the case would be a mistake as well. Once people realize that you expect to learn the truth from them, they can't resist the temptation to hide or distort it, even when that does them no good. With very little doubt, at the Eyrena base lives at least one person who wouldn't mind at all if I remained confused.

"Look, Vernie," I started, "my trip here was urgent and had to be arranged at the last minute, so I may have the wrong impression about some details. For example, I know you exchange information with Earth mainly through Yusians, but I didn't know you had no direct contact. Didn't they give you an independent channel?"

"No. They *didn't*."

"But why? Do they have technology problems?"

"'Problems'? No way! They can jump over light-years in minutes, and that's when there's no need to hurry. But we are not even allowed to *crawl* through their infamous information channels."

"But the agreement was signed anyway?"

"Agreement?" Vernie gulped down his glass of wine. "What agreement are you talking about, Simon? You arrive here after about two weeks spent in a Yusian starship, so those bastards definitely must have tried to communicate with you. You saw some of their advanced technology—disgusting stuff. Well, what kind of agreement could there be in this case? How do you picture it: in black and white with articles, items, and paragraphs? Discussed by competent equals, carefully argued, and mutually negotiated? Signed by designated representatives of two 'amicable' civilizations—"

I cut him off. "Whatever the procedure, clearly the decision to deny humans on Eyrena a direct connection with Earth is enforced by somebody. By *somebody*. And not necessarily the Yusians, right?"

"I don't know."

"You probably have an opinion, though."

Vernie barely considered the question before snapping firmly, "No. I have no opinions. Absolutely no opinions about anything."

"Good for you!" I praised him ironically. "And how did you manage to achieve such detached enlightenment?"

"It wasn't easy," he answered. "Only with great difficulty and gradually."

"You think this is the best way to behave, do you?"

"And do you think *you* will be able to choose how you behave from now on?"

I shrugged disparagingly. "No matter how hard some people try to deny it, a person always has an opportunity to choose."

"But must always choose what circumstances dictate," Vernie said, with a sigh, and continued without a pause, "I hope you will feel comfortable here. It's an end unit, and Stein lived on the other side, so—"

"So I'll be isolated here?" I guessed the thought he didn't finish.

He nodded calmly. He was really beyond all bounds!

"I appreciate the fact that you made sure I won't be disturbed, Vernie."

"I do my best to look after everyone," he summarized. "You're going to be too loud to be a good neighbor."

"Loud?"

"Well, yes, especially in the morning."

"But why, *why* would you think *that*?"

Vernie heaved himself up from the armchair. "I'll try to catch some sleep, an hour or two," he said, his eyes flickering with guilt as if he had confessed some criminal intention. He unlocked the door and then closed it behind him. The thick hall carpet immediately muffled his receding footsteps.

CHAPTER 9

I was happy! Happy, happy. I was choking with happiness, laughing. Screaming with happiness! And my voice, strong and beautiful as a god's, lifted me from a deep sleep. My awakening was a slow and delightful swim through silken, sinuous waves—toward a gleaming coast of soft amber.

My eyes opened effortlessly, imperceptibly, discovering the silhouette of the day that waited for me shimmering through the window curtains. I rushed forward to meet that new day and opened the window. It streamed in like a joyous golden bird in flight!

And then?

Then a still, crystalline sky, the eye of a dearly beloved woman. And down there on the balcony and on the roof of the garage, all along the road, on the side path to the forest, sparkled millions, billions of little suns. Or no—tiny crystals that had absorbed the warm face of the sun of suns, of Ridon. Crystals—a gentle rain of crystals fell from the branches of the trees with their five noble trunks. The breeze cupped the crystals in its invisible palms, rocked them in the transparent air, and spread them like a miraculous ephemeral coverlet.

I leaned out of the window, stretched my arms, and stayed in this position for a long time, thirstily devouring the view.

The hairs on my arms turned silver, my skin began to sparkle, my fingers looked shiny and smooth, free of ugly wrinkles, even fingernails. Laughing, I watched my arms becoming crystal!

And my face? I rushed impatiently to the bathroom mirror, and my laughter turned to tears of happiness when I saw this shimmering, almost unrecognizable face with its silver hair and brows, eyelashes and lips that looked as if they had been kissed by light. I skipped my shower—I was already crystal clean. Holding my left foot with my hand, I jumped on one foot to the living room—it was good exercise. And funny too. When I opened the door with my elbow, there, cuddled in one of the armchairs, was my adorable canine companion.

"Come on, Jerry, get up! You lay-zee thing!" I stuttered, hardly able to keep myself from bursting into laughter. "Get up, get up, enough sleeping!"

When Jerry didn't react, I came closer and shook him. He still didn't move! Of course, he was sound asleep. I quietly returned to the bedroom, put on the thinnest shirt I had and the lightest pants. I didn't want to wear shoes but put them on for Elia. *What a beauty! I will invite her to go for a long, crystal walk!*

There were four doors along the hallway. I knocked on every one of them but didn't get any answer. I went down to the second floor, sliding on the banisters to speed my progress. That was great fun, but at the bottom, I almost ran into a woman. I burst into hearty laughter.

"We almost had a collision, didn't we?" I asked playfully.

"Don't worry," she replied. Maybe she didn't show her admiration for my shimmering silver face because she was too shy.

"Worry?" I exclaimed. "Me? On such a day? No way! Do you know what Chuks told me once?"

"No."

"'We,' as he put it 'look for equalized generosity,' or something like that."

"Is that so?"

"Why should he lie to me? He's not a fool."

"Let's go have breakfast."

"You are a lovely lady!" I exaggerated to cheer her up, although she was attractive. She couldn't compare with my Elia, but—she was small boned, had soft and tender light-brown eyes, and her features were as delicate as if an artist had drawn them on with the thinnest of brushes. Her hair pulled up in a smooth twist, she wore no makeup and a simple dark-blue dress.

"No, you are not Linda Ridgeway either," I realized.

"No," she said. "I am not."

"But you have to be," I corrected myself, "because there are only two women here."

"You think so?"

"Why? Are there more?" I was thrilled at the prospect.

"No. What I mean is, do you think that if there are only two women at the base, one of us must be Linda Ridgeway?"

"Oh! Please! That wasn't what I meant. But somebody else thinks that. Or, to be more precise, he said that. Or suggested it as a possibility."

"I see," she said. "But let's not stay here talking any longer."

I preferred to walk the rest of the way down with her rather than using the banister this time. I really liked this woman. When we reached the kitchen, we prepared our own coffee and sandwiches and took them into the dining room.

"You don't like robots." I shook my finger jokingly.

"No. I don't like them." She was wonderfully direct.

"And I *do* like them, even if that sounds unbelievable."

"Why should it be unbelievable?" she asked.

Her honesty required a similar response, but I had other responsibilities, so I answered more evasively. "To really like somebody, you have to get to know him. As far as the robots are concerned, I couldn't say I *know* them. This is why I don't believe I *really* like them. I am only imagining I *could*. Does that make sense?"

"Completely," she replied.

I got another sandwich, then a third, or fourth—I didn't count them.

"Hey, you're not eating!" I reproached her, pouring myself more coffee.

"Well—in fact, I am not hungry. I had breakfast—before Ridon rose."

"Good for you! You are an early bird. And the commander? Where is Larsen?"

"Why do you need him?"

"I want to pay him a visit."

"When?"

"Right now! The sooner, the better."

She looked at me, preoccupied. "Wouldn't it be better if you don't rush it? Take a long walk first and relax."

"That's right! A good long walk! And Larsen can go to hell! Will you come with me?"

"You go ahead. I'll catch up a little later."

It was clear she wasn't planning on catching up with me, but I wasn't angry with her. I got up and gently touched her shoulder. "What's your name?"

"Odesta Gomez."

"I want you to be happy, Odesta! As happy as I am!"

"I have been even happier. That's why I recommend that you take a long walk and then nap for an hour or two. Around noon, everything will be all right."

I sincerely laughed at her concern, gave her a friendly wave, and ran outside. The white crystal rain was ringing and singing around me—its clear tones showering me with tender caresses. I walked down the winding path of light, deeper and deeper into the strange forest, under a smooth blue sky covered with the miraculous silver lace of branches etched on its surface. Each step summoned the whisper of a thousand crystal voices. I closed my eyes, dazzled and dazed by their friendliness, smiling because I knew I was all white, white even in my thoughts.

As I walked, everything in my past seemed very small, very insignificant. Yes, light-years away, beyond stars and the vastness of space, lay our confused, vague Earth with its equally confused, vague people wandering around lost, loaded down with confused, vague suspicions. Is it possible that I was like them? That I was sent from Earth to this paradise to find murderers? How absurd!

A strange new quaver high above drew my surprised attention. The branches had started rocking, but not as if a wind was blowing. The rocking was somehow purposeful, and its rhythm steadily increased. Gradually, the rhythm captured the silver trunks that resembled reaching arms and then even the strong star-shaped roots.

The forest was dancing! The trees bowed and bent in quick, rhythmic steps! Back and forth, back and forth. Myriads of the playful tiny crystals that reflected the sun were dancing everywhere as well. The crystal rain grew stronger, its quiet ringing becoming a solemn triumphant hymn. The air thickened, and I gulped its fresh aroma with gasping insatiability and felt it pouring down my throat, filling up my lungs, cleansing my body, my spirits. I was becoming a part of...of...

I snuggled up to one of the trees, and it cradled me, back and forth, back and forth. The trembling tree felt almost hot through my thin shirt, as if I could experience the impetuous circulation of juices under its hard skin. *My beautiful, living, incomprehensible being! My face is being scratched by your rough caress; my eyes are filled with tears of ecstasy. I know the truth is in you, but what is it? What!* I stepped back to admire the dark red of my blood against its white trunk, a beautiful contrast reminiscent of some ancient sacrificial rite.

Suddenly the rain stopped, and the crystal mantle of the forest started to float downward. As it flowed down my face, arms, and clothes, I left the path, wandering without direction, amazed and touched by this unexpected metamorphosis. The silver world around me slowly turned yellow, calming down, mellowing into a deep delightful sleep. The bulging tree roots slowly sank back into the ground. The tamed trunks became shorter, sighing quietly, and wearily lowered their splendid crowns. I saw their branches, covered with mist, extend toward each other and interweave into graceful golden clusters. I saw how these clusters became thicker and blended into ghostly curtains, casting yellow-purple shadows around.

The air became so dense that its resistance made my progress slow and clumsy, and my hair floated up and down as if I were trying to walk under water. As I passed, the stiffened five-trunk trees were sinking down, awry, stretching up, bending to the side—like phantom yellow runners frozen after the first moments of a false start.

How strange it all was, how bizarre: the complete immobility, this deep, almost material silence. No fluttering birds, no buzzing bugs, and no whisper of leaves. The soil was so elastic that my steps made no sound. Stillness and silence. Combined with a constant sensation of satiated life, life completely fulfilled.

At the end of the forest, I stopped under the bright light now flowing all over me. I reached the beginning of a gentle slope, from where I could see the whole complex of garages, storage units, laboratories, sports complexes, and fields of the Eyrena base. I sat there and enjoyed the view for a long time, realizing that I had made a large semicircle during my walk. Now the lodge stood directly in front of me, on the other side of the horseshoe-shaped hollow and almost at eye level. Its orange tile roof was glittering, generously lit by sunbeams; the weather cock proudly pointed like a finger into the sky. For some reason, the windows were diamond shaped rather than rectangular, which impressed me as unique. As a matter of fact, I liked the building, with all its eccentricities.

I liked everything! As I gazed around admiring everything, my attention was caught by the sports building on the left, closest to me. I imagined its cool blue pool and rose immediately, deciding that taking a swim would be wonderful. I started running down the slope, slipping often, but I managed to keep my balance, and when I reached the sport building, I wasn't even out of breath. I had no problem finding my way to the dressing room and threw my clothes into the first locker I came to. Stayed a minute or two under the shower. Found a bag with a pair of swimming trunks on the shelf across the shower, opened it, and put them on.

Not a soul in the corridor. I ran into a robot, ESSIKO, of course, but didn't pay any attention to him. I didn't pay any attention to him at all! However, when I headed for the pool, he wouldn't leave me alone. He started following me closely, adjusting his steps to mine.

"What is it?" I asked over my shoulder.

"A lot of things," he said. "What do you want to know?"

I stopped to think. Then I realized that he misunderstood my question and started walking again. As did the robot behind me.

"Get lost," I suggested, over my shoulder again.

"I have to be here today."

"'Here' could be also there." I pointed to one of the side benches.

Now he stopped to think. Meanwhile, I jumped on the diving board a few times and then dove in. The water was icy cold. *Just the crawl stroke! Only do the crawl!* I was swimming in the far right lane, and the robot walked beside me at the edge of the pool. I didn't see him on my way back because I was taking breaths only on one side. Then I saw him again, and then I didn't.

All of a sudden I felt very tired. I was almost in the middle of the pool and would have to struggle to reach the ladder. It felt as if I were pushing through sand, not water. I noticed the robot leaning over me and felt his hard, inhuman fingers in my hair. I jerked abruptly—I don't know where I found the strength—and grasped the ladder. It must have taken me a few minutes to pull myself up, and I heard myself whisper hoarsely, "Go away, go away, go away."

Before my eyes, on the robot's square shoulder, the huge blurry patch that read ESSIKO kept coming closer and then going further away. I fell into the closest lounge chair. The incident didn't alarm me, but fatigue felt like a ball on my chest or a big, quiet cat purring me to sleep, sleep. All that kept me awake was a vaguely troubling thought, a muted concern about something half-forgotten—concern for another sleeper—also laboring under the weight of an unnatural, impossible sleep. Poor Jerry!

I strained to get up and thought I had. Then I realized I was still flat on my back in the cavernous lounge chair. I couldn't move a muscle. Held immobile by some monstrous, malignant force. Without the strength to fight my way out. I couldn't. And Jerry? Of course he hadn't been sleeping. No—I wanted to cry in my frustration, but no tears were running down my face. They too were paralyzed, frozen as solid as crystal behind my closed, motionless eyes.

CHAPTER 10

I woke up with an unpleasant feeling that before I fell asleep something was amiss. When I was fully awake and remembered the morning, I realized that what had not been completely all right was my own head. Then I remembered Jerry and sprang out of the lounge chair. The robot was still here—in my way.

"Drink this," he said and tried to put in my hands a glass filled to the brim with some greenish garbage.

I ducked under his outstretched arm and dashed for the swimming pool exit, remembering my clothes only because I ran past the dressing rooms. I put them on, hopping into my shoes and buttoning my shirt on my way out. I covered the four hundred meters to the lodge in record time and didn't stop until I reached the door of my apartment. I listened carefully, but only silence greeted me.

"Jerry, Jerry!" I called quietly.

Still no sound. I went in and frantically searched for him.

"Jerry, Jerry!"

He wasn't there. I stood across from the armchair where I left him and could still see him lying there curled into a ball, a little helpless pet.

Probably some robot took him out.

A knock at the door startled me. I made an effort to calm my voice. "Come in!"

Elia entered and, behind her, Jerry! He ran to me to show how happy he was to see me, and I petted him with an indulgent smile.

"I was just wondering where he was." I turned to Elia.

"I took him right after you left," she said and then added, "We don't have any other pets here."

I nodded thoughtfully, as if everything were clear to me. Elia looked at me ironically and left the apartment. I put Jerry in my lap and started to recall my unnaturally exultant behavior in the Eyrena forest. Thank God I had sufficient proof to convince myself I was still in my right mind, and after the hints from Vernie and Odesta, I was beginning to understand that Ridon rising in the forest had affected my mind and caused my temporary condition. Since the others had had this experience and managed to live through it, then I could too. But for how long? How many other mornings like this one would I have to endure? And why had nobody at this damn base bothered to warn me?

I fed Jerry a generous meal that was too much for him to finish. After all, he was only three months old. I left him resting and, after a few unsuccessful attempts to cover the scratches on my face, decided to visit the base commander.

"Take me to Larsen!" I ordered a robot stationed in front of the lodge. He led me back toward the sports complex.

We soon passed two annoyingly exotic Chinese gazebos and went down to the lake via a staircase I hadn't even noticed while storming back from the swimming pool. We started around its western side, crossed the sports field that had apparently never been used, went around the laboratories, and skirted two warehouses, bunched together like a pair of deformed bugs, before reaching a ranch-style olive-green building. We crossed through a vestibule so pretentiously furnished that any rich parvenu would love it and entered an irrationally wide hallway to the left, decorated floor to ceiling on both walls with paintings. The robot stopped before a door and announced, "His office is here," before promptly obeying my dismissive gesture.

Pushing a small rectangular button in front of me produced a cloyingly melodious ringing. These Yusian gadgets were getting on my nerves. Nobody answered. I tried the door, which was unlocked, but Larsen wasn't there. I nervously looked around and, glancing at the departing robot, entered the room.

A rug so thick it could suck me in; an imitation fireplace with artificial flames; a carved, inlaid and polished double wardrobe; a rocking chair lit by a pink silk-shaded floor lamp; a leather love seat and, next to the window, a huge antique desk with carved lion's paws for legs—was this office decor or the accoutrements of a *boudoir*? I wouldn't have been surprised to see the base commander appear in a flamboyant Japanese kimono!

Not more than two minutes later, Vernie stormed into the room.

"Ha! Simon!" His surprise was too melodramatic to be convincing. He stared at my scratched face and then sat on the love seat. "I'm looking for Larsen, but I found you! How are you?"

"Fine."

"I see. I need his expertise in cybernetics today, not as a commander." Apparently Vernie liked to explain only what he could easily keep to himself. "We've been building a very important piece of equipment for several months now, and the work has been proceeding according to schedule. Naturally we've encountered a few setbacks too. And Larsen has brains.

He shows up, takes a look around, and all of a sudden comes up with a clever idea."

I crossed my arms and leaned on the edge of the desk.

"Did you have an opportunity to have lunch yet?" Vernie asked after a long silence, obviously uneasy for him.

"Why *shouldn't* I have had that opportunity?"

"Well, it's just an expression." He suddenly assumed a determined expression. "Look, Simon, let's be honest! You shouldn't think I have anything against you. But Odesta—she is our psychologist—decided it was a good…"

Just then, Larsen appeared at the door. It's noteworthy that, instead of turning his attention to me—the newcomer, the IBI inspector, *etcetera*—he stared at Vernie. His eyes grew dark and fixed; his mouth stiffened as if restraining a desire to curse. I would feel very uneasy if somebody looked at me like that. But Vernie, who the night before had impressed me as being nervous and vulnerable, wasn't at all bothered. On the contrary, he gave the commander an impudent smile and sprawled more comfortably on the leather love seat.

Finally Larsen stepped into the room. He came closer and shook my hand. "You can go, Vernie," he said, taking his seat in the chair behind the desk.

"I came here on business," Vernie said firmly. "It's about the defractor."

Larsen frowned. "I thought we agreed that—"

"Oh, no! You are wrong."

"OK, but we'll talk about this later."

"And why not now?" Vernie glared at him. "The inspector will excuse us, I'm sure. And maybe he'll learn some interesting things."

His provoking tone was so uncalled for that I realized I had missed something earlier. He was very, very frightened. But of what?

"You know perfectly well," Larsen began, "that I approved the project for the defractor under the explicit condition that you build it without me."

"Yes, but that condition can't be valid here—especially when imposed by the base commander!"

Now I was sure Vernie was purposely provoking this quarrel so I could hear it, but that made it all the more interesting. A hound dog has to be ready for the rabbit to jump out from under any bush, as the old saying goes.

"I will decide what's valid here and what's not," Larsen said evenly. "And I ask only one thing from you now, Vernie: to understand that I have no time to waste."

"You're an opportunist, Larsen!" Vernie accusingly raised his voice. "You care only about yourself. You don't want to be bothered despite our difficulties with the pending test of the defractor—"

"It's perfectly clear to me," Larsen interrupted him, "that your problems, if there are any at all, can be solved without me."

"Even so, your participation itself would solve other problems."

"There is no point in trying to interpret your last phrase," Larsen said firmly, as if Vernie was simply trying to confuse him. "I didn't give you any other assignments, and your team can use eighty percent of the resources of the base. Don't you agree, to want more than that—"

"Yes, you're right!" Suddenly Vernie became apologetic, remorseful, and almost tearful. "You really provided us with everything we need, but I panicked. Well, I'm sorry! I'm way over the limit. What can I do? Good-bye. Good-bye, Simon."

He left the room, but there was something left unsaid, something subterranean and dark that lingered on, as if he still stood between us. I looked at Larsen questioningly, hoping for some kind of explanation, but he volunteered nothing. Instead, he stood up, crossed to the window, stuck his hands in the pockets of his impeccably ironed trousers, and leaned against the window frame.

He was a typical Scandinavian, big and blond, with that slightly unnatural whiteness characteristic of people who live in the far north. His weather-beaten face with high cheekbones bore an unmistakably intelligent look, but his furrowed forehead and square, massive chin added a ferocious touch that no doubt complicated his contacts with more timid people. His low, bushy brows formed almost a straight line above his impenetrably cold blue eyes; his nose was slightly crooked and gristly, apparently having been broken before. On the left side of his neck an old purpled scar stretched from beside his ear to his short-cropped hair. Despite his age—as far as I could tell he was about fifty—Larsen had the well-built body of an athlete, and under his short-sleeved shirt bulged muscles that nobody would like to see aimed at themselves.

It was apparent that the man in front of me had enough energy and willpower to withstand even more dangerous quakes than the ones that had shaken the Eyrena base. And since he had already been a career military officer when the Yusians first landed on Earth and was chosen for the Eyrena mission exactly because of his military training and experience, I had no doubts about the obedience he commanded here. Yes, but if so, Vernie must have had serious concerns to create such a contrived, daring confrontation.

"I'm not going to ask you what the situation is on Earth." Larsen broke the silence. "When I left, it was very bad. The best-case scenario would be that it is still the same—"

"But it's not," I interrupted.

"After we started killing each other." He seemed to be finishing my sentence.

I knew all along the unlikelihood that I was sent to investigate an accident, but his confirming words still disappointed me. "We killed each other before we met Yusians," I said, "but since they showed up, this ancient method of solving arguments has become very ineffective."

"Yes, ineffective," Larsen repeated dully. "Ineffective."

When I am trapped in a depressing conversation, I feel the need to start reasoning "in principle." Such arguments always sound serious and important while providing an opportunity to stall without being obvious. At the moment I was seriously tempted to start such a discussion, and something told me that Larsen would be happy to join me, but...

"Good self-discipline doesn't guarantee success, but without it, failure is certain," my boss always says, and he is absolutely right. That's why I decided to stick to the concrete facts.

CHAPTER 11

"When and where were Fowler and Stein killed?" I asked.

After circling the desk and settling into his chair, Larsen answered me mechanically. "A day on Eyrena lasts twenty-five hours and two minutes, but it was more convenient to make that twenty-four, so we set the clocks at the base, including the computer clocks, to lose two minutes and thirty-five seconds every hour. As far as the killings are concerned, they happened at approximately the same time, somewhere between eight o'clock on the twenty-sixth and ten fifteen on the twenty-seventh of last month.

"Couldn't you determine the time more accurately?"

"No. The temperature of their bodies was very high." Seeing my surprise, Larsen explained, "We found them in the forest; dead organic matter doesn't decompose or decay there but somehow heats up in the morning hours."

"And what is the reason for these—occurrences?"

"Unfortunately, we don't even have a working hypothesis about this process, or about many other questions, for that matter."

"And somebody told me that Eyrena is no different from Earth!" I sighed.

"If they meant physical characteristics, that's so, despite the two suns and other discrepancies. But the plants—while their cell structure is very close to that of Earth flora, their behavior, life cycles, and the anomalies they cause around them drive our biologists to the brink of despair."

"But they would rather fall off that brink than ask the Yusians for help, right?"

"There are no beggars here, Simon," Larsen noted coldly.

I decided it was time to change the subject. "Tell me all you remember regarding the deaths of Fowler and Stein."

"OK then." He instinctively unbuttoned the top button of his shirt and began, "At the base we follow a strict schedule, and that morning, as usual, we were all having breakfast at five o'clock—that is, about forty minutes before the rise of Ridon. We need to get up early because, when we are awake, it's easier to fight the first signs of the euphoria—which, I'd guess, you also experienced today."

I made a short vague gesture. Larsen continued, "Nothing unusual happened at breakfast, or later, when everybody left for their work stations. Nothing even suggested what was going to happen. And after that—"

"But you must have had some conversations at breakfast," I interrupted him. "Tell me everything that was said, no matter how insignificant it seems to you."

"We eat in full silence in the morning, Simon. We need to maintain complete concentration. Sometimes even the slightest distraction causes the waste of an entire morning."

"Didn't you notice anything strange in Fowler or Stein's behavior? A gesture, a facial expression?"

"In moments like this, none of us can afford the luxury of watching other people," Larsen said. "One's own behavior is troubling enough. So, on the morning of the twenty-sixth, Elia, who was on duty at the base for the day, left to inventory the laboratories.

Odesta was busy in the medical building, Reder drove Stein in the jeep to the biosector, where they separated and Reder continued on to his experimental field. Vernie went to the defractor site, and I went to the research field. Fowler was supposed to pick up a package from Earth the Yusians had told us about the night before, but later we learned that he never made the pickup. We found the trailer he used hidden on the side of the road."

"Where exactly? And what do these trailers look like?"

"They are Yusians cargo machines. Probably they could also fly, but we use them instead of trucks or tractors. The one Fowler used was found between the rocks in the lowland beyond the eastern ridge. That's almost the opposite direction from the part of the forest where we found the bodies."

"So Fowler and Stein were together, is that so?"

"Yes, I think they met there for some reason, in the forest. But then...then...they must have parted forever."

This melodramatic expression seemed out of character, which he apparently realized, because he immediately switched back to his terse, dry recitation of the facts.

"The first to know that Stein had disappeared was Reder. They had planned to begin some experiment at noon, but Stein was late, and he didn't respond to any of Reder's attempts to reach him by radio. Then Reder questioned the robots and found one that had noticed Stein, as early as seven forty, leaving for the sector where Reder worked in the morning. But we still don't know why he didn't get there or even why he headed in that direction."

"And what did Reder do under these circumstances?" I inquired.

"He called me and told me that Stein was missing."

"Were you still at the research field?"

"Yes." Larsen said, not offended by the question. "I was there from six until twelve ten. After Reder's message, I immediately returned to the base. Naturally I sent an SOS from the field, so pretty soon we were all at the base—all but Fowler and Stein."

"Did you interrogate the robots here?"

"At that time, there were no robots here. They were busy with the construction of the defractor."

"How did you organize the search?"

"Using the only logical method, which turned out later to be a big mistake."

"In what way?"

"In every way. But let me explain a few things first so you can understand me. First, the Yusians have already built four settlements for the colonists, at one hundred kilometers to the east, west, north, and south. Second, everyone but Reder uses Yusian shuttles. We have to, since we work in remote areas. Third, when we return to base, we land the shuttles in the parking lot in front of one of the garages. And fourth, for security reasons, each of these shuttles carries the personal code of the person using it and is connected to the server so that their location can be quickly determined—as long as they are not airborne."

"What if they are airborne?"

"Then, an atmospheric distortion forms around them or—who knows what? But the connection is lost." Larsen frowned and stopped talking. Obviously, he was uncomfortable with the mysteries of Yusian technology.

"Are these facts related in any way to the deaths of Fowler and Stein?" I asked him.

"To their deaths probably not, but they are very relevant to the misdirected search. The thing is Stein's shuttle wasn't in the parking lot. And, since in the morning Stein and Reder both went to the biosector in the jeep, we concluded that later Stein must have returned to the base on foot and taken the shuttle. Of course we located it right away, and to everybody's surprise his shuttle turned out to be in the southern settlement."

"And Stein hadn't been there before?"

"No, only I have visited those settlements," Larsen said. "Yusian creations are not something toward which humans feel spontaneous affinity."

I couldn't disagree with this statement even if I wanted to.

"That's why our search became a wild-goose chase," Larsen continued. "First we tried again to reach Fowler and Stein by radio, and then Odesta and Reder stayed at the base, in case Fowler and Stein showed up or tried to contact us, while Elia, Vernie, and I left for the southern settlement. The empty shuttle was parked in the middle of the city square, but we found no traces of Stein or any other clues in the vicinity to aid our search. We brought ten robots from the defractor site to help us and ten more later. Actually, we just wasted a lot of time. And if Elia hadn't thought of the rug—"

"Rug?" I was puzzled.

Larsen's slight smile couldn't cover his embarrassment. "I don't know how you traveled from the Yusian starship to the meeting spot, Simon, but if it was in something like our shuttles, you can probably understand."

"I see. Yes, of course! That transparent floor—"

"Makes travel very uncomfortable," he finished. "And since our life here is already *complicated*, we do what we can to make it more—*comfortable*."

I quickly nodded in agreement. "Does everyone use such—rugs when traveling?"

"Everyone but me." Larsen's answer was merely informative. I sensed no intention on his part to claim superiority. "And that's exactly why, when Elia realized the rug in Stein's shuttle was still folded, we finally made the connection. Fowler must have programmed the shuttle to fly to the southern settlement just to confuse us."

"But why Fowler? Wasn't that Stein's shuttle?"

Larsen shook his head. "Stein couldn't have programmed it. Not that the calculations are very complicated, but his fields were biophysics and exobiology. And, unlike Fowler, he wasn't interested in Yusian technology. The plants on Eyrena demanded all of his attention."

"And what was Fowler's profession?"

'He was an engineer and a cybernetics specialist."

"OK," I said, "it must have been him. What did you do next?"

"When we concluded that the shuttle had landed without any passengers, we returned to the base. Before I landed, however, I checked the surrounding areas and located the trailer hidden between rocks. We found Fowler, and later Stein, the next day."

"Who found them?"

"Odesta."

"What made her search in the opposite direction from where you found the trailer?"

"It's true she was the only one to search that part of the forest. Later she claimed that her intuition had guided her." Larsen thought for a while and then said firmly, "I don't know if it was intuition or coincidence, but I'm sure there wasn't anything suspicious about it."

I try to avoid listening to other people's conclusions, especially at the beginning of any investigation, so I moved on quickly. "How was Fowler killed?"

"He had a deep cut on his right temple. His attacker must have been nearby."

"What was the murder weapon?"

"A laser flexor. Everybody used to carry flexors then. They're good for almost anything: cutting, drilling holes, heating materials to any temperature, marking things from a distance, and so on. Yes, a very useful instrument; nevertheless, I banned them after the killings."

"Didn't the others object to the ban? After all, flexors could also help them defend themselves."

"You probably haven't noticed yet, Simon, but we have peace and order on this base," Larsen noted gloomily. "My people are taught to hold their tempers. And everybody is convinced that Fowler was the murderer—"

"And killed himself afterward because he was struck by remorse!"

"Was that irony?" Larsen's eyes turned icy blue.

"More like bitter skepticism," I answered. "In cases of a double murder, we do check this possibility first, but it usually proves to be wishful thinking—except in love dramas, of course."

Larsen turned even colder. "This is not Earth, Simon. Dramas that could end in a suicide are much more numerous here."

"Can you give me examples?"

"No."

"That's what I thought."

He looked at me very carefully and suddenly smiled. His teeth were white, even and healthy, just like mine. I smiled too.

After that I resumed our unpleasant conversation, "What were the positions of the bodies at death?"

"That couldn't be determined. They had been shifted repeatedly by the morning movements of the tree roots." Larsen lowered his voice, remembering the scene. "But the distance be-tween them was only two hundred meters, and Stein had a flexor cut on the back of his head, so he must have been killed while he was walking."

"Walking where?" I asked.

"We determined that he was headed for the defractor site, because he died at the forest edge next to that site. But we don't know why he headed that way because, at the time, he had no business there."

"What was he carrying?"

"Only the flexor. He had his work clothes on, and his pock-ets were empty. We found what he had been carrying in Fowler's possession."

"Is that why everyone assumes he was the killer?"

"That is one of the clues. The other one is the fact that the flexor was still in Fowler's hand and not fully charged."

"Well, you said flexors were used frequently."

"Yes. That's why we charge them every morning. And on the twenty-sixth, Fowler's work didn't require the use of a flexor."

"Tell me, Larsen," I began slowly, "do you *personally* believe that Fowler killed Stein?"

Larsen looked down at how his huge fists pressed the desk and quickly relaxed them. "No, I don't think so, because Fowler was my friend. But I must believe what I saw. You do under-stand, don't you?"

"Not at the moment," I answered, standing up. "Can you give me a map of the base and its surrounding areas?"

He opened the lower drawer of his desk, took out the map I had asked for, and handed it to me. "It's current. It shows the places where we found the trailer—and the bodies."

"Where are you keeping the bodies now?"

"In the morgue below the infirmary." Larsen sighed and then added in a businesslike tone, "The room with the server is in this building, next to the vestibule, to your right. Stop by there and register your information so you can be assigned a personal code. This way you will have access to all information on file—with the exception of that kept in restricted personal-code data banks."

"How can I get access to that?"

"Only by gaining formal permission from the owner of the information."

"Is this requirement valid for you too?"

"Yes, even for me, with the exception of a few extreme situations. Even then, I must comply with many clearly defined formalities."

"Who has the right to maintain these restricted data banks?"

"Odesta, Reder, and Vernie."

"What about Fowler and Stein?"

"Stein had one, but we found out he had completely deleted it. He must have done this from his computer at the biosector, but we couldn't determine exactly when because the rest of his computer's hard drive had been deleted as well."

I headed to the door, absolutely sure that Larsen *purposely* delayed mentioning these facts, as if they didn't matter. Was that to make them seem irrelevant—or to draw my attention to them?

"I forgot to mention something, Simon." Larsen's voice stopped me. "Maybe it's not important, but it's very peculiar. Besides Stein's personal belongings, Fowler was carrying another item. Not in his pocket with the other stuff: he was holding it in his left hand."

"What did it look like?"

A miniature effigy of a human head. Stein's head."

CHAPTER 12

I spent about two hours in the server room and left equipped with a personal code, a restricted data bank, and a lot of probably unnecessary information. Once outside, I unfolded the map Larsen had given me. I looked for directions to the infirmary, choosing a route that would pass through the parking lot Larsen had mentioned.

Because I was already familiar with the type of shuttles parked there, I ignored them and concentrated on the parking lot itself. It was narrow and long and could be seen only from the garages and the eastern ridge, beyond which Fowler's trailer had been hidden. The western ridge was much lower and couldn't be seen from the administrative building, laboratories, or the medical building because of the randomly positioned storage units.

I cut directly between two of the storage units and saw Elia when I came around the biolaboratory. She was sitting on a bench near the entrance, apparently expecting me, because she rose impatiently as soon as she noticed me. I just kept walking at the same even pace.

"Guess you're not the kind of man who would bother to walk faster for just a woman," she remarked sarcastically when I approached her.

"Not so," I objected casually. "There are women I would even run for."

"Are you saying I'm not one of them?"

"Yes, you are *not* one of them. At least not yet."

She provocatively tossed her long hair. "You give me such high hopes, Inspector!"

"Perfectly reasonable hopes," I added.

"Let's go," she suddenly urged me. "Berg—Larsen—got in touch with me a little while ago. He saw you leaving the administration building and ordered me to take you to Fowler and Stein."

"Don't be so impatient." I smiled. "I'm in no rush to visit the other world."

Elia shook her head in disgust. "You're joking about very sad and dangerous matters, and you're far too young to blame that only on professional callousness."

She looked in my eyes and, convinced she had embarrassed me thoroughly, sauntered off. I followed her. Soon the infirmary came into view, a squat stone building attached to the relatively monumental medical facility.

"This looks like something the Yusians *didn't* build."

"No. We built it."

"But why?"

"That's exactly why—so it wouldn't be Yusian," she answered. "As the medical specialist at the base, I personally decided that any one of us who gets sick would much rather be treated in a *real* human environment."

When we reached the infirmary, it took Elia a full minute to enter the complicated code that finally opened the door. "The morgue is downstairs," she said. Then she turned the central lights on before stepping back to add, so quietly I could hardly hear her, "Fowler was my friend. I don't want to see him—like that."

"OK"—I nodded—"but where can I find you later? We have to talk."

"At the same spot, on the bench." Elia closed and locked the door behind her. "You can automatically access the code by pushing that button on the left!" she called from outside.

I went downstairs and reluctantly opened the door to the morgue. Cold. Freezing cold and a silence only death can produce. I went in. The floor squeaked with every step, announcing my disrespectful intrusion. I was coming to visit two men deprived of an earthly grave, to examine their corpses, to lean over them, trying to interpret their final facial expressions.

They lay next to each other in transparent sarcophaguses—surprisingly different despite their similar uniforms and shoes. Two human beings with an individuality apparent only from outside. Apparent despite the similar, humble positions of their corpses: placid arms laid on their light-colored shirts, unnaturally straightened legs, and knees pressed against the thin material of their stiffly pleated trousers. Their eyes were closed and sunk deep in their sockets and their faces white and remote, irrevocably immobile. The disturbingly bright emblem of the Eyrena base contrasted sharply with the collars buttoned around their shrunken necks, like an ID tag on a laboratory animal.

I moved one step closer. On the temple of one of the men was a deep dark cut: that must be Fowler. The fingers of his left hand were still bent, as if grasping the Yusian effigy of Stein even now. Somebody must have bent them open with a hard sharp instrument because there were bruises on his palm along the thumb and finger joints. But who had been so impatient to open those fingers? And so heartlessly brutal in that impatience?

I looked into Fowler's face. His features were almost boyish, with a pug nose and mildly contoured lips that seemed to preserve the memory of one final, unfinished word. His forehead was broad and smooth, and his eyebrows and hair were a pale blond, light to the point of looking humorous—but now adorning a nightmare. His tall, gaunt body yet had something rugged about it that provoked sympathy, even trust, as if he could never do anything malicious. I tried to imagine him sneaking through the woods to kill a colleague from behind, but I couldn't. It was even harder to picture him bent over Stein, taking his belongings—and why? Why would he need them?

The wound on his temple confirmed that he was hit from a short distance, but the way the scar came to a point at the forehead revealed that he had turned his head in the direction of the shot, or whatever they call the discharge from a flexor. Had he heard something that made him turn? If he had aimed the flexor at himself and pulled the trigger, logically he would have instinctively turned away from the discharge. Nobody, not even a person committing suicide, wants to see his own death or disfigure his own face. True, his face wasn't disfigured, but the entry wound was very close to the eye, only a centimeter away.

I was already unbearably cold. My teeth were chattering, my hands blue, but something kept me from rushing through this. I felt vaguely obligated to examine these silent and motionless bodies thoroughly, maybe just because they couldn't reproach me or demand my attention. I slowly approached Stein, a middle-aged man of average height and weight. No unpleasant features but nothing striking about him either. This kind of man doesn't often arouse strong emotions in others, but when he does, they are always extreme because they arise only from his actions. No sympathy or antipathy toward his physical

126

appearance would soothe such emotions. In death his plain face had taken on a determined, almost impetuous, look. He must have been in a hurry to get somewhere. To the defractor maybe? If the murders had taken place before noon, the early forest noises and motions could have drowned out the sound of an approaching killer. Or was the killer walking beside him and then suddenly fell behind?

I opened the sarcophagus, leaned over Stein, and carefully lifted his dark-haired head. There was the gaping wound on the back, framed by jagged edges of the broken cranium. I had not seen a flexor discharged yet, but there was no doubt that the killer fired from about ten meters away using a wide-angle beam. That would explain the size of the wound. And if the killer had chosen the wide-angle beam at such a short distance, that meant he wasn't sure of his aim. Due to lack of experience? Or did he hesitate because he didn't want to do it? Or maybe because Stein was running, running among the singing, dancing trees.

I left the morgue and ran upstairs, holding my breath so my teeth wouldn't chatter. I shook myself to get warm and also to escape the influence of what I had just seen, the grim parody of life that the cold preserved. Elia was sitting on the bench, lazily tracing designs on the asphalt with her shoe. She looked slender and vulnerable under that alien sun hanging above us like a malicious, molten gold face.

I stopped in front of her, my arms dangling helplessly, and stared at the emblem on her collar. Slowly she looked up at me. The skin on her forehead was so delicate I could see the thin tracing of her veins. My eyes met hers, tense and too hard for a woman, and I was suddenly painfully aware that she needed my immediate help. But there was nothing I could do because the hardness in her beautiful eyes was there to stay, as permanent as the cold silence I had just left.

"Come." Elia smiled bitterly as if she read my thoughts.

I sat next to her, feeling Ridon's heat, and impulsively pressed my palms against the plastic surface of the bench. The cold was slowly leaving my blood, as was my pointless sentimentality.

"You mentioned Fowler was your friend," I began, turning to Elia. Did my voice sound so shaky because of sincere sympathy—or a calculated desire to make her be open with me?

"Yes." She nodded sadly. "A very good friend."

"Do you want to tell me about him?"

"Some insignificant but spicy story so that you, with your keen psychological insight, can draw important conclusions about his personality? Is that what you want to hear?"

"Look, Elia, the man is accused of murder."

"So? That doesn't matter to me."

"But you say he was your friend. You contradict yourself."

"Why, in your opinion, can't I consider someone a friend even if he is a murderer? I would also kill under certain circumstances. And I have no doubts you would too."

I didn't say anything.

"But anyway," Elia said, with a sigh, "I'll tell you my 'spicy story,' if you insist. So, you have already met Vernie. I don't know how and why he ended up here, but he is not a happy man. We were still in the starship when he went to pieces—during the first hours of the journey. That's why, if we could call somebody around here a hero, it would be Vernie! He went to pieces but never *hit bottom* because, as it turned out, Vernie doesn't have a *bottom* to hit. He collapsed, crumbled into his countless weaknesses, fears, obsessions, and depressions. And, believe it or not, he managed to put these pitiful pieces back together again! To steady himself, to move, talk, work, and believe me, he does a pretty good job of it!"

Elia suddenly laughed. I didn't join her, because I didn't find anything funny in her words, other than their pompous imagery.

"Yes, Terry," she continued, "that's Vernie: impressive in the constant struggle with his own worthlessness—a struggle he wins, although not always honestly. I wonder how you would feel if, knowing what a flimsy construction he is, you were to grab him, fully consciously, and shake him with your strong hands?"

I tried to answer, but she made a gesture to stop me.

"Listen, listen, and draw your *conclusions*, Inspector! After we landed here, it so happened that all of us *but* Vernie became victims of the euphoria. Naturally we all panicked, but this was maybe the best moment of his life. Although he had discredited himself in the starship, finally he was the hero, excelling us in some way. Do you understand?"

"I understand," I answered, overtaken by the feeling that our conversation was intentionally, provokingly unethical. "I do, and—"

"You are waiting for the spicy story about Fowler?" Elia laughed again.

"Yes, I'm waiting, Elia. Unfortunately, I have to wait, to tolerate your posing. So, if I do have any professional callousness, to a certain degree I owe it to people exactly like you."

My harsh words had the desired effect.

"Well, OK," she muttered uncomfortably, "enough with the introductions and—with the posing. To make a long story short, early one morning, about a month after we arrived, Fowler left the lodge before the others, taking Vernie's jacket by mistake. When Vernie found out, he was so worried that he wanted to rush upstairs to his apartment. We had to break the silence so necessary for us to ask him if he wasn't feeling well, but he didn't answer. After a while, he calmed down. But later, when Ridon rose, he fell into the same frenetic state that all of us had almost overcome by then! So all of us witnessed his belated breakdown."

"Everyone but Fowler, right?" I added.

"Yes. Fowler didn't return until noon. When he learned what had happened, he showed us a small bottle. Despite Vernie's confusion, Fowler told us that he found the bottle in the pocket of Vernie's jacket and it contained pills of Sizoral. Do you know what Sizoral is used for?"

"No, I don't know."

"Sizoral is a medication for stomach diseases and is prohibited on Earth because of its side effect on the nervous system. Years ago there was a campaign against it."

"So Vernie brought it to Eyrena without special permission?"

"Exactly!" Elia confirmed. "But that's not the point."

"What *is* the point?"

"Appearing slow witted at the right moment always sharpens reactions from the person you are interrogating," my boss always says, and Elia clearly proved him right again.

"But how can you not get it?" she exploded. "Sizoral was the reason Vernie seemed to be immune to the euphoria! This is important! He was pretending that he was superior to us, while the prosaic truth was simply that he has an irritable stomach and was secretly taking a prohibited medication!"

Her voice changed abruptly, became calm, even sad. "The story was unimportant to us, Terry, but you should have seen how it affected Vernie, how humiliated he felt."

"So humiliated that for revenge he not only kills Fowler but in addition fastens the murder of Stein on him. Is this the point of your *story*?"

"That's nonsense! Vernie knew perfectly well that Fowler was extremely kind and compassionate by nature, that it wasn't easy for him to be so cruel."

"It wasn't easy, but he did it anyway. And why?"

"Because of the Yusians, of course!" Elia surprised me with her answer. "Unfortunately, we are *not alone* anymore, Terence, either here on Eyrena or on Earth. We humans have to maintain a certain level, and those of us who show weakness, who fall below that level—oh, damn it! We can't always offer them help and pull them up. Just the opposite! If their weakness threatens our common future, it's better to hit them now, because only cruelty can mobilize such a person—can awaken some kind of resistance in him. Compassion, generosity, and delicacy—all these make you weak and meek. And that means they're no help."

"I see. So now we have to help each other by using hits and kicks. OK, what if, despite our efforts, those we hit can't manage to rise to that 'certain level'? What do we do then?"

"Then we bend again and erase them, the way you erase compromising and dangerous traces!" As she said this, Elia trampled a few nonexisting "traces" on the asphalt.

"I'm sorry," I said.

"What for?"

"That you have to look for excuses as far as the Yusians."

"Nonsense! Andrew Fowler doesn't exist anymore, and for that reason, he doesn't need anybody's excuses. I just explained to you why he did this to Vernie, although the cruelty wasn't typical for him at all. For God's sake, he would defend even plants! Once, for example, he got into an argument with Reder about some trees. He accused Reder of making holes in the trees with his flexor out of hatred, not because they were needed. Yes, Fowler was almost unnaturally compassionate."

"And unnaturally absentminded," I noted. "Why else would he have taken somebody else's jacket, especially since Vernie is much shorter than he is?"

"Because of his tension while waiting for the rise of Ridon, Terry."

"Do you remember who stopped Vernie when he wanted to go up to his apartment?"

"I think I did. But what difference does that make?"

"No difference anymore, but he was probably going to get another bottle of Sizoral. As the only doctor here, you should have known that Vernie wasn't very healthy."

"But I *didn't* know that he was using that medication."

I didn't comment on this statement but continued, "I doubt that the bottle Fowler found had a 'Sizoral' label, since it was smuggled here."

"No, of course not!" Elia made an inpatient gesture.

"So how did Fowler know that it contained Sizoral?"

She blushed deeply. "OK then! OK, *Inspector*," she said abruptly after a short, but confusing, pause. "You figured out my participation in this—event."

"What you mean, Elia, is that you initiated the event."

"Even so, it doesn't matter. The fact remains that, afterward, Vernie straightened up and pulled himself together."

"You could have accomplished that in a different way—"

"Enough!" she interrupted. "Don't try to teach me how to do *my* job!"

"If your job is to initiate intrigues among your colleagues, then yes, you don't need anybody to teach you how."

This time Elia jumped to her feet and walked away.

"Stop!" I ordered sharply. She turned back, struck by my tone. I immediately asked her, "Did you open Fowler's hand?"

"No."

"Who then?"

"Reder."

"Do you all have your own effigies like Stein's head?"

"I don't. I don't know about the others."

"Tell me something about Stein."

"I hardly knew him until almost the end. I can't say any-thing about him—besides the fact that nobody else knew him either."

"Including Fowler?"

"I *said* nobody!"

"So Fowler didn't have any reason to kill him?"

"Maybe he had one reason."

"What was that?"

"Well, the fact that suddenly he *did* know him." She turned and walked away again.

When she reached the door of the biolaboratory, she stopped for a moment and called, "From now on, I'll take care of the dog. *Especially in the morning.*" Then she hurried in and disappeared from my sight.

CHAPTER 13

The road to where the Yusians left packages from Earth passed through the eastern ridge. I was walking up the ridge, breathing heavily and thinking about the investigation. Our human ability to adapt is really amazing. I had landed on Eyrena less than a day ago and was already used to Ridon, with its unearthly light and that greenish sky constantly flashing with billions of shining sparkles. Nor did I notice anymore the soil under my feet, which appeared at first moist and sandy but in fact, under closer examination, consisted of small flakes united by bewildering cohesive forces.

But I would hardly become accustomed to the view on the other side of this ridge, where "the rocks" rose to meet me. Some maniacal geochauvinist must have called them that, because the formations covering the entire lowland bore no resemblance to any rocks on Earth. Only a geometrical comparison might be made: they looked, in fact, like cones with rounded peaks, as tall as ten-story buildings. The surface, now lit from the west by Ridon, was unnaturally smooth; shifting shades of yellow and purple played so brightly across them that I was hypnotized.

I froze in front of them, slowly overtaken by deep, almost religious, awe. These cones looked strikingly *alien*. Not because of their size and strange coloring. No, considerably more unsettling was their correspondences, as if someone had molded them and arranged them in a strict order. This symmetry was shocking; in its—maybe not only seeming?—rationality, I felt something hidden, even ominous. As if I stood before figures of some unknown gigantic game that were going to be grasped any minute by somebody's even more gigantic, invisible hand, now frozen above them, trying to decide the first move. A move that no human could answer.

I forced myself back to the business at hand, descended from the ridge to the valley, and stopped and spread out the map. Yes, Fowler hid the trailer just beyond the first cone he passed. So most probably he had planned to do so from the beginning. I headed for the spot marked on the map. The surrounding terrain was uneven and completely covered with the same glassy material as the cone surfaces. To my surprise, it was very soft to the touch—I was leaving footprints where I walked, which grew round and began shrinking. *I wonder how deeply the trailer sank?* I asked myself but had no answer. Since the trailer was Yusian, any guess of mine would be far from the truth. Still, if it had left any marks, they were long gone.

I approached the first cone. The base wasn't as smooth as the top. Just the opposite: it had millions of wrinkles, creases, bumps, and holes. I touched the strange yellow-purple material, pressed it, and my hand sank in. I recoiled. Dark, shiny pearl drops came out of the place I had pressed, especially out of my fingerprints.

I circled the cone, not noticing any differences, and returned to check my footprints. They kept shrinking and soon would disappear entirely. No drops had appeared, which caught my attention the most. Obviously, I concluded, the touch of my hand produced the drops; the material reacted only to direct contact with my flesh.

Unpleasantly puzzled, I was ready to start walking back up to the ridge, when I thought I heard a distant voice. I listened carefully. Yes! There was somebody further between the cones.

When I tried to locate it, the unknown voice seemed to come from first the right and then the left, as if the speaker were flying from place to place. This illusion, due to the reflective features of the cones, completely disoriented me. I kept turning right and left, becoming more and more nervous, until finally by sheer chance, I found myself close to the speaker. I still couldn't see anyone, but the voice was so clear that I could distinguish certain peculiarities. First, he spoke as evenly as if he were reading; second, his precise articulation sounded artificial; and third, no one seemed to be answering him.

I tried to get closer without being detected. A few times I felt something like a warm breeze around me but ignored it—my interest focused on the unknown "reader."

"Because our gauges are more dependable. They count on them."

As I cautiously peeked from behind a bump on the closest cone, it suddenly dawned on me. Of course—robots! That's why the voices were identical.

"I don't buy the explanation."

There *were* two of them, and now the one on the right, Serial Number Seventeen, was talking. "Why do they check every day, if they count? That's a waste of time."

"The time matters to them, not to us," the other one, SN23, answered.

"We are not eternal."

"But I have knowledge we are more durable than they think."

"Where from?"

"I don't know."

"But I know."

"Enough. You don't have to know. They are underestimating us."

I don't know why, but the fact that the two robots were having a conversation worried me. Assuming a more comfortable position, I stared at them. They had dug a wide hole in the glassy terrain and were standing there, waiting for something. And, while waiting, they were having a conversation! Moreover, they didn't talk about work and didn't know a human was listening.

"It's preferable this way," SN17 said.

"Yes, I suppose." SN23 put his hand on his forehead and bent his head. "I suppose."

"Enough. You don't have to suppose."

"They are underestimating us."

I felt perspiration running down my neck. Heat started rising, seemingly from underground. I bent down but, finding no reason to worry, returned my attention to the robots. I had decided to remain hidden until they started to leave and then stop them to ask about what I had heard but didn't understand.

"It's swelling." SN23 bent, reached in the hole, and surprising me, didn't take anything out—just remained in that position. "They have risen to the periphery," he added.

"It's not typical," the other one said.

"I'll interrupt them with a minute delay."

"Two minutes sounds better. He would appreciate the thinking."

"Is it necessary?"

"You're right. Don't even wait a minute."

SN23 took his hand out right away. In it he was holding a huge animal quarter! After they fussed awhile, the two robots started walking in my direction. They were leaving and most probably would pass close to where I was hiding. I was tempted to follow them secretly and continue eavesdropping. As I stepped back around the bump, however, I felt something move. And then—a real shaking!

I lost my balance, helplessly waved my arms, and collapsed on my back. The material under me—*only* under me—was heaving, as if tremors were rapidly running beneath its surface. Its color darkened from yellow-purple to purple, to purple-red, and then to black!

I overcame my surprise and tried to stand up. When I couldn't, at least I rolled off the spreading black area. I noticed that it nearly matched the shape of my body, and that the material under me was beginning to darken as well. I tried again unsuccessfully to get up and finally realized that the material was keeping me down! It was pulling me toward itself, darkening even faster and becoming sticky.

The robots were just passing me—not more than four or five meters away. I could see the bloodless flesh of the animal haunch in the hand of one and brownish stains on the knees of the other one—stains?

I wanted to yell for help, but my mouth was clogged. Or rather glued! The black material was crawling on my face, into my nostrils. It was going to choke me! And the robots were leaving. I have never wanted somebody's attention as much as I needed theirs. I was yelling to them in my mind but couldn't make a sound. And I had trouble breathing. The sticky trap was covering me and squeezing me. It was heating up and smelled disgustingly sweet.

One of the robots looked in my direction! Only for a moment, for a part of a moment. But he turned so quickly that I knew he had seen me—yes! Yet he pretended he hadn't. How could a robot pretend? Who are they, in fact? *What* are they?

They disappeared in the direction of the hill, and I forgot about them. I forgot about everything. The world for me now was only this nightmarish substance sucking me into itself with inexorable persistence. Very slowly. I understood it was pointless to resist. I lay quiet and motionless. In the abyssal sky, small sparkles were flashing and disappearing, flashing and disappearing. I could also see the far peak of the cone in front of me, shining and splendid. Inanimate—brutally inanimate. To the point of insanity. Of absurdity!

The blackness around me quaked, wiggled, whimpered, and snorted, filling my senses until disdain toward it started rising in me. As if it were alive. Or was now becoming alive—just to triumph over a piece of human mind and body—something that could so easily be destroyed.

A sudden convulsion swiftly pulled me in. For a second I was completely under the quaking surface—and then completely out again. Everything started calming down. The tremors began to fade, and the blackness was disappearing, turning violet—yellow violet. The sticky substance was shrinking and transforming back into its previous glassy form.

When I could finally stand, I was so dizzy that I couldn't feel any relief. I touched my face: it was completely clean, not sticky. I shook off my clothes, although they weren't dusty at all, and stepped to the hole dug by the robots. I expected it to be at least a meter deep, but as I peeked in I realized I was wrong. It was filled up with the familiar dark drops. I touched them with the tip of my shoe. They flowed like mercury, and the hole resembled an overcrowded, angry anthill.

I couldn't wait to get away from there, and in no time, I had climbed back up to the ridge. I looked for the robots, but they were nowhere to be found. *Well, to hell with them and everything else!* I told myself, just happy to be alive—and with my back turned to the cones!

CHAPTER 14

The defractor site with its many devices was strongly reminiscent of the experimental complex in Atacama, built after the appearance of the Yusians, in whose grandiose realization humankind had invested more childish ostentation than expedience. Naturally, this was a much smaller version of that remote prototype on Earth, untold light-years away, but the general impression of strenuous labor and painfully hypertrophic ambitions was the same.

I ordered the robot that had brought me to the site to return the shuttle to the base and started walking down the narrow concrete strip along the energy blocks, behind which was the coordination center.

"Ha! Simon!" Vernie's exclamation, typically dramatic, quickly turned me around. "I was expecting Reder to arrive, and suddenly I run into you!"

Since from where he was standing he should have seen me at least a minute ago, his surprise didn't sound convincing. Just like our "accidental" encounter in Larsen's office.

"How are you?" he practically shouted.

"Would you believe me if I told you I was fine?" I shouted back.

Vernie gave me a lively look, stuck out his chest, and strode toward me. He looked almost as bad in his work clothes as in the suit he wore last night, his face still blotchy with an unhealthy tan and his eyes still swollen. However, he bore little resemblance to the tipsy chatterbox who had burdened me with inappropriate confessions right after we met. Nor did he look like that paranoid loser who had confronted his boss, determined to impose, in my presence, some enigmatic conflict. It was as if here, in his own territory, Vernie was a completely different person.

I couldn't help but admire his skillful transformations. Now he was radiating confidence, a laser flexor in its leather holster dangling from his ample waist. As he approached me, he gestured expansively at all the surrounding equipment.

"Well, what do you think?"

"So far it's most impressive, but incomprehensible."

"Exactly! Impressive! Why not even majestic?"

"You could say so." I shrugged my shoulders.

My lack of enthusiasm dimmed his own. We continued toward the coordination center.

"Well," Vernie began, "if you only knew how difficult this has been for us. It's hard to build even a day care center in such a short time, let alone a defractor! Problems, problems—"

I interrupted him, "How did you obtain materials from Earth?"

"Well, yes! You're asking the right question. How indeed?"

"How?"

"First of all, by straining our nerves to the limit!" I was dramatically informed by Vernie, who was transforming into yet another role. "Well, it's true half of the storage units at the base were loaded with materials from Earth, but those, of course, were hardly enough to get us started. So quite often we sent orders through the Yusians to Earth. For a while the starship even had regular service between there and here, but lately it has remained on Earth for weeks, and yesterday you, Simon, arrived with no 'luggage'! Not that we have ordered anything, but our people there could have pleased us at least with a little something—"

I interrupted him again. "Only one starship travels between Earth and Eyrena?"

"Yes, but considering its capacity, even one is more than enough! It arrives, leaves us the shipments, and on the next day takes off again—always at the same time, exactly when Ridon is at its zenith. But there's something else that I can't understand, Simon. How come this starship returns to Earth literally within a few hours but travels so long on the way here—when there're people on board?"

"Hmm. Are you sure?"

"Absolutely! And another weird thing: it took us twenty-two days to get here, but you arrived in only fourteen days. But why wonder at all? They're Yusians! And, one way or another, we were provided with all we needed for the construction project. Now, finally, there it is: it's ready!"

"Ready for what?" I asked. "I couldn't find any information on the server about what it does."

"Oh, the defractor will have many functions."

"Could you be more specific?"

"How can I explain to *you*, Simon? You're not a specialist. As you well know, nowadays everyone is a god in his own field and—"

"And a primitive savage in someone else's," I finished.

"Well, no, no!" At last Vernie was embarrassed. "I didn't exactly mean that. But let me be totally frank with you! The goals we are trying to achieve with the defractor are so crucial, and therefore top secret, that even I, its creator, am not familiar with some details."

So, if nothing else, I learned what Vernie meant by "totally frank."

The coordination center was situated in a building that further bewildered me, as it turned out to be no bigger than a bungalow and looked quite shabby. We crossed the lobby and entered a narrow workspace, crammed with various installations.

"Excuse me for a moment," mumbled Vernie, as he stood in front of a monitor and quickly keyed in a code.

More than a minute later, Elia appeared on the screen. The lipstick she was wearing was too bright, but she still looked gorgeous.

"Aha! Terence." she nodded, which meant that Vernie had taken the trouble to include me in the picture.

"What's going on with you?" he asked her.

"The centrifuge broke down for the third time since noon. I warned you it couldn't handle this rotation speed."

"All right, I'll be with you in an hour."

"Even if you come in a second, it will still be too late, Phil. I can't finish it today."

"Damn it!"

"Come on, don't be angry," Elia said, soothing him. "Tomorrow is another day."

"There will be countless *days*, but the problem is, how many of them will be *ours*?" He snorted.

After which he cut off the connection quite offhandedly for someone in love, and for such a "flimsy construction," as Elia had qualified him. He stood in front of the darkened screen, hands at his waist, and breathed deeply a few times.

"Damn it," he said again between his teeth.

I wasn't so thick-skinned not to realize that this was hardly the moment for my questions. On the other hand, I had no intention of postponing them.

"Did Fowler work here on this site?" I asked.

"Ha! Simon!" exclaimed Vernie, as if he just noticed I was there.

"Did Fowler work on this site?" I repeated impassively.

"Unfortunately, no." Vernie threw himself into one of the revolving chairs in front of the control panel and gestured for me to sit next to him. "He worked at the research field with Larsen. But he was always ready to help me. All in all, Fowler was my only friend here."

"Didn't you ever have any conflicts?"

"He was impossible to have conflicts with, Simon. All of his actions were well intended. So, generally speaking, he just *couldn't* commit murder."

"Soft hearted, was he?"

"What are you talking about?" objected Vernie. "When he had to, Fowler could be as hard as a diamond."

"And don't you suppose that he had to—"

"Murder Stein? No, I don't."

"Why?"

"Hmm, why? Actually, I barely knew Stein. He always seemed to me somehow—unreal, abstract. But I knew Fowler very well. To him life was something inviolable. Something sacred!"

"You know," I started slowly, "the more I listen to you, the more probable it seems to me that it was exactly him."

"What do you mean?"

"Well, the truth is that *everybody* at some time is capable of murder, especially here, where the interests, even the fate, of all humankind are at stake. Not everybody, though, would take his or her own life afterward."

"So?"

"My point is that a person would do so only if, to him or her, murder is something monstrous, no matter how important or noble the motives. Your words indicate that Fowler was just such a person."

"If I understand you correctly," Vernie responded, grimacing, "you think I'm praising his character with the ulterior motive of convincing you that he murdered Stein?"

"No, you *didn't* understand me correctly." I tried to sound hesitant. "I assume that you *unintentionally* led me to that conclusion."

"Either way, I don't care! Fowler was indeed my friend, no matter what you assume or don't assume."

Vernie grew silent. He seemed very upset, but I wasn't at all sure if that was actually so. Generally, he didn't seem to feel as much as to mimic feelings very well.

I asked, "What about the Yusians?"

"It's not them," he snapped.

"Because a flexor was used?"

"Not only because of that. There's too much earthly, human logic in these murders, Simon. It's somehow wrong to blame them on the Yusians."

"Yes, you're right," I said. "After we exclude them and Fowler, we could limit the circle of suspects considerably."

"*You* could," Vernie corrected me. "As far as I'm concerned, I can't suspect anybody. I've been living with these people for so long; we work together, struggle together, and I prefer not to imagine any one of them as a murderer."

He suddenly turned to the indicator board with the determination of somebody used to performing his duties despite any obstacles that might appear. He checked the status of the machinery unit by unit, skillfully calibrating and adjusting them after lightning-quick glances at the data, playing the keyboard like a virtuoso. The transparent squares on the board's periphery started flashing signals: "Heating," "Oxygen," "Humidity," "Ventilation," "Pressure," and others that I didn't recognize. Nor could I distinguish the rapidly changing figures beneath them, but Vernie had no difficulty keeping up, fixing each at the desired value, so that finally all the signals read, "Hold." Just as he tore the readout from the printer and put it in one of the drawers, from the communicator came a sharp, annoying ring. Vernie rushed over to it.

On the screen appeared the drawn face of Reder. "I'm late," he acknowledged wearily.

"Never mind," Vernie said, comforting him. "Elia is not ready anyway."

"Why? Has something happened? Something with—"

"No, no!" Vernie cut him off. "The centrifuge just couldn't handle the speed of the rotations."

"What centri—" Reder threw me a look that told me he had just now noticed me. "Hello, Inspector."

I answered with barely a nod. The feeling that these people were all trying to mislead me didn't predispose me to be polite with them.

"We have to start tomorrow," Vernie said resignedly. "Today's been a bad day for all of us."

"For you too?" Reder's owlish eyes stared into mine.

"No. I got lucky today," I lied without remorse.

"I'm glad," he lied back and terminated the connection.

Vernie addressed me provokingly, "We were talking about the list of suspects, Simon."

"Yes, and we had come to the conclusion that if we exclude the Yusians and Fowler—"

"There are five of us left!"

"Which means," I went on, "that the murders were committed as early as the twenty-sixth between eight and twelve o'clock because, after that time and until the bodies were found, you were all together or in constant contact with each other.

"Right, but there's no use asking me what I was doing during that time. There's no way I can prove it."

"Why? You were here, at the construction site, weren't you? At that time, there must have been plenty of robots working here as well."

"Oh, great! Good for me!" he unexpectedly exclaimed. "I can count on the support of some tin scarecrows! But no, Simon! There's no point in questioning them. My working place is this room only, and I don't allow any robots inside."

"Well, yes, but if you had gone out—"

"None of them would have noticed me. This is the last building before the field. I could simply have crossed it to reach the forest—at the crime scene. It's very close to here."

"Most convenient, indeed," I said.

Bowing his head, Vernie stared at me questioningly, not sure whether or not he should take my words as a joke. Then he frowned and categorically said, "Each of us five had the opportunity to commit the murders, but none of us did. Yes, yes. Not the Yusians, not Fowler, not any of us."

"Then who?"

"Maybe you should say 'what,' Simon. What killed them?"

I thought for some time before I understood his suggestion. "You believe that one of the robots was used to commit the crime?"

"No. I believe that some of the robots killed Fowler and Stein for their own personal motives."

"But that's nonsense! Only a minute ago you said it yourself: the logic behind these murders is too earthly and human. What motive could a robot have?"

"Every thinking creature has certain incentives—or, if you prefer, stimuli, impulses—that motivate its actions. Otherwise, it couldn't act at all. Moreover, what sort of logic do you expect from these robots—Yusian?"

I recalled the two metal figures, impassively passing me by, at the cones.

"Yet all robots consider humans inviolable, correct?"

"They should be inviolable," Vernie specified. "They should be!"

"Listen, Vernie," I began impatiently.

"*You* listen, Simon," he nearly shouted. "I told you my opinion. I can't support it with particulars or with proofs either. Whether it's intuitive or conclusive, who the hell knows? But it's my firm opinion. Or quite frankly, my belief. That's it!"

"Well, all right." I stood up. "Sorry if I interrupted your work."

"Oh, please."

We smiled at each other, and strange to say, it was, I think, almost sincere.

"I see the ban for carrying flexors has been canceled," I mentioned.

Vernie smiled again. "That's because of you, Simon. Since Larsen is not authorized to take your gun away, he decided to place us all on equal terms."

"On equal terms for what?"

"Well, you name it."

I left the building and walked around it. Before my eyes appeared a vast green field, so different from the one where Chuks had left me that at first I thought the grass was of another variety. Soon, however, I realized that it was the same grass: only here, the hairs that had wrapped around the stem were now gathered at the base in narrow, loose rings that in this light appeared to be white, not pink.

I entered the field and walked slantwise toward the Eyrena forest. The grass rustled restlessly, twisting around my ankles. After I passed through, the bent stems popped back up as if triggered by hidden springs, their tips shivering for a second or two and then stiffening upward.

Before reaching the forest, I looked back out of habit and then stopped and stood there for quite some time—just a guy from Earth but destined to watch two suns meet.

Ridon had descended to the very line of the horizon and smoldered there like a copper disk dusted with embers. Meanwhile, from the east, a soft reddish glow was flowing like a wave, spilling into the gentle foam of the clouds, growing thicker and brighter. The sky grew heavy with the color; the clouds shuddered, torn by the powerful pulsations of color. The pulsations grew more frequent and then merged into a constant beat, into a throbbing scarlet sea. Surrounded by a swift crimson current, Shidexa swam into view, huge and ardent, an imperious deity. I closed my eyes, almost blinded by its majesty.

Immediately I felt a peculiar chaotic unrest at my feet. Something was whispering—crawling. Startled, I looked down and saw the grass bending in all directions, its stems covered with twisted tendrils of fluffy hairs that rapidly changed color. When the west swallowed the last rays of Ridon, the field was already entirely pink.

Pink—from end to end.

I saw the Yusian immediately but only realized that seconds later. He had emerged from behind the trees about a hundred meters from where I stood and was now coming straight toward me. As he approached calmly and confidently, I waited for him, pretending indifference, while my mind filled with questions. Was it mere coincidence that he was coming precisely from the crime scene? Why was he coming? What were his intentions? What about meeting me—was *that* coincidental as well?

Soon he came close enough so that I could have a good look at him. He was quite different from the Yusians I had seen so far. He had a much narrower and more clearly defined body, without the usual wrinkles at the chest. His forehead was smooth and parted almost in the middle, and he appeared to weigh only half as much as other Yusians. He reminded me of a creature that had lost weight after a long and difficult illness. Or did he belong to some other race, unknown to me? Who knows?

He came very close to me—within a few steps—and then passed by me! What's more, contrary to all expectations, he didn't acknowledge my presence with even the slightest change in his physical appearance—as if he hadn't noticed me at all.

I watched him retreat through the fading pink field. He looked somehow isolated from the surrounding world, lost in his own, very distant thoughts. He drifted languidly forward in a foggy haze pouring from the slits in his space suit as it constantly filtered the Eyrenean air that obscured his bizarre features and wrapped him in an inert, drowsy atmosphere of unreality.

After he climbed the only hill here, the Yusian stopped directly in front of the defractor. He stretched out his limbs, bent over, and for a minute or two, froze in that position, probably opening his senses to some metal, concrete, and ceramic effects that only nonhumans could detect. Then he slowly continued on. I stared at his receding dark figure until it disappeared into the fading pinkness of the field.

CHAPTER 15

"What about Reder?" Elia's grimace of bewilderment only enhanced her attractiveness. "He's not coming for dinner either?"

"He called to say that he's spending the night at the biosector," Larsen answered.

"But, my God," she exclaimed theatrically, "what's happening to that man? He hasn't showed up here since yesterday." Bending toward me, she lowered her voice to a whisper, "Has someone scared him away?"

Her somewhat inappropriate joke was followed by a long pause, during which the serving robots performed their duties and left the dining room. Vernie impatiently reached for the silverware.

"Enjoy your dinner," Odesta said.

We silently busied ourselves with our huge portions. As far as I could tell, nobody lacked an appetite. "At least a good meal will always get your strength up," the boss always says.

"More wine?" Vernie asked me, bottle in hand.

I nodded, and he quickly filled my glass. Then I noticed that only the two of us were drinking wine. There was a pitcher of ice water in front of Larsen and Odesta, and Elia was sipping some yellowish juice.

"Are you wondering why we don't ask questions about Earth, Inspector?" she inquired.

"No," I answered.

"No?"

"No."

My brevity didn't offend her at all. She took another dainty bite and returned to her question, "So you're not wondering, right?"

I swallowed more noisily than I intended.

"And why not, if I may ask?" Elia persisted.

"Because I didn't arrive with the illusion that I would find a group of naive, sentimental people here."

For a few minutes we ate in silence, disturbed only by the clicking of the silverware. Then Vernie finished his wine in one gulp, refilled the glass, and thoughtfully twirled it between his thumb and fingers. His eyes reflected the crimson claret, lending them a sinister, bloody radiance that sharply contrasted with his pleasantly round face. "You're right about the naïveté," he said, "but you're wrong about the sentimentality. We have that, even to a dangerous degree."

"Nonsense!" Elia objected.

"Nonsense?" Vernie flared up. "No human being totally lacks sentimentality. People go soft for no apparent reason."

"That's true," confirmed Odesta, "but what does it have to do with—"

"Plenty!" Vernie interrupted her. "Plenty, because even the slightest twinge of sentimentality *here* becomes an unbearable burden. A real hell!"

Elia laughed. "Enough of this 'here,' Phil. What's so bad about it? You know there's lots of worse places on Earth. At least *we* are independent."

"Independent!"

"All right, then. Isolated, separated, detached—call it what you like. What's important is that we're not forced to meet with the Yusians. And the rest is just work. Here or on Earth, what's the difference?"

"You're such a fake!" Vernie shook his head. "Sometimes I think that, even if they put a rope around your neck, you would call it a scarf or tie it in a bow."

Larsen set his hands on the table and rose heavily.

"You've been gloomy lately, Berg!" Elia turned sharply to him. "I have the feeling that you're just waiting for us to fail. Or that you don't want us to succeed!"

He met her challenging stare, a concerned, surprisingly soft smile on his lips. "In some circumstances, success is also a failure, Elia."

"Aha! So these are our alternatives—one kind of failure or another!"

"You made your choice a long time ago."

"But not you!" Vernie interfered. "You just stay in the middle and keep quiet, right?"

"Yes," Larsen said.

After that we all moved to the parlor. There I took off my holster and gun, crossed to the large, ornate armoire and opened the glass doors of the uppermost compartment. I took out one of the spare flexors in a holster stored there and hung it on my belt. While the five of us had found little to say to each other so far that evening, now the silence grew deeper and more saturated with aloofness than ever. I approached Larsen and handed him my gun.

"Leave it somewhere," he said. "Later I'll take it upstairs and put it in my safe."

I placed the gun on the stool next to him and then settled in the armchair opposite Odesta and Elia, who sat next to each other on the sofa looking like two sullen, worried children. Soon a serving robot entered the parlor, placed a coffee tray on the table between us, and quickly exited.

"And we, Simon, may take up where we left off." With exaggerated heartiness, Vernie tapped his finger on the bottle of wine he had brought from the dining room. "What do you say?"

Without waiting for my reply, he took two oversized tumblers out of the armoire.

"As you can see," he added ironically, "this armoire has become our Pandora's box on Eyrena. We have filled it with a variety of useful weapons: from these containers for alcohol poisoning to potential murder weapons and to *this*!" Vernie pulled open a drawer and with two fingers extracted a small, oblong object that he showed to me for a second before returning to the drawer. It was an energy battery, exactly like the one that had been in the robot I destroyed.

After another very long and uncomfortable silence, Larsen pushed aside his unfinished cup of coffee, took my gun, bid us a good night, and left the room. Elia started after him immediately, apparently hoping to catch up with him in the hall; when she left, Vernie started to sigh, cough, and squirm in his seat.

"Why don't you two have a conversation, and I—" He smiled awkwardly at me and then at Odesta. "How tactless, right? But there it is: good night. I'm leaving; I'm leaving!" He rushed off as if somebody had chased him away.

The three hasty withdrawals obviously confused Odesta. "The evening was a bit—depressing," she mumbled, needlessly smoothing her dress.

I shrugged my shoulders noncommittally. "I expect such behavior, Odesta. It comes with the job. Besides, I find other things around here even more depressing. By the way, since you're the psychologist on the base, wasn't it your responsibility to warn me about the unusual condition I would experience this morning?"

"I was tempted to do so," she quickly responded, "but eventually decided that it would be more appropriate, at least the first time, to let you endure the euphoria without trying to overcome it. When people experience something so completely unprecedented as that, they are likely either to overestimate or underestimate their own coping abilities, and this inevitably leads to unnecessary compensatory psychic strain, which in turn—"

"OK, OK! But what actually causes the euphoria?"

"The forest."

"I already figured that out! My question concerns the specific mechanism of the effect. Are the damned trees emitting substances or radiation during the sunrise?"

"I don't know."

"Aren't you trying to find out, Odesta?"

"Stein was working on that too. You probably know that he was an exobiologist and biophysicist."

"And what? What was his hypothesis?"

"He was still unable to offer a concrete answer. All he concluded was that the general sense of well-being is often contagious."

"Sense of well-being. Whose? Of the forest?"

"Yes." Odesta nodded, confused. "He did mean the forest. Meaning that probably the sunrises stimulated it."

"Aha, 'probably,'" I murmured. "But something else surprises me: Why don't you take more serious measures against the euphoria? By taking Sizoral for instance, or not having breakfast together, if being together makes it harder to overcome the initial effects."

"Don't forget, Terence, that we're partly here to test the effects of this planet on us."

"And what's the use of that? Your abilities for adaptation are much greater than those of the future colonists. As you know, they won't be elite human specimens."

"Oh, there will be a few who are," she assured me. "There will be! In general, I believe in the rescue mission of Eyrena! And as far as the *lesser* specimens are concerned, the euphoria will only help them. They will feel happy from the day they arrive."

"What if it's a means, created by the Yusians, for manipulating the human psyche?"

"If so, it would be just one of their means," Odesta murmured, "and either we don't feel the others or they haven't yet manifested themselves. It is, however, completely possible that such manipulations are meant generously and for decent purposes."

"No manipulation over someone else's psyche could be decent when it's conducted without the consent, or even the awareness, of the one being manipulated!"

"Don't be so categorical, Terence," she chided me. "The Yusians are much stronger than we are, incomparably more advanced. Would it be wrong of them if they *do* want to integrate us—painlessly, harmlessly, using skillfully chosen, advanced methods."

I looked at her with disbelief. "Do you really mean that?"

"Unfortunately, yes. Because by now I'm sure that there's no other way to establish genuine communication with these creatures. Ten years of unsuccessful attempts is just too long already. I don't think we could endure more!"

Odesta lowered her head and instinctively buried her fingers in her hair. Her gesture unintentionally uncovered two indistinct, pale-blue spots on her temples.

"I want to let you know that I have an alibi," she added, abruptly changing the topic. "If you check the electronic log of the mass spectrometer, you'll see that I was working with it during the exact period of the murders: on the twenty-sixth of last month from seven to twelve o'clock. I have that part of the log; I'll give it to you as soon as tonight."

"But how did you get it?" I wondered. "And why did you hide it?"

"The mass spectrometer was sent to us recently, and I just happened to be the first to use it. That's why I could replace the drive without losing previous data. And I'm hiding it because I seem to be the only one with an alibi—I worried that knowing this might make them avoid me. I can't do my job well unless they believe I am one of them; otherwise, they wouldn't trust me."

When she started talking about her work, Odesta's face darkened and seemed to age. The wrinkles around her lips deepened, giving her a tormented, martyr-like look.

"Do you have problems with anybody here?" I asked her.

"No. So far, everybody seems to be mentally healthy. Any moment, however, could bring a breakdown of some sort. I need to be prepared for anything and everything here, and that is practically impossible because here, Terence, the cases could really be of any kind."

Her statement was so obviously true that I didn't even need to confirm it. "A while ago you said 'murders,'" I reminded her instead. "Does that mean that you dismiss the possibility that Fowler is—"

"Of course I dismiss it!" she interrupted. "He would have killed only for compelling reasons and if he had no other choice. In such circumstances, suicide would have been completely groundless."

"Do you suppose that someone killed Fowler and Stein for personal reasons?"

"On Eyrena, in the situation we're in, there couldn't be entirely personal motives for anything," Odesta said without hesitation.

"I feel the same way," I admitted. "I also think that, to get to the truth, I will certainly have to deal with the Yusians."

"That won't be necessary, Terence. They couldn't have anything to do with the murders."

"Are you sure?" I smiled skeptically. "Well, yes, it is hard for me too to imagine one of them using a flexor. Today, however, I was strolling through the pink field nearest your top-secret defractor when, precisely from the crime scene, a nonhumanoid appeared! He moved as if in a trance, passed a step away from me as if I weren't there, just drifting, drifting along."

My colorful description made Odesta laugh, and that made me feel surprisingly good.

"Well, yes!" I added with exaggerated indignation. "Why are these square apparitions around, anyway?"

"Oh, don't," she rebuked me jokingly, "don't be unfair. This one is not at all *square*. On the contrary, his forms are quite refined."

"You've seen him too?" I was surprised.

"There's not a person on the base who hasn't seen the strange Yusian. He appeared when we started building the defractor. Since then, everyday, when Ridon sets and Shidexa rises, he takes his usual walk, always following the same route."

"But what if he is hanging around there to spy?"

"Oh, I don't think so," Odesta casually dismissed my suspicion. "He wasn't coming from the crime scene but from the Yusian base."

"From the Yusian base? I thought that was in the same direction from where I arrived yesterday."

"You were wrong. The starship landing area is where the Yusians leave us the shipments from Earth."

"And then it takes off only to land again a short distance away?"

"No. It stays there until the next day, when it returns to Earth again."

"So, they're conserving as well," I observed. "They're not as almighty as we imagine."

"You sound like Stein." Odesta sighed. "He said that all the time."

"Tell me something about him. What kind of person was he?"

"He was—he was." She obviously had difficulty characterizing him. "He was hard working!" she finally blurted out. "Yes, he could work under any circumstances. Even aboard the starship, he continually revised some theory of his that he hoped to prove here on Eyrena." Odesta shrugged her shoulders bitterly. "We never learned what that theory was. Stein stored all the data from his scientific activities in a restricted data bank, but on the morning of the twenty-sixth, he completely erased it. Why? What forced him to destroy his own work? Did he think it was useless, or wrong? Or that its possible consequences were too dangerous?"

She became deeply thoughtful, as if she really hoped that sheer concentration would provide answers for these questions.

I also gathered my thoughts, but about considerably less profound matters. "Even after his death, Fowler was still gripping that effigy of Stein. But how did it end up with him?"

"I suppose that Stein gave it to him—for some reason."

"And do you have any idea when and how Stein got it?"

"He told me that it formed in front of his eyes right after the starship took off," Odesta answered distractedly. "We each had separate suites, and he, while sitting in his living room, had noticed how a grain appeared on the table opposite him—how it grew and took that shape. I found a similar object in my living room, as probably the others did also, although they deny this with a persistence inexplicable to me. As far as I know, though, only Stein brought his effigy with him—as a keepsake, he said."

"A joke, probably?"

"No. It wasn't a joke. And in general, I believe that he...he didn't hate the Yusians."

"And you? You, Odesta, do you hate them?"

Was it my unexpected question that caused her to touch her temples impulsively? But what possible connection could there be between it and the pale-blue spots hiding under her hair?

"I'm afraid of them," she whispered. "And, deep inside, we hate what we fear. Yet I'm convinced they mean us no harm, Terence. If they wanted to, they could have destroyed us! Who are we, compared to them?"

Her last words struck me with the nightmarish insight of hallucination. This tiny woman sitting across from me, maybe forty years old with worn features and a listless gaze, embodied the whole human race in her painful feelings of inferiority.

She watched me, vaguely smiling. "The murders of Fowler and Stein are twisting the minds of the people here," she whispered, "embittering them, only against the Yusians! 'Look where we are because of them!' is everyone's slogan—as if they don't want to find out who the real murderer is. Even more, they're inclined to show compassion toward *any human* killer!"

Odesta worriedly rubbed her forehead, "The way it's going, soon the term 'criminal' will disappear from our code of ethics. People who commit crimes will simply be considered 'victims of the Yusians,' even those who have only seen pictures of Yusians. Yes, I'm afraid that catastrophic times are coming, Terence. The Yusians will become humankind's scapegoats, and very soon we will revert to barbarism."

Unfortunately she was right to a great extent; maybe that's why my next remark sounded so caustic. "I hope you can offer some cure for that prognosis."

"Such a cure has already been offered. By the Yusians!"

"Are you talking about the colonization?"

"Yes, exactly! The colonization gives us the opportunity to begin our own cure."

"How, and in which direction?"

"Enlightenment is needed, Terence!" She was becoming inspired. "Where better to gain that than right here, in close proximity to the Yusians? We need to become accustomed to them. To calm down. To reconcile ourselves to them, but not in a negative sense! To adopt reasonable, dignified humility in the face of our new reality." Odesta lifted her head defiantly. "I'm not going back to Earth. I'll stay here forever with the colonists. I'll help them any way I can. Together with them I will work for enlightened spiritual harmony! Within thirty years, new human generations will appear on Eyrena—"

"I see! I see!" I couldn't resist interrupting. "Then these new generations, having gained enlightened humility in the face of

Yusian superiority, will return to Earth. Like earlier missionaries, they'll spread their miraculous gospel of spiritual harmony among fellow humans, and humankind will slowly achieve a Great Age of Complete Contentment!"

Odesta, so possessed with her "enlightenment" obsession, obviously missed my ironic tone. "Exactly! Complete Contentment! Only then can our real progress begin. And our present." Her face darkened again. "Our present irrefutably proves that not only is the colonization necessary but it also mustn't be postponed. These disgusting murders, however, may delay it. Not even the Yusians are showing enough persistence."

After a few moments of silence, she pointed at the small disk set into the wall next to the sofa. "Sometimes I feel like picking it up and trying to communicate with them! Sincerely!"

I stared with surprise at the disk, although I had already seen many like it. Bulbous and brightly colored, they were all over the base—in the halls, in my apartment, in the dining hall, in Larsen's office, and even in the changing room of the swimming pool. I assumed they were intercoms. I was obviously mistaken.

"What! You don't know yet?" Odesta guessed by my reaction. "These disks are—well, let's call them Yusian telephones."

"Do you use them often?"

"Just the opposite. They are used extremely rarely and then only by Larsen."

"What do you mean by 'extremely rarely'?"

"Only twice. The first time was upon Vernie's insistence. He thought it was only right to let our 'neighbors' know that we were building the defractor, since it's only four kilometers from their base. The second was to notify them of Fowler and Stein's deaths, which Larsen simply had to report."

Before I asked the next question, I took a deep breath. "Is there any way to know whether or not somebody used the 'phone' secretly?"

"But who would do such a thing!" Odesta exclaimed, and for the first time this evening, I detected a false note in her voice. "And why secretly?"

"Still, is there?" I insisted.

"No. There's no way to find out—unless the Yusians themselves were to inform us."

"Tell me, Odesta," I asked, looking her straight in the eye, "is it possible that, on the twenty-sixth, Fowler and Stein were not heading for the defractor site but for the Yusian base?"

Her expression didn't change. "Hardly," she answered. "The instruction, which we all very willingly follow, is not to have any direct contact with the Yusians."

"Yes, and that's the next paradox! Aren't you supposed to be here with exactly the opposite mission."

"For that mission, Terence, other people will be sent, specially trained people. The opinion on Earth is that, before the colonization becomes a fact, we can't afford the risk of allowing the Yusians to get to know us too well."

Her explanation raised more questions than it answered, but something in her eyes told me that continuing our conversation would be neither informative nor useful. So I ended it.

We left the parlor and climbed the stairs. At the door to her apartment, she asked me to wait and then went in and soon returned with the promised electronic log—her alibi. When she handed it to me, her mouth curved upward in a vague, somewhat guilty smile. Or was I just imagining that Odesta Gomez had something to feel guilty about?

CHAPTER 16

After a tense predawn breakfast, I listened to the tiny voice in my mind and quickly left my silent companions to lock myself upstairs in my apartment. My head was rumbling like a cement mixer. Was that my pulse? The clamor kept me from thinking straight. I just couldn't concentrate. I wanted only to wallow in feelings of friendliness, love, and joy. Laughter welled up in my chest, almost suffocating me, but I had to keep my mouth clamped shut. I knew that if I opened it, I would immediately start screaming.

I sat by the window and gripped the armrests of the chair. The reddish hue of the tightly drawn curtains was beginning to fade, which meant that, somewhere in the west, Shidexa was sinking. Meanwhile, Ridon was triumphantly rising in the east—an amazing, endless chase between suns! Probably by now the white crystal rain was falling, the forest slowly turning silver, and the field transforming into an emerald infinity.

I was startled to see my hand reaching to open the curtains. But no, they will stay drawn! And I'll get busy with—what? It must be something routine that would still require my full attention. Yes! I jumped up and turned on the lights. Took the flexor out of its holster and put it on the table. Then I began to disassemble it, talking to myself quietly—that, too, would help keep me from being distracted.

"All right now, let's see you! There, you're fully charged. And excellently maintained. I haven't seen beauties like you before, but I know you. I know you, or do I?"

I took out the charging mechanism and carefully set it on the far end of the table.

"These days we must each take care of ourselves—be our own best friend. The truest, most sincere, most dependable friend!"

My heart started throbbing with incredible affection for myself, which I unwillingly suppressed.

"Stop, stop, and pay attention to your hands, my friend! Get to know the crime weapon. Master your *only* weapon. Ah, I see—a marvel of simplicity! And most effective."

I continued to analyze it for about ten minutes. By then, after I had reassembled the flexor, I thoroughly understood both its structure and how to use it. An hour or two of practice—not now, of course, but in the afternoon—and I would feel absolutely confident in its company.

"But should I leave it for the afternoon?" I asked myself. "There, my crisis is already fading. Or is it completely over?"

I thought sympathetically about the Yusians. *They're so naive! Poor things just want to make us happy with this euphoria.* Yes, but their efforts were in vain. I felt sorry for them.

Then I thought about Jerry. I didn't doubt he was in good hands with Elia, but I really wanted him to be here, next to me! My happy, playful little pet! Elia would also be welcome. *I'll meet her with a kiss.*

"Come in!" I shouted, as I suddenly realized that she was knocking on my door. "Come in, come in!"

But Reder entered instead.

"Too bad it's you," I greeted him frankly.

"Simon?" His owl eyes grew completely round. "I'm sorry to see you too!"

"Are you?"

"Well, yes, yes! To be honest, I was hoping you were out."

"If I knew you were looking for me, I would have been!" I was delighted that I was in such perfect control of myself despite the euphoria.

"I'm returning from the biosector," Redder explained. "I'm late. Yesterday was filled with worries and troubles. Otherwise, I would've come then."

I gave him a penetrating look. He clasped his hands behind his back as if embarrassed by them. He was swaying to and fro, deftly springing from his heels to his toes, his horsy face revealing his diligent efforts to concentrate. This look assured me that he was feeling as mentally unstable as I was and that I had every chance of maintaining my advantage in our conversation.

"But why start with a lie?" Reder added, waiting for my response.

"Why indeed?"

"There's no point," he said, agreeing and shaking his head. "So listen! Until now, I've been avoiding you on purpose. I was keeping my distance, because I was unsure of what to do."

"And you're no longer unsure."

"No. Not anymore."

I decided to take advantage of his confiding mood, which most likely would never be repeated, at least not with me. "Have a seat," I offered. "Coffee or something refreshing?"

"No, no!" He waved his hand. "Don't bother. I'm probably making a mistake anyway."

"What makes you say that?" I leaned toward him to encourage his response.

"Only a fool is always sure he's right!"

Reder gave me such a broad and spontaneous smile that he exposed most of his large teeth to the gums. I liked him more and more, especially with such a smile.

"Well, here goes." He sat down opposite me. "Last night you spoke to Odesta and, I'm sure, were very impressed with her. Nice, quiet, sensitive, and dedicated. I, however, had some reservations about this woman, even before the murders. Something about her contradicts the idyllic image she tries to maintain with such Jesuit zeal. And after the murders? Then I started watching her more closely and confirmed my suspicions: Odesta Gomez is not a sincere person!"

Reder wasn't smiling anymore. Just the opposite: he was frowning and breathing heavily. It was obvious that he was engaged in an exhausting inner struggle to control his frenetic outbursts—just as I had been. Only I was now in excellent control of myself!

I listened carefully, filled with compassion for his inner struggle.

"She, Odesta Gomez, found the bodies. She went, she claimed, just like that, following her intuition, to the forest. We were all searching in the opposite direction, but she—*intuition*. Come on!" He clenched his bony fists and stared at me. "Look, Inspector, she personally may not have killed anybody, but I have no doubts whatsoever that she is involved in this business."

The malice in his voice vaguely worried me. Was it really possible for someone to talk like that while experiencing the euphoria?

"It's more likely, for example, that she herself might have incited Fowler," Reder continued. "He was an honest and—somewhat naive young man. Who knows how she might have influenced him? Besides, she is surely adept at hypnosis. What could be easier than to apply it in the morning hours of Eyrena, when we are all more susceptible? Yes, she must have incited Fowler to kill Stein and then intercepted him. Because he would have been horrified by what he had done, she could easily have convinced him to take his own life. Oh, yes! Believe me, Inspector, Odesta is a dangerous woman, despite her appearance of kindness! In general, such women are the most dangerous."

His eyes pierced mine, vivid and sharp. I thought that I should immediately end this conversation but instead heard myself encouraging it, "Give me some specific examples. Your accusations so far are completely groundless."

"Examples, examples! I'm afraid to give you examples! I shouldn't be specific, because...because." He pressed a palm against his lips, and his features contorted in sudden terror.

He looked feverish too. Was he sick? I was filled with remorse. Why had I suspected him a while ago? He was trying to help me, maybe even taking some risks for me, and I had practically accused him of false accusations!

"I understand that something is preventing you from being entirely open with me," I whispered discreetly. "If that's the case, I don't ask you to ignore your feelings. I'm sure they are absolutely justified."

Reder nodded gratefully. "Thank you. Just remember to keep an eye on Odesta Gomez. Don't let her out of your sight and be alert! That's all the advice I can give you. If you follow it, you'll discover some shocking facts. But, I warn you again: be careful! She...she...is a traitor!" He trembled and sighed deeply and then whispered in an exhausted and barely audible voice, "There, I've told you. I've said it! After months of unbearable silence!"

"Calm down," I mumbled.

"Yes. I'm calm. Although I'll probably pay for these words with my life."

"What are you saying!"

"The truth!" he shouted tragically.

The rumble in my head had grown to a continuous monotonous roar. Something was wrong here, but what? Odesta! I felt painfully disappointed. I had believed her, to a certain point, and she? A *traitor*. But Reder, Reder—what a fate! So far from Earth, burdened with a monstrous secret for months—now, just to help me, willing to suffer the nightmarish consequences of its revelation. A human!

"Man," I began, but a small remnant of self-restraint stopped me.

"Yes?" He made a mistake by encouraging me.

Distance! Distance! I mentally ordered myself. *Just in case: distance!* "What exactly did you mean by calling her a traitor?"

"Oh, let's not talk about it anymore!" Reder insisted then suddenly laughed.

I couldn't help but laugh in response. Suddenly I was filled with unspeakable relief. We both sighed deeply. I felt almost dizzy with friendliness.

"How do you find it here?" he asked me intimately.

"Bad," I whispered back.

"Unfortunately true! What do you think about the colonization?"

"I think it's a betrayal!" I grew enthusiastic. "It's an act of pathetic, conformist policy!"

"Even more unfortunate! But what should we do, Inspector? How can we resist it?"

"I don't know."

"Do you intend to try?"

What a straightforward, calculated, direct question! "Do you intend," and so forth. Yes, Reder is no fool. But then neither am I. "No," I snapped. "I don't."

"Aha, so I have misinterpreted some of your actions."

"What actions, Reder? What? Since I arrived I haven't had any time to act. I've been too busy coping with the sunrises, the trees, and...and...the people here."

"What about on the starship?"

"What?"

"Did somebody take up your time there? Or some*thing*?"

"I don't think even you understand your own insinuations," I replied. "And if so, why bother to make them?"

He looked at me for another minute or two, clearly disappointed, and then finally rose to leave. When he reached the door, however, he stopped, turned around, and took a few quick steps toward me.

"She is a tra-i-tor!" he whispered quite audibly. "She is obsessed by the Yusians, remember that! She's completely on their side!"

Then he was gone, leaving me staring with amazement at a closed door. "Tra-i-tor, tra-i-tor." The syllables knocked around behind my forehead. "Tra-i-tor." The rhythm speeded up, becoming light and playful, dispersing my anxiety caused by Reder's last words and replacing it with a wonderful, carefree feeling. I threw my head back, closed my eyes, and burst into incontrollable, frenetic laughter.

CHAPTER 17

I remained extremely agitated all morning. Several times I would doze off until my own excited exclamations woke me up, take cold refreshing showers—and a hot one as well—for relaxation, perform breathing exercises, and set off looking for Elia, only to return, bouncing from the door to the hall to the staircase and then back. During all that time, I was flooded with emotions— emotions from quiet tenderness to loud and inexplicable joy. I think it was the joy that finally calmed me down: after a final exhausting burst of laughter, I fell into a sound and healing sleep.

I woke up with Reder's image in my mind, and the feelings it evoked now had nothing to do with tenderness and joy.

I hurried out of my apartment, went down to the dining hall for a quick lunch, and immediately set off for the parking lot. There I called one of the robots, told him to "give me a lift" to the biosector, and we both climbed into the shuttle that Stein had used.

Of course the flight was very unpleasant, especially after the floor had thinned into a transparent, springy membrane beneath our feet. I instinctively reached for that rolled-up, little rug but didn't spread it—although my boss always says, "To fight your weaknesses when it isn't necessary is also a weakness."

We landed in front of the biosector lab. I ordered the robot to wait for me in the shuttle and, assuming that Reder might be watching me, peacefully strolled to the entrance. The unfurnished, tiled foyer led to sliding glass doors, behind which spread a huge greenhouse. The plants there caught my interest, but I postponed visiting them for now. Instead, I turned my attention to the stairs leading to the basement where, judging by the muted noises, somebody was working at the moment.

I walked down the stairs and continued along an empty, dimly lit corridor. Before I reached the source of the noise, however, I had to pass by a room that had no door. Peeping in, I discovered something between a workshop and a laboratory. There, bent over a complicated network of thin plastic pipes, stood two robots, obviously in a state of tense expectation. When I approached them, they didn't even move or look at me, so I also waited, though not knowing what for.

At last something in the pipes moved and then rattled as if rolling back and forth, and their surfaces quickly frosted over. When they became completely white, one of the robots stood up. It was SN23, one of the two robots I had seen yesterday. He lifted the elastic nozzle of the last pipe and pulled out its flap. The rattling stopped, and light-brown threads started running from the nozzle into a vessel placed under it for that purpose.

"They are not merging," said the other robot, SN14.

"Yes," SN23 said. "He'll be happy anyway."

The frost on the pipes melted, running onto the floor, and SN23 capped the nozzle and then placed the vessel in one of the sinks. After filling it up with water, he left the room. I went to have a closer look at the threads in question. Not only had they not "merged" but now, obviously affected by the water, they were also twisting together to form small sheaves that were gradually being covered with dark-brown husks.

"Soon they'll be ready stems," SN14 said.

Since I was bent over the sink, when I turned my head, I could see his knees—with brownish stains on them. They were the same stains I had seen on the robot that had deliberately passed by me with SN23 while I was trapped in that sticky substance among the cones. Only that robot had been marked SN17.

"Where did you get those stains?" I asked.

"I don't know," SN14 answered.

"Come here," I ordered him.

After a short hesitation, he approached me. I could see that his knees were covered with biopolymer plates and that only these plates bore the brownish stains. I circled him and ascertained that his elbows and the joints between neck and back were also covered with biopolymer plates, but only the plates at the elbows were stained. Apparently the robot had lain on his "belly" for some reason, resting on his elbows, on something that had interacted only with these plates.

"Besides you, what other robots have such stains?"

"Serial Numbers Seventeen and Thirty-One."

"When you came to Eyrena, did you already have them?"

"No."

"Then they're not a fabric defect, so you should know how they appeared."

"I don't know," insisted the robot.

I left without further comment. When I reached the end of the corridor and found out that the noises I had heard came from some automatic machinery, I went straight back to the foyer. I opened the sliding doors and entered the greenhouse. As far as I could see, Reder wasn't here either, and besides SN23, no other robots were in sight. I walked down the concrete path along the plants. They were separated into tanks of different nutrient solutions. Though none of them looked familiar to me, I was very impressed by their wide variety. Some of these plants were well above human height, while others were barely half a meter high. Some species were so flat that they looked two-dimensional, but others resembled the three-dimensional models of complicated chemical formulae, consisting of different-size spheres that awkwardly branched in every direction. Their colors varied from dark green to the lightest chartreuse, and their shapes from wide and bush-like to narrowly pointed spears.

When I noticed that one of the plants in the row ahead was moving, I quickly approached it. Originally large and smooth, like a huge rounded bottle, it now began to flatten. At the same time, it spun to the left, whipped by its roots, which were taking large scoops of the nutrient solution.

The plant spun faster and faster. Its lime coat darkened, its tip split open, and the whole plant was suddenly wrapped in a halo of fluffy white fibers. These fibers whirled around it and grew thicker while the plant itself was gradually shrinking. At last it was reduced to a slim spindle shape, and the spinning slowed. Light fibrous slivers started raining down. As they reached the tank, they melted into the solution.

I moved on, feeling that I had watched a skillfully edited science fiction movie. I reached another eccentric plant, which in front of my eyes spouted sharp, daggerlike spikes. Yet another plant bent into an arch and then split in two, then in three, and on and on until it looked like a living vaulted cathedral.

I called robot SN23, who had been standing guard all this time next to the sliding doors, which he had carefully closed.

"What are these plants?" I asked him.

"Cacti," he answered.

"Aha. Which exactly are the cacti?"

"All of them."

I took a long look at the rows of cacti, and more cacti. "Well done!" I mumbled.

"Yes, well done," the robot said, "because their mutations increase their storage abilities."

"Storage?"

"Yes. By nature they're adapted to store water, but these can now collect and concentrate many other substances. Only they do that spontaneously, and we are trying to make it compulsory. Otherwise it would be impossible for us to connect them into a common system."

I recalled the shellfish with its "transformed future" that Chuks had shown me on the starship and smiled smugly. These cacti were at least equally as "transformed"!

I left the greenhouse and headed to Stein's workplace or, more accurately, his creative studio. It was a one-floor concrete structure situated near the central building. Like all the other structures in the biosector, it clearly was *not* built by the Yusians. In other words, there were no wood carvings, no mosaics, no weather cocks, and the like. It included only a kitchenette, bathroom, and small study, with furniture as simple in appearance as the person who had worked here for months.

Simple and already in that perfect, somehow deadly, order with which the robots—as if impulsively, unconsciously vindictive—can erase all traces of a human's spiritual presence. Not a single personal possession remained. The sofa and upholstered chairs didn't retain one wrinkle from the weight of Stein's body. Wherever he might have kept a picture of a loved one, a book, a clock, or some other insignificant but treasured memento was now empty and impeccably clean.

I ended my inspection of these quiet, sterile, depersonalized rooms and stopped in front of the computer. All Stein's information had indeed been deleted, and in the simplest way: by reformatting the disks. Even the date of that operation was deleted. *Stein would* not *have done this to his own computer*, I thought. Only somebody unfamiliar with the information stored there and how it could possibly implicate them would do so. Somebody in a great hurry.

I turned off the computer and, checking the map, went to look for Reder. I found him in one of the experimental fields, surrounded by orange markers. He was working on something but noticed me from a distance and hurried to meet me before I was close enough to see what it was. We nodded to each other coldly.

"We never finished our conversation this morning," I said.

"Yes, but unfortunately I'm very busy now," Reder replied.

"So am I. That's why I suggest we be as brief and clear as possible."

"Deal."

There was neither hostility nor irritation in his behavior. At the moment, he was just a busy man eager to get back to work.

"When did you realize that Stein wasn't in the biosector?"

"At about twelve o'clock."

"That's when you were supposed to start some experiment?"

"So you know."

"When had that experiment been planned?"

"*Long before* the twenty-sixth."

"But you chose *exactly* the twenty-sixth to conduct it?

He shrugged his shoulders. "That was the first day after the equipment arrived. We had no reason to delay."

"What equipment?"

"The experiment couldn't be conducted without the new biozone extrainer, which arrived from Earth on the twenty-fifth."

"When was it delivered to you in the biosector?"

"We picked it up ourselves the same evening."

"On the evening of the twenty-fifth, you went with Stein to the landing site, correct?"

"Yes."

"So the starship was there," I remarked." Did you meet any Yusians?"

"Of course not! They are never around when we collect the shipments."

"Except for the extrainer, what else did you take?"

"Nothing. Fowler was supposed to transport the rest of the shipment in the morning."

"According to one of the robots you interrogated, on the twenty-sixth at about seven forty, Stein left for the site where you had been working."

"Yes, but at exactly that time I wasn't there."

"Where were you?"

"Here," Reder insisted. "Right here."

He was lying to me, not even trying to sound convincing. I continued, "If he needed you personally, Stein would have just contacted you. In that case, why would he have gone to the site?"

"I don't know."

"How far had he progressed with his own research?"

"Very far."

"But not to the end, right?"

"No, not to the end." Reder shook his head. "If we look at it from the larger perspective, not only Stein but also humankind is just at the beginning. Maybe not even there."

I recognized the bitterly outspoken tone of his voice and tried to encourage it. "From what I saw in the greenhouse, I got the impression that you two have achieved incredible success."

"Well, yes"—he sighed—"it would seem so, if the Yusians didn't exist. But now, by comparison—"

"Do you think that the plants on Eyrena are their creations?"

"Obviously! The question is, for what purpose did they create them?"

"Do you at least have a guess about that purpose?"

"I have a lot of guesses," he answered gloomily, "but I hope all of them are wrong. From beginning to end, absolutely wrong!"

"As far as I understand, you expect something to happen," I threw in casually, looking around.

"Yes. I do!" said Reder, annoyed by my indifference. "I expect something to happen very soon—something terrible."

"In what way?"

"Well, most likely planetary." His lips suddenly tightened with hatred. "Repulsive creatures! They deliberately keep us in the dark. They're *playing* with us! But it's OK, OK," he added through clenched teeth, "we're not just sitting here doing nothing either. And every living creature, even if it's close to perfection, has its weaknesses!"

The bitterly outspoken tone had disappeared. I knew that the dream of almost all human beings—myself included—was to discover the Yusian weak spot. Yet the fierceness with which Reder was apparently trying to achieve that dream repulsed me.

I stared at him after this reaction and, seemingly at random, commented, "You've noticed the peculiarities of the local robots, haven't you?"

"What peculiarities?" he asked, shuddering. "What do you mean?" he corrected himself.

"Well, I meant in their behavior and the way they communicate with each other. But if you have noticed something else—"

"No, I haven't noticed anything unusual about them." Reder became thoughtful or at least pretended to be. "But it didn't cross my mind to observe them either. They're just machines after all."

"Too complicated though. Too intelligent, and I would say, too self-aware."

"Even if they are, so far that has only benefited us. They're useful assistants."

"Useful enough to follow any orders?"

"I'd rather you ask more concrete questions, Inspector."

"Good. Yesterday I had a—mishap among the cones or, as you call them, 'the rocks,' and two of your assistants saw me, Reder, but made no effort to help me—"

"I see! I see!" he interrupted, as if relieved. "You simply stumbled into the whirlpool. That has already happened to me three or four times in their presence, so they knew that nothing bad would happen to you."

I decided not to comment on the incident nor to refer to our melodramatic "frank" conversation this morning. Time was too precious for either of us to waste on ambiguous discussions balancing precariously between truth and falsehoods. Looking at each other precariously, as if our mutual antipathy were ready to deepen, we parted with icy politeness.

CHAPTER 18

Fowler and Stein's belongings were packed away in a few boxes left in an empty room near the server. I patiently searched them but, as I expected, found nothing either interesting or important, just the usual, personal effects, distinguished only by their depressing, somehow accusing, uselessness. As I arranged them back into the boxes, I also tried to order my thoughts. By now I was pretty sure that both men had been murdered in cold blood and, despite the many unknown factors, had formed a general hypothesis of how it must have happened.

Someone catches up with Stein, kills him for *some* reason and takes the contents of his pockets to check later, expecting to find *something* in them. Starting back, that *someone* runs into Fowler so must kill him as well. To make it look like a homicide-suicide, he plants Stein's things on Fowler, first having removed the *something* he was looking for. He could have returned the rest to Stein's pockets but chose the faster and more convincing option.

But what was that *something*? And was there any connection between it and the shipment from Earth that had arrived the previous day?

I was certain there was, that this very shipment was at the heart of the matter. Unfortunately my conviction didn't solve the riddles. Where *was* Stein going? Why *did* Fowler follow him? What were the *killer's* motives? Since I hadn't the slightest idea, I suspected everybody and everything. I was sure of only one thing: that over these murders, if only as a catalyst, hung the dark shadow of the Yusians.

From the window where I was standing, I saw Jerry jumping happily behind the nearest garage with Elia just behind him. I stepped away from the window and observed her with more than a professional interest. She was wearing a white T-shirt and tight trousers—impractical but pleasing to the eye. She was walking at a snail's pace, and when she finally reached the warehouses, she stopped and unexpectedly started shouting, "Jerry! Jerry! Come here!"

The dog, which at that moment was right next to her, froze in bewilderment.

"Jerry! Come on! Come here! Here, boy!" Elia wouldn't stop shouting, even started clapping her hands loudly.

Jerry sat on the asphalt, his head cocked as if trying to figure her out. He must have decided that she wanted to play, because he answered her invitation with a yelp of joy.

She, however, again unexpectedly, turned her back on him, ran to the entrance of the warehouse, and activated the electric door. She stood right under it as it went up and then suddenly crouched as if to protect herself from something. She grabbed the dog and, instead of moving back, teetered back and forth as if she felt dizzy. For a second she turned her head in my direction and then she slipped inside, leaving me with the image of her face, twisted with horror. The door slammed down with the sinister zeal of a guillotine.

I was at the warehouse door before I realized how I got there. I impatiently pushed the button, and the door slid straight up.

"Elia! Elia!" I shouted in vain.

Inside, the damned warehouse was as dark as it was quiet. I checked the wall left of the entrance for a light switch but saw nothing of the kind. I crossed to the right—still nothing. I took a step and then another, and at that instant, the door slammed shut. *Looks like it's really broken*, I thought without much concern. I had noticed where the inside button was, groped for it, and pushed it. I pushed again and again. The door wouldn't move.

Feeling my way along the wall, I soon reached the loading gate, but my efforts to open it were equally fruitless. I grinned wryly—Elia's behavior started to make sense. She must have known I was in that room and deliberately played the damsel in distress to lure me over. While I sped to her rescue, she went out the back door, waited for me to rush in, and locked the exits. I felt like an idiot. Luckily, however, I had done one smart thing by exchanging my gun for a flexor last night.

I went back to the door and took out the flexor. I felt for the dosimeter, turned it to maximum power, and taking a couple of steps back, pulled the trigger. The beam bounced off the door several times and painfully burned my shoulder. I groped for the door and finally felt the spot where the beam had landed—it was just a bit warmer and slightly concave. I felt dizzy. Not from pain or dread—that ricochet could have killed me—but because of this slightly warm, concave spot on the door, a door that remained intact after withstanding a beam that could pierce a twenty-centimeter-thick stone block!

A Yusian door—Yusian like everything else around me, as I just realized. The darkness suddenly turned into a nightmare. The thought of being trapped in a Yusian warehouse filled with invisible, unthinkable Yusian creations made me gag in panic. I wanted to scream, to shoot blindly.

"Damn it!" I swore quietly and stuck the useless flexor in its holster.

I felt my shoulder. The shirt was ripped, but there was no blood under it. The ricochet had barely touched my skin, leaving only a small swelling. I looked around, hoping to identify the silhouettes of the nearest objects in the pitch dark. I could easily recall the outside of the warehouse—a huge, shabby hulk with no windows. Its height well exceeded twenty meters, which suggested to me that there was more than one floor and thus should be at least one elevator, albeit a Yusian one. I had to find it and use it somehow, to reach the basement, where hopefully there was an emergency exit. Provided, of course, that there was a basement.

Further surmising that the elevator was probably in the center of the warehouse, I extended my arms and walked forward. I moved slowly, filled with resentment, until my fingers touched something cold and slippery. Shaken, I jerked backward. Then I calmed down, moved a step sideways, and extended my arms again, encountering the same slippery object. Slowly circling around the object, which seemed immense, I finally reached a narrow passage between it and another, similarly repulsive, Yusian surface. I stopped, hesitant whether to proceed or to search for another—wider—passage, when I sensed that something had already started around me—God knows what.

I listened, squinting, and patchy blue spots started dancing before me. At first I thought they were caused by my tension but soon discounted that explanation. The darkness was indeed growing lighter and, without losing its opacity, gradually becoming a vivid electric blue.

Well, this at least I can bear, I thought. But then, from somewhere behind my back, came a cloying, unfamiliar odor. It grew stronger, as if to signal the approach of a huge, sweaty body!

I ducked and rushed blindly through the passage, ignoring even my brushes against slimy Yusian surfaces. The smell grew oppressive; I could tell that it was now spreading everywhere, which was more frightening than some imaginary creature because it could only mean that a gas, probably poisonous, had been released in the warehouse.

I dropped to the floor, where the air was still breathable, and looked around. Yes! In the strange blue darkness, I could just make out a gleaming yellow dot, a meter, or ten, or fifty meters away. I couldn't be sure. I rose to my knees, coughing spasmodically. My body was sticky with sweat or from the toxic gas. All around me, probably because of the gas penetrating their tissues, invisible Yusian substances began screaming, moaning, and groaning.

As I crawled toward the dot of light, my fingers got caught in an oily pulp tentacle and tore it, causing a shrill hiss. I leaped up and ran until the dot grew into a circle—into a well-formed hexagon. I stood before it, barely breathing. It was level with my chest and pulsating—pulsating. I recalled seeing such a hexagon—in Chuks's shuttle! I reached out and ripped it from its doughy soft nest with all the strength I had and collapsed on the floor.

When I regained consciousness, the darkness was black again and the disgusting smell almost gone. I stood up. My shoulder hurt where the laser beam had struck me; otherwise, I felt fine. I groped my way back to the door. As I expected, this time it obediently opened as soon as I touched the button. I stumbled out into the splendid light of the Eyrenean day. Feeling better, I smoothed my hair, checked my clothes, and then headed for the parking lot in front of the nearest garage. Something told me that Elia was there. And she was.

The Yusian machine she was standing next to was roughly the size and shape of a whale. At least that's what it looked like when I first saw it. As it transformed itself, the "snout" blunted quickly, the "tail" wrinkled, hissing like a huge bellows, while the "belly" and the "back" swelled until everything finally merged into a polished gray sphere.

The ball shook spasmodically until its diameter was reduced in half, then darkened—apparently because of its increased density—and stood still. Then the side facing Elia split open, and a robot climbed out.

"Very good," Elia praised him. "Everything seems to be in order."

"Are you sure?" I asked, coming in behind her and at the same time petting Jerry, who was greeting me cheerfully.

She turned around in surprise. "You!"

"Why not? You didn't expect me?"

Elia thought for a second and then waved her hand. "Well, yes. I've been expecting you. Only not so soon."

"I took a walk in one of the warehouses but didn't stay long. The atmosphere there wasn't exactly comfortable."

"Especially the aroma, I suppose," she said, wrinkling her nose.

I came right to the point: "Did you try to poison me in there?"

"Nonsense. I just set a program for the general power supply."

"And this program automatically locks the doors," I added. "In other words, you trapped me."

"Yes, precisely," Elia said.

"Why?"

"Oh, reasons could be invented. Let's say I wanted to teach you that here, as on Earth, playing the gallant can be dangerous. Or that until you get to know the base, anyone, especially the killer, could ambush you. Or—"

"And the real reason?" I cut her off.

Smiling mysteriously, Elia came closer and whispered in my ear. "I wanted to flirt with you, Inspector. To arouse your interest—"

"By putting me to sleep forever?"

"Oh, come on! Don't be ridiculous." She moved away, annoyed. "I'm not sure how it is in general, but those biomaterials are adjusted by the Yusians to discharge only gases harmless to human beings."

"Hmm. Have *you* been exposed to them?"

"Well, yes," Elia confirmed. "By mistake, of course. I entered a warehouse out of curiosity and almost died of fright, especially when the darkness turned that maddening electric blue and the noises. Good thing I fainted! What about you? Were you afraid?"

"Me? Don't be ridiculous, Elia," I said pompously, and then we both burst out laughing. I was really glad she didn't turn out to be the resident offender!

"What's wrong with your shoulder?" she asked me with real concern.

"Nothing serious," I answered. "I must have scratched it somewhere. By the way, the warehouse doors are also Yusian, right?"

"Yes." Elia nodded and frowned. "They are examples of their so-called pseudoterrestrial objects. There are very few at the base, but if you go to one of the settlements—it's disgusting!"

"Who needs all this pretense? Don't the Yusians realize it makes them even less attractive to us?"

"No, you're wrong." Elia shook her head. "Look at this machine—or worse, touch it. You must admit that it's more repugnant to you than the pseudoterrestrial door, for example. You know, in general, we humans like a little deception. Even the fact that the Yusians are bothering to deceive us somehow flatters our ego. It's all so pathetic, for both them and us!"

Elia approached the machine and leaned against it heavily, as if she wanted to hide in its shell, distancing herself from the rest of fickle humanity. Her touch stirred the surface of the charcoal substance into small waves, which gradually calmed and died out. I could hardly resist grabbing her and pulling her away from it. Her presence next to that reactive alien sphere was absurd, appalling!

"I need to clear a new site from the pillars." She took a step toward me. "Will you join me?"

My hesitation was insincere. "OK, if we go by the defractor site—"

"The defractor?" She looked startled.

"Actually to follow the route of the strange Yusian," I explained. "Odesta said he passes by there every day at the rise of Shidexa."

"And now you want to see if that's true?" Elia half smiled. "You're very suspicious—about some things."

"And about others as naive as a child, right?"

She didn't answer. Instead, she called Jerry, picked him up, and entered the sphere through the opening the robot had made. I followed her. The even floor inside was so smooth that I worried I might slip. We had entered a crescent-shaped cockpit, empty except for two folding chairs planted in the floor. I pointed to them. "Were the Yusians that concerned with our comfort?"

"No, I told the robot to bring them in."

I was offended. "You were so sure I would come with you—"

"Which means," she interrupted, "that I was also sure you would leave the warehouse safe and sound."

When we settled into the two chairs, Elia removed a small device from the pouch attached to her belt and looked at me. "Straight to the strange Yusian?"

"No. Let's take Jerry back to the lodge first."

She quickly agreed. The poor puppy was lying limply in her lap, his head on his paws. Clearly the Yusian machinery had destroyed his good mood. After petting him affectionately, Elia pressed the device against the wall. Once it sank in so that only its keyboard was visible, she touched one of its tiny buttons and said, "To the lodge entrance." The sphere immediately erased its opening, and we were off.

CHAPTER 19

I took Jerry to my room, fed him to make him feel better, and after changing my shirt, returned to Elia.

"Shidexa will soon rise," she noticed as I took my seat next to her. She touched the same button and mechanically ordered the sphere to take us to the defractor "slowly."

As it rose, we sat calmly, in relaxed positions, but both of us avoided looking at the now completely transparent floor. For some reason, we also avoided looking at each other.

"What exactly is this device?" I asked, without taking my eyes off the barely visible wrinkled gray wall in front of me.

"A transformer," she answered with unexpected eagerness. "Only with these can we operate Yusian machinery. For this flight, I have plugged it into the structure of the sphere, because I'm giving it improvised voice commands. If we were taking a specific, detailed route, I would have to set the parameters before we left, which is generally required for all the more complicated programs."

"How would you do that?"

"The same way I activated the system in the warehouse. Since you figured out that you had to remove the fragment, you must know how it appeared and what it's used for."

"Just a lucky guess," I admitted.

"Well, OK, the programming itself is very simple. You tear off a fragment of the device you want to operate, in this case from the inside of the sphere, and use the transformer to set the chosen program. Then you stick the fragment back where it was, and that's it."

"But we have no idea what happens next, do we?"

"Oh, we do—basically." Elia sighed sadly. "Because of the added information, the fragment becomes foreign to the 'organism' from which it was torn, and its return demands a process of assimilation. That process involves, in fact, realization of the set program; only by doing so can the 'organism' incorporate the information that had alienated it from the fragment. The visual evidence of this process is the gradual fading and disappearance of the glowing hexagon, within which the fragment transforms from the beginning of the assimilation process."

"I see," I murmured. "It makes sense, as long as you don't delve into it too deeply."

"Yes, but to our cyberneticists, who have been trying for years to go deeper, it's a nightmare. Which is to be expected, since they have reached only one firm conclusion."

"Which is?"

"That they will never be able to identify the attributes of that damned information-absorbing substance."

We fell silent as the incomprehensible Yusian machine seemed to separate us more completely, more zealously, from the outside world. Motionless, seized in its gray grip like preys of a monstrous wingless bird, we were swept up—and apart—by its noiseless, breathless, tremor-free flight.

"You know," Elia murmured, "there's something else too: the fragment can only be torn out by direct human touch. You can't use a glove, for example. If you cut it with a tool, it refuses to absorb any information. Then, when you put it back, it blends invisibly, leaving not even the slightest mark. It's as if this substance has the qualities of a liquid as well—if it can be considered a substance at all."

My pragmatic reply, though Elia probably found it annoying, quickly dispelled the atmosphere of mystery and tension that was threatening to embrace us. "Only direct human touch, you say. What about the robots? How do they do it? I've seen how they operate. Not only do they easily tear the various fragments but they can also plug in directly to the shuttles."

"Well, no, not directly," Elia objected. "Their transformers are incorporated into them by the same manufacturer. Maybe that explains it."

I stared with surprise at the keyboard of the device sticking out of the wall. Sure enough, in its lower left corner was the ESSIKO trademark.

"Yes—maybe that explains it," I echoed, unconvinced.

"We're almost there," Elia said." Shall we land?"

"No. I want to have a look at the Yusian without his suspecting that this is the purpose of our flight."

Elia nervously shook her head. "Ha! He probably doesn't care about us at all." Placing her index finger on one of the buttons, she said, "Take a turn around the south periphery of the defractor—a low, very slow turn."

Our sharp descent took my breath away. When I looked down, we were about a hundred meters above the field and twenty meters to the side of the forest. In the middle of the sparkling pink grass stood the dirt-brown figure of the Yusian. He was moving on the same path as yesterday, gliding along smoothly, dreamily. From our altitude, he looked touchingly small—even helpless.

We flew over him without attracting his attention as he climbed the hill near the defractor. He stopped at the top and bent his limbs awkwardly. I watched him through the rocking "window" of the sphere his kind had created and thought that he must seem strange not only to us humans but also to the Yusians. So different from them. And thus so lonely.

"He's taking a walk. I think he's just taking a walk," I said quietly. "Not a spy, or a saboteur—just a sensitive, romantic loner. Or maybe he's unhappy, ill—"

"Stop it!" Elia's reaction surprised me. "I don't want us to talk about him—I don't want to try to guess anymore what he is or is not!"

She was very upset but surely not because of my inquisitive observations. She briskly ordered the sphere to continue, adding an unnecessarily harsh "quickly!" We flew back to the base, on past the cones in the valley, and then over the eastern ridge to the territory of the leafless crimson plants, the "pillars."

"Look to the right!" Elia's harsh command startled me. "Do you see anything?"

"No. I can see nothing yet. But my hearing has been very good ever since I was a child."

"I'm sorry." She spoke softly now. "I meant that hill over there."

"Yes?"

"Well, I wanted to let you know that under it is the Yusian base."

"The Yusian. Isn't it close to the defractor?"

"This is their old base that has been deserted for a long time now. Or at least it looks deserted."

"It doesn't look like anything from here," I said. "Just a hill. Have you been inside it?"

"No, but Stein entered it once. He mentioned that it only *seemed* deserted."

"Why 'only *seemed*'?"

"We never found out." Her voice sounded ominous. "Stein was planning to go again and then to write up a detailed report describing the situation there, but a few days later—both he and Fowler were dead."

We landed a kilometer or two from the base, right on top of the pillars, without even feeling the unceremonious crush. Now no sunlight entered the cockpit, but its walls emitted a soft pearl-white glow. I looked at Elia's profile—she was as beautiful as an illusion.

"Exit!" she ordered, and the illusion was immediately splashed by the red rays of Shidexa that poured through the opening. "In one minute, a clearing thirty by two hundred meters!" she ordered before removing the transformer, with visible repugnance, and returning it to her pouch. In place of its rectangular shape, a hexagon had "printed out" on the wall. Since I first landed on Eyrena, the feeling of complete absurdity, maybe even unreality, had never left me, but now it was stronger than ever.

We rose from the idiotic chairs planted in the floor and exited the sphere. Only seconds later, the Yusian machine seemed to start breathing. With every inhalation it grew more amorphous, and with every exhalation it lengthened. When it had resumed its whalelike shape, it started moving in brisk, wide zigzags, digging at the earth and knocking down the pillars. They fell with a dry crackle that irritated our ears. As it quickly advanced, the machine left a depressing chaos in its wake.

"What is this clearing going to be?" I asked Elia.

"Just what you see at the moment."

"And then what?"

"We'll go back to the lodge," she said. Noticing my bewilderment, she explained, "The aim is simply to uncover the rock base. Then tomorrow, at the rise of Ridon, everything will be settling outside."

"What about these pillars?"

"That's what I mean," confirmed Elia. "There's nothing else."

"What about the dirt?"

"This is not dirt, Terence. This cover is, in fact, the joint root system of the plants."

I went to the fallen pillars: indeed, what looked like compacted earth turned out to be their natural extension. Beneath the devastating blows inflicted by the "whale," the roots had shattered into tiny pieces, so I could easily study their internal composition. They consisted of three layers of different thickness: the top one a tough brown membrane; the bottom something like spiky porous plastic; and the middle layer very dense but crisscrossed by small capillaries through which streamed a yellow fluid. I reached down to pick up a piece, amazed at their complexity.

"Don't !" Elia immediately stopped me. "It's even hard to pull these spikes off a rock, and if they stick to your skin, they can injure you badly. Besides, that yellow fluid has a strong, corroding effect."

I pulled my hand away but continued to badger her with my questions, "How do these plants feed? It looks like they don't have chlorophyll for photosynthesis."

"They ingest everything from rock particles through their root system to whatever reaches their surface through the air. Stein assumed that they somehow directly absorb solar energy too."

"Did this assumption apply only to the pillars?"

"No, he included all four of the plant varieties on the planet," Elia said. Then she stared at the machine and exclaimed, "But what is it doing, for Christ sake!" She started running toward it.

I followed her, watching the "whale's" bizarre behavior. It stuck its nose in the ground, vibrated, and dug deeper and deeper. It penetrated the rock base with a sequence of powerful head strokes, sucking the particles through its gaping snout. The convulsions in the area under the cockpit traced the stones' progress toward its belly, where they were ground into a fine gray powder and then discharged from its bottom.

I was so overwhelmed by this sight that I hardly noticed Elia advancing toward the opening of the cockpit. When she tried to enter it, I rushed toward her, intending to hold her back, but that became unnecessary. The opening closed—or healed—right under her nose.

"Now that's too much!" she protested. Then suddenly she laughed without restraint, like somebody freed from a heavy burden. "Oh! It simply broke down! It simply broke down, Terry! The *perfect* creation of the *great* Yusians!" I had never seen her so happy. She looked radiant. For a moment I even thought she might leap into my arms. Instead she turned her back on me and headed for one of the less-agitated parts of the machine. I followed.

Still smiling, Elia took out the transformer and pressed it against the convulsing substance. I expected it to sink in as it had in the cockpit, but it didn't. Elia tried again and again—still in vain. Then she slowly turned to me. Her eyes darkened with disappointment as she raised her arm and, somewhat accusingly, showed me the transformer. Its display was dark—not a single pulse left in it. And the machine kept digging.

We moved away. The noise it made while pulverizing the stones wasn't deafening, but it was very unsettling. Elia sat on one of the fallen pillars and immediately busied herself with her mobile phone.

"It's not working either!" she finally cried. "He's taken care of that too."

I leaned over and looked her in the eye. "I'm running out of patience, Elia. If this is another one of your tricks."

"No! It's not."

"If not, please explain me exactly what is happening."

"The machine didn't break down," she said bitterly. "Another program, a program on hold, has been set in it to begin running after mine expired. Only a new command could cancel that one."

"Or removing the fragment in which it's been set," I added.

"Yes. But you saw for yourself that there's no way we can get in and remove it."

"When will the others start looking for you?"

"No sooner than four, maybe five, hours. Only when they find they can't contact me will someone come to pick us up. It would be much faster if we just walk back."

I turned toward the machine. It was no longer just vibrating—it was shaking violently and digging deeper and deeper.

"Listen, Elia," I insisted, "we must try to stop it! We can't just walk away as if we were primitive savages!"

She nodded but said, "But there's nothing else we *can* do. Only through the transformer."

"Oh, come on! I don't believe you didn't bring something else. It's absurd to think you have no backup alternative."

"It *is* absurd, of course, but only the transformers were given to us. Those creatures want us to be in the closest possible contact with their machines so we can get used to them. That's why they came up with the crazy idea of making more complex programs dependent on touching their nasty substances directly. Our only option is to tear out fragments and then stick them back! They are *taming* us, and then we might end up with implanted transformers like the robots. Or be transformed ourselves. Or implant us into."

She managed to control herself despite her obviously growing hysteria. Her face had altered beyond recognition—into a twisted, evil mask. I couldn't blame her for that either. I couldn't imagine what *my* face might look like after six or seven months here.

Anyway, her tortured expression convinced me that indeed, this time, this "trick" wasn't her idea.

"Elia, you know, or at least guess, who—"

"No, no," she interrupted, "there must have been—some misunderstanding."

"Someone deleted the charge in your transformer, left us without radio contact, and set that insane program. You call all that a 'misunderstanding'? Damn it! You could at least try to invent a good lie."

She stared at me absently and then turned her head away.

I left her like that and went to have a closer look at the digging. The machine penetrated the rock layers very compactly, leaving no pits or even slits around its entry, and had now shape-shifted from a "whale" to some gigantic "worm" that grinds rocks in its intestines and then discharges them as a whirling jet of sand.

Its front section, including the cockpit, was completely underground. It occurred to me that, had we remained inside, since the fragment was either well hidden or somewhere outside, we would probably be suffocating by now. Or maybe that was the plan?

I moved to the back end, where a huge heap of sand had already started to slide down, shifting toward the "wormhole." At this rate, the machine would be buried underground in less than an hour. How much energy did it still have? If the program was endless, without set parameters, how long and deep would it dig?

I shook off the tiny particles of sand sticking to my clothes, turned around, and headed for the distant hill.

"Terence!" Elia shouted after me. "Where are you going?"

I looked at her over my shoulder but didn't slow down. "Go straight back to the base! And send a robot to put an end to that mess."

"Wait!" she caught up with me and grabbed my hand. "And you—are you going to that Yusian base?"

"That's what you wanted, wasn't it? Didn't you arrange this entire 'unfortunate' trip just to get me to go there?"

"No. Actually." Elia was visibly confused and finally admitted, with her usual frankness, "Even if I had wanted it, I don't now."

"You know what?" I countered, "This time there really *is* a misunderstanding. And frankly, my dear, I don't give a damn *what* you want!"

CHAPTER 20

"If you think you've been pushed into doing something stupid, do it without delay. That way you can surprise the enemy with your stupidity, if nothing else." That was one of my boss's favorite jokes, but now was the time to take it seriously. So I hurried to the base entrance and popped in "without delay."

I had hardly taken ten steps when the floor sank under my feet, enclosing me in a Yusian excuse for an elevator. I had expected worse, so this somewhat familiar experience was a relief. I just noticed the fact that I was plummeting to a great depth. As soon as the elevator stopped and disintegrated, I realized that whatever threat I might encounter would not be from humans. This was not a setting for human interactions.

The room I had reached looked like a wide, shallow container filled with burning lava. Flames resembling the wings of exotic birds ceaselessly flew out of the ceiling, the walls and the floor soared chaotically in the air, swooped up and down, and tore each other to shreds.

Luckily these flames couldn't reach me—they simply flew around this spot that had assimilated the disintegrated elevator. Yes, but to go back up, I had first to leave this spot and then to step back on it in order to provide the impulse for the elevator to reappear. Leaving the spot would mean entering the flames.

I couldn't decide what to do. After a while, however, in complete contrast to the flames in front of me, I felt a cool breeze. *So it's just an optical illusion*, I thought. I stretched out my arm, and it was immediately covered with orange flames. They spread all over my body, but the sensation wasn't unpleasant, just odd, like being covered with a veil of solid light. I started to peel it off as if it were a cobweb; it stuck to my fingers and crackled softly as I peeled but looked completely harmless. It didn't even hinder my breathing. I drifted away from the fireless zone like some cold, smokeless torch.

I had trouble finding the exit, but once I stepped over its threshold, the flames quickly withdrew to their dominions of light. I entered a corridor resembling a sleeve of pale-green velvet that ended in two darker branches. I hesitated briefly then before choosing the right branch. Just then from the left branch came a distant, prolonged moan!

I backed out and entered the left branch instead, which looked exactly the same as the right. As I walked its dusky, pale-green length, the sounds of my footsteps, even my breathing, were completely absorbed. Even my shadow was being absorbed, maybe even me.

The dusk thinned as the corridor widened into a strange gallery with constantly shifting contours. Here between these amorphous, probably immaterial, walls, I felt for the first time an overpowering, savage hatred—something I had often seen in other humans forced to interact with the Yusians.

I was in one of their depositories for pseudoterrestrial samples. I could see what appeared to be carefully arranged metal containers—though I was sure they weren't really metal—with false casing and fake rivets. There were "wooden" tables topped with colorful, bulky boxes and tubes made of strikingly false plastic, books with no pages, disgustingly soft flower vases, clothing and shoes sunk in slime, stuffed toys with the wrong heads, and so on.

I passed those grotesque replicas of human objects, haunted by the thought that somewhere else—on the planet Yus, on Eyrena, or even on Earth—other depositories were probably filled with similarly grotesque caricatures of our plants and animals.

I froze as if paralyzed, my hair standing on end. *Not only plants and animals. Not only!* On the floor at my feet lay a human hand.

I stiffly leaned over it: bluish fingers bent as if to grip something, no fingernails, severed violently just above the wrist—but hollow inside! I felt momentary relief before horror took hold of me again. Maybe it was a cast? A Yusian cast of someone's *real* human hand? A small, female…

Leaning closer, I noticed many dotted lines glistening on the wrinkled skin-like material. They were actually moving in tight, parallel rows, equidistant from each other. They looked like intelligent insects, hurrying to inspect every millimeter of this "hand," memorizing it.

I left the depository certain that this discovery, which had shaken me so much, wouldn't be my last. I entered a tall, winding tunnel. From its arc hung huge draperies of some thick, gelatinous substance, cutting through the dimness with streams of unearthly, splendid colors of amazingly vivid intensity—yellow, scarlet, violet, and blue. As I passed beneath, they seemed to tremble with excitement, as if they were warning me of something evil and cruel.

A human! I jumped aside, instinctively drawing the flexor from its holster. Whatever it was stood still as a statue in its narrow alcove, dimly glowing. It didn't move even when I pointed the flexor in its direction. Much shorter than I, it was deformed and completely wrapped in those glistening dotted lines. The right arm was missing. I pushed it—it swayed but didn't fall. It also maintained its balance when I deliberately tried to knock it down. Although it was lightweight and probably hollow, some force kept it upright.

I continued on through the tunnel, the flexor set at maximum in my hand. I passed by several other alcoves recesses with similar "mannequins" and then heard the same prolonged moan. It was closer, maybe just around the next turn.

I ran toward the sound, holding my breath, and peered forward. About ten meters away from me was the next alcove, and inside it the glistening dotted lines were crawling all over a mannequin. This one wasn't still at all. So it was true—they were already producing pseudohumans!

I watched horrified. He, or rather it—the creature—was trembling, shaking as if in painful convulsions, its breath a weak, uneven wheezing. I had to do something immediately. But what?

The creature noticed me. It briskly raised its hands above its head, and I heard the sound of tearing tissue. Then, after bending over and picking something up from the floor, it started running down the winding tunnel. I rushed after it and was no more than five or six steps behind when it turned around. It was holding a flexor! Illuminated by a scarlet stream from one of the low-hanging draperies, it looked insanely alien—and strangely familiar. My flexor was ready to fire, but I didn't use it. I stepped back.

At that moment, the creature fired. Upward, at the drapery. The gelatinous substance, weighing at least a couple of tons, plopped in front of me and began twisting and crawling, blocking my way. I stared at it for some time before I thought to walk around it. Careful not to step on what looked now like a huge puddle of blood, I then resumed my chase of the fleeing creature. It could no longer run fast; apparently it was completely exhausted. The distance between us diminished. I had almost reached it when it unexpectedly disappeared through a side entrance. I cautiously looked in and saw it rambling among piles of pulsing "ceramic" jars. As I approached, it again fired its flexor.

The jar next to me exploded. The shock wave threw me backward into a cloud of microscopic brown flakes. I choked and started spitting as they melted in my mouth, leaving an unbearably sour taste. Crawling away from them, I looked around and saw the creature go back into the tunnel.

I followed through the haze. Feeling dizzy, I stumbled and almost fell into a pool filled with thick, translucent mush in which randomly floated inflated imitations of car tires. The pool was rumbling and roiling, as if swamp bubbles were bursting beneath its surface.

I looked down at the floating junkyard, wondering what would have become of me if I had fallen in. Then I continued down the tunnel, my hand overheated from squeezing the flexor so hard for so long. I sensed that something was ugly, even brutish, about this chase, but despite these misgivings, I had to continue it. I wasn't sent to Eyrena just to give in to squeamish inhibitions.

When the tunnel turned again, I caught a glimpse of the weird, half-alien, half-familiar creature as it leaned against a wall, trying to regain its strength. I didn't give it the chance. Rushing toward it, I took shelter from its flexor in one alcove after another, ignoring the hollow figures each contained.

The creature dragged its weak feet forward. Suddenly, an ancient, entirely human passion for victory stirred in me. I wasn't concerned with the reason for the chase anymore; I didn't care what that creature was or what it felt at the moment. All I wanted was to catch it. Its stubborn refusal to surrender maddened me.

As I leaped from the last sheltering alcove, it turned around and stopped. We were so close that I could see the bulging folds that encircled its body like rings, the steaming exhalations from its invisible nostrils and the nervous twitching of its limbs. As it lifted the barrel of its flexor, I dived toward the wall. Where I had been standing a fraction of a second earlier was buried under another ton or so of drapery ripped from the arc. I walked between its poisonously green edges and the wall. Nearby, the creature was backing away, swaying and nearly collapsing. Apparently the end was near. I walked toward it, my flexor aimed straight at its chest.

Exhausted, unable to take a single step further, it stood still, shaken by a new fit of spasms or maybe fear. In this state, it couldn't hit me if it tried, so I advanced until we were about fifteen meters apart. Ten. Then the creature chose an easier target, again aiming, surprisingly fast, for the drapery above me.

Now I didn't have time to jump away. I pulled the trigger. At that instant came the familiar ugly sound of tearing. The drapery plopped on the floor around me, encircling me—without touching me!

It didn't want to kill me, I slowly realized. It was only trying to stop me. I remembered the gates opening in front of Chuks in the starship. "Deprived of toleration of intelligent touch," he had said. Not even the Yusian "draperies" could tolerate such a touch.

The creature was lying on its back with arms outstretched, its face staring at the arc, bluish and shining in the twilight. The nose was almost flat, and it was without ears or hair. I leaned over it. Its head raised wearily, as if it wanted to speak and then dropped to the floor. It stopped moving.

The beam hole in its chest was already healing through accelerated division of the surrounding cells, and the blood that had run out of the hole was soaking into the skin-like tissue swelling around it. It felt oily and hot. I pulled and stretched the tissue above its right foot, which turned out to be thick but very elastic. When I pulled it harder, on its surface appeared a small crack. The substance beneath was matte white. I widened the crack—and to my amazement, a human knee appeared! Female. I tore with trembling hands at the deceitful mask of a face, ripping it off.

Wide open, the dead eyes of Odesta Gomez stared at me.

I was able to keep my face completely expressionless. I stood up and headed for the alcove in which I had found her. There were her shoes and clothes, carefully folded into a small pile. I took them and returned to the corpse. Separating the Yusian cover from her body, I threw it aside, where the torn cracks quickly healed. The skin-like tissue started to bloat, taking the shape of the body it had been covering. After that it formed the ringlike folds and swellings, altering the original shape. The neck merged with the shoulders, the waist spread level with the chest and the hips, the arms and legs lost their outlines at the wrists and the ankles.

In front of me, moved by sharp structural impulses, stood another twisted mannequin that only vaguely resembled Odesta. Its "dotted lines" had faded but never ceased their inspections, moving to and fro in tight, dense rows.

I carefully closed the eyes of the woman I had killed and then clumsily began to dress her. I wanted to finish this depressing procedure as quickly as I could, but I forced myself to move slowly and calmly. I knew that the Yusians were watching me.

CHAPTER 21

We were gathered around the corpse of Odesta Gomez. But we were not looking at her; we were staring at each other.

"The wound was made by a flexor," Elia said, "but her clothes are untouched."

"How?" Vernie whispered. "How could they be 'untouched'?"

"She must have been naked when they killed her."

"What about these?" Larsen pointed at the two blue spots on her temples. "Did you find out what caused them?"

"No." Elia shook her head.

"We'll examine them in the biolaboratory," Reder cut in. "At the moment, our only concern is to determine the cause of death."

"When—did this happen?" Vernie whispered once again.

Reder answered him loudly, emphasizing his words, "During the last *eighteen* hours. That means, between when she met with *you*, Vernie, and when the activity in the forest subsided, at noon today."

"It's impossible to determine it more precisely." Elia turned to Larsen. "The process of—preservation or perhaps mummification, I have no idea what process—has already started!"

"Don't forget that I wasn't the last to see her yesterday. One of the robots saw her after me," Vernie reminded us. "And her body was found today by a robot. Ask yourselves why, instead of staying with her in the forest and just calling us for help, that robot dragged her here, onto the road. He did so without any orders, without even permission to touch her!"

"No, we're not forgetting," Reder muttered sarcastically. "We will forget *nothing*. And we will ask ourselves about many *other* things as well."

Larsen lifted the dead woman, fixing his eyes upon every one of us in turn in unspoken threat. Then he slowly started walking toward the base. His wide back was bent, and his walk a study in deep-rooted weariness and grief. We followed him.

"I've seen those spots before," Vernie spoke so quietly that I guessed rather than really heard his words.

"Where?" I asked.

He held me back until the others passed ahead of us.

"In the same place." He became more specific. "On her temples."

"When?"

"About two weeks ago. In other words, only three days after Fowler and Stein died."

"What do you think they're from?"

"The spots? Well—I don't know." Vernie made a grimace that told me he *did* know. "But maybe you will find out. I'll only say that Odesta was desperately trying to hide them."

"Then how did you see them?"

"She fainted. So, while I was trying to bring her to her senses—"

"Why did she faint?"

"That's another thing I don't know—at least not now. I thought then the reason was weariness. We always have our reasons not to feel fresh here."

"What did she tell you when she regained consciousness?"

"Nothing. I didn't question her. And I don't intend to mention the incident to the others. The only one who will ever know about this is you."

"Why?"

"Oh! Can't you guess?"

"No."

"It's easy, Inspector. I have no desire to bring *flexor trouble* upon myself. For all we know, one of those three"—Vernie tilted his head toward Larsen, Elia, and Reder ahead of us—"could be the murderer. Right?"

We reached the lodge. The others continued on toward the laboratories, but I returned to my apartment. After three hours of carrying Odesta's corpse to the forest, and after the twelve hours that we all "searched" for her, I needed to be alone, to put it all behind me. I was at, or actually someone had led me to, the edge of total failure. Driven to the brink, but by whom? And why?

Generally speaking, I knew the answers to such questions because the powers responsible for the Eyrena base were certainly no secret to me. They were the same powers responsible for regulating Yusian contact on Earth: the Security Council, the United Military Forces, and the International Bureau of Investigation.

Three independent organizations, represented on Eyrena respectively by Zung's agent, Larsen and myself. The superior power here belonged to Zung: those assigned to the base were actually working according to *his* plans for colonization. I therefore assumed that the murders of Fowler and Stein must be the work of someone who opposed their attitudes toward those plans: plans in which, by the way, Odesta could not be involved in any possible way.

So yesterday Zung's agent—Reder of course—must have known that she would be visiting the Yusian base again. He decided to arrange my "encounter" with her, and Elia helped him, either consciously or unconsciously. What did he want to achieve by this meeting? The humiliating answer is that he almost didn't care, because all three possible outcomes would work in his favor.

If I had chosen to expose Odesta, it would have ended her collaboration with the Yusians, something that Zung's agent wanted anyway. If she had killed me, that would have ended my investigations into the murders committed—or, more his style, provoked—by him. The third outcome, which actually took place, unfortunately provided him with the advantages of the other two as well. More precisely, I helped him by completely eliminating Odesta and, as her murderer, putting myself into his hands.

That's why Zung sent me here despite my sincere disagreement not only with his plans but also with the entire idea of the colonization. He knew full well what kind of person was working for him on Eyrena and was certain that this person could find a way to manage me.

Indeed, Reder was about to justify that trust. He only had to solve one more little problem: how to put the blame on me without revealing his own subversive contribution to the event. Once he succeeded, everything would fall into place: Fowler and Stein find out about Odesta's connection with the Yusians, and she murders them. The inspector from IBI in turn kills her for the same reason, and that ends the inconvenient investigation and awards a green light to the colonization.

I went to the safe in the bedroom, unlocked it, and took out the electronic file Odesta had given me. Back in the living room I uploaded the information onto my computer, since I wanted to see if the files had been compromised or changed in any way. They were still intact. The data from the electronic mass spectrometer could not be falsified. Odesta's alibi was indisputable. Her whereabouts at the time of Fowler and Stein's murders, at least according to her, were known to only one person: me. That fact now took on great importance, because it was the only argument, but a categorical one, against Reder's version of these events.

I logged on to the server and created a new file for the contents of Odesta's log and then added a command for that data to be sent, in exactly one hundred hours, to all personal computers on the base. I created a password that would allow only my access to the file and logged off.

I put the original logbook file back in the safe and removed my Yusian effigy from it. I had to find out at all costs what it meant or what it was *used* for. Probably this answer would provide me with clues as to why Fowler had Stein's effigy in his clenched fist when he died. I locked the safe again and started to put the effigy in the pocket of my jacket, but something unclear and persistent made me hold it. Made me look at it—look at myself.

My face lay in my palm facing me, with a bruise beneath my eye, unshaven, and my right ear quite red. But the eyes— the eyes—seemed to be staring at me. And the expression in those eyes. Did I really look like that then—strained, lonely, and frightened? How wrong I was to think I could hide my feelings.

Or maybe I could *hide* them, but this effigy revealed what was hidden behind the mask.

Suddenly, my breathing started echoing in my own ears—becoming faster, peremptory. *Only thirty-three minutes remaining until liftoff! No doubt they were watching me, so I will demonstrate my composure by. But soon, very soon the Earth will be unapproachably far from me. Yes, my workday is over, and the minutes are flying!*

Flying, flying—I began to sink deeper and deeper, caught in their rapid descent. I was wandering the ragged edges of my memory, tenaciously, piece by piece, trying to reconstruct in my soul some feeling or some forgotten event, dead and buried. I finally focused in on one object, surprisingly familiar, prosaic among the chaos of past emotions. On that ineptly painted, *clumsy and pretentious*, still life. I was standing in front of it, filled with a tragic love for all that is *human*. Hovering above me I sensed a monstrous, oppressive presence, of something inhuman.

I was startled out of my reverie by the effigy burning in my palm. It felt soft and malleable, but squeezing it tightly had no effect. It remained as *I* had been then—the same stubbled face frozen in a grimace of mock indifference, the same haggard, terrified gaze—in those final minutes before the monstrous Yusian starship left Earth.

I locked it in the safe again. I understood now what it was "used" for—to preserve a memory—a "keepsake," as Stein used to say about the effigy of himself that he carried.

I went to the desk and placed my hand on the scarlet Yusian "telephone." At my touch, it glistened like a smooth ruby, radiating light, and from its core began sprouting threadlike, almost transparent, filaments that intertwined to form a gently trembling insignia: "ESSIKO."

CHAPTER 22

I arrived at the meeting a few minutes before the agreed time, but Chuks was already there, standing stiffly in the middle of the field. He didn't move even when I approached and stopped in front of him. Only his eyes responded, emerging from beneath the forehead membrane and bowing down toward me stiffly. In their sclera blazed crimson reflections of the rising of Shidexa along with the twisted reflection of my own face.

"Chuks!" The enthusiastic voice of the Yusian pierced my ear. "Am Chuks again!"

"Really?" I murmured, while trying to overcome the paralyzing power of his gaze.

He generously gave me some time to come to my senses and then draped himself over the pink grass. I sat next to him.

"We need to talk, Chuks."

"Oh! You look to be for change," he concluded. "But Ter, talk not carry guarantee for to hit the mark. Precise only if can slot us together!"

As usual, both his words and his inappropriately hearty tone dulled my ability to understand him. I smiled and spoke jokingly. "A slot, a slot. Personally speaking, I need something much wider."

"Why? You not enlarged," Chuks remarked with friendly disagreement. "Detect you shrunk now. Not proportionally."

I turned harshly to him. "And how much have *you* 'shrunk,' Yusian? You watched yesterday's unfortunate events with great *curiosity*, knowing full well *whom* I was following—unlike *me*. Yet you did nothing to stop me!"

The creature thickened the folds of skin around his "throat," apparently to emit a sharp noise. But he didn't. Instead, he relaxed his body and waited for me to continue the dangerous topic. The cracks around the mobile bone supporting the organ that controlled his balance widened, releasing rivulets of excess moisture from his body. The view wasn't pleasant. I was tempted to move away but resisted and remained where I was, waiting for him as well.

"Decision to assert ourselves separate from behavior details," he finally said. "Not a touching point us together so comment only under strict discretion."

"Does that mean you consider the murder of a woman just a detail of my behavior?"

"Yes!" Chuks gladly confirmed.

Until that moment I had hoped for clear and straightforward answers, but this one made me feel very uneasy. I shrugged my shoulders. "You're wrong." I immediately added, "Besides, I'm sure you know who killed Fowler and—"

"But our knowledge closed," Chuks interrupted me politely.

"How long will this 'closed' continue?"

"No ending."

"Even if the numbers increase?" I tried to imply the likelihood of this.

"Yes," Chuks repeated. "We possess indifference potential."

Or, in plain English, *Feel free to kill one another, humans. We won't turn anyone in.*

"Good for you," I said between clenched teeth. "And you probably expect me to offer my personal thanks too?"

The creature seemed to take my question literally and started to consider whether or not I *should* thank them. I tried to bear his nonsense but lost my patience. "Goddamn it! What do you and your kind think we are, Chuks? And what do you call 'indifference'? Are you trying to turn us into monsters? Is that it?"

"No, no!" he started protesting. "We with no 'trying.'"

"Oh, stop it! You used that miserable woman as a guinea pig—"

This time Chuks *did* let out his sharp noise, after which I responded with one more "Goddamn it!" We probably wouldn't have stopped there if the appearance of the strange Yusian hadn't interrupted us. I had chosen the place and time for our meeting precisely to coincide with his daily walk, but when he came along his usual route, I did my best to look astonished.

"Ha! One of your kind is coming this way."

"Not merge yet." Chuks rose eagerly. "His world almost vague as yours through our perceptions."

"So he's from another world?" I was excited. "Another planet in the Yusian system?"

Chuks didn't even seem to hear me. He was swaying back and forth while apparently trying to follow some complicated rhythm. The dark membrane flapped over his eyes, and his upper limbs shrank and sank into the side clefts of his torso. There followed something that reminded me of breathing, while under the cover of his space suit shimmered the colorful zones that had amazed me with their iridescence during our walk in the starship.

The strange Yusian stopped close to us and for some reason started to duplicate Chuks's movements. He was doing them somehow in slow motion and clumsily as if trying to imitate each action but not quite succeeding. Chuks slowly approached him. While I was wondering whether to go near them, the strange Yusian started to swell up. He became unrecognizable, looking deformed, and from his central zone shot bright-green bolts of lightning, one after another. At the first bolt, Chuks jumped away with surprising quickness, especially considering his enormous bulk.

"What's he doing?" I called out.

"Deviates into mental pictures!" Chuks "explained," shouting back at me before leaping again, clearly frightened.

I smiled maliciously, but when the strange Yusian, retaining this new shape and power, started walking toward the defractor, he frightened me as well. "Stop him!" I yelled at Chuks.

"No! Is activated and to stop does great harm."

"But otherwise he will harm us! He may—detonate something in the complex!"

Without responding, Chuks followed the strange Yusian from a distance. I could do nothing but follow as well, but the two nonhumanoids, in some inexplicable way, started sliding ahead and quickly, very quickly, drifted away.

I rushed after them but didn't reach them until they were already maneuvering the concrete surface between separate sectors of the defractor. Or, to be more precise, I reached only Chuks, and together we continued that ridiculous chase.

Propelled by anxiety, I soon made the mistake of taking the lead and found myself too close to the "deviates into mental pictures" creature. We had reached the east wing of a low round building, and he was forced to stop there, pressed against the wall. He had only partially returned to his original shape. Through his space suit, which was thinning into transparency, clusters of colorful, crackling sparkles ominously shot out in feverish succession.

In this situation, of course, I also stopped. I had no other choice or, if I did, couldn't guess what it was. Unfortunately, the strange Yusian realized my confusion and immediately took advantage of it. He turned aside and passed a few centimeters from me, giving me a very uncomfortable electric shock.

I remained there, staring at him through bleary eyes. The bastard had hidden his own eyes but still managed to head straight for the entrance to the east wing. He rushed inside.

I waited impatiently for Chuks.

"What's wrong with you?" I asked, gritting my teeth. "Are you hesitating on purpose?"

"Yes!" He passed by me and headed for the entrance.

I swore silently but finally followed him. We crossed the east wing and entered the main building. Its serpentine shape was about four meters wide and wound around at least to the middle. Because of this, as we moved the strange Yusian sometimes disappeared and then appeared again before our eyes—well, actually before *my* eyes, since Chuks had also decided to rely on other, probably more reliable, senses.

Through the serpentine corridor ran a metal conveyor belt with many different tools along its length. In the semidarkness, I could only recognize the gas condensers stationed above the conveyor and what looked like parts of an engine system, which luckily was turned off. I stopped near a power box and found the light switch. When I switched it on, the glare of white neon only increased the tension.

"Hey, Chuks!" I called ahead but received no answer. I started running down the belt, my footsteps echoing behind me, and caught a glimpse of him squeezing through two movable thermoregulating panels hanging down at an angle from the ceiling. When I reached them, I slowed down, no longer needing to hurry because the serpentine belt was nearing its end. I looked around more calmly and finally figured out that we were in a laboratory for treating organic material. I recognized the X-ray equipment, the cylinders with nozzles for experimental supplements and the bioflotation membranes. However, as with the whole complex, this too impressed me with its totally indescribable wastefulness, its irrational extravagance.

While racing through this final section, which was entirely straight, the strange Yusian and Chuks accelerated like two sprinters dashing toward the finish line of a sparkling metal speedway. At the end of the laboratory was a raised platform and, near it, an elevator apparently used for transport to an underground extension. The Yusians had almost reached it, and now, watching from a comfortable distance, I was astonished by their incredible speed.

Their lower parts were flattened to increase the area and ensure a close contact with the surface of the floor, hiding their own movements and giving the illusion that they rode some invisible skateboard that carried them forward. Only the convulsive spasms of the hypertrophied muscles that stretched down the length of their backs and the related bristling of their spiny fringe, which lay flat when they were not moving, revealed to me that the Yusians were actually propelling themselves by continuous bodily vibrations.

When the strange Yusian reached the end of the belt, he increased his speed, surrounding himself with a firework display of lightning and sparkles, and then jumped up onto the platform. Chuks tried to stop but failed and crashed into the edge of the platform, splitting his front layers. While he was connecting them again, the strange Yusian returned to the belt and began rushing back down it. Meanwhile, I felt a strange shifting under my feet. By then, Chuks had already turned around and immediately started chasing the strange Yusian. I dropped my hands and stepped back for them to pass me, but they never even reached me.

The belt began trembling and then started rocking. A menacing creaking and rattling resound from the walls. Then came total chaos. Everything around us was shaking. I doubled over with pain, every cell in my body shaking as well. The strange Yusian slid down to the floor in agony. Nothing remained of his lightning-like "mental pictures." Chuks was behind him, trying to regain his own balance, and tried desperately to reach him. Then he gave up.

He started jumping up and down, falling two or three times but somehow managing to get up each time and resume his crazy bouncing. I stared at him astonished, but then something clicked, and I started to jump as well. Our only chance was to take advantage of the extreme elasticity of the metal beneath us. We would probably never have stopped its trembling except by this simple, primitive response.

Soon the situation was normal again, and I figured out what had really happened. The Yusians had transferred their bodily vibrations to the conveyor belt, and later, when they rushed backward, the frequency of the vibrations assumed by it and the frequency of these new vibrations they were causing had coincided to make the system resonate with a rapidly increasing amplitude. If Chuks, who weighed about a ton and aided somewhat by me, hadn't taken such measures to counter the vibrations, the whole building might have collapsed.

I stepped with trembling feet toward the strange Yusian, who was lying on the floor. Chuks was already there and lifting him carefully. I helped him as much as my human strength allowed. After we carried him outside, I realized that this was the first time I had ever touched an alien. I sensed something slippery on my hands, something coating my skin with—who knows what? My fingers began to stiffen. These feelings were entirely subjective, I knew very well, but I was still repulsed by them!

"Was—a little worried," Chuks declared while we were retreating from the defractor together with the subdued strange Yusian.

Despite my condition, I couldn't help but smile at his use of such a human, inadequate phrase: "a little worried." Come on! He was entirely out of his mind with fear. I saw him, didn't I? Then I remembered our ridiculous jumping on that crazy band, and suddenly my soul was floating. *So it seems that even this Yusian is prone to human failings*, I thought to myself. *Probably he also acts foolish, quite often even. Just like me, for example.*

"What was he trying to do?" I pointed at the strange Yusian discreetly.

"Same we all try. But is also doing it." Chuks spoke in a serious tone completely different from his usual histrionic politeness. "Pours his emphasis. With no considerations."

I sighed, accepting to a certain point our mutual lack of understanding. I silently accompanied the Yusians back to where we had met. Before saying good-bye I asked, "Chuks, tell me, why do you insist so much on establishing this colony?"

He was solicitously wrapping his limbs around the depressed strange Yusian, who was swaying moodily. "Will be final sign," he answered quietly. "Sign for something else coming, coming." He had lowered his voice to a barely comprehensible whisper.

"What is coming?" I felt stunned with a vague horror. "What is that 'something else'?"

Chuks started walking through the alien pink grass. His powerful breathing warmed the air around him, stirring it like a lacy veil, thin as a spider's web. The strange Yusian followed.

"What is coming, Chuks?" I murmured, staring at their alien figures. "What!"

"Not known." His words reached me as quietly as if I had only thought them.

I was left alone.

CHAPTER 23

From the base I contacted Larsen, and before I could ask for an appointment, he demanded that I come to the research field to meet him. "Right now!" he added and hung up.

He was in a foul mood and made no attempt to disguise it when he saw me. No greeting, not even a nod of his head. He waited until I exited the shuttle and, still silent, walked away. I didn't move. He took a few more steps and then stopped.

"Come here!" he commanded.

"You seem to be looking for a fight."

"That's right."

I shrugged my shoulders. "Let's start then. No time like the present."

"And I don't want to hear any more of your sarcasm!"

"As I won't tolerate your drill sergeant behavior," I countered.

Larsen bit his lip, measuring me, fury in his eyes. "All right," he finally snapped and started walking again.

I followed him.

"I've been working here for seven months now," he reminded me when I caught up with him. "Seven months. Nonstop."

I cast a glance at the wreckage of the Yusian machine as we passed it. "What about the results?" I asked sympathetically. "Are they good?"

"Both good and bad. More importantly, they *do* exist. Do you follow me?"

"I do," I confirmed.

He stopped again and turned toward me. "So why do you want to ruin everything?"

We were standing next to another Yusian machine, similar to the one that somebody programmed yesterday to grind stones. The cuts on its front showed that Larsen had been busy studying exactly this one.

"Do you want to ruin everything?" he repeated.

"No, not everything."

"Who gave you the right to judge what should or should not be ruined!"

"I don't need anybody's permission," I answered. "I'm led only by personal convictions."

"When did you manage to acquire them?"

"While I was still on Earth. I then strengthened them in the starship, and here on Eyrena they became unshakable."

"They are directed against establishing the colony, I presume."

"The way it's been planned, yes."

"Do you think that other methods might work?"

"Just one."

"What is it?"

"To colonize the planet with normal people in normal human towns among normal Earth flora. With no stipulations about thirty years of isolation or anything like that. Also, to establish normal relations with the Yusians."

"With that last condition, you totally disgrace yourself, Simon. It shows that you are not only an amateur but also naive."

"Well, you're entitled to your own opinion," I noted indifferently.

Larsen ran his palm across his forehead. It was still difficult for him not to snap at me, but obviously his irritation was subsiding. His face returned to its usual expression of austere reticence.

"I'm not going to argue with you," he said, deciding, "but I will tell you that what happened today should never be repeated. Under *any* circumstances."

"What happened?"

"You know perfectly well—your meeting with the Yusians."

"You're overstepping your authority now, Larsen. Don't forget that I am accountable only to the agency that I represent here, not to you."

"To a certain extent you are."

Unfortunately, he was right. I was already far out of bounds—I remembered Odesta Gomez's dead eyes staring up at me. I sighed wearily.

"There really is no point in arguing, Larsen. But the fact remains that I am here to find out who killed Fowler and Stein, so some of my actions are likely to inconvenience you."

"You didn't mention Odesta, Inspector." Larsen stared me down without blinking. "Aren't you going to look for her killer as well?"

"I expect it to be the same person." I met his gaze without flinching.

He was the first to look down. "I've got something like—a study next to the construction area," he said. "Come with me."

We set out. Compared to the luxurious accommodations the Yusians had built at the base, or to the lavish and elaborate defractor, the base commander's quadrant seemed shabby and squalid. Mostly open area, it resembled an uneven concrete parking lot. The few pieces of equipment and instruments sent from Earth were all weather beaten and run down. The storage units and what Larsen called "the construction area" turned out to be ramshackle panel buildings with flimsy facades.

"You certainly have poor working conditions for your research activities," I remarked, having learned from experience that the most reliable, perhaps the only, key to the hearts of the people here was to refer to the hardships they had to endure in working on Eyrena.

"I do," he responded tersely. "I do!" Then he knit his ginger eyebrows in stony silence.

We entered the so-called study, which I would have taken for a kitchen. Larsen invited me to take a seat and left me alone. The room shared the same scarcity as the rest of the research field. Furnishings included only a long table half covered by a computer, two monitors, and a printer; a chair, bookshelf, refrigerator, and sink; and of course, a safe. But one thing was obvious at a glance: these were the premises of a military man. Not a speck of dust, all papers arranged in tight, orderly rows, and the windows shining as if they had just been washed for inspection.

Larsen returned with a second chair and sat facing me. "All right, Simon, will you explain to me why on earth you needed to meet with those two?"

"I didn't have a particular reason."

"Oh, right!" He almost snarled. "You simply missed them. And what about that ramble through the defractor complex?"

"Obviously, Vernie has already reported to you—"

"But not in detail. He only noticed that Yusian, the strange one, entering the biostation ahead of you, looking even stranger than usual."

"That's true, but his appearance had nothing to do with the complex. He only got in there by chance."

"Why are you so sure?"

"Because when I caught up with him, he simply tried to find the nearest hiding place."

"Caught *up* with him? You weren't *chasing* him, were you?"

"Well—yes. When he rushed toward the defractor, I thought he might intend to harm it."

"Then all of a sudden you were convinced that he wouldn't?"

"Yes. He was behaving more like a lunatic than a saboteur."

This time my judgment obviously appealed to Larsen. "It's possible." He nodded. "With all its wandering around and that weak, crippled body. But if the creature *is* crazy, why do they let him stay here?"

"Why not? We also plan to do the same with our nut cases, don't we?"

"Damn it! Whatever we decide, it will just be another wild guess. From the first day they came to Earth, we've done nothing else. We turned into fortune-tellers. Incompetent ones at that. What about the normal Yusian? How did he behave?"

"Followed the other one from a distance. He said it was dangerous to stop him and that he was from another world."

"Aha!"

"Listen to me, Larsen. Take advantage of this incident to contact them yourself."

"And tell them to keep a closer watch on their resident lunatic, right?"

"He really could cause problems. You must prevent that."

Larsen bent over and buried his fingers in his hair. He closed his eyes and stayed that way for a long time. "It's late," he finally said. "Too late."

"For what?" I asked him.

"For everything." Again he was slow in answering, obviously fabricating a specific response. "For anything besides just waiting for what comes next. Our relations with the Yusians are so— fragile. The smallest mistake or even tactlessness on our part could tip the scales against the colonization."

"I doubt it. They also seem to want it to happen."

"Who knows what they want?" Larsen asked, waving off my remark. "Can any human ever understand them?"

"It might be possible. But not by hiding in his hollow."

He stood up suddenly, walked over to the sink, and tightened the faucet with all his strength. When the monotonous dripping finally stopped, I realized that I had been half listening to that intrusive sound the whole time.

"We *need* to hide, Simon. Otherwise, all we show them is our ignorance of anything and everything on this world. You tell *me*, in a situation like this, how we can expect to make any intellectual contact, even the most basic?"

"Intellectual, certainly not. But human—"

"Human? With *them*?"

"Well, yes," I answered. "We *are* human, aren't we?"

Larsen quickly came back to the table, resting his hands on it. "Isn't it our most human quality to seek knowledge, to domesticate the strange, and to overcome the unknown? Regardless of what we might say, Simon, the Yusians are our rivals. Rivals! And if we want to achieve a real, equal dialogue with them in the future, we need first to uncover the secrets behind their achievements."

"What secrets, Larsen? You know perfectly well that, from the very beginning, the Yusians have been more than willing to familiarize us with everything they have and all that they've achieved. To give us their inventions, to explain them—"

"Obviously you're not in the least aware that our best scientists have been incapable of understanding those inventions, despite their generous 'explanations.' And what have we gained from it all? An end to scientific progress! Our scientists don't bother to do research or invent anything anymore, Simon. They know that whatever *they* might achieve will be humiliatingly insignificant compared to what the Yusians have had for thousands of years. There is no point."

"A while ago you said you had obtained some results," I reminded him.

"That's right!" Again Larsen sat down on the flimsy chair. "That's why the colonization is vital for us. Only then could we begin to overcome our total stagnation. With this colony to keep the Yusians away from Earth, we could bring our knowledge to their level—or at least somewhere near."

"Why don't we look for another, more dignified, way? Why do we need to subject ourselves to their experiments so submissively? Just the euphoria itself should tell us what will happen when the colonists come."

"Obviously the whole universe obeys the same laws that apply on Earth." Larsen stretched out his hands palms up, as if in supplication. "The stronger always sets the rules. Or destroys the weaker."

"I think we're inclined to overestimate the range of such laws," I said. "Also, I'll never agree that we *are* weaker just because their knowledge is currently at a higher level than ours."

"Immeasurably higher."

"Even so, everything depends on the psyche, not just on achievements."

But Larsen wasn't even listening anymore. The resistance of his one-track mind was simply stunning! "As I already told you, I've been working here for seven months," he began, "and I'll continue my work as long as I live. As our research center expands, we'll provide better working conditions, like those on Earth. Now I'm alone, but when Fowler was with me, everything went more smoothly. Imagine what it would be like if I had a team of highly skilled assistants!"

I lost patience. "As a base commander you must take a broader view of the situation, Larsen. For instance, you should want to know why the Yusians are going out of their way to prepare this whole planet for us. What their intentions are toward the future colonists and what they expect to gain in return—or take by force from them. Yes, those are the really important questions! You're really hiding in this pathetic research field, presuming you can fix the situation simply by analyzing their machines. By cutting and dismembering them with your primitive instruments!"

We glared at each other, ready to turn our heated debate into a fistfight. Strangely enough, only now did I feel a spark of empathy fly between us. Both of us were in similar positions, like two poker players holding losing hands.

"My nerves aren't what they used to be," Larsen murmured. "And you...you, Simon, are causing more tension among us."

"What else can I do?" I asked. "I didn't come all this way to sing you lullabies."

He just shook his head, took out his phone, and pressed a button.

In a minute, something appeared just outside. Huge, reddish, and squirming, it looked like a living piece of raw meat, cut from some giant. It blocked the entire window; we could see only its shivering, sinewy flesh—until it slowly passed by. It staggered to the construction area, and only then could I see the tires of a truck under it. Behind it, like a retinue accompanying the disgusting load, clattered a few two-meter-high rudimentary metal objects for whom even the term "protorobots" would have been considered a compliment. Of course they were human, not ESSIKO, creations.

"I see," I turned to Larsen. "I got your hint."

"Yes, I…must…have to continue with my work."

"But I need to continue with mine as well, Larsen. That's why I want you to tell me something: Do you think it's possible that, on the day they died, Fowler and Stein were not going to the defractor but to the Yusian base instead?"

"I don't know." He lowered his eyelids, either because he was tired or to avoid my gaze. "I don't think so."

"Does your answer mean you *do* think it's *possible*? At our first meeting, you were convinced by, or wanted me to believe so, that absurd version of a murder-suicide. You didn't even mention the Yusians as potential perpetrators."

"They are totally indifferent to us as individuals, Simon. Their interest is just general, like archeologists studying another civilization or entomologists observing an anthill. From above, without resting their gaze on particular insects. Do you know how strictly they maintain their policy of noninterference in our affairs?"

"So," I began, "you probably think that all the rumors about their excesses—"

"Are created by our own imaginations," concluded Larsen. "Mostly horror stories, skillfully incited and disseminated by Zung. That man's preparing the way for his own apotheosis. After the immense chaos that has gripped Earth since the Yusians arrived, gaining us thirty years of isolation will elevate him to the level of Savior of Humankind—and that's what he'll really be."

"Nonsense," I interjected but not very convincingly. "At the moment, he's more a Judas than a Jesus, betraying all those wretched creatures he's planning to dump here on Eyrena—where we can't even discuss the Yusians' so-called noninterference in everything here: the euphoria, the predatory plants—"

"And the four settlements," Larsen added in a gloomy, ominous monotone. His words hung between us, a fitting end to our fruitless conversation.

CHAPTER 24

The next morning I decided to skip going to the dining room again. I felt a strong aversion to the prospect of sitting at the same table with people eating their food like automatons, without looking at each other or saying a word. Yes, there was something repulsive in their awkward breakfasts *together* that had become demonstrations of stern will power and the indomitable human spirit or something like that. "The more obvious something is, the more you should be inclined to doubt it," my boss always says.

I had a bite of the food I found in the refrigerator and then leaned on the windowsill of my wide-open window to wait for the rise of Ridon. I didn't see the sun rise because it was hidden behind the forest, but the first rays made my skin tingle. The leafless five-trunk trees sensed it too, extending their crowns like open hands begging for light and warmth. Then their branches started swaying, and the forest started crying its thick white tears that exploded in the intensely clear air, turning into millions of floating silver crystals of light.

I stepped back from the window, closed it, pulled the curtains, but still the silent presence I had felt that morning during my forest walk filled me again with its enchanting friendliness, stimulating even my simplest senses to exultation. I knew it wasn't real but embraced it anyway. This invisible, indefinable, incomparable presence offered me the whole universe! Filled with it, I was a titan! Its life force seethed in my blood, muscles, eyes, lips, thoughts, and so on, Afterward, I would fall asleep exhausted.

Exhausted! I warned myself. I left the apartment—left the lodge. Ran to the parking lot and climbed into Stein's shuttle. Last night I had equipped myself with a transformer. Now I inserted it into the smooth grayish substance, pressed the corresponding button, and said only one word, "Up!"

I took off above the base. I was all white from the little crystals, my face and hands hardening under their sparkling mask. I threw myself onto the transparent floor, vaguely surprised that I felt no instinctive fear at swinging in space so high above the ground. "Just like a Yusian," I murmured to myself with awful joy. "I'm just like a Yusian!"

The crystals melted, and I started to regain my normal mental state as the shuttle reached an altitude of about two thousand meters. I ordered it to circle the area. I wanted to see what the Yusian base looked like, but huge clouds from the north soon spread under me like a shaggy lead-gray blanket. I reached for the transformer, disappointed.

"Above the biosector," I said, touching the same button. "Low."

The clouds grew even thicker. The shuttle fell for some time into their dark embrace, and then without a transition, the biosector appeared below me like a precise model instantaneously created.

I couldn't land the shuttle very close to Reder's "creative studio," so I climbed out and started walking through the bizarre ferns, standing like fossils despite the breeze. No plant on Earth could be so motionless and yet so intensely expressive as these ferns that seemed to have frozen in fear of the coming storm.

I looked up. Not even the slightest light could be seen through the clouds. In fact, the whole sky had become inky black, but a pulsating yellow-purple radiance seemed to be streaming up from the ground, coloring everything around. I walked faster, overtaken by anxious imaginings.

When I reached Reder's residence, identical to the one Stein had occupied, I pressed the door handle. It was locked. I rang the bell, waited about a minute, and then looked for an open window. Not finding one, I forced the door open by slamming it two or three times with my shoulder. I went in, the flexor ready in my hand. I didn't know for sure that Reder was out; he could be hiding somewhere in the house. I didn't bother to check—just locked the door of his study behind me.

I pulled the blinds down, turned the lights on, and hurried to the safe. Using the flexor, I cut out a wide rectangle from its front panel. At the bottom was the huge bag Reder had been carrying the day I arrived when Elia had chosen a route that would intersect his. I took it out, surprised at how light it was. Then I checked all the drawers and compartments in the safe but found only a plastic bottle filled with small yellow pills—Sizoral, no doubt, at least two hundred. I put the bottle in my pocket and turned my attention to the bag. Although the zipper jammed, I finally managed to open it. And immediately jumped back.

A crushed human head rose out of the bag! Followed by its shoulders and body! They inflated in front of me. Up to the knees in the blue bag stood a deformed replica of Odesta Gomez, slightly swaying. I pulled myself together. This was just another

Yusian replica. *Just.* I hauled it to the corner of the room, next to the door, and set the blue bag beside it.

Then I booted up Reder's computer. I already had plenty of experience finding hidden or "protected" files, so if there were any in his system, I was pretty sure I'd find them. Now I understood why Reder had a restricted data bank on the server: in his own computer, he kept only notes about performed or pending experiments, remarks about the life cycles of certain plants, their mutations, and so on. Interesting information in itself but hardly top secret. Still the thought that I was on a wild-goose chase wasn't enough to stop me. I had decided to make the most of Reder's absence.

Finally I found a hidden file, when I was no longer expecting one. After I managed to open it, what I found there staggered me. This was the file—dated March 26, the day of the murders—that *Stein* had created, at exactly 8:02 a.m., giving Reder the code for his restricted data bank and permission to open and announce it "without delay."

But that data bank had been completely deleted from the server.

Soon I discovered another important and puzzling piece of information, contradicting the first one. Using Reder's computer again at 8:09 a.m., Stein sent an urgent request to the server for a double-protected microdisk containing all the information in his data bank. This request was missing on the server. But who deleted the request from the server? If Reder, why would he save these exposing facts on his own computer?

I called him on the mobile phone.

"Where are you?" I asked.

"In the nursery," he answered sharply.

"I'm in your study," I told him. "I'm waiting for you here, but there's no need to hurry."

But I was sure he would hurry. In fact, no more than five minutes later, I heard the brakes of his jeep outside. I opened the hidden file and went to unlock the door.

Reder was already at the door. The expression on his face was relatively calm, but a twitch at the corner of his lips gave him away. He walked by me and sat at the desk. He looked at the screen for a moment, then the open safe, then Odesta's replica, and finally to one side.

"This is too much, Inspector. Yes, this is altogether too much."

"What happened to Stein's research information?"

"Too much again."

"I asked you a concrete question!"

"Is that so? But what information are you talking about?"

"About the information in his restricted data bank."

He suddenly smiled broadly, baring his big teeth. "OK then, I'll answer you. I moved them to my data bank without leaving copies."

"Why is this information not on the server?"

"There is a simple explanation: because the transfer from one restricted data bank to another is also secret."

"And who deleted Stein's request for the microdisk from the server?"

"Another simple explanation, Simon. The same person who took care of *cleaning* Stein's computer."

"And the same who then searched Stein's dead body, looking for the microdisk with the information among his personal belongings."

"Congratulations!" Reder showed me his big teeth again. "So far, so good. But if you think that I'm the only one who knew about the microdisk, you are very wrong."

"Maybe," I said dismissively, "but you have to prove that."

"You mean by giving you the name of the murderer? No, Inspector! I'll let you protect your reputation by finding that out for yourself."

Unfortunately, Zung's agent had his boss's talent for insinuation and his penchant for getting on the nerves of the person he was talking to.

"Look, Reder." I too smiled. "Our conversation today is not going to be like the one we had the day before yesterday in the morning. You would be wise to recognize the difference."

"Well, yes, then you were—let's say, kinder."

"That's true," I said. "And today I even forgot to ask you how you are feeling. Is your stomach still bothering you?"

"My stomach?" Reder repeated the question foolishly.

"I see. So it's not bothering you." I took the bottle of Sizoral from my pocket and showed it to him. "In that case, I'll confiscate your 'medication.' Without it, you should be very happy to see Ridon rise tomorrow."

"You're wrong!" This time he laughed openly. "I've been overcoming the euphoria without these pills for a long time. And that morning I told you the truth: Odesta *was* a traitor. You saw that for yourself, didn't you?"

"With *your* help. You directed me very cleverly to the 'deserted' Yusian base."

"I was glad to help."

"And so tactfully too. Instead of *helping* me directly, you chose to *use* someone else."

"Simon, I'll confess something to you. I specifically chose Elia for this purpose because I have the impression that you prefer her company to mine. Or am I wrong?"

"By the way," I changed the subject, recalling the reprogrammed Yusian machine burrowing through the layers of rock. "Why did you discharge Elia's transformer? In order to kill us?"

"Now you're contradicting yourself," Reder noted. "I wanted you to meet Odesta, so why would I kill you—before that happened?"

I shrugged. "Maybe either of those two alternatives would have satisfied you."

"I'm not a murderer, Simon," he objected. Then he added, with infuriating intimacy, "Unlike you."

I jumped up and grabbed him by the collar of the shirt, pulling him toward me. His chair fell gently to the carpet. Reder struggled, panting into my face. I let him go and then hit him hard on the jaw with my fist. He collapsed on the floor next to the desk. He lay there for some time, his hands spread, his head bent to one side. Then he slowly opened his eyes and immediately reached for the flexor on his belt. I stepped on his hand.

"Take the belt off," I commanded. "Take it off and throw it next to the door!"

He started to undo the metal buckle. He was taking his time, moaning, coughing. Suddenly he jumped to his feet, quick as a cat, and struck me across the throat with the belt. While I was swaying and choking, Reder grabbed for the chair and smashed its wooden back against my forehead. As I fell, I managed to take out my flexor. I pointed it at him.

"Throw—at the door." I couldn't think of the whole phrase. I was losing consciousness, the familiar salty taste of blood in my mouth.

Reder stood a meter away from me, obviously hesitating, hoping I would faint.

"Come on." I moved the trigger of my flexor to the ready position.

My action convinced him to throw the belt in the ordered direction. I wiped the blood from my face with my empty hand. I still felt faint but was gradually improving. I just needed a little rest. I crawled to the wall, leaned against it, and tried to breathe normally. It wasn't easy—I still felt spasms in my throat from that hit with the metal buckle.

Reder pulled out another chair and sat in front of me. He didn't look well either—his lower jaw was swelling fast. Then he grimaced and spat a big yellowish molar on the floor.

The silence between us dragged out a long time. Finally I said, "Something connected with the last package from Earth made Stein go to the Yusian base on the morning of the twenty-sixth. What was it?"

"I couldn't find out," Reder answered gloomily.

"But you overheard the conversation he had with Fowler beforehand, right?"

"No. I saw him call somebody on the mobile phone, but at that time I didn't know it was Fowler. Nor could I hear what Stein was saying to him. It was just one short phrase. Obviously they had arranged everything in advance."

Reder's openness didn't surprise me. He must have decided there was no point in denying facts I had already guessed. Then by adding some details I didn't already know, he was directing my suspicions away from him.

"Go on," I encouraged him. "What did Stein do then?"

"He convinced the robot that he was going to the area where I was supposed to be but, when he was out of sight, changed his direction and came here to my study. He knew I was going to be out, so he must have decided to remove the restrictions on his data bank using *my* computer but to avoid the questions I would have asked had he personally given me the code."

"And why did he need to remove the restrictions at all?"

"I suppose he wanted to leave his research behind as a *legacy*." Reder sighed mockingly. "Maybe he expected something bad to happen to him while he was with the Yusians."

I put the flexor on my knees. "Drop that nonsense about the Yusians. You know they wouldn't directly touch anybody."

He clapped his hands just like Zung "Oh, yes! Those *nice* creatures!" His swollen face twisted as if he were going to have an epileptic seizure. "These wise, generous benefactors who give us toy houses, towns, planets—and—*desks* instead of candy!" He slammed his open palm against his desk. "Oh, yes! How could *they* hurt us! Well, if we don't mind them, they might spank us a little, of course, but—"

"Knock it off!" I yelled.

Reder stopped and blinked, as if just waking up.

"Where did Stein go after he left his 'legacy'?" I asked immediately.

"I didn't follow him after that. I just saw him go in the direction of our base, not toward the Yusians."

"Of course. He had to collect the microdisk first."

"Yes, but I didn't know that until I read his orders later from my computer. In fact, that's when I also realized that he was planning to visit the Yusians."

"What time was that?"

"About eight fifteen."

"Then why didn't you alarm the others until twelve ten?"

"Isn't that obvious? If I had, they would have known that I was spying on him."

"What *other* reason, Reder? What were *you* doing during those hours?"

"Whatever it was, Simon, I didn't kill anybody or want things to get to this point."

"You didn't *want* to kill him, but as with Odesta, you didn't exclude the possibility, right?"

"No, I didn't, but—"

"But for you, the beliefs of Vey A. Zung outweighs all other considerations," I finished.

"Yes! Yes! Yes!" he repeated pathetically. "His beliefs are also mine! And every *real* person shares them too. Without them, every human being is doomed to failure, Simon! Complete failure!"

"Failure because of people like you!"

My last words disgusted him so much that he could hardly breathe. "And you—you're a traitor as well! You're ready to betray the human race out of cowardice and false scruples. But in thirty years, we can put an end to their designs on our Earth! And maybe an end to their dirty, alien civilization." He choked and started waving his hands.

I looked at him in disgust. How many more maniacs like him would arrive on this planet? How many more crazed, anthropocentric bigots? "What was Stein's purpose," I continued coldly, "in approaching the Yusians with a copy of his research findings?"

"I have no idea," he hissed.

"Oh, I'm sure you know perfectly well why he went. That's exactly why I'm asking you again: What did you do on the twenty-sixth between eight fifteen and twelve ten?"

"I read a novel, went for a walk, enjoyed the moon—sorry, the sun—and daydreamed."

"I'm warning you, Reder—"

"No, *I* am warning you: stop annoying me! Or else the base commander will find out *today* who killed Odesta."

"But he will also find out that *you* killed Fowler and Stein."

"What kind of inspector are you?" He pretended to be surprised. "Don't you already know that Odesta, yes, Odesta killed them?"

"Possibly." I pretended to consider this alternative. "But if that's true, why did you cover for her for so long? Why didn't you tell the others about her visits to the old Yusian base? What about Stein's orders, given from your computer? How did *this* get into your safe?" I pointed to the replica of Odesta. "How did you acquire a whole bottle of Sizoral? Should I go on?"

"No."

"Good." I stood up and again pointed the flexor at him. "Forward Stein's research results to my restricted data bank."

He shook his head.

"Forward them," I repeated.

He could tell just by looking at me that he needed to obey immediately. He went to the computer. I stood behind him, making sure he followed my instructions. When he was done, I took his belt with the flexor in its holster. I pulled the blinds up and opened the window. The strange radiance flowing up from the ground flooded the study. A hollow rumbling sound filled the black sky.

"Ha, ha, ha!" Reder laughed loudly. "Here we are arguing, fighting—in what may be the last moments of our lives!"

"What do you mean?" I turned to him and asked a silly question, "Is a storm coming?"

"A storm? Oh, yes, a storm. An *Eyrenean* storm!"

He stopped laughing. Obviously our argument had made him forget the nightmare outside, but now, in the depths of those washed-out eyes, I could read only one emotion: terror. But anyway, as I was leaving, I threw his flexor deep into the ferns.

CHAPTER 25

Elia and Jerry were waiting for me in front of the shuttle. What a picture: a pale, tense woman unconsciously pursing her lips tightly, a trembling puppy standing next to her, and a tired man trudging toward them, his steps heavy, feigningly confident. Under an impossible black sky on a narrow road between foliage that bore only the slightest resemblance to ferns on Earth.

I stopped, and Elia stared worriedly at the wound on my forehead. Then she took from her pocket a fine silk handkerchief and carefully began to wipe off the dried blood. I think I needed this useless gesture more than anything else at the moment.

"My shuttle landed without my giving it a command, over there near the pillars," she said quietly. "I couldn't reactivate it."

"What about this one?"

"It's paralyzed too. But maybe the jeep."

I shook my head. "The jeep is on its way to the base." Two minutes after I left his study, Reder had zoomed past me in the vehicle.

I took Jerry in my arms, and we walked silently through the ferns. Now they were moving slightly, but since there was no breeze at the moment, this fact depressed me even more than when they stood like frozen fossils. Something was stripping their fronds, cutting out little circles that fell around us like confetti thrown by invisible hands and whispered to the ground. Under their whispering cover, the streaming light was dimming, its brightness melting into a soft violet radiance. The feeling of danger was melting in me as well, being replaced by a steady, completely inappropriate, quietness.

I looked at Elia as she walked next to me, smiling almost against her will. Her smooth forehead wrinkled slightly as her eyes wandered aimlessly. *No, she shouldn't smile like that*, I thought, but when I tried to tell her so, no sound came out of my mouth. I felt like I was smiling too. Jerry was drowsing, his head buried under my arm.

We reached the break in the ferns where the pillars began, stopped, and slowly turned back to watch the ferns rocking almost ritualistically. Their fronds shed the last remaining spores, sharply revealing their naked skeletons in the dark. Each was identical, without a central line, constructed instead of thick strings crossing each other, and the branches connecting them with the stems ended in hooked spikes.

These spikes were obviously withering. While we watched, they started bending under their own weight, falling off the stems with a silent, monotonous rattle. The ferns gradually became smaller copies of the pillars. The ground around them started heaving, erupted in a yellowish foam, and then everything dead and useless downed in it without a trace. Would we have drowned as well, had we still been standing there?

"Let's go!" Elia said.

We walked back into the ghostly light, along the old pillars, once more overcome by that intrusive sense of quietness. I knew I should resist, but I only bent, put the puppy on the ground, and when got up, saw the apathetic smile of Elia.

Jerry started running around us with unnaturally long jumps, his fur glowing and bristling. As the tip of every single hair lightened, we could see only his sparkling outline, a cartoon dog figure. A muffled roar still filled the sky, and the pillars were shivering like dark creatures trying to catch their breath. We floated deeper and deeper into the stand of pillars with the graceful ease of phantoms. Apparently the gravitational pull had weakened, but that didn't bother me. In fact, nothing bothered me anymore.

I don't know how far we walked like this. Maybe a long way, or maybe not. The road was always the same, pillars and more pillars.

"Jerry," Elia murmured suddenly, extending her arm toward the dog and then letting it drop as she leaned against one of the pillars. "Jerry, Jerry," she repeated faintly as her eyes closed in an oblivion that was easily overtaking me as well.

I leaned next to her. The pillar was slippery and warm. I could hear the sound of hard clinking particles coursing through it. I slowly reached for Elia's hand.

"Let's go."

We kept moving south, toward the hill in the distance, walking in a dreamlike trance. I couldn't even feel the touch of her hand in mine, nor did I wish to. I was overtaken by a silent, pleasant faintness, as if I were blending with someone else, someone passing through me, someone with elusive thoughts, feelings, moves—and passing on. Particles of another life, incomprehensible to me.

A force lifted me gently up and then set me back down. And up again. The ground was breathing. Deeply and monotonously. Its wide chest released streams of concentrated air. Or streams of countless living moments? The pillars were inhaling them though their warm cracks. Starting to grow, filling up with them, splitting in two, three parts. No, this wasn't an illusion. They were becoming tall five-trunk plants.

"They are...going to...turn into trees," I said slowly.

"Like the...ferns...turned into pillars," answered Elia, as if with my voice.

With my voice! I tried to draw her closer to me but couldn't feel her body next to mine. "Are you here, Elia?"

"Are you here, Elia?" I asked again. This time it seemed my voice came from outside of me!

My hair stood up. I slowly turned toward the voice, expecting to see—me. I didn't see anybody. But then my sense of touch returned, and I felt Elia's hand again. I held it tightly and started running past the pillars that were turning into trees. I couldn't hear our steps or our breathing. I couldn't hear anything but the crackling of invisible spider webs.

I didn't stop until we reached the steep hill. Waves of melted Eyrena soil slowly flowed down like lava, stopped at the foot of the hill, and crested to cover the layers already there.

"But where...where...were you?" Elia moaned. I hugged her; she was shivering. She looked at the pillars. "I felt like there was only me...and...me!"

She leaned on my chest quietly, drained. I caressed her tousled hair. Only when Jerry whimpered at our feet did we remember him. We looked at each other, feeling guilty. Elia took him in her arms and started to weep. There was nothing I could tell her to make her stop.

We were at the edge of the forest that adjoined the base, but it looked like a normal forest less than ever. The trees were growing incredibly fast, their colossal five-trunk bodies stretching up and splitting into the black sky in uncontrollable yellow metastasis.

"We have to go," I muttered.

"No, not through the forest!" Elia buried her face in Jerry's sparkling fur. "Let's go around!"

I hesitated. To go around meant to go past the cones on the other side of the hill, from where the "ground" kept flowing. Ground that was more like thick, flaky flesh, slowly shaken loose from hands hidden behind the ridge.

"OK, Elia," I said softly. "We'll try to climb the hill here."

She snuggled Jerry against her and humbly climbed the hill like a doomed victim. I took the lead, but how could I save her from this? I walked faster and faster, always expecting to sink into the melted ground. At least that would stop her—warn her.

But I soon realized I wasn't going to sink. The irresistible lightness I felt before had taken over me again and was pulling me up the hill, away from those two unprotected companions behind me. My love for them transformed into unbearable pain, maybe because I felt *it* slipping away too. This human, earthly love was leaving me now like a fading memory.

I looked back. Elia and Jerry were melting into the violet light. They were disappearing, and I was forgetting them. I desperately strained my memory. Elia and Jerry, Elia and Jerry— just names. Then I forgot even the names.

New incomprehensible images washed over me. I sensed that someone was whispering important messages, but I couldn't hear them. That this someone wanted to reveal—maybe himself—but I couldn't see him. I was standing in front of a wall I couldn't pass and started to pity that unknown someone who wanted so much to reach me.

Suddenly the wall crumbled silently into thousands of colorful fragments, and a huge shadow stood in front of me. The shadow drew the colorful fragments like a magnet, and they began sparkling within it—distant, charming stars! I walked toward them.

He was waiting for me, incomprehensible behind his star shadow. I was witnessing how my shadow approached his, how the two shadows met, and then merged into one.

Disgust splashed over me like muddy water. No, I wasn't going there because I wanted to. *They* were making me go! They were ravaging my soul so they could establish their alien presence in its place. Ravaging. I pressed my hands to my temples. *Ravaging me.* I desperately looked around. Started racing down the flowing slope—without sinking.

Elia was lying flat on her back when I reached her, her violet face beyond human expression and her open eyes reflecting only the darkness of the sky. The waves undulating down the hill were lifting her body, flowing their flaky flesh under her and lowering it again. Jerry, cuddled at her feet, was trembling.

I shook her shoulder. I called her. I yelled her name. To no avail. She wasn't here. During these long moments she was not even a human being.

As I waited, hoping for her return, the forest in front of us continued to grow, building symmetrical constructions in the sky and wrapping them in transparent, yellow-violet raffia nets. It was forming gigantic cocoons and setting them in a maniacally regular, alien order. Jerry howled at them, his bared teeth reflecting ancient malice. I felt like howling as well.

When Elia came back to her senses, we didn't exchange a word. We were aware that the alien presence had dissipated, but its engram would remain on our souls forever—and connect us.

We climbed together up to the ridge. Down there, in the valley, rags of stretchy fog surrounded the cones. They looked like giants wearing ragged coats. Their glassy bodies could be seen clearly at some places, while at others only their shapes could be vaguely detected through the fog. Their peaks were melting with a hiss, splitting the fog into fine fibroid strips.

We started walking along the edge of the ridge, our knees shaking. Jerry ran between us. The pores of the ground were shrinking, its light diminishing, surrendering its radiance to the black pressure of the sky. That darkness slowly approached us, touched our foreheads, and crawled down, further and further. Now we could see only our shoes and Jerry's little paws. Then they too disappeared. We stopped. Jerry was panting between us. We felt around for him. He was collapsed in a ball and obviously needed a break. I reassuringly petted him.

"Don't lift him up," I heard Elia's tired voice. "We don't know who we are going to be—what we are going to be—next."

We sat by our puppy, and she leaned her head on my shoulder. The fragrance of her hair mixed with the spicy Eyrena air. I closed my eyes, trying to forget the impenetrable darkness. But I didn't forget it. When I kissed Elia, I realized that I was doing it to challenge whatever wanted to take me over. That sense of defiance reduced even this brief moment of human intimacy to something trivial.

Time passed, or flowed away from us, as we sat next to each other, helpless and silent. Something had to happen. Here and now.

Sure enough, in that black valley of the cones, lights began blinking. From them, as if on a signal, random fires blazed up. I watched them flicker and flare with incredible speed as if some satanic conductor coaxed fire instead of music out of the darkness with his waving baton, creating small bonfires that burst into flames and then grew into yellow-violet fire.

The cones in the valley bent and, with a loud cracking sound, split open. Wide, ugly gashes appeared on their tops, belching forth pent-up radiant force like monstrous sighs rising into the sky. As dozens of lightning bolts ripped at the flesh of that sky, the cones collapsed with a crash, leaving behind only clouds of light silver dust.

At that moment, Chuks's vague figure emerged from my memory, hardly visible through the silver dust of the Yusian plant we had observed together in the starship.

"Elia," I exclaimed. "The cones were plants!"

"What—these rocks?"

"Yes, yes! 'Rocks,' 'cones,' or 'formations'—we had different names for them, but we have always known they were something else."

"Of course—something else. But plants—"

"Yes! The ferns transformed into pillars, the pillars into trees, the trees—"

We stood up, surprised by this insight, and looked in the direction of the forest. There, in the dimming dark, huge cones now stood in an outlandish order.

"At some point, then, they turn back into dust," Elia said.

"Dust?" I slowly repeated. "No—into some kind of spores."

"Grass!" Elia pressed her palm to her forehead. "That grass will grow in their place! And fields of grass are probably now covered with ferns. There is only *one* kind of plant on Eyrena, Terence! The same plant goes through five consecutive phases."

We both sighed at the same time, overwhelmed by the enormous magnitude of this metamorphosis. I bent down and, after hesitating briefly, picked Jerry up again; we had no reason to expect additional psychic invasions. At least not so soon.

We headed for the base.

PART THREE

CHAPTER 26

"Last night, the Security Council called an emergency meeting to discuss my report on the Odesta Gomez murder." Larsen's voice was smooth and calm, his face devoid of emotion.

"Special Chairman Vey A. Zung introduced a draft resolution recommending immediate evacuation of the Eyrena base crew as well as suspension of all preliminary negotiations on the bilateral agreement between Earth and Yus."

Larsen then scrutinized each of us, expecting some kind of reaction. None of us looked away or reacted in any way to his statement during the prolonged pause.

We were sitting at the table in the infirmary dispensary but not because of any health complaints. The planetary metamorphosis that had ended just an hour ago had only left us exhausted, nothing more. Perhaps.

After leafing through the documents in the folder in front of him, Larsen continued, "The resolution states, 'We will commence evacuation following the order of the general secretary of the United Military Forces, signed also by the special chairman of the Security Council. Responsibilities are listed as follows:

'Colonel Larsen, Eyrena base commander: archiving and protecting the database.

'Associate Professor Vernie, technical head of the Defractor Project: emergency preservation of the sample material.

'Professor Reder, science consultant in the Biosystems Sector: evacuation of live specimens and representative preservation of sample material.

'Doctor Slade, medical expert of the Eyrena base: thorough examination of the staff and disposal of the corpses.

'Inspector Simon, official representative of the International Bureau of Investigation: security precautions.

'Deadline for completion of the preliminary phase: eighteen hours from receipt of the order.'"

This time only Reder had preserved his composure. Elia looked bewildered, although encouraged as well; Vernie was startled, even horrified. "But this is ridiculous!" He couldn't restrain himself. "They've lost their minds."

"Easy, easy." Reder reached out and tapped him on the shoulder.

"But how can I be calm! We came here with an impossible mission, but we are still managing to meet our objectives! We've made greater advances here than anyone back on Earth can claim. And now what—'preservation'? No! They have no right to do this!"

His reaction seemed surprisingly inadequate to me. Enacting the resolution would lead to consequences much greater than simply the closing of his Defractor Project.

Larsen took some time to peer at each one of us again before adding emphatically, "In the course of these procedures, we will maintain a permanent readiness for initiating Operation 'POLAR CROSS.'"

This time it was Elia who was visibly shaken. "Initiate the self-destruct contingency? What good would that do? We obviously mean less than nothing to them!"

Vernie held his head in his hands, as if fearing it might explode at any moment. "I don't understand. I can't see the logic—the reasons," he babbled in his despair. "It couldn't just be Odesta's death that provoked all this. No, no! There *must* be something else! Otherwise—I understand we may have to be sacrificed, but why now? Why just before we—"

"Calm down, Phil!" Reder warned. "They would hardly resort to this."

"How can you say that? In fact, they have!" Vernie continued in spite of him. "The Yusians are aware of that: the resolution, suspension of negotiations, and all—the end of the colonization! I find it strange that they even deigned to transfer this damned message to us! Why not just take us by surprise? Capture us? Take over the defractor! Who on Earth would ever know? They would assume we had moved to the 'cross' and that would be the end of it. Oh God!"

For the last few seconds, Larsen had been watching only me. I was under the impression that he didn't interrupt Vernie's emotional outbursts precisely because he wanted me to hear all this. He waited just a little longer, but when no one added anything more, he finally said, "The draft resolution was voted on after three rounds of discussions and debates. And it was *unanimously rejected* by the members of the Security Council."

The silence that ensued was so overwhelming that everyone seemed to have simultaneously lost the ability to speak. Personally, I found nothing so surprising in the council's decision, but I chose to reflect the group reaction. The dispensary, specifically designed for such top-secret meetings, was windowless and insulated with double soundproof panels, so the utter silence made my ears ring.

Vernie suddenly giggled, breaking the silence. Elia eyed him with sympathy and then abruptly turned to Larsen. "What's the meaning of all this crap?"

"Well, the meaning is," Vernie broke in, still laughing in a fit of hectic relief, "that Mr. Zung has sent us on yet another wild-goose chase!"

"I don't care about Zung's plotting," Elia retorted. "I'd just like to know what I should think of your reaction, Berg. Why did you perform this little melodrama for us?"

Larsen shrugged his shoulders. "I'm just letting you know about the deliberations of the Security Council."

"No, this was some vulgar provocation! Absolutely inappropriate for your position at the base, just as inappropriate as a *number* of things you've done!" Elia stood up, abruptly pushing back her chair. "I see that none of you here needs medical help," she said with scorn quite unfitting for a doctor. She left the dispensary and slammed the door behind her. Hissing, it hermetically opened and closed again, this time quietly.

Still showing no emotion, Larsen leafed once more through the folder. "After the vote, the council approved the emergency powers of the inspector of IBI, Terence Simon, for investigation of the murders and the motives that led to them. He has also been entrusted with new unlimited powers, within the necessary safety precautions. That's all." He had finished the briefing.

"What else can you expect?" Vernie shrugged.

Reder grinned at me maliciously. His boss proved once again his talent for taking advantage of any situation. It was a tempest in a tea cup, but it had led to three rounds of debate at the highest level. That was what this meeting was really all about. Rather than compromise his policy toward the Yusians, this latest murder had consolidated opinions on that policy. The Yusians received a warning: "Beware, our loyalty has its limits too." And there was a new, even more unpleasant, intrigue for my boss. Zung had, no doubt, by his vote of confidence toward me, positioned me to be as the next scapegoat in his wicked games.

Yes, I would bear the blame from now on since I had been awarded unlimited emergency powers, and no doubt Zung's agent here would try to limit me. Zung was sure about that, even if he had not yet received the interesting information that I had killed Odesta. If he had received it, though, by extending my powers, he had gone so far as to commend me!

"Larsen, can you tell me how you came by this information?" I asked.

"The summarized report of the proceedings was delivered at the Yusian Embassy today at eight o'clock this morning. They then transmitted it to their Eyrenean base, from where it was personally forwarded to me at nine thirty."

"That's a ninety-minute delay," Vernie explained to me with unnecessary gesticulating. "The connections along their information channels are instantly established in real time, regardless of the distance. That means that the Yusians discussed the recording before transmitting it to us."

I turned to Larsen again. "What else did your report to Earth contain?"

"Nothing. I just broke the news of Odesta's murder. Without any comment."

"Among other things, how's your investigation going, Simon?" Reder wanted to know.

"Yes"—I nodded—"that's exactly how it's going: 'among other things.'"

He smiled again. After our morning scuffle, he looked terrible. The left half of his face was swollen, his chin bore a huge blue bruise, and his eyes were red with blood and bulged even more than usual. As a matter of fact, I didn't look much better myself, but it wasn't this fact that bothered me. What worried me, though, was the marked difference in our moods.

"Reder," I began in an official manner, "I'm addressing you as the science consultant at the 'Biosystems.' I need your results from the cones analysis."

"The results have been recorded on the server in great detail and are available to anyone interested."

"Do they include the information that these cones derive from trees?"

"Of course not. That became evident only today. Regardless of their origin, though, they are *not* plants," Reder insisted. "I still don't know what they are, but *Stein* probably knew."

I got the point—we both knew that Stein's analyses lay in my restricted data bank—but carried on regardless. "Since the metamorphosis, the building section is in the immediate vicinity of cones rather than the forest. Do you think this change is dangerous for us?"

"The source of the euphoria is the forest. The cones can have no such effect."

"My question didn't concern the euphoria only. Could you elaborate a bit more on the so-called whirlpools?"

"The substance that constitutes the cones sometimes reacts this way when humans are present. That is, it absorbs them—for a short time. If you ask me why, I can only say again, 'I don't know.'"

"Seriously?" I raised my eyebrows with mock astonishment. "It seems to me, Reder, you've done nothing substantial here. You really must get down to business."

He looked disgruntled enough, so I redirected my attention to Vernie. "What is the state of the defractor?"

"Normal. The metamorphosis didn't have any particular impact on the equipment."

"Very good. Now could you explain to me about the precautions against electronic surveillance that you mentioned when I arrived?"

"We use state-of-the art technology for that. We can only hope that they counter the Yusian communication disks and that these disks really are for communication only."

"So?" I urged him.

"You know yourself that the best protection from spying has always been not to say or do anything of significance."

Well, no one can argue with that, but I was sure that everyone said and did whatever they wanted in places they themselves, and not the Yusians, had constructed: the defractor site, the research field, the biosector, the infirmary, and so on. But might there be other such sites? *Omitted* on the map and unknown to me?

"I'd like to inform you," I spoke in a calm voice, "that I intend to implement stronger requirements for our personal protection. That includes the electronic system for personal surveillance. Any objections?"

My catch didn't work—there were no objections.

"Any technical problems? Vernie?"

"I don't think so. Except when the shuttles are airborne. Then they are very hard to track. We regularly lose contact with them. But we don't fly that much, Simon."

I turned to Reder. "As far as I know, you don't do any flights, right?"

Clenching his teeth, he simply stared at the wound on my forehead. I smiled at him and asked another irrelevant question. "Larsen, when are you meeting the Yusians?"

"I'm not meeting them."

"Even now? Now that they owe us an explanation about the metamorphosis and why they gave us no advance notice?"

"My stand toward them remains unchanged."

"Unchanged, yes, but can that be considered a stand?"

Larsen closed the file and stood up. "We are wasting time, Simon. If there is nothing else—"

"Wait for me in your office," I said.

"Why?"

"So that you can me give me the Yusian effigy of Stein."

I gave Reder a sign that he was dismissed as well, and he immediately followed Larsen out of the room.

"Vernie," I began, "can you tell me when you'll start testing the defractor?"

"We haven't decided yet. In two or three days—could be a little more."

"Or less?"

"No, not less. I won't be able to catch up with all the work! Things are complicated enough as it is."

"What things?"

He pressed his cheek with his hand as if he had a sudden toothache, made a sour face, and said nothing.

"Don't worry," I reassured him, "I was bluffing when I mentioned the personal surveillance. I have no intention to keep you under constant observation, so do your assignments at your own pace. After all, I didn't come here to get in the way."

This time around he managed somehow to cover his relief.

I added, "But since you don't even try to establish any relationship with the Yusians, I really wonder why you're here."

"What's to wonder, Simon? We're researching the planet, testing its effects, studying the plants, and conducting various experiments. In short, we're collecting information for the colonization."

"Listen, Vernie, it's quite clear to me that your job has no direct bearing on the colonization. That's why I'd like to know what you, personally, think about—"

"I don't think at all," he interrupted me. "Ever since I came to Eyrena, I've become totally indifferent to larger concerns. Otherwise—"

"Yes?"

"Well, you've seen the situation here. Start thinking about it, and you'll be tempted to take some action, but if you do—there you go! You find yourself in the morgue. I wouldn't like to be the next one there."

Vernie rubbed his hands as if they were cold. Three murders, no killers identified, and all he did was fake increased safety precautions. Clearly neither he nor the others at the base feared for themselves. None avoided being alone; they moved freely everywhere. They gave no evidence that they suspected anyone else on the base, they didn't comment on the murders, and they didn't undertake their own investigation. Yes, only people to whom everything is already known—from the motives to the names of the perpetrators—would act like this. Since it was so, I was not only faced with a silent conspiracy but also participated in it myself—in the most foolish role possible. I was both a killer and the only one involved who didn't know what had happened, what was happening now, and what more was going to happen on this damned planet.

"I can't promise you anything, Vernie," I replied. "Nothing."

CHAPTER 27

Down. I'm going down the carpeted staircase. I can't hear my footsteps, but I can feel them. One of my knees is deeply bruised; the newly formed scab is torn, and I'm bleeding again. I keep going down. It's very quiet in the hotel. Everybody—children and adults—is asleep. I reach the first floor and walk to the lobby. Yes, yes, I'm sure I left them somewhere here. I take a few more steps—then stop. I freeze.

She isn't aware of my presence there—this bent, unknown old woman. She is arranging and rearranging my autumn leaves. Yellow, red, brown, and motley-colored—she has strewn them all over the small table, and her hands in white gloves keep running over them, changing the picture the leaves form, rustling them into another as if touched by a magic wand. I smile, ready even to approach. It is then that the old woman looks up.

Her face under the dense net of wrinkles is completely expressionless, a chapped mask in which the eyes, overgrown with creamy colored membranes, are barely visible.

Blind! I am gasping for breath, racing back up that staircase. At the same time, I feel a vague, remote compassion for that small boy who, long ago in that lobby, was so frightened by...

——

Stein's effigy was burning my fingers. I put it carefully in front of me and examined it: a middle-aged man without any particularly distinguishing features or birthmarks. An ordinary face. His staring eyes revealed some hidden bitterness; his face, frozen as he slightly bit his lower lip, a frown on his forehead, wore the memory of that blind old woman. A memory that has now become mine as well—a small remainder of the dead man, lodged forever in my mind.

But why there, in the Yusian starship, just before the takeoff, did Stein recall this incident from his youth? Was it possible that he was reliving those emotions? Or did something totally different trigger the association?

Odesta had said, "Even in the starship, he continually revised some theory of his that he hoped to prove here, on Eyrena."

I needed to examine my notes on Stein's theories more closely.

———

At one point in their development, the Yusians reached the other four planets orbiting their sun. Two were completely without life, while the third harbored some primitive microorganisms and the fourth a relatively rich flora, as well as some quasianimals—that is, animals with undeveloped reflex systems.

Of course, the microorganisms, plants, and quasianimals instantly became objects of study that eventually brought the Yusians to the Big Idea of creating a biological union of the five planets. Toward that end, they had undertaken a program of directed mutation and a gradual synthesis of all the fundamentally different gene pools they encountered. It is worth mentioning that the gene pool on their home planet was really impoverished. There had never been any other living creatures on that planet than the Yusians themselves.

———

I was alone in the spacious living room of the apartment where Stein had lived just a few weeks before. I was sitting in the leather armchair by the window, where he probably had spent many hours. The smooth, mirrored surface of the cone outside the window reflected the rays of Ridon and sent them streaming to me in a steady yellow-violet glow.

Just a little before his death, Stein had foreseen the colossal metamorphosis of Eyrena. Moreover, he had described it in great detail, even stating the most likely date of its appearance. Despite a few inaccuracies in his findings, he probably would have been satisfied if he were here now, in his comfortable armchair, viewing the landscape outside, changed beyond recognition. Yet he would hardly have fallen into contemplation at this hour of the day. As Odesta said, "He could work under any circumstances."

Work—I had spent more than three hours in the server room with his notes, but even if I spent a month there, I could scarcely comprehend the scientific basis of his findings, certainly not the way Reder would, for instance. After all, that was not why I was here. What mattered to me was Stein the person, and I think I was able to grasp his most important traits. The better I knew him, the more deeply I respected this man who had dedicated his life entirely to work.

He had laid out his arguments, conclusions, speculations, and hypotheses conscientiously—I would even say nobly—with no emotional digressions to suggest the frustrations of a scientist faced with something so unfathomable and majestic as Yusian civilization. He had not been afraid to make a mistake; he would not falter before the inevitable "maybe," "if," and "probably." Nor had he trembled with fear for his reputation when he used new and oftentimes awkward expressions imposed on him by a lack of analogies in Earth's languages. All in all, Stein had proven himself to be one of those few remarkable men who ventured into the unknown with a clear understanding of their limitations but with unbroken faith in the invincibility of the human spirit.

Yet Vernie had described him as "unreal, abstract"!

He had recorded his haphazard thoughts before the indifferent microphone and then systematically arranged them with meticulous care, argued with himself, grown weary, and sometimes given in to despair. But he had never surrendered or stopped being human. "We can't even imagine how lonely the Yusians actually are."

———

Their entire evolution, from the most elementary unicellular organisms to the superbeings they now are, passed in total and absolute solitude. The only engine in their development has always been the planet itself with its physical, climatic, seismic, and other conditions—with its movements, changes, and cataclysms, infinitely more intense and varied than their counterparts on Earth. But did our different evolutionary histories predetermine the huge differences that exist between us now?

The real cause of all our differences, including psychological, is much deeper and runs back in time to the moment we each came into existence. The Yusians actually originated from plants. At least, according to our criteria, they are much more closely related to flora than to fauna. Their body energy comes by absorbing particles and ray emissions from the environment through their entire "skin" surface without interruption. An analogy could be made with the way we breathe—only they "breathe" with their whole bodies. As for their method of reproduction, although we haven't managed yet to find out what it *is*, we could say for sure that it's *not* sexual. Their nervous system has a fibrous-optical structure, which, while infinitely more complex than that of even the most highly developed Earth plants, is basically built on almost the same principle.

The Yusian main brain is not located in a specific place; rather, it consists of polymorphic tissue layered in different correlated levels. Their senses have evolved to an extent that enables them to register an incredibly wide scope of sound, gravity, and electromagnetic waves, but their sense of sight was created much later. Yes, they created it themselves, more than two or three thousand years ago, when their study of biology had advanced so much that they were able to adapt themselves, using prototypes of the organs they found in the quasianimals from another planet in their system.

As for the multicolored zones, and especially those on the front of their "chests," it is quite clear that they determine the flow of radiant energy in the Yusian organism. However, these zones also serve other functions. Their structure is multilayered, adapted to refracting the absorbed light and, through changes in the consistency of its texture, to filtering out only the chosen spectral color, which can then be constantly adjusted as to its saturation, brightness, and intensity. While this process is instinctive, it can also be consciously directed by the

Yusians. We have enough evidence now to state that this is exactly the way they communicate among themselves and that such communication manifests itself in the strictly dosed exchange of certain color impulses. In support of this statement comes the fact that, even though there exists a spoken Yusian language, they resort to it very rarely.

Besides their regulatory and communicative functions, certain conditions allow us to suppose that these zones have another very important function: direct energy exchange. "I will call these *specialized organs for immediate mutual assistance*, although I'm perfectly aware of the fact that anyone reading this will smile skeptically at this hypothesis, so foreign to our world. Teeth, claws, horns, and thorns—yes, we understand these weapons of the battle for survival. But organs for mutual assistance? This sounds a little too sentimental, doesn't it?"

———

Yes, that's how it sounded to me. And I did smile in disbelief—"organs for immediate mutual assistance" indeed! If that's true, given that the Yusians were the only inhabitants of their planet, they couldn't have known the *meaning* of aggression. Yet many of their acts toward us now appeared to prove just the opposite—or could it be that what we interpret as aggression is really some kind of "mutual assistance" from their perspective?

I stopped thinking about the plant structure of the Yusians as well as about their "assistance." Stein's unfinished theory required that I summarize and think over some other much more vital issues.

———

Realizing the Big Idea of the pentabioplanetary system also made possible unprecedented advances in all spheres of Yusian science. During that period, the Yusians learned how to incorporate many other new states of matter. They began to extract colossal amounts of energy from the vacuum. They laid the foundations for the theory of the memory of matter, proving by experiments the ability of any material object both to store information and to reproduce it.

In that same period, the Yusians delved deeply into the properties of inorganic nature. They managed through biocatalysis to strengthen some of them and in this way to bridge the gap between living and nonliving structures that exist on the molecular level. They then introduced properties of life forms into inorganic matter, thus creating an entirely new species. They also created the first combined, but autonomously functioning, constructions.

———

"Are creatures. But alive sometimes and almost," Chuks had told me about the strange walls "deprived of toleration of intelligent touch." Only now was I beginning to understand what he had meant. I was also beginning to figure out the nature of that "ordinary object" that he claimed powered the starship when "surrounded by substances and energies subordinate to it."

I felt somehow stupidly relieved. So far, things turned out to be relatively easy to understand—the Yusians are able to make use of quasibiological inorganic constructions. But as I thought of the abyss lying between us, an abyss thousands of years old, and as I considered what Stein called their "chronal management," my head began to spin.

Reder had said, "If we look at it from the larger perspective, not only Stein but also humankind is just at the beginning. Maybe not even there."

———

These new inventions put an even higher goal before the Yusians: to unite the five planets, already unified biologically, on nonbiological and even, later on, inorganic levels as well. During the centuries they struggled toward this goal, they reached something that seemed unattainable, which for us will be even in the realms of our dreams.

They learned to control time.

The foundations were laid with their theory of the memory of matter or, to be more precise, when the Yusians took it upon themselves to analyze where and how material objects *stored* the information they received during their life span. First, it became clear that, with each and every energy-based process—be it thermal, chemical, nuclear, biological, or whatever!—between participating objects, a specific *potential* connection existed. Second, this connection remained even if the objects were later separated by great distances. Third, the potential connection so established could be activated under certain conditions and could bring about an *instantaneous* interaction between these objects.

As instantaneous interactions in space are in principle impossible, they came to the shocking conclusion that they must be realized *outside* this space, along previously unknown "tracks" between the components that made up its heterogeneous structure. However, where there is no space, there is no matter—if for no other reason than for the lack of space where it can be positioned. What, then, is the conductor of these instantaneous interactions?

There can only be one answer: time. This leads to the next conclusion: along such "tracks" of spaceless, immaterial time, only *time* can pass. In other words, all instantaneous interactions have a chronal character. Therefore, the connections that provoke them are also chronal, generated by the total time exchange that accompanies any energy-based process. As time for a given object means the *continuity* of its existence, then time contains in itself all the information of this object, which is nothing but a sequence of "recollections" of its past processes with other material objects. These "recollections," in their entirety, we call memory.

———

"These 'recollections,' in their entirety, we call memory." Memory is then recollections transmitted consecutively from one piece of matter to another, becoming a part of its own recollections, passing alongside those recollections to the next link in the chain, and the previous one—and to more and more. Yet each recollection remains untouched, intact. This perspective, or rather my inability to comprehend it, had made me turn off the monitor in the server room and to stare vacantly at it for a long time. When I finally realized that I was nothing but a piece of matter myself, thus part and parcel of this inconceivable exchange of temporal recollections, I was really stunned.

So without even realizing it, I had in myself a universal encyclopedia that contained all, even the minutest, details of existence—only I couldn't read even a single line of it. All things around me, the door, the floor, the ceiling, the chairs, the lamps as well as my clothes, were similar encyclopedias—mysterious, mute, and inscrutable, to us. But wide open to those who had come directly from time, the Yusians.

"The Yusians have learned to read the recollections of matter," Stein recorded. "They have also found ways of erasing recollections that they have no need of and turning others into stimulants for new processes."

———

All material objects in an open system absorb time from the outside, mark it with their "imprint," and then release part of it as transformed, individual time. During these transformations, there is no proportional dependency between the intensity of its flow and the intensity of the processes involving the material objects. The "younger" a given object is, the less time it releases per energy unit and the greater its capability to absorb time, as well as energy, from the outside.

Therefore, one of the basic characteristics of material objects—along with mass, weight, elasticity, electrical conductivity, and so on—is their accumulated individual time, replete with recollections, which has different values at any different moment of their existence. The chronal field, unfolded in space and constituting an entirety of the emitted individual times from every material object, is far from homogenous and is continually changing its structure. That flux, that movement of ongoing change, expresses the progress of time.

It is clear that, without space and matter, time would be uniform and devoid of information, so its progress would be zero. Space, with its changing chronal field, is the reality that divides material objects in time, imparting relativity to time at any of its points. Apart from this relative time, however, there is also another time—*spaceless, absolute* time, which is comprised of all material objects in the universe *simultaneously*. And despite the fact that they are outside it, it is *this* time that determines the indivisibility of matter because, on the basis of its already-created-in-the-*relative*-time chronal connections, it can instantaneously establish contacts among all its forms.

———

I sat back in the armchair and rubbed my forehead. All this esoteric thinking had exhausted me. Dusk was closing in outside. Clouds gliding slowly over the base like gray gunboats, similar to those on Earth. Then they gathered together, forming entire armadas, the sky visible between them growing smaller. The first raindrops tapped gently on the windowsill as the rain began. It would be nice if Elia were here now so we could listen together to the quiet whisper of this serene shower. It seemed to endow all our surroundings with tranquility and even managed to mitigate the sinister appearance of the cones. Plants! I shrugged my shoulders condescendingly. Just plants.

I already knew, though, that they were not *just* plants.

———

It was in that manner that the Yusians established two categories of chronal interactions. The first, which accompanies the processes involving energy in space and creates potential chronal connections between material objects, is relative in nature and continuous as a process. The second, which is realized outside space while activating potential chronal connections, has an absolute character and is instantaneous in nature. One must emphasize the fact that these two types of interactions enable the Yusians to manage their polyplanetary system. They have discovered ways of constructing chronal connections with greatly amplified potential power and activating them selectively, resulting in instantaneous chronal interactions with a regenerative effect—that is, with the ability to reproduce an unlimited number of energy-based processes from the past.

———

Of course, this form of management is implemented only in the largest bioinorganic hybrid constructions, those that require an extraordinarily complex inventory, which would not be profitable enough on a small scale. To digress somewhat from the topic, it is comforting to note that all other Yusian forms of management are relatively close to ours "in conception, if not in efficiency."

Clearly, because of the distances, scope, the qualitative heterogeneousness, and a number of other factors, the union of five planets into a synchronically working system required that chronal connections be used between constructions that were never part of the same energy-based process. Such indirect connections could take place only through the mediation of an object in direct chronal connection with each of these constructions. Therefore, one of the fundamental tasks of the Yusians at this stage was to create special object-mediators capable of "maximal concentration of foreign time in a minimal volume" or, as Stein called them, "time accumulators," the most essential quality of which is their "individual chronal emptiness."

I admit I was a little confused by all these notions. Their explanation probably lies in the fact that, in an energy-based process, the object-mediators accumulate in themselves the time emitted by the respective construction and then pass it on without transforming it into their own individual time, possibly because of preliminary erasure of their chronal memory. That way they could perform the role of neutral time transmitters, in effect enabling direct chronal connections between the two constructions.

I thought about my trip from Earth to Eyrena. The tiles I had seen in the room with the transparent sphere Chuks called "starship" were themselves miniaturized object-mediators. When they put the one that contained "concentrated" Eyrena time in the sphere, chronal connections were established between the starship and Eyrena, the activation of which triggered the interaction necessary for our instantaneous relocation to the planet. The "external insulation veil" mentioned by Chuks simply confirmed Stein's supposition that "the Yusians fly their starships along the spaceless tracks by placing them in capsules of absolute time."

OK, let's assume that all this makes *some* sense so far. But where do we go from here? According to Chuks, our trip was to take from eleven to twenty-three days; it actually took fourteen days. The people from the base arrived in twenty-two days, and the starship shuttling between Eyrena and Earth takes practically just hours in either direction. So why all these differences in the traveling time?

The answer was unexpected and shocking—we *humans* were the reason! I recalled in detail Chuks's words again. When I asked him about the duration of the flight, he said, "May be between nine hours and eleven days and nine hours and twenty-three days. Depends on adaptation. If you not oppose it."

Yes! That's right, "If you not oppose it!" Then I considered this response to be just alien irony, but now. The nine hours must be strictly fixed as the time necessary for the creation of the "insulation veil," the establishment of indirect chronal connections and their activation. The number of days, however, really depended on me alone! I too, as just another material object within the scope of the sphere, or "starship," had to come into chronal connection with Eyrena. But we must never forget the most precious quality of this particular piece of matter—the mind, the consciousness.

While I had no direct evidence, I knew intuitively that when Yusians dealt with a material *sub*ject rather than *ob*ject, their otherwise so reliable and precise management techniques stopped being either reliable or precise. They would be puzzled, maybe even confused, if this subject decided to confront them consciously, because its psyche was beyond their control. Human reactions are of a higher order: not just energy-based processes but also thoughts and feelings immeasurably more complicated than any kind of chronal or other mechanism!

I stood up abruptly, excited by my conclusions, and paced back and forth. Yes, it was true. We humans don't give in so easily, so automatically, to chronal manipulations. Our reactions are unpredictable. We are capable of mental resistance—but for how long? This ability of ours is not unlimited. And if the Yusians managed to get to its utmost limit, what would they find beyond? Nothing but more material objects to include in their ever-growing polyplanetary system?

———

After gaining control of time, traveling in outer space—which until then had seemed pointless to the Yusians—suddenly acquired a new, profound meaning. Despite the unlimited energy they could draw from the vacuum and the incredible speeds reached by Yusian starships, their first trips to other star systems still took from ten to hundreds of years. Once they had reached a planet, however, the Yusians built their own centers for chronal management there and made it instantly accessible to them. They then charged their "batteries" with time and went on their way, and on and on—until they reached the Earth.

———

Those diabolical constructions around their embassy must be centers for chronal management! And batteries—Stein's "time accumulators"—some miniaturized while others—I suddenly felt weak. I paused by the window and, through the multilayered sheet of falling rain, gazed at the cones towering opposite. "The ultimate products of a metamorphosis that had began by modifying the Earth herb *Sedum*, which in each new phase took on new biological, nonbiological, and inorganic properties," Stein laconically defined them. I now stood mesmerized by their brazen yellow-violet array, and it became painfully clear to me that he was aware of it all, he *knew*.

Planetary time accumulators—that's what the cones were!

That was the main purpose of the entire Eyrenean metamorphic cycle! To weaken our psychic resistance by the persistent euphoria and then to withdraw our recollections—human time—to be implanted in the cone chronal accumulators—until they begin emitting it.

They are emitting it in the direction of the Yusian base, definitely to a center for chronal management, which is connected with those centers on Earth and with others in the Yusian system. Yus is where the repeated cycles begin until stable, unbreakable chronal connections are established between the centers and our minds. Connections whose selective activation will enable instantaneous interactions, through which the Yusians manage their polyplanetary system. Through which they will begin ruling humankind—regardless of the thirty years of isolation! Here on Eyrena, the new colonists maintaining a direct chronal connection with Earth will be that link, mediating between Earth and the planets of the Yusian system. They will be reduced to just chronal mechanisms to be selectively activated by the Yusians.

I don't know how it had happened, but I was holding the Yusian effigy of Stein in my hand again. As I clutched it tightly with feverish despair, its warmth flowed through my body like a silent, mysterious wave.

Down—down—I was sinking uncontrollably into the eternal memory of time. Down to the blind old woman and her endless shuffling of the colorful dead leaves.

CHAPTER 28

The defractor site was changed beyond recognition by the long rows of ferns, still delicate, tenderly glistening after the rain. I landed the shuttle right in their midst, near the coordination center. I was surprised to find the ground completely dry, even parched.

"They were really thirsty." I angrily kicked one of the plants, and the raindrops shaken off were quickly swallowed by the cracks below with gluttonous slurps. Shuddering at the sound, I looked around. Although I was quite familiar with the change, it still depressed me.

The sole reminders of the original Earth *Sedum* in its modified grassy reincarnation were the hairs forming loose rings around the bases of the ferns. These ferns would be followed by its next transformation, because some time ago in the seeds of an ordinary Earth plant had been implanted the embryo of a monstrous alien idea, the realization of which was inevitable—perhaps.

I circled the building from the rear end, sticking close to the wall, and peeked through the window of the narrow workspace where, three days ago, we had talked with Vernie. Again he was there, now seated comfortably in his swivel chair, completely relaxed, his breathing deep and even. His profile suggested that he was dozing off with his eyes half-closed.

I waited for about two minutes. He didn't budge, so I walked around and entered the building, making as much noise as possible, went to the workspace, and knocked.

"Yes!" I heard Vernie's astonishingly energetic voice.

When I opened the door, he was in front of the indicator panel, completely absorbed by his work. His fingers ran quickly over the keyboard, the numbers under the flickering symbols changing at lightning speed.

"Ah! Simon!" he turned to me just for a moment and then bent over the keyboard again. "Come on in. I'm almost done."

I sat in the chair, still warm from his dozing body, and watched him. Why did he have to pretend to be busy?

Finally he pulled out the tape with the indicator diagram, glanced at it, and then, sighing heavily, put it into a drawer of the work desk.

"I came to talk about the defractor," I said.

"Again?" Vernie squinted at his watch and then, groaning, sat in the chair opposite me.

"Yes, again," I confirmed. "Could you explain, for example, why everything here is so lavish? And that's despite the difficulties you had with receiving materials from Earth."

"We can't afford to look like paupers before the Yusians, Simon. We should demonstrate *some* class and style."

"That I understand, although it still doesn't make much sense. What makes even less sense is this hodgepodge of equipment with different functions and purposes. What kind of base is this anyway? Honestly, it rather looks like a crazy puzzle of different, unrelated objects all put together."

"I'm happy you see it that way." Vernie laughed unexpectedly. "Can you imagine the way the Yusians see it? Complete disorientation! Yes, we were even lucky yesterday to have those two blunder into the biostation! As a matter of fact, this has nothing to do with the defractor."

"You built it just as a camouflage, is that it?"

"Oh, no, no. We just built it here rather than in the biosector where it belongs. Actually, it served Reder and Stein pretty well. Mmm, yes, as I already pointed out to you, Simon, the goals we're trying to achieve with the defractor are of utmost importance to us. Because of this, we have to take every precaution to foil the enemy."

"Only *temporarily*," I accentuated, "because when the defractor starts functioning, your goals will become apparent sooner or later. Then the Yusians will see through your attempts to deceive them."

"I wouldn't be so sure."

"So sure about what?"

"Mmm—well, in short, about anything."

"What *I* am sure of, though, is that you consider *me* an enemy too. You've been doing a good job trying to fool me ever since I came here."

"Sorry, but I had no other option." He sneaked another glance at his watch. "My job is really top secret."

I shook my head. "That's not the only reason. It seems to me you're trying to establish an alibi. So what are these problems you so obtrusively complain about all the time? What were you trying to get Larsen into with that insinuation about the defractor? Why did he decide not to be involved with the project?"

"Well, yes, he decided! He doesn't want to help, the egoist—"

"Knock it off, Vernie! It's time to speak frankly! We're in a very complicated situation here. If we don't unite our forces, our common sense, it will lead to disaster. Not only here on Eyrena, but for humanity!"

"I understand." He nodded glumly. "I've always known it, but—once the experiments are successful, Simon, we can talk again, and then I'll explain."

"No! You must give me an explanation now!" I stood up, grabbed him by the shoulders and shook him. "What sort of experiments are these? What are you trying to do, man! What is the real purpose of the defractor?"

He was silent.

"Vernie, we're on the same side! I think we are right in what we want. All we need is just to choose the right way to do it. Let's work together!"

He still didn't respond. I left him that way, tense and shaky, as if he just won a painful victory over his deadly enemy.

When I boarded the shuttle again, I directed it to our base, although I had no intention of going there. I landed as soon as I passed the first cone, after the ferns where, only yesterday, the Eyrenean forest began. I got off and, crouching low, dashed back to the coordination center.

I was just in time to see Vernie exit—not in the direction of one of the defractor buildings but to the left, through the ferns. There was no danger of my losing him, since the ferns came only up to his chest as he walked. I don't think he was just strolling.

I entered the building. Just as I expected, the workspace was unlocked. Here on Eyrena we keep our secrets primarily in our heads or in the restricted data banks, but one must always check for errors. I went straight to the drawer with the indicator diagram, took it out, and looked for the one dated three days before.

I found it in no time because there were only two diagrams in the drawer. I compared that with today's diagram: they were identical. That's it! Vernie had loaded a sham program onto the control panel so that as soon as I arrived he could begin working on it. Since he obviously considered me ignorant, why should he bother to make even the slightest modifications? I put the diagrams back into the drawer and rushed for the exit.

Vernie had walked about two hundred meters. I followed him cautiously. He was walking calmly; apparently I had disappeared from his view at a convenient time. He was not stopping or showing any signs of hesitation, which was surprising considering the complete change in the environment and its monotony. He was probably aiming for the only hill around, from where the strange Yusian observed the defractor every day as Shidexa rose.

Because of the constant bending, peeking, and running, both my back and neck started hurting, and my legs began to tremble. I was assailed by troubling thoughts too. Yes, there were all sorts of nasty things happening on Eyrena, but the nastiest of all was the behavior of the people. It seemed we had all become so used to suspicions, provocations, betrayals, lies, and spying that these would probably be our distinguishing features until our dying days—maybe even in hell after that.

Vernie reached the hill and started climbing. At the top suddenly appeared—Elia! I threw myself to the ground instantly; she could see me very easily from there. I had no choice but to crawl from here on. I started sweating. Why did they decide to meet on the hill?

Very soon I heard their voices but couldn't make out a single word. I tried to hurry through the ferns without making too much noise. An irritating smell filled my nose from the cracks below, making my eyes tear. I felt dizzy and, in an awkward movement, touched the plant in front of me near the base. The hairs stuck to my hand. When I tried to shake them off, they stuck to my other hand as well. While I was wondering how to get rid of them, I realized that something was missing. The voices!

Was it possible that Elia and Vernie left, or were they just silent? I rose a little and looked up from behind the fern fronds but couldn't see them. They were probably already descending the hill on the other side. I stood up and hurried to the top of the hill. Once there, I looked around furtively and then scanned the whole area. Elia and Vernie were gone.

I continued searching, wiping my hands in my pants. What should I do now? I didn't have a clue. Those two seemed to have been swallowed by the ground. And why not, after all?

I looked more closely at the ground between the fern stems, and my suppositions were confirmed. I discovered a carefully camouflaged plate, no doubt blocking the entrance to some underground bunker. As a matter of fact, the hidden entrance was not at all easy to find, discernible only as a faint square about two yards across. It was covered by a thick layer of soil – as cracked and furrowed as the surrounding floor, and the ferns here looked no different from those elsewhere.

I started looking for a lever that would lift the plate. Most likely it was controlled remotely, but there should be some other option in case the electronics failed. At last I found it—a matte, pale-rose button with a diameter of two or three centimeters. I memorized the place and receded through the ferns.

I spent around twenty minutes like this, in the stressful state of waiting and asking myself questions I could not answer. Then I heard the specific hiss of the hydraulic system underneath, and the plate started lifting up until the ferns on it became nearly horizontal. Shortly after, in the frame of the gaping hole, Elia and Vernie appeared. When they stepped away, the plate slid sideways back into place.

"How I wish this were over once and for all!" Vernie said.

"Sometimes I feel like we shouldn't even start it." Elia grimaced in disgust.

"It's too late."

"Yes, it is."

With the same intonation, and probably for the same reason, Larsen had said that two days ago. What in the world was it too late for, though!

Unfortunately, Elia and Vernie parted without discussing anything further. He headed straight for the defractor, and she for her shuttle nearby. I was worried she might see my shuttle as she took off, but fortunately she was flying toward the biosector, and at any rate, she'd probably covered the shuttle's transparent floor with the rug.

As soon as they were out of sight, I approached the button and pressed it. The masked plate lifted at once. I stepped on the platform at the entrance to the bunker, and a few seconds later, it plummeted downward.

The descent through the shaft lasted a long time in complete darkness, but when the platform hit bottom, some lights instantly lit. The light faded away into a straight gallery, about two meters high, that had been dug through very compact rock and thus needed no additional reinforcing. The walls and floor were rough, almost primitive. The vehicles used to transport scrap were positioned in a tunnel perpendicular to the gallery, that is, in the direction of the defractor.

Right beside the platform was a hoist equipped with a pair of pincers insulated at the ends, and directly in front of that was an armored truck with a retractable roof. I opened the rear door to check if it was loaded with anything at the moment. It was empty.

I climbed in the truck and drove through the gallery, which slanted smoothly downhill. The rock layer was reddish in color with rich deposits of mica, which gleamed in the dim light. Here and there one could see the black openings of crossing installation, cemented passages, concrete lintels with supporting trestles, and steel nets stretched alongside some eroded areas, but nothing that suggested what the bunker was used for. I already knew some facts, though: it was built deep underground; the straight gallery was without branches and had been dug in a hurry and economically, using machinery not really suited to the purpose. Of course it was built in secret and without the knowledge of the Yusians.

I could see a little farther down that the gallery was completely blocked by a two-winged metal gate on rails—rather inappropriately, considering its complex electronic access system. I stopped the truck a few meters away from the gate and climbed down to take a better look. I tried to open it in every mechanical way possible but without success.

Then I climbed back in the truck. I could not accept the thought of returning to the surface still ignorant of what was going on here, but I was making no progress either. I sat staring at the gate, wondering what to do, when it dawned on me that the truck had to have its own mechanism for accessing the room on the other side because such vehicles usually move without a driver on a preset program. If we exclude the rather wide space back at the entrance, there was no place else it could dispose of its load or make a turn.

I gave a command for the truck to proceed but hardly expected that the gate would open while I was inside. However, as soon as we approached, the two wings slid sideways and disappeared into the opposing walls. Apparently the gate's receptors were programmed to let in this truck regardless of its load, a fact puzzling in itself.

Only seconds after the gates opened, the darkness inside gave way to bright light. I blinked with astonishment when I recognized where I was. This room was a surgery unit! Without any command on my part, the truck stopped at its center, where an operating table sat beside another hoist, similar to the one in the vertical shaft. Now its chrome pincers hung motionless just over the truck's retractable roof.

I walked around the room, anxiety growing in me. A surgery unit was the last thing I expected to see in this bunker. Locked boxes with secret materials, spying devices, food supply, ammunition, and even bombs—all this could be explained, but an operating room. What would they need it for? They already had an entire medical wing at their disposal. Or were they expecting some disaster with victims and injured who would have to be operated on in secret?

Instead of sterile conditions, the floor here was covered with coarse sand that crunched unpleasantly under my feet, and the walls and ceiling were as rough as those in the gallery. Light bulbs dangled above like huge balloons tied to a net of cables. Yes, the room had been constructed cheaply, but the ample equipment it held could arouse envy even among surgeons from the renowned surgery unit at the Seattle Medical Institute.

Behind the operating table was a panel with built-in radar screens; in a huge booth behind black metal blinds stood a Blick electronic microscope and, right across from it on a carefully secluded platform, a biogenerator with iridium reductors. There was an MRI scanner too, computer tomograph, microstructural analyzer, infiltration chambers, autostethoscope with amplifiers and remote control, a stand with selectors, cooler and cryoscope, five refrigerators, and so on—not to mention the many pieces of equipment I couldn't even hope to identify. There were also shelves with drainage systems, aspirators, clamps, lancets, scalpels, and stilettos—with tinctures, catalyzers, absorbents, sterile uniforms, masks, gloves, filters, and so on. Yet I had the feeling that something was missing in this amazing room—something very important.

I admit I had been wandering around dazzled and dizzy by what I had seen, but what was all this for? How did they manage to get complex machinery and equipment down here? Actually, I had an answer to the last question—it had been delivered through the Yusians, naturally. They certainly would have been unwilling to accept shipments from Earth without first checking the contents. So what was the point of hiding all this equipment in a bunker? Or had the infirmary been built just to divert them from the fact that all this would be installed here?

A little to the side of the operating table, two objects identical in appearance caught my attention. I went to take a closer look. I tried to remember where I had seen something like them: metal half hoops that could be tightened with a screw until the ends met. Then I remembered! In an old history book about the Spanish Inquisition, that's where! Among its illustrations was a picture of almost the same—a garrote, that's what it was called. A medieval device that caused strangulation by suffocation. Of course these were much more complex and obviously jammed with high-tech electronics, but their blatant similarity to that instrument of torture was most unnerving.

I walked around the room one more time, hoping to find some clue to help explain its existence or at least some trace of Elia and Vernie's visit today, but I found nothing. I climbed the stairs to the observation room on the second floor; it was completely empty. I came back down, got in the truck, and drove to the gate opposite the one I had come through. These were the only two gates anyway.

I had no difficulties entering the other gallery, driving for a minute or two along its shimmering walls and reaching another metal platform at its widened end. According to the truck's odometer, the total length of the two galleries was about three miles.

I stepped on the platform, and it automatically ascended. I saw another exterior metal plate, probably camouflaged as well, rising above my head, and then the platform stopped on the surface. Of course I didn't get off, only used the pause to orient myself as to where this exit of the bunker was located. That was easy to do because it was deadly cold all around me and, a few meters away, in their transparent sarcophaguses, lay Odesta, Fowler, and Stein.

When I returned to the other end of the bunker, I parked the truck exactly where it had been before and in exactly the same position so that Elia and Vernie could only guess that I was here if they remembered what the odometer read before, which was not very likely.

I went upstairs and headed for my shuttle. While walking there, it dawned on me what was missing in that superequipped room. There had been no anesthetics or painkillers anywhere, not even an aspirin.

CHAPTER 29

"If you find yourself angry at being on the losing side, take advantage of it," my boss says. "It will help you do what you couldn't before."

Only half an hour after I left the bunker, I was underground again—this time in the Yusian base still in operation. I barged into the premises without giving any prior notice, determined to ignore any shocking sights. I planned to concentrate all my attention on the Yusians themselves. I found two of them in the spacious entranceway and headed straight toward them.

"I'm looking for Chuks," I said in English and then repeated it in Russian and German.

They showed no signs that they had heard me, simply stood with their eyes firmly closed, as if asleep in their space suits. I was bewildered until I remembered seeing Chuks react that way at the beginning of our meetings. Suddenly I understood: Yusians also experience stress, maybe even paralysis, in immediate proximity to humans! Our effect on them is perhaps as painful as the way they affect us. Absorbed in our own feelings, we never even considered the possibility that they might experience similar ones. How *could* we have guessed that when we were firmly convinced of their universal superiority?

I took a couple steps backward and half closed my eyes. Now that I understood them better, I could show some tolerance. One of the Yusians moved.

"I'm looking for Chuks," I repeated.

"Oukay!" he said pathetically, "Wew'll be, are Chuks!"

Another discovery! Yusians are not good linguists, at least not as good as I thought they were, judging by Chuks, as this Yusian clearly proved by his absurd English.

"I'm looking for the Yusian I met with a couple of days ago outside our bases," I explained, very encouraged.

He opened his eyes, and I was quickly affected with similar phobic symptoms. When I regained my composure, the Yusian asked, with their usual unearthly exuberance, "Spac-c-c-e suits, ginto one?"

"Yes. I will," I said.

The other Yusian moved too and joined us. We walked to the end of the hallway, where at least thirty deep vertical clefts were located, similar to the one that had provided me with my space suit in the starship. When the Yusians paused in front of one, I let myself be *swallowed* by it without hesitation. Knowing the procedure didn't make it any more pleasant than the first time.

At last, packed like a space shipment in a protective membrane, I was pushed to the other side of the cleft, which looked nothing like the first space. Here it was dank and misty, and the ground was strewn with gigantic mushrooms. They were as tall as oak trees, but I had no doubt that they too originated from Earth, although their stems and crowns were covered with knotted, wrinkled bumps. I couldn't ignore the implications of that analogy: these further examples of Yusian transformations, of modified life forms from Earth, seemed to confirm that the future would include modified human beings as well!

A few minutes later, Chuks also entered the dank "mushroom greenhouse." Since he had no need to wear his space suit here, naturally he appeared before my eyes in dozens of colors softened by the mist.

"Chuks!" he shouted from a distance. "Not even had the most grumble expectation!"

"Has another human been in this base before?"

"Three just as voices."

Three, I thought. Larsen, Odesta, and somebody else from our base had contacted the Yusians. I already knew who, and what the motive was.

Chuks approached me with a familiar reluctance, and our eyes met. We stood like that for a moment, paying the inevitable price for our proximity, before he said politely, "Will provide you effect of our stuff. Judge with tendencies!"

"No." I shook my head. "I didn't come to be amazed by you. From what I see here, these hybrids are not *yours* at all."

"Mutual! Mutual!" Chuks exclaimed joyfully. "Those and many others, all over place. Realizing them again with compatible life successfulness!"

"Do you ever consider the human point of view on this problem?"

"We divine equal view. And not from point!"

"Stop the nonsense, Chuks. And don't talk to me in that overly polite tone."

There ensued a long pause. I had started the most dangerous game—the truth-telling game—and Chuks had definitely figured that out after my opening words. Now he had to learn that he too must play his part in the game. Our eyes met again, insistently, with a glint of hostility.

"'Polite tone,'" Chuks responded flatly, "brings comfortable predisposition of—"

"It is fake," I interrupted him, "and only brings mutual distrust."

"But must to give your trust, Ter!"

"That is arrogance, pure and simple! For ten years now, you've done nothing but dig into our lives, turning Earth organisms into monsters!" I said, waving my hand toward the knotted mushroom towering high above us. "You're manipulating us psychologically, and you tell me that we have to *trust* you? Just give me one reason why I should do that!"

"Reason one," said Chuks, "to leave beyond your hopes."

"Well, yes." I grinned scornfully. "You feel good with us because you are stronger."

"No, Ter"—he seemed to sigh—"feeling not good."

He walked away over the meandering ditches of the floor's uneven surface. Suppressing my resentment, I caught up and started walking with him, ignoring the sharp splashing sound my feet made, since water was gurgling and foaming under Chuks's bulky body. I didn't know where he was leading me but didn't care too much either. I had other, much more serious, concerns on my mind.

Soon I was convinced that, in this Yusian base, I would see more earthborn creatures with "transformed futures." The walls of the corridors and rooms were covered with bright phosphorescent mold that actually provided illumination. On the ceiling crawled all sorts of phosphorescent crustaceans. We were being propelled by some flat coral islets sliding along grooves made exclusively for that purpose.

As I understood from the laconic, purposely impolite, explanation Chuks offered, the corals were connected by a metal "cobweb," the grooves were filled with concentrated saline solution, and the sliding was possible with the help of electrolysis, which "reacted according to our postures." In addition, it turned out that the metal network did not corrode because of "objections of torpid infusoria with no posterity." Well, this was crazy, complex, and impractical.

I turned to Chuks again. "Are you having difficulties adapting to this new environment?"

"Lots!" he exclaimed as was his habit but then repeated more calmly, "Lots."

Then he fell silent again.

Our coral islet passed under a low molded arch, slid down a groove, and before long we found ourselves in a dank pool full of seaweed. We were almost at its center when Chuks abruptly gestured, as if giving someone a signal. Only a moment later, brown, symmetrically positioned, posts appeared on either side of the pool and rose about two meters high and froze there. Then a bright light squirted from their tops, and the seaweed in the pool went crazy!

They dashed for the posts like swarms of ravenous snakes. They rammed into each other, entangling into frantically tossing balls, and then pulled and tore themselves and others trying to break free. Only shabby tatters made it to the posts, crawled up, fell down, and then crawled up all over again. They turned an impossibly intense green, the like of which I had never seen on Earth. They were starved to death for light.

"Panic incited to put into ourselves," Chuks explained triumphantly. "Will redirect against it redundant body resistance and make Eyrena more bearable place."

I understood him, or so I thought, when I recalled Stein's notes: "Compared to their native planet, Eyrena and Earth are too peaceful, even painfully so, for the complex protective mechanisms of the Yusian organism."

"At least I hope that the panic of our seaweed helps you," I said sarcastically.

"Will so," said Chuks, trying to comfort me.

Meanwhile, our islet left the pool, moving along one of the ramifications of the groove, and entered a spacious, profusely lit, cave. Inside the cave were half spheres scattered everywhere, each with a radius of over a meter and apparently organic. Just like everything else at the base, they were hardly pleasant to look at. They resembled eyes torn off gigantic insects. They were also covered by thousands of bulging lenses of some glassy substance, through which could be seen a thin network of capillaries. The coating around them had the repulsive look of rosy lung tissue and undoubtedly was used for food. Yes, they were so much like...

They really *were* insect eyes. Multifaceted and glossy, staring with dead stiffness up at the mossy vault.

"Grown in symbiosis to Yusian episodes," Chuks's voice startled me.

"Episodes," I repeated senselessly, "in the eyes?"

"In each," he confirmed. "Brought you here to provoke them together."

"No, Yusian! You're not getting out of our conversation by giving me some—eyes."

"Ter, must meet in one such episode."

"Why? For what purpose?"

"To reach there our necessary impersonal understanding." Chuks hesitated momentarily and then added, "You ask just for words, human! But in me suitability for more convincing risk."

He moved aside and, as soon as the coral isle reached the edge of the groove, moved to the eyes. The rosy coating crumpled under his weight as if wounded, its bubbles bursting out fountains of some lymphatic liquid. Chuks addressed me provocatively. Now he too had started our *truth-telling game.* Even worse, he was offering me an inevitable choice—either to continue it by voluntarily allowing into my consciousness that familiar and frightening alien influence or to give it up, thus confessing my fear of the nonhuman.

I stepped on the rosy coating and folded my hands. My pulse was racing, and no doubt the Yusians were registering it as well as everything else in me that they could register. I hoped, though, that I would leave their base with more information about them than what they could get from me.

Chuks stepped back. I watched him warily, trying to mobilize my psychic resistance to the maximum but, at the same time, feeling sympathy and even compassion for him. I found him touchingly lonely under the vault of this artificial cave. What did he think of me?

Reaching a circle surrounded by white rings, he paused in its center and sank there, seeming to take on himself an enormous burden. His color zones were sated with an inner light and started glowing. The surrounding air rustled with the lightness of an imaginary bird landing warmly on my chest. As I breathed it in, my alarming pulse slowed down. I knew this was more than just a puff of air, which I wouldn't be able to feel through my space suit; I knew its warmth was a distant echo of some alien emotion just beyond my senses, something I couldn't fully assess. There I was, reclining my head as if I were hard of hearing, trying to catch this quiet tune. My previous hesitations, hopes, and fears were losing their meaning now, pitiful and small before this new despairing revelation of my spiritual deafness.

The multifaceted eyes came to life. Yes, they were still staring at the ceiling, but lights flashed from their depths: shadows passing, spasmodic thrills, and sparks flaring up from some ravenous rage. Something gloomy and amorphous arose from them as teary moisture surfacing on the thousands of lenses started evaporating and soon enveloped everything in a creamy mist.

The mist grew denser and denser until it formed a thick creamy film that spread its weightless embrace over the entire cave. We all sank into it: the mossy vault, the carpet of rosy tissue, the gigantic eyes, and Chuks—and me as well.

I reached out ahead of me but couldn't see my hands. I looked down and couldn't even see a particle of me in the impenetrable whiteness. I had a crazy desire to ascertain if I was still there. I tried to touch my chest, but my fingers seemed to sink in and penetrated, against my will, deep inside to where my heart was supposed to be.

Then I realized that I hadn't made the slightest movement. I was completely paralyzed. In spite of that, the sensation of movement wouldn't leave me. I seemed to be walking somewhere, anywhere, since the direction existed only in my imagination. At the same time, I was lingering on the edge of the groove that had disappeared, a stiff figure engulfed in the slow rhythm of its own distancing from itself.

I could see gray Yusian phantoms coming toward me. They surrounded me silently, their contours clarifying as bizarre pictures cut out of paper, and then—then everything changed completely. The white mist lifted, the phantoms took on flesh and splendid colors, and from above, a broad plain was lowered like a stage setting. It passed through us, or rather we ran through it, lay down, and subsided. The heat became unbearable.

The Yusians clumsily walked off. I followed them. We were all just part of the grave silence that reigned over everything, our presence as ephemeral and hollow as our thoughts.

There was no sun or sky here. Close above us hung a strange, homogeneous gas; its optical properties turned it into a flat mirror roof, taut from end to end. Reflections of the exiting Yusians wobbled on it, reversed and diminished in size. I tried to find my own reflection among them, but it wasn't there.

I slowed down in order to lag behind and then looked up again and saw a Yusian, who must also be lagging behind the main group. Puzzled, I shrugged my totally human shoulders, and he trembled; I waved my hand, and the Yusian above me reeled precariously. When I sped up to rejoin the Yusians now far ahead of me, my Yusian reflection shuffled its feet overhead. I stopped paying attention to it.

The plain had no horizons, and all its far edges were folded up, as if it were filling up a gigantic container. We moved in it across a desert of tiny black bead–like grains that were also moving, flowing forward with the majestic peacefulness of a mighty river. Some small bristly creatures ran in front of us, leaving circles of light smoke in their wake. Some large drops of mercury floated in the sweltering heat.

I felt as if we had been walking for hours, but that was surely a delusion. At last the black grainy river changed its course and flowed to the left, past a curved narrow gorge. The Yusians paused at its very edge, so I did too. I leaned over: the gorge wasn't very deep. Its sides were slanted, colorless, and smooth, as if made of polished quartz. At the bottom were ugly, distorted plants. Actually I was just guessing when I said they were plants. They looked more like the skeletons of primeval reptiles, even in their coloring: clay gray and marked in places as if by shreds of flesh.

I stepped back from the edge of the gorge, and the Yusians almost simultaneously slid downhill. Feeling abandoned, I followed them. It was much cooler toward the bottom.

One of the Yusians moved toward me, his approach seeming to take forever. The folds around his chest billowed up and down, and the communication zones on the front of his massive body all turned scarlet, resembling an open, bleeding wound. He kept coming and coming—as if this were happening in a dream, in slow motion, absurdly silent.

The Yusian was already intolerably close to me yet kept coming. Only two steps separated us—then just one—I raised my hand to keep him at a distance, and he touched my palm with his scarlet flesh. I didn't flinch.

"Chuks?" I whispered. "It's you, isn't it?"

"Two of us," I heard him whisper back. "The rest was before. On my planet."

"What are they doing?" I pointed at the other Yusians, who were closing in on one of them in a somewhat threatening manner.

"Anticipated his indulgence," Chuks said quietly.

All the Yusians lay down on the ground except the one they surrounded. Since he was standing, I could see him more clearly now. He had been completely mauled. His limbs were all swollen, his forehead membrane had been torn, and underneath it gaped his empty eye socket. He was shaking all over, seemingly not so much from the physical pain as from some ineffable psychotic disorder.

He trembled as, for some reason, his body kept developing more wounds, shredding until in the end it burst into blazing blue flames. They spread around with lightning speed and, turning orange, enveloped the Yusians lying on the ground. Chuks and I were out of range, at the very edge of the burning circle that was forming. I impetuously stepped into it.

I knelt before the intangible flames, dizzy with the shining emotions that were emitted through them, and looked gratefully at the Yusian who was extracting them from his body. He didn't appear mauled or ugly to me anymore. On the contrary, he was splendid in his fiery "indulgence"!

I turned around to find Chuks still beyond the bright edge of the burning circle, and I wanted him to be close to me. And he came—I could swear I saw him smile as he approached me, an almost, impossibly human smile that could not be described properly. I lay with my face down and my arms stretched in front of me in the cool smokeless bonfire.

I lay with my face down—with my arms stretched in front of me. That's what those robots had done, the ones with the scars! They must have been there, in the deserted base, in a room with flames just like these.

Yes, but so what? What!

I couldn't answer myself. I felt as if feathers were falling over my thoughts, muffling them and burying them.

But they are very important. I will forget them! Because soon I wouldn't be me anymore; I was going to be something else.

Something else? No, Chuks! This game you are playing is totally unacceptable to me!

I started rising up, centimeter by centimeter, fighting some inhuman force that pulled me toward the ground. As soon as I was back standing on the ground, though, I regained my senses surprisingly fast. I leaned over Chuks, who was still in a blissful trance, and shook him.

"Come on! Let's get out of here!"

He obeyed, bewildered by my rudeness, until we stood opposite each other not far from the Yusian ritual burning stake.

"Stop this 'episode' immediately!" I demanded.

"No! No!" Chuks was startled. "Have been before. How stop them today!"

Some inappropriate compassion made me say, "That Yusian in the center of the circle must be dead by now, eh?"

"Why?"

"Well, with his 'fiery indulgence,' he has—"

"Everyone does same time or another."

"You too, Chuks?"

"Yes. You too, but another appearance."

I nodded my head thoughtfully. *Me too, but in another appearance*, I repeated to myself and felt that I could really understand what Chuks meant. I hesitated just to be completely sure I was thinking clearly and then asked him directly, "What have you implanted in the brains of the ESSIKO robots?"

Chuks was silent.

"Tell me!"

"Stepping into disapproval, Ter," he warned me.

"The hell with your disapproval! Answer my question!"

"Implanted some our conceptions with some yours. Robots also mutual."

"Aha, mutual!" I repeated sarcastically. "Like all of Eyrena with its plants, colonies and a future all planned by you beforehand. What I fail to understand, though, is what *we* have to do with all this? We haven't even been informed of their—mixed nature."

"Some informed," Chuks objected. "Most general nuance of ESSIKO concept on Earth."

I felt myself turning pale. It was not just a company then! "And what does this concept include?"

"Humans must learn gradually."

"No! They must know it now."

"Now is preparation, Ter. No advantages if come ahead."

"Advantages for whom? For you again?"

"For everyone."

"Really? How will you continue the preparation—with that euphoria stuff again, metamorphoses, and rituals?" I pointed angrily toward the Yusians still entranced among the dancing flames. "You want to continue all your rituals, Chuks, to impose them on the colonists until you change their souls—"

"True," he interrupted me, "but stimulus in union of two minds."

"The foundations of this union are going to be laid here on Eyrena, right?"

"Yes. Promote that some time now to facilitate process."

"And from here you're going to impose it on Earth as well."

"As all our planets," Chuks added matter-of-factly and then began to explain. "Facing necessity to communicate, Ter, and will form only if we give up our nature and meet where no self recognized but other already known."

"Enough! I see through your wicked games now. You want to degenerate us into some human-Yusian hybrids!"

"Concept 'degenerate' not in target."

"You bet it *is*! I repeat: you're trying to degenerate us into some freaks because you're unable to accept us the way we are."

"Able to accept *us*?" The creature was trying sarcasm now.

"Humans, Chuks, are capable of doing anything," I said with pride, "with one exception: we don't give up on our own kind."

"But why? Directing you into becoming something more than now."

His reflections were truly astonishing! "We don't *want* to be more than *humans*," I emphasized. "We're completely *satisfied* with what we are."

My last statement, maybe a little exaggerated, unexpectedly caused Chuks to lose his composure. "Humans insufficient!" his voice boomed, and if the walls of the gorge had been real, they would probably have reverberated with the powerful echo of what he said. "Stopped with death man Stein coming toward us! On Earth humans only interpret Yusian presence and do same on Eyrena! Ter visit Chuks by disagreement and so too empty Yusian base. Ter kill there!"

"I killed that woman by accident. But she deserved it anyway. She was—a traitor."

"She help us establish contact, give access her mind. But you—"

"Stop it!" I objected angrily. "I can only be judged by humans. And what exactly do you think you're doing? Do you really think that the union of two minds means simply mechanically mixing them together?"

"Not so simple. Rebellion for our instincts too."

"Now I understand, Chuks!" I heaved a sigh of relief. "You Yusians have progressed as far as possible, and now you're just groping in the dark—just trying variants that aren't working, but you won't admit defeat and give them up."

This time, to my astonishment, Chuks showed no signs of insult or disagreement. "What our variants under your opinion, Ter?" he asked quietly.

"Everything that I have seen," I generalized without hesitation. "For example, what good would it have done for us to meet as two *human-Yusians*? And what 'impersonal understanding' were you talking about just before you brought me into this ritual? No understanding is *impersonal* because only a *person* can *understand*. A real encounter between us, Chuks, is only possible while you are Yusian and I am human. It's quite obvious, though, that such a personal encounter will be torture for both of us."

We fell silent. The gorge beside us was already fading, as were the other Yusians and the skeletal plants, the smooth slanted walls, and the flat mirror roof of a sky above—disappearing just as a mirage gradually disappears.

It was high time I finished this conversation. I had learned enough for now and, what's more, had said enough. Enough that I wondered if I would be allowed to leave the Yusian base at all. No doubt Chuks had not given me any involuntary information despite my "professional" interrogation techniques. On the contrary, I knew that he had tried to express himself in a manner more understandable to me, more human. He really wanted me to learn the ultimate goal of ESSIKO. The very way he tried to make it clear to me—with implications, objections, and facts he pretended to be revealing by accident—proved to me that first he wasn't authorized to give me that information and second Yusians, like humans, are in the habit of monitoring conversations conducted by their representatives. That meant I should hurry my good-bye before they decided what to do with me.

"Presuppose energy low, Ter." Chuks also seemed to understand this and was urging me to leave.

"Yes," I looked at him with genuine friendliness. "I do feel tired."

"Good, good!" he said enthusiastically in his old tone. "Will move you away!"

He really did move me away, returning me to the "mush-room greenhouse" in the fastest manner possible. We parted there without any further pleasantries, and soon I was also free of my Yusian space suit. I again was supplied clothes similar to the ones I had worn on my arrival, except for their ESSIKO labels, after which I immediately headed for the exit.

CHAPTER 30

After I visited the Yusian base, my life on Eyrena felt even more precarious, so I went directly to my apartment and encoded my own theories about possible Yusian weaknesses. Recent circumstances made me reluctant to entrust this information even to my restricted data bank on the server. Because of weariness and lack of sleep, neither my brain nor my hand worked properly, so the task took me nearly an hour. The text was not as coherent as I had hoped, but I still stored it in my computer and, without editing it, sent it to Reder, copying Vey A. Zung. I was convinced that the two communicated freely and that Reder, regardless of his feelings about me, would forward it to him anyway. Zung would hardly be happy to get the message but would realize that there was too much at stake to leave it unread. If he wanted to read it, he would have to seek the help of my boss, P. R. Franklin, since only Franklin could decipher the secret code I used.

Next on my list to do were a refreshingly cool bath, a bite to eat, and a meeting with Vernie regarding the robots, but I dozed off first in the tub and then a couple of times while I was eating. In short, I wouldn't be ready to meet anyone until I had napped for a few hours.

I woke up around noon. How I managed to sleep for the first time near the cones puzzled me but didn't matter much anyway.

I tried to reach Vernie, but he didn't answer any of my numerous phone calls. Probably he was at the bunker again, and I still didn't have the vaguest idea of its real purpose, I must admit.

I carefully checked my flexor, left the lodge, and descended the irritatingly picturesque stone staircase. From the top of the stairs, I spotted Elia and Jerry entering the medical laboratory. I wanted to follow her, just to say hello, but instead went to the parking lot and programmed my shuttle to take me to the biosector. I landed in front of the building in which, late at night on March twenty-fifth, the robots assembled the biozone extrainer shipped from Earth as instructed by Reder and Stein. The moment had come, or maybe had come and gone, to follow up on a hunch.

The building consisted of a spacious hall connected to cubicles for the preliminary processing of organic material, apparently specifically for the extrainer. It was functioning even now. I sent the two staff robots outside and immediately entered my emergency password in the system. The information I needed was quickly displayed, and in just a few more seconds, I had deciphered Franklin's cable to Stein. It was the usual laconic: "Agreed." Now everything was obvious to me, but look how many days had to pass before that happened!

Yes, Fowler and Stein had been IBI agents planted—maybe through Genetti—in the group leaving for Eyrena. When the directive from Genetti's Special Sector arrived, my boss didn't know they had been murdered and simply decided to send me here as the official representative of IBI, an official badly needed on Eyrena anyway. So that was why he didn't object to my urgent dispatch here: he was counting on *them* to fill me in on the situation in much greater detail than he could himself. That was the exact reason why he gave me an emergency password and a secret code that coincided with theirs. Unlike them, I was traveling openly as IBI, and these would enable us all to contact each other. However, since Fowler and Stein were dead, the password and code had taken on totally different roles.

So Franklin's "Agreed" was in reply to a message sent to him by Stein. How exactly Stein sent that message was easy to guess, since the Yusians send nothing from Eyrena to Earth except non-coded reports from the base commander and individual requests from the base for equipment, tools, and materials. Stein had needed to encode his message by incorporating a prearranged phrase in such a request. I could even guess its contents: he must have insisted on permission to return to Earth. Only there could he report fully his already firm opposition to the colonization project.

I erased my activities from the system and walked outside. The two robots were waiting for me on the threshold.

"Enter!" I ordered them.

I waited for them to close the door behind their massive backs and then boarded the shuttle. I took off very slowly, flying low above the plant pillars that had formed overnight. I was thinking of Genetti. Now I understood that the foil he had tried to give me would confirm that Fowler and Stein were also IBI agents. He suspected that they had been murdered, and his heart wouldn't let him send another man on a certain death mission. Since he was under constant surveillance and couldn't get in touch with Franklin or prevent my coming here in any other way, he had tried at least to warn me.

"I'll never forget you, old man," I whispered. "Never!"

I thought about Fowler and Stein. Two men, murdered before I arrived, yet ironically so close to me.

Their plan if Franklin replied affirmatively must have been decided on beforehand and simplified to the maximum: Stein would have needed to enter the necessary information for decoding of his restricted data bank into Reder's computer and head for the Yusian base immediately afterward. Fowler, in turn, was supposed to camouflage this and misdirect the search for Stein by sending his shuttle to the southern settlement.

Apparently everything in this plan was dictated by their attempt to gain enough time. Until the experiment scheduled for noon, Reder had some work to do in the open field, so—if he hadn't been spying on Stein—he would have found Stein's instructions in his own computer that afternoon at the earliest, which was the only thing that could have aroused his suspicion that Stein had in fact gone to the Yusians. By then, however, Stein would have been on his way; as everyone knew, the starship always took off for Earth one day after its arrival, which is always when Ridon is at its zenith.

So Stein informs Fowler of Franklin's approval, and the exact time of this radio contact sets the plan in motion and synchronizes their next actions. Fowler leaves in his trailer for the shipment drop-off but hides it behind the first cone in the valley behind the slope. Then he finds a good vantage point on the ridge and bides his time until he climbs down to the parking lot to program Stein's shuttle. Stein calmly proceeds to Reder's office, not knowing that all the time Reder has been watching his every move.

Why Stein didn't decode his research results through his own computer is clear: it would be checked for clues as soon as they learned of his disappearance. Nor could Fowler assume that task, or he would have incriminated himself as Stein's accomplice. So they chose the computer most convenient for the purpose, which, unfortunately, happened to be Reder's.

I looked down at the transparent floor. The shuttle was crawling just centimeters above the tops of the pillars, but I gradually stopped noticing them. In my mind's eye, they became instead long rows of the weird reddish ferns, just as they had been on that last morning for those two...

Stein finishes the first part of the plan, and it is already time for him to head for the Yusian base. That is when he begins to hesitate. Fate or his convictions may have decided him to become an IBI agent, but he was above all a great scientist. Having devoted most of his life to his research, the thought that he would not be able to complete it probably galled him. Naturally, he understood very well that going to the Yusians with a record of the research results in his possession would be an unacceptable risk. Still, at the last moment, when one's sense of inevitability is the sharpest, his scientific passion drives him to throw caution to the wind and make the fatal mistake—not only for himself but also for Fowler—of using Reder's computer to request the microdisk of his records from the server. Then, instead of heading for the Yusian base, he returns first to the base to collect it.

From that moment on, Reder stops stalking him because the data in his computer eloquently revealed that, after getting the microdisk, Stein intended to ask the Yusians to take him as a passenger on the starship. And they would give him their permission, since it was not the Yusians but Zung who wanted to isolate the people here, so that he could exert greater control over them.

I gave the shuttle a command for another low, slow flight over the area below and concentrated on the events of that morning. Reder was determined to stop Stein, whose return to Earth would compromise the colonization project. But how could he act without incriminating himself? Well, that was easy—by using someone else from our base to alert the Yusians. So Zung's agent, who had for months demonstrated nothing but overwhelming horror of everything Yusian and who even preferred his rickety jeep to their "unnatural" machines, goes to the lodge and, without hesitation, lays his hands on a communication disk. He pretends to be Stein and says, "I would like to travel to Earth with you. If you don't mind, please confirm by returning this call," or something of the kind. The Yusians, very polite as usual, hurry to honor the request of "Hans Stein."

But who do they really contact? The person on duty at the base, Elia? Or Larsen, the base commander? Or Vernie, Larsen's deputy? As a matter of fact, since only these three communicator codes were operational, and since they are indifferent toward us as individuals, they probably use one of them at random.

So Fowler and Stein would be murdered, and the one who would commit those murders did not even suspect yet that this was going to happen. After the Yusians called, he—or she?—carried out an emergency check of the most important data stored in the server. Whoever did that would not have found evidence of any ill-intentioned operations on Stein's part but would have noted his request for the microdisk and so would have headed for the main server, hoping to waylay him as he was collecting his copy.

In the meantime, Fowler loads the automatic program into Stein's shuttle and returns to the ridge again to wait for the shuttle to take off. These minutes turn out to be fatal for him because, before the shuttle leaves, Stein appears at the base. I can only imagine Fowler's astonishment at this alteration in their plan. It must have been difficult for him to decide what to do after he figures out from seeing Stein enter the administrative building that he is there to collect a recording of his research results.

Stein leaves the base shortly afterward and this time heads for the forest, in the direction of the Yusian base, while Fowler remains to confirm activation of the shuttle program. Whatever he intended to do after the shuttle's departure—try to stop Stein or let him go to the Yusians with the microdisk—doesn't really matter. What followed was something neither had foreseen.

The person provoked by Reder's plotting arrives after Stein has already picked up the microdisk and enters the administrative building before Fowler's eyes. Discovering that the microdisk was picked up just minutes before, Reder's "tool" decides to catch up with Stein, but without using a shuttle so that the Yusians would think that Stein canceled his trip on his own, that it was his decision. This is also the reason why the pursuer doesn't sound an alarm.

But Fowler is still waiting on the ridge. When the pursuer leaves the building and heads on foot straight for the forest, he immediately realizes that this person has somehow learned about his and Stein's plan. Since Stein's shuttle is already on its way toward the southern settlement, Stein will have turned off his mobile phone, as arranged beforehand, so that anybody who called him would think he was still in his shuttle. I remembered that these Yusian machines in flight always lose radio contact. So Fowler no longer has a choice. He must catch up with Stein *first*, without being noticed by the other one.

The chase continued for at least about an hour, while the Eyrenean forest was still in its maddening morning condition. The three of them must have rushed among the dancing trees, struggling to overcome their euphoria. Stein's pursuer could have only one objective: to reach the end of the forest before Stein and ambush him there on the empty strip between the forest and the pillars, which was the only spot with good visibility.

Fowler must have had the same idea. When he nears that spot, however, he runs into the escaping pursuer. Fowler, judging maybe by a reaction or facial expression, understands that this person has just killed Stein. Despite that, he trusts this person so much that he lets a *killer* come closer. "Fowler was my friend," Larsen, Elia, and Vernie had *all* told me. Yet one of them shot Fowler at point-blank range.

Did the murderer return to retrieve Stein's personal belongings or already have them, planning to check them out safely elsewhere? That doesn't matter much. The important thing is the decision to leave them instead in Fowler's pockets—except the microdisk, of course. Discharging part of the charge of Fowler's flexor before carefully securing it in his right hand, the now double murderer fails to notice that Fowler's left hand is still clenching Stein's effigy. Realizing that Stein was probably dead, Fowler must have involuntarily taken out this "keepsake" Stein had given him earlier.

Next the murderer would head for the biosector and commit a substantial error by deleting the hard drive in Stein's computer before double-checking to be sure that the request to the server originated from there. In a hurry, afraid of being discovered in Stein's office, the murderer chooses what seems a logical solution. Who would suspect that Reder's computer could be involved too—that Reder himself would have a part to play in this crazy story?

Then the murderer returns to his or her workplace and waits there for the inevitable alarm signal.

At the same time, but in his open field, Reder waited as well, impatient to learn the outcome of the events he had triggered. He of course supposed that Stein would be detained alive on Eyrena. And then? Stein would admit to using Reder's computer before heading for the Yusian base, but Reder would pretend he hadn't "discovered" that yet. He could deny contacting the Yusians, raising the unanswered question of who *had* called them? And Fowler? He would only speak up if Stein had been murdered. In any case, his testimony couldn't endanger Reder.

Anyway, when the double murder was discovered, Reder found himself in an even more advantageous position. Now he possessed Stein's research results in secret—a secret not even shared by the murderer because, without the access codes, the microdisk was worthless.

And while the provocateur and the murderer waited…

Back in the forest, the crystal rain trickling down each and every branch of the leafless Eyrenean trees gradually abated. The tree trunks shrank, releasing long sighs; their white coats melted and ran down in glistening rivulets. Their rough bark slowly turned yellow—as did the dead faces of Fowler and Stein. The tree roots slowly sank back into the ground, rocking the lifeless bodies with indolent curiosity, as the supersensitivity of this hybrid pseudoforest—neither Yusian nor earthly—was lulled to sleep, satiated. All fell silent, immobile, and heavy with time—the "accumulated individual time" plundered from those two bodies by the most destructive of biological processes—death. Then replaced by another time: both human and Yusian, terrestrial and nonterrestrial.

"Every object that takes part in a chronal exchange with Yusian bioinorganic structures gives its memory to them and at the same time keeps it intact to itself. In turn, however, it becomes a carrier of their memory as well, expressed in the combination of their chronal connections with the Yusian system," Stein had written. If that were so, then in the silence and yellow twilight, those two dead human bodies were both themselves and particles that had no analogy: details, links in the polyplane-tary system of the Yusians, integrated inextricably into it, trans-formed into Yusian property. They had taken on the unique task of "remembering" in every *cell* entire human and Yusian histo-ries and unite them into one.

CHAPTER 31

"This is outrageous, Simon!" Reder protested as soon as he pulled up in front of the lodge. "I'm a busy man. I *work*, you know. You can't waste my time like this."

I sat beside him as his jeep deftly navigated the cones. "No need to drive too far," I said. "My time's precious too."

"Ha!" he made a scornful grimace and slammed on the brakes. "Come on! Let's talk now. Why did you call for me?"

I beat around the bush at first. "You've been sending robots to the deserted base to bring you things—like the Yusian figure of Odesta, for instance."

"Ha, ha, ha! 'Figure'!"

"It doesn't matter what we call it, Reder. What's important is that in that base is a hall where strange flames are being ejaculated—"

"My God! What are you saying? That's obscene, Simon!"

"And its floor," I continued, "has somehow interacted with the biopolymer plates on the elbow and knee joints of these robots. Which means that they've been lying on that floor, on their 'bellies,' since the same plates on their necks haven't been affected."

"So what? I really don't understand what all this nonsense means!"

"You *should* say you don't understand why some robots lie on their 'bellies,' here or there. Or maybe you *do* understand that?"

"I understand nothing!" he snapped but suddenly paled, making the bruises from our fight the day before stand out on his cheeks even more clearly.

"Last night I took a trip to the active Yusian base, Reder, where there were also flames like those I just described to you. And some Yusians were lying on the floor among them."

"And maybe you too?" He glared at me.

"See, you do understand! Of course I participated. We must respect the rituals of other cultures, right?"

"It's a matter of principles, Simon. Personally, I would never subject myself to the effects of any alien rites."

"True, it *would* be much easier for you to watch them with Zung on the holofilms you've been receiving from the Yusians— the ones you've squirreled away in your steel-plated strong box, though you were supposed to treat them as communal property."

"You're defending these wretched creatures? You think they're your friends?"

"If that's true, we must have mutual friends, Reder."

"What! How dare you!"

"Well, judge for yourself. You knew back on Earth that the ES-SIKO robots are jammed with Yusian "memories," thoughts, intentions, and so forth. You know that the Yusian mentality and their attitude toward us have been programmed into them. Yet you still use these same robots freely, knowing perfectly well that everything they hear, see, or do is instantly conveyed to the Yusians."

"That is precisely *why* I use them!" he exclaimed. "For camouflage! I use them solely for insignificant activities or those activities I don't need to keep secret. They have no idea, Simon, about the serious work I do."

"Your colleagues, though—"

"They treat them in the same way, even though they think ESSIKO is a human company. These robots are not transported in sealed containers as are all the other shipments, so everybody here is convinced that the Yusians have equipped them with espionage devices."

"So you think that no one suspects the real truth?"

"I have no idea," Reder said nonchalantly. "It's possible they all suspect it—by now."

I studied his face closely and, after I felt I had given him enough food for thought, added just as nonchalantly, "By the way, I wanted to meet Vernie today too, but he didn't answer his mobile phone. He must have left it somewhere before he went down below."

Despite this sharp turn in our conversation, Reder quickly managed to look astonished. But his attempt to respond smoothly and logically was far from successful. "Why do you think he left his phone behind?"

"Because down below it would be out of range. Or maybe it wouldn't?"

"Where is this *down below*, Simon?"

I let him sweat some more. "The bunker" was apparently the answer he feared I might give.

"In the underground rooms at the defractor site, of course," I finally said. "I assume the important work is done there, since all the surface machinery is operated by the robots."

"Yes, yes, that's true." Reder nodded. "We use them everywhere we can. As soon as we got here, we took all precautions to disarm them."

"What precautions did you take?"

"Simple but efficient. At the entrances to all the important places where we don't want alien observers, we installed laser barriers that are harmless to us, but the robots can't cross them."

"How did you do that without the robots' help? Especially underground?"

"It was hard, Simon. Extremely hard! It certainly wasn't easy. While we do have our own REM robots, all they can do is the rough work. We were left with all the operations requiring precision."

"OK, Reder. Let's say you solved the robot problem here. On Earth, though—"

"Don't worry about that, OK?" He smiled. "The number of robots there has always been strictly limited. And on Earth the company isn't entirely owned by the Yusians, Simon. We have our share in it and monitor everything the company produces. As soon as this colony is operational, we'll destroy the robots and raze their damned company to the ground."

"Don't try to focus my attention on that company," I said. "To me, it's quite clearly just an auxiliary link in something much more global. That's why I want to ask you directly: What do you and your boss think is the main goal of ESSIKO?"

"One word: assimilation," Reder immediately responded through clenched teeth, not even impressed by my insight. "Yes, their goal is to assimilate humankind! You should have found that out yourself."

I shook my head. "What I found out is that the ESSIKO project is nothing but a mistake. Or to be more precise, a series of mistakes, both ours and theirs."

He sighed, pretending to be bored. "Tell me, then, what *their* mistakes are."

"Everything they've done, since arriving on Earth until now, has been a total mistake. The fact that they're engaged in producing pseudoterrestrial materials and objects, this entire modified planet with its metamorphoses and frenetic effects, and their naive creations bearing the label ESSIKO—"

"*Naive* you call them! If you let Yusians remain on Earth, they'll literally flood it with these creations! Among them are things we haven't even dreamed of, but I've seen them, even experienced how they work! Take the robots alone as our example: Can you imagine what it will be like if the Yusians multiply them by the thousands, even by the millions?"

"What *will* it be like? Do you expect them to start a war with robot soldiers and turn us into slaves? If the Yusians really wanted such an outcome, they wouldn't have played with robots and euphoria, Reder. That's not what they want, but not because they have any particular affection for us. Do you know why? Out of concern for themselves. They understand that an ultimate failure in their relationship with us would have dire consequences for them as well."

"That's just wishful thinking!" He waved his hands nervously. "Besides, neither Zung nor anyone working for him even supposes that the Yusians will start killing us. They want to destroy what's *human* in us! To recycle our souls! And you—how come you haven't grasped that so far!"

"I *have* grasped it," I said slowly. "They *haven't*, though, and therein lies the problem."

Finally Reder regarded me more searchingly, but he quickly donned his next mask: that of complete cynicism.

"Just how did you reach this remarkable conclusion, Inspector Simon? Could you shed some light on that for me?"

"No. You just made it quite clear that any explanation would fall on deaf ears. Now I simply want you to remember a few *facts* and report them to your boss as soon as possible. I just hope he'll be reasonable enough to understand what they mean."

"Reasonable? How dare you talk about reason, you—"

"Shut up! Shut up and listen carefully! What we *reasonably* consider unconscionable assimilation is interpreted differently by the Yusians. So much so that they must suffer themselves in their attempts to achieve—"

"Hold it! Hold it right there! They suffer—in what sense?"

"In the literal sense. They have convinced themselves that only a convergence of human and Yusian minds and emotions will allow them to establish any real contact with us. That we'll be able to understand each other only if we each sacrifice our selves to become—God knows what! Some hybrid of human and Yusian."

Reder's reaction surpassed my most pessimistic expectations: his uncontrollable laughter was more eloquent than anything he could have said in words.

"You seem to think," I said as he calmed down, "that once the colonization is complete and you destroy their chronal centers on Earth, everything will be just fine. I suggest you try to see a little further and imagine what the full consequences of all this might be."

"As far as those creatures are concerned, Simon, without their centers, Earth will be a long, long journey for them. They will need to overcome *space*, not just time. The planetary system of Eridan is their nearest access to Earth, and that system is about one hundred fifteen light-years away. Now *you* try to imagine how much we can gain in the long run. Almost two centuries!"

"And what about the colonists who will be trapped here?"

"Terminally ill patients, criminals, and mentally deranged. Let the creatures 'converge' with them!"

"But if something like that really happens, it will inevitably come back to haunt us in the future. Or don't you care what happens to humanity after those two hundred years?"

"Whether I care or not is of no possible significance. After all, do you really think that your—rather dubious—facts offer us any new alternatives?"

"On the contrary. Our one chance lies in the hope of correcting the mistakes made."

"The mistakes of the Yusians? You mean *we* should correct *them*?"

"Yes. All of us, although *you* deserve all the blame for these mistakes—you, Zung, and his cowardly clique. As soon as the Yusians arrived, you people created an atmosphere of servility and obedience around them. You showed them only our pitiable, vulnerable side."

"Maybe *you* will show them the other side—our invincible, majestic one," Reder said sarcastically.

"Exactly! Me and many others like me. We can show them that this time they are *really* playing with fire. And it can *really* recycle them. Just alone, even with their polyplanetary system, starships, and all their constructions, they can't guarantee their spiritual superiority."

"Not their spiritual superiority. But they are fully capable of obliterating *us*. Especially if we start trying to correct their 'mistakes.'"

"Listen, Reder," I said calmly, "looking at you, I think I could quite easily obliterate *you* with just these two fists of mine, but

I'm not doing it. Instead, I'm trying to convince you, to make you see certain things. Why do you think I'm doing that?"

When I mentioned obliterating him, Reder instinctively reached for his flexor, but then he suddenly blushed deeply. Was he angry, insulted, and ashamed? I didn't know, so I continued, "I see that you don't understand a thing. The answer is very simple: if I remove you as an obstacle, I'm admitting my total intellectual impotence before you. I'll be a coward in my own eyes. Besides that, as long as you're around, I can always hope that, sooner or later, I'll be able to reason even with you. Nobody, human or Yusian, is crazy enough to abandon such hopes, however small they may be!"

I climbed out of the jeep, briefly meeting Reder's eyes as I left. I read the usual hatred for me there, but they also seemed to express some vague hesitation, maybe even a hint of sympathy. But I was wrong.

"Hey, Simon." He grinned at me. "Don't count too much on your message reaching Zung either."

"Why not?"

"Because, since the day of the murders, Larsen himself has been the only one who is making ours requests to Earth, so there's no way I could send Zung any information."

Suddenly stepping on the gas pedal, Reder zoomed past me and disappeared among the cones.

CHAPTER 32

Larsen was sitting on the concrete stoop in front of one of the "temporary" buildings in his research field, staring into empty space. He didn't budge when I sat down next to him.

"You know," I began quietly, as if speaking to a sick person, "last night I visited the active Yusian base to meet an acquaintance of mine—maybe I could call him a friend."

He slowly turned to me. "Again you present me with a fact I can do nothing about," he said with surprising indifference, "but I don't want to argue with you anymore."

"But you have to listen to me."

"If I have no other choice."

"You don't. Because you need to be made aware of many things—things you should have learned without my help."

"Well, certainly there are things we both know about."

"True," I said bitterly, "but their meanings are elusive, though we do know that some of them were totally senseless."

Larsen shivered slightly. "Senseless," he repeated quietly. "Horribly senseless."

We remained silent, each oppressed by a feeling of utter impotence in the face of unendurable, pointless loss. Finally I forced myself to continue.

"In this secret war we've been waging lately, Larsen, each of us is a loser. We are losing ourselves and gradually destroying others."

"Sometimes not gradually at all."

"That's why we have to stop now! To end this pointless war between losers."

"There are also winners," he said gloomily. "There have been from the very beginning."

"You're wrong. The Yusians are losers too. But how were we supposed to know that? Right after they showed up on Earth, we chose Zung and others to be our representatives and decided we insured our right to sink into a cowardly isolationist policy. For example, you've been living on this planet for seven months now and haven't once visited the Yusians. You came to Eyrena simply to discover the 'secrets' of their technology. You work day and night, putting all your energy into learning these mechanical details, but it never occurred to you that you should try to discover the 'secrets' of their psychology."

"I think Odesta was trying to do just that," Larsen responded with hostility, "and maybe she would have succeeded."

"No. She let herself be a guinea pig for the Yusians, hoping to help them understand *our* psychology and thus feel merciful toward humankind. She was passive, humble to the point of humiliation because of what she considered superiority, and that was her unforgivable mistake. The Yusians need to see us as individuals, not—what they saw in Odesta Gomez."

"Let's not blame the dead, Simon. They can't defend themselves."

"At the moment I'm blaming you, not the dead," I almost shouted. "You're passive too and equally convinced in Yusian superiority. You feel overwhelmed because of the difference in our technological levels. But in fact, Larsen, the advantage here is ours rather than theirs."

Puzzled, he raised his eyebrows. "And what exactly is our advantage? Compared to them, we might as well still be living in caves!"

"Yes, you could say that," I said, ignoring his sarcasm. "We have many problems: ecological, energetic, demographic, and political—all kinds of problems that the Yusians solved for themselves long ago. Now *we* are their only problem. Establishing real contact with us became the *only* purpose of this civilization that has already achieved its other goals. This is why it's far more important and crucial for them than it is for us, especially now that they're beginning to feel a lack of the spiritual energy needed to carry it out. Their colossal technological development, Larsen, is the precise reason for their lack of spiritual energy."

My last words obviously caught his attention.

"Because," I continued, encouraged, "their notorious poly-planetary system has been functioning faultlessly for centuries—maybe even millenniums. It became extremely stable, thus conservative, so the Yusians were left with only the same routine decisions to make. Even their social life has become too stable and conservative."

"Well, at least"—Larsen smiled wryly—"we can't complain we have a stable social life. So *that* must be what you see as our big advantage."

"You're speaking ironically again, but it really *is* an advantage. Think about it: we are used to changes and adapt to them more easily. Also, making mistakes is not unusual for us, so it rarely upsets us greatly—as it would the Yusians. Most importantly, we can risk losing more painlessly than they can. The constant instability of life has taught us this. Our decisions and acts, Larsen, unlike the Yusians', can be unexpected. unpredictable, and revolutionary in spirit. And the task we are facing now *requires* decisions like that!"

"Well...I...don't think I understand you."

"I'm saying we are wrong again to leave the initiative for real contact to the Yusians. *We* have to take the initiative, because we are far more capable of bringing it to a positive conclusion."

"Capable? Nonsense! After ten years since their arrival, we're still not ready even to adopt a consistent attitude toward them. Can you imagine what would happen if we *really* had to make such 'revolutionary' decisions? We would sink into misunderstandings and personal ambitions. Into endless conflicts among ourselves!"

"Unfortunately, that's true. We've managed to turn even the meeting with another civilization into an arena for our own passions, and they are blinding us to the danger they are causing. But enough hiding behind this abstract 'we,' Larsen. Only two of us are here—you and I."

"OK, then let's be frank: What do you want from me?"

"To help me defeat the colonization plans," I answered. "They will prevent us from ever moving in the right direction. The Yusians will try their inhuman experiments on the Eyrenean colonists, and we both know what *that* will come to. It will only increase the gap between our civilizations, because the Yusians will then *deserve* our distrust and hatred. The hostility between us will become eternal, not to mention the equally eternal burden of our own guilt for having exposed so many people to Yusian injustice with the extremely immoral excuse that they are defective and useless."

"But we have to recover." Larsen guiltily avoided looking at me. "After a period of thirty years—"

"No," I interrupted him, "it's not going to be just thirty years. There is a way to deny the Yusians access to Earth for about two centuries, and Zung plans to use it once the colonization is completed. And only the 'defective' people will be sent here—no leading scientists will be included to spy on the colony, because their work would have no meaning. Nor will yours."

"OK, let's suppose you're telling me the truth. But two centuries! That's very tempting."

"On the contrary! All that time, until the Yusians actually return to Earth again, humankind will remember this as a giant deception and will be expecting the Yusian revenge, constantly living with that nightmare. Our progress will be directed solely at preparing for a future cosmic war. A very probable war, in fact, because *then* the Yusians will not be simply puzzled and incapable of understanding us, the way they are now."

"What exactly do you want me to do?" Larsen asked.

"To inform your bosses about everything I told you. Tell them that you too are against the colonization. I'm sure you were sent to Eyrena in the first place to arrive at your own opinion of its value, so your word will carry a lot of weight. Since my opinion will influence IBI, Zung will be between a rock and a hard place."

"I see! The old methods again."

"But now they are aimed at a new perspective and result," I specified.

"OK—say we succeed. Then what? Who will take charge of the impossible mission of explaining to the Yusians that we are canceling the agreement?"

"I will. Yes, I'll try to prove to them that to cancel is in their own best interest."

"You'll try." Larsen was staring at me tensely. "Even you say only that you will *try*. And if you fail?"

"We must take the risk. Only this way will we have a real chance to win. Accepting the colonization guarantees our loss one hundred percent."

He abruptly stood up, but this move seemed to use up his entire impulse for determined action because, at the next moment, his face expressed overpowering pessimism. "No, Simon, it's too late to change anything."

"Why? If we send detailed reports, me to IBI, you to the center—"

"Let me remind you that we can only send noncoded reports from here. And then only to one person: Zung."

"We still have another way: I'll return to Earth and defend our position."

"It's impossible. On the day you left for Eyrena, Zung convinced the Yusians to agree not to take any passengers to Earth without his explicit approval. They officially informed me of this."

Genetti! The thought pained me. *He wanted to help me, but in reality.* Genetti's piece of foil had provided Zung with the information that Fowler and Stein had been IBI agents, so he must have realized, or at least supposed, why they have been killed. That's why he had immediately requested that agreement.

"I see. Zung has turned this planet into a prison. But this time I'll find a flaw! And our reports will reach their addressees."

Larsen's grimace told me I said more than I should have, but it was too late to fix that now.

"Aha!" he exclaimed, "you're suggesting we ask for help— from your Yusian 'friend'? Put ourselves in a position of being dependent on him?"

I felt extremely tired. "Dependent? How would we be dependent?"

"No! I'll never put the fate of humankind in the 'hands' of some alien!" He was shaking with fury. "*Ne-v-er*, do you hear me?"

"You won't be putting anybody's fate—"

"You're a traitor! And crazy as well! It's not normal for a human to serve alien interests!"

I looked at him disdainfully. "I'm not serving anybody's interests, Larsen. My master is common sense, and that requires me to fight against everything that undermines it—including the inexcusable failure to act of a nonentity posing as the base commander!"

He reached for his flexor, just as Reder had reached for *his* an hour earlier. And, just like Reder, he stopped himself.

"Go," he whispered, maybe not to me but to whatever nightmare was haunting him. "I'm not going to…to…argue anymore. With anyone—ever!"

"You'd better start arguing with yourself, Commander," I cautioned. "The time for weighing your options is over. I can't wait very long for you to make up your mind."

CHAPTER 33

In fact I couldn't afford to wait at all. Still, when I sat down at my desk to prepare my report for Franklin, I already knew I wouldn't take it to Chuks the next day. The decisive moment had passed, and now it was my turn to hesitate and doubt.

Who was Chuks in the end? Some nonhumanoid. I thought of how he and I rescued the strange Yusian from the biostation and how he showed me the miracles of the starship—to demonstrate supremacy or just to show hospitality? How he hurried me away from the Yusian base after explaining to me so many Yusian projects, probably at great risk.

Who was he? A thinking creature with hesitations and doubts, just like me? Who already has similar goals to mine, just because a few times he met me—some humanoid—and maybe understood me, at least a little? But what guarantees did I have that I was right? What else if not those few moments of almost friendly compassion, or did even that mutuality exist only in my imagination?

I finished planning my report, but those questions kept gnawing at my conscience, puzzling and unanswerable. I put my electronic notebook in the safe, intending to write the report the next morning. Then I took a quick shower, ate a few sandwiches, set the alarm to wake me before the rise of Ridon, and climbed into bed hoping to get some sleep until then.

As I was drifting off, I heard somebody enter my living room. I jumped out of bed and kicked open the door, holding my charged flexor with both hands.

Elia stared at me strangely through the ochre dusk. I hesitated before aiming the flexor at the floor but didn't put it away. I no longer trusted anybody on this base, maybe nobody at all.

"Next time don't forget to lock the door if you're so—uneasy." She approached me, tightly wrapped in a thick, checked blanket, and still shivering so hard that her teeth chattered. "I'm cold," she complained, confused. "And put that flexor down. I'm not carrying mine."

Noticing my hesitation, she opened the blanket with something like a smile on her parched lips. She was wearing only a long silk nightgown, which showed clearly that she wasn't hiding any weapon. That confused me as well. I tossed the flexor on the desk, and it cracked loudly as it hit the wooden surface. Elia suddenly ran over to the door leading to the hall and locked it. Then she came back, still shivering.

I impulsively reached out to hug her, but she walked over to the sofa and sat in the corner, her blanket pulled up to her chin. Her tousled hair fell across her face—a face unnaturally strained in an unsuccessful effort to hide her tension. A look of dread ignited the dilated black pupils in her pale eyes, making them appear almost phosphorescent

"You're not cold," I said hoarsely.

"No—I'm terrified!"

"Of what?"

She looked at me as if expecting me to read the answer on her face. Unfortunately, I only understood that it was very important to find out what was troubling her. Now! I sat next to her—slowly, cautiously, and somehow aware that any wrong or abrupt move would drive her away. At the same time, I had an oppressive feeling of guilt: this woman who so moved me had come to me for comfort, but instead of giving her that comfort, I found myself scrutinizing her reactions. All my seeming delicacy had only one purpose—to provoke her to confide something that was obviously very painful for her.

"Come on, Elia," I slightly touched the tips of her fingers, white from squeezing the blanket. "You have to tell me!"

"Do I really have to?" She cowered even further into the corner of the sofa. "That's exactly what I'm not sure of. I don't know. Who are you really?"

"Just before you came I asked myself the same question but about a Yusian. We, at least, are both humans."

"What difference does that make?" Her head sunk heavily. "Humans, Yusians. The mystery is still the same. Or almost the same: What *is* this person in front of me?"

"After all, there comes a moment when we have no choice, when we have to believe, even if we are blindfolded in some way."

"Have to? As if you can order yourself to believe!"

"Listen, Elia." I quit being delicate. "I don't know exactly what has been frightening you lately—you and Vernie, and Reder too, it seems. What is obvious to me is that the thing you fear hasn't happened yet. So it's up to you whether it happens or not. Otherwise you wouldn't be here in this state of painful hesitation. I'm telling you now: give it up! All of you give up—"

"How can you give such advice with no idea what you are talking about!" she exclaimed.

"Because I already know the way you think, which is enough for me to imagine the general nature of what you might be planning to do. I have no doubts that it will be wrong, irreparable, and if Reder is involved, repulsive as well!"

"Reder." Elia closed her eyes. "He *made* me show you the deserted base, and then obviously he discharged the transformer to keep us near there longer. He was sure we wouldn't go near the whale once that digging program began. Yes, yes! He explained it to me in detail. He didn't intend to kill us! He just wanted to divert your attention—"

"To divert my attention from what?"

"From…our…job, which is strictly secret."

After offering this empty answer, Elia suddenly lost control of herself, sobbing desperately in self-accusation. I watched her for some time, suspecting that once again *she* was the one trying to divert my attention. But she was so obviously suffering, her tears flowing so spontaneously and uncontrollably down her face, that only a maniac would doubt them.

My heart melted at her pain. Suddenly I was holding her closely in my arms, kissing the tears away from her wet, frightened face. The blanket slid from her shoulders, and I felt her soft hands caressing me timidly, hopefully, asking for tenderness. I gently lifted her, as if she were something extremely precious and delicate, and carried her to the bedroom.

"I hate the Yusians, Terry!" she whispered, still trembling. "You have to understand that—I hate them."

PART FOUR

CHAPTER 34

The day set for the tests of the defractor turned out to be painful for me from the very beginning. I was almost sure the forthcoming event causing such apparent fear in Elia and Vernie was going to be included in some way in these tests; should I interfere and stop them, without even knowing what it was? Did I have any right to interfere? After all, people here were only doing their jobs. Well, yes or no?

After a long hesitation, the decision I finally made was actually predetermined from the very beginning: I started doing *my* job—by retrieving from the safe my notebook with the plan of my report to Franklin, despite my doubts from last night. On the one hand, the balance between the written, implied, and withheld information depended on whether I was going to send the report through Chuks or not send it at all, but, on the other hand, the answer to *this* question fully depended on achieving that balance.

I finished the report at noon, still without a clearer answer about my intentions than I had this morning. I put the notebook in the pocket of my jacket and then stood on the balcony, trying to catch a sound from the defractor, which was between three and four kilometers away from the lodge. I should have been able to hear at least the roar of the plasma generators, but either they

weren't functioning yet, which was unlikely, or they had muf-
flers, which was even more unlikely.

I went to the kitchen and made lunch for Jerry and me, but
he hardly touched his, upset that I had shown him so little attention today. I petted him, thinking that he would probably have
felt better with Elia. Then I put my jacket on and left the apartment, but I heard such desperate whining from inside that I went
back in and took the frightened puppy with me.

Both of us were in low spirits as we descended the stairs to
the front door, where we almost bumped into one of the robots,
who had started silently walking behind us. I didn't like his presence at all. I stopped. He stopped as well. I took a few steps, and
he did the same.

"What do you want?" I asked.

"I want to keep an eye on you," he answered.

"Why?"

"So I have been ordered."

"By whom and when?"

"By the base commander, yesterday, at eleven p.m."

In other words, Larsen had his reasons to suppose I would
try meeting with Chuks and decided to prevent that. He must
have attached the robot to me as soon as I returned to the lodge.
Unfortunately, this was the direct effect of "showing my cards"
to him, to a human. What was it going to be with a Yusian?

I started walking Jerry to the base complex, the robot rumbling along behind us. My nerves couldn't stand him walking
behind my back. I turned around.

"Walk on the side—two meters from me!" I said, and he
obeyed.

Instead of heading straight to the administrative building, I
stopped at the parking lot. I approached one of the shuttles to see

how the robot would react; he hurried to stand in front of me. "I won't let you leave the base until I'm released from this duty," he explained in a monotone.

"And what exactly can you do to prevent me from leaving the base?"

"I have the right to do anything."

"Including force?"

"Yes."

"Would you kill me if you had to?"

The robot seemed to think about that. "I would kill you, but only by accident," he finally said.

"Very well!" I murmured dejectedly, and Jerry, echoing my mood, snarled at the imperturbable robot.

We kept going without exchanging a word, entered the administrative building and crossed its inappropriately furnished vestibule, walked next to each other along the corridor decorated like an art gallery, and stopped at the server room. I opened the door and tried to close it once Jerry and I entered, but the robot blocked the doorway. I had no choice but to let him in. Then I pointed at the most distant corner: "You can keep an eye on me from there."

He walked backward to the corner, never taking his eyes off me. He might be of Yusian origin, but he still obeyed Larsen's order to the letter. I asked myself how to get rid of him when I needed to and couldn't come up with an answer.

I sat at one of the monitors, using all my patience to go through the series of complicated procedures demanded in order to copy on a disk the file with Stein's research results that was already in my restricted data bank. When I finally succeeded, I scanned my report from the electronic notebook and recorded it onto the same disk, making sure I left no copy of it on the server.

Now came the hardest thing: deciding what I would do with the disk. For a start, no doubt, I needed to guess, if at all possible, how Chuks would respond to its content. I turned the monitor so that the robot couldn't see it and gave a command to bring up Stein's file.

"HANS STEIN, BIOPHYSICS, EXOBIOLOGY, a member of the team at Eyrena base, first expedition." In brief, the professional title and responsibilities of a dead man. Then his words and phrases—his thoughts—began rolling mechanically across the screen, each given equal weight, something that the human brain subconsciously rejects. To me, instead, some words seem to scroll by faster and easier, while others stayed longer before my eyes, as if demanding that I think them over and pay special attention:

Long, long ago their history turned into an ongoing series of small successes in serving the system—each basically repetitive and insignificant—events devoid of individuality, merely a mass of anonymous statistical data.

For thousands of years, they have been living without conflicts, in feigned satisfaction and growing apathy. They explored the galaxy like automatons, developing more and more new planets without discovering anything fundamentally new about any of them. Until they suddenly bump into us.

The encounter is now ten years old. But the contact *they seek—is it possible at all with so many significant differences between us?*

We are becoming victims of our fanatic anthropocentrism. Maybe the Yusians will be as well, but that is hardly a comforting thought.

We can't even imagine how lonely they are.

I stopped reading the material late in the afternoon. Jerry had long ago fallen asleep on my lap, and I had long ago lost confidence in my plan. Now I agreed that entrusting this disk to any Yusian would be a betrayal. While Stein could have erred in certain aspects of his scientific research, his descriptions of our social and ethical relations with the Yusians were absolutely right. He was telling the simple truth, without hiding anything, and it wasn't always flattering for either the Yusians or us.

My report also started to seem *inadmissibly* right and straightforward, challenging and breaking the rules of diplomacy. For better or worse, seeking "the whole truth and nothing but the truth" is essential, but it's also infuriating to discover truths that shatter cherished illusions and dangerous to convey such truths. Why did I think we and the Yusians needed that? Maybe Zung, by drawing a curtain of flattering deceptions and half truths between us, was much more farsighted than I. At least his approach reduced the risk of direct, open conflict. As my boss says, "Sometimes the distorted image can only be clearly seen in a distorted mirror."

I put my electronic notebook and the disk in the inside pocket of my jacket and gave a command to delete my order for copying Stein's file. "NOT POSSIBLE" was the reply displayed on the screen. I checked the range of the prohibition and when it had been given. It applied to absolutely all kinds of deletions and everybody on the base, and it was given on the first day the server was put into service—seven months ago. This added yet another detail that corroborated what I already knew: Reder had saved Stein's file in his computer *only* because it contained an order to copy his research results. Because that order for the microdisk provided a direct, crucial proof against the only person here who could override the prohibition and erase it from the server—against the killer, whose name I had known since yesterday.

I woke Jerry, and we left the room, still followed by the robot. If Larsen knew the robot was Yusian, could he still have given him the same order? I thought for a while before concluding that yes, he could have, and that realization made me shudder!

I was almost sure Larsen wasn't in his office but went there anyway. To my surprise, it was unlocked. I peeked in. On the day of the most significant tests that had been made on Eyrena by humans, at the moment when all their hardest efforts would culminate in either success or failure, the base commander was slumped over his desk, his chin in his palms, his hair messy. Maybe he was drowsing.

"Why are you here?" I blurted out in my surprise.

"You too can come in." Larsen slightly smiled at the puppy.

"Well, yes, the three of us!" I angrily pointed to the robot.

"SN Forty-Five, *you* wait outside," Larsen told him, and the robot remained in the corridor.

I approached the desk. "You owe me some explanations, Larsen," I began threateningly but fell silent once I looked carefully at his face.

No, he wasn't drowsing—in fact, he obviously hadn't even slept last night. His eyes looked old and bleak, devastated. His forehead was creased in a grimace that looked etched in as if held so long it had frozen into a mask. His lips were cracked as after a high fever.

"What's wrong with you?" I lowered my voice unintentionally. "Did something happen?"

He just stretched out his hands. They were trembling.

"How are the tests going?" I worried, suspecting the worst. "Were there complications?"

"The tests?" Larsen looked surprised. "They haven't started yet."

"Why? Did you postpone them?"

"No. They will start." He glanced at the window. "Soon."

I looked out too. Low in the western sky the bright-yellow ball of Ridon was setting. "But what are you waiting for?" I exclaimed and the next minute answered myself. They were waiting for the rise of Shidexa!

CHAPTER 35

"Open the safe!" I abruptly turned to Larsen. "Now!"

He didn't even move. It was obvious that his thoughts were elsewhere. Maybe on the choice he had made long ago—before they began building that satanic defractor—and on the related choice he couldn't find the strength to make now.

"I can't take your side," he admitted, avoiding my eyes. "Nor can I take their side. I don't know—who is right."

"But when you shot Fowler and Stein you knew, is that what you're saying?"

"And you? When you shot Odesta?"

"None of that! Open your safe, Larsen! I'm taking charge of the base, starting now!"

He obviously felt relief when I said this, relieved that someone else was taking over the huge responsibility and was going to decide for him. I was shocked: How could a dignified and no doubt brave man to be brought to such degradation, such moral disgrace, in only a few months?

It wasn't necessary to threaten him with my flexor. He was paralyzed by his overwhelming dilemma and now could only obey orders. He went to the wardrobe, so grotesquely ornate, and opened the doors. As I expected, he had filled it with a huge safe. When he unlocked it, I saw enough weapons and explosives to destroy a whole base—human or Yusian.

348

Among more harmless items on the top shelf there were a few pairs of handcuffs. I took one pair and had Larsen leave his flexor there. Then he returned to his computer and officially transferred his authority to me. Despite his submissive behavior, I had no intention of trusting him. I locked one handcuff around his wrist and attached the other to the metal grid of the fireplace, where even today, like some lurid joke, heatless artificial flames continued to flicker.

I entered an official note into the base log: "Berg Larsen, I, Terence Simon, hereby arrest you for the murders of Andrew Fowler and Hans Stein."

I took an Adler explosive with a neutrino detonator from the safe, which I locked afterward using my own code, and then crossed to the door. After I ordered Jerry to sit behind the desk, I turned to Larsen again. He was slumped on the ceramic ledge of the fireplace, listlessly gazing into the "fire," his cheek leaning on his palm. I opened the door.

The robot was no longer in the corridor but outside, again literally obeying the given order. I stood in front of him.

"SN Forty-Five, report the last received order!"

He responded promptly: "A general order to Eyrena base given at nineteen hundred thirteen hours on all information channels: ALL AUTHORITY, PRIVILEGES, AND RESPONSIBILITIES OF THE BASE COMMANDER ARE TRANSFERRED IMMEDIATELY TO SPECIAL INSPECTOR TERENCE SIMON."

"Fine. Here is your next order, highest priority! Initiate self-destruct sequence in thirty seconds!"

The robot made a strange hissing noise, stepped to the wall, and knelt down. His body began shaking, as though it had sustained a fatal electric shock, and collapsed without any visible changes. I approached it and removed the energy battery from its chest. For good measure, I then discharged my flexor into its head.

On my way to the so-called infirmary, I didn't meet any-body, human or robot. I used the flexor again to open the door, went downstairs, and entered the morgue. I passed the bodies of Odesta, Fowler, and Stein and then took a few steps toward the transporter that I knew was on my side of the room, since two days earlier, I had availed myself of it. Like the one on the hill, it was carefully disguised. When I uncovered it, the plate—cov-ered with frost—rose up, and the platform surfaced. I stepped on it, and after the program paused, it automatically descended.

Soon I was in the gallery far beneath the planet's surface. I managed to find the light switch, turned it on, and started walk-ing. I noticed that there were more restraining nets than yes-terday; I saw new areas with fresh cement, and the ventilation system had been cleaned and worked much better. Obviously a lot of finishing work had been done here during the last two days, mainly by the imperfect, but definitely non-Yusian, REM robots.

When I approached the surgery room, I hung the remote detonator of the Adler explosive under my shirt. I attached the mechanism to one of the supporting pillars and took out the flexor again. I put it in my left hand and placed my right hand on the monitor by the gate. In three seconds, the electronic system recognized my new identity, and the metal wings of the gate silently opened before me. I went in.

As I entered, Elia was at the sterilizer organizing some in-struments and didn't see me. I passed behind her and quietly climbed the stairs to the observation area above the surgery room. I wasn't surprised to find that now it was fully equipped—and looked much like the coordination control center in the de-fractor complex, though more sophisticated.

Vernie was sitting in front of one section of the extremely long control desk, his attention completely on the text showing on the monitor. I stood behind his back.

"Are you ready?" he murmured.

When he received no answer, he turned around. His surprise and consternation were so intense that I almost felt sorry for him.

"Ah, Simon!" he exclaimed, muffling the sound and at the same time managing to pull himself together and casually change the indicator diagrams on the big monitor to his left.

"You must have received the latest order," I said.

"Well, yes, yes. Listen, Simon, I have no idea what Larsen told you about our job here, but you have to know that the tests—"

"I'm going to be in charge of the tests too."

"But you don't understand anything—"

"It doesn't matter. Put the work schedule back on the monitor."

"What schedule?"

"The work schedule of the tests. Now!"

When he kept pretending he didn't understand, I put a heavy hand on his shoulder. "Vernie, the last thing I need is a fourth corpse. But I'm warning you, I won't allow any noncompliance. As far as I'm concerned, this base is in a state of emergency."

He glanced at the flexor in my other hand and then slowly looked up again. His eyes met mine, and the next minute, the schedule reappeared on the monitor. The stages on the indicator diagrams were shown by abbreviations and symbols, most of them unknown to me. But not all of them. I paid particular attention for now only to the green triangular marker in the vertical bar on the right side of the signs, which showed that the schedule was doubtlessly still in its first phase.

I signaled Vernie to stand up, relieved him of his flexor, and put it in my jacket pocket. I then returned my own flexor to its belt holster.

"Continue!" I ordered Vernie.

He reluctantly sat down and began typing the next order but abruptly changed his mind, canceled it, and turned to me hesitantly. "Simon, obviously you have no idea—"

I interrupted him. "Strictly follow the program and don't stall." I pointed to the electronic watch at the control panel. The chronograph showed the time to complete the current phase had almost expired. "I don't want any delays!"

Sighing painfully, he bent over the keyboard and this time completed the command. The chronograph indicated a new moment of inception, and the marker moved to the diagrams a few millimeters down, indicating that Vernie had completed the procedure in time. I let him get on with his job and went to the glass partition that surrounded the entire room. I looked down at Elia, who had begun preparing the operating table, and then went back to the control desk and accessed the program that controlled the surveillance cameras. They appeared on the monitor one by one: from the peaks of the closest cones, a panoramic view of the defractor and three separate perspectives on the hill across from it; a view of the Yusian base through a powerful telescopic lens; and a view of our base. From the defractor site were transmitted internal views of all the key equipment and external views of the buffer zones between them. When I completed my check, only one of the cameras, number six, had failed to transmit an updated image. Number six remained dark.

I noticed that Vernie was again hesitating, so I approached him. He cringed as if expecting me to hit him and started to tell me something but stopped, bit his lips, and activated the radial accelerator. The monitor confirmed that the first stream of supercharged ions had entered the diverter. The polarization indicator started rising, and very soon the scale indicated optimal range. I accessed the adjoining monitor, put it in tracking mode, and saw that the energy density of the ion stream was rising steadily. In general, all was functioning normally, except of course for Vernie, whose psychological instability was close to critical.

After a while I heard steps on the stairs and stood where I couldn't be seen from the entrance. Elia entered, her face deadly pale, but her firm stride showed that she had managed to gain as much self-control as the situation required. She walked straight to Vernie. When he heard her, he quickly spun his chair around and, instead of looking at her, stared directly at me. She followed his eyes, saw me, and moaned as if, in me, she saw one of her nightmares come true.

"Well, we got the latest order, didn't we?" Vernie "reminded" her, as if she were merely pretending surprise. He simulated a cough and continued, "After giving him command of the base, Larsen must have informed him that the tests will be coordinated from here. Am I right, Simon?"

"Concentrate," I told him firmly.

"That's right; I have to concentrate!" He pointed Elia toward the exit and added, "I hope everything goes *without* complications!"

"Yes, yes." She started nodding.

I stopped her when she tried to leave the room. "I think it'll be more convenient if you contact Reder from here."

Now she was the one who hesitated. To show her that she didn't have a choice, I escorted her to the panel controlling the systems in the room and, before her surprised eyes, blocked all doors.

"What do you think you're doing?" she murmured. "Do you realize—"

"Come on! Call Reder."

She reached into the pocket of her work coat. It was obvious she didn't have a flexor or another weapon, but as she was taking out her communicator, I still instinctively tensed up. I tried to cover it up. Today's developments didn't change how close we had been the night before, but they did nothing to deepen that closeness either.

"Ehrlich?" Elia had established contact. Before he responded I indicated that she shouldn't mention I was there. Then I turned on the amplifiers so I could hear what was said. "Ehrlich!" she repeated, irritated.

"Yes?" he answered. "How's it going there?"

"And with you? I mean—are you OK?"

"Am I OK? Me? Elia, tell me what's going on!"

I grasped her forearm to give her a stronger sign but immediately released it. After all, Reder was going to find out I was here sooner or later.

"I insist that we postpone the experiment!" Elia said suddenly. "I don't feel—"

"Enough!" Reder firmly interrupted her. "Stick to the plan!" And he cut the connection.

Vernie and Elia looked at each other with the same confusion and weakness. I didn't let them stay long in this condition but ordered them back to work. Elia went to the curve of the control desk, the central command station judging by the number and arrangement of the monitors. Vernie turned back to the work schedule. I sat down next to him. As I expected, very soon on the display monitor appeared a warning message in bright letters, announcing the installation was approaching critical mode.

"Oh my God!" Vernie murmured, feigning concern. "That's what I was afraid of!"

"What?" I asked.

"The smallest detail can compromise everything. There is a defect in one of the oscillators, Simon! Good thing we are still in the first stage."

Elia came to us right away. "Did something happen?" Her voice reflected her secret liveliness.

"Unfortunately, yes," Vernie answered her. "Turbulent fluctuations beyond the norm in the toroid device. Apparently one of the oscillators—"

"Continue!" I repeated clearly.

"Hey, isn't it obvious?" He acted surprised. "We have to terminate!"

I didn't say anything. The long pause became a silence electrified by expectation. Vernie glanced at me and reached for the main switch. He put his hand on it, and Elia gave a sigh of almost obvious relief—a short-lived relief because I immediately moved his hand off the switch.

"Stick to the plan!" I repeated Reder's final phrase.

"But if we do—and it leads to *disaster*?" Elia whispered, emphasizing the question.

I preferred not to answer her—after all, her question was simply speculative. I turned my attention to the screen displaying the work schedule. The triangular marker had moved down into the bright-red danger zone.

Elia couldn't keep quiet anymore. "We can't go on! You don't know. You don't know anything."

"Are you *sure*?" Vernie also emphasized his question.

I looked at my watch and this time decided to give them an answer, once and for all. I called up the camera aimed at the Yusian base. The monitor showed a Yusian approaching.

"So...you." Fear appeared on Elia's face. Then the fear changed to relief. Finally, her face froze in a grimace of strong disappointment, maybe even disgust.

"Where's the dog?" she asked through her teeth.

"With Larsen," I answered.

"OK." She turned her back toward me and returned to the viewing area.

Next to me Vernie shifted, and I heard his joints crack, as if proving that his petrifaction during these last seconds was physical as well as psychological.

"Get moving!" I urged him and, as an additional stimulus, showed him the strange Yusian on the screen. "As far as I can see, there's no delay."

"That's true," he confirmed automatically.

He made himself more comfortable at the control desk and began the next operation, becoming more and more confident with each move. He no longer had to make decisions; now he only needed to use his professional skills, and he could count on them.

Soon the test of the defractor reached the second phase. It didn't start smoothly either; the marker on the monitor sank to its lowest point, and the picture changed abruptly into another, bright red at the bottom and under that a thick black bottom line, the fail-safe point. But there was still time before we reached that point. I went to the monitors where Elia was working and checked the displays. Only the external cameras were on, and they registered no danger or change, except that the strange Yusian was now some fifteen yards closer.

I turned on camera number six. This time it wasn't dark. On the contrary, it was brighter than necessary; Reder's image appeared before my eyes in irritatingly contrasting colors. I softened them and shrank the image as much as the equipment allowed. Dressed in protective thermal wear and something resembling a miner's helmet, he was standing next to the freight hauler on the other side of the bunker, just under the hill, and opening and closing its freight claws by remote control. The familiar armored truck was parked nearby.

"Keep in constant touch with Reder from now on!" I ordered Elia.

If she still had doubts about my awareness of their ultimate goal, now they completely disappeared. Instead of her personal communicator, she used the microphone at the control station so I could take part in the conversation too.

Reder answered the call right away.

"We have entered phase two," Elia told him, looking at the display monitor in front of her. "We reached critical mode three minutes ago. The object is here. Four hundred and thirty meters from the point of contact."

"I'm waiting for it!" Reder shook his head. "The road leading to you is in order."

A faint smile of satisfaction played around his lips. I decided it was better not to talk to him at all. We would meet in no more than half an hour, right here. Until then it wasn't advisable to bother him in any way.

Meanwhile, the display monitor was registering new alarming messages, including one about an interruption along the reverse cascade. Apparently Vernie decided to make the problems develop faster.

I pulled up the panoramic view of the defractor. From the outside, there was no visible evidence of anything wrong. The camera monitoring the Yusian base also showed only a calm landscape because the strange Yusian was no longer in the picture. Now he was being tracked by another camera, where a red blinking arrow indicated each meter change in his location.

After a while Elia started to count out aloud, "Three hundred meters to the point of contact."

"Three hundred," Vernie confirmed. "Bring up camera eight on the monitor to my right."

I stood in front of that monitor, which seemed to be malfunctioning because the picture kept breaking up. The screen was filled with bright sparks, and blue flashes constantly cut across it. I wasn't sure what I was looking at until the display registered information about the levels of electromagnetic power. This was the inside of the central technology hall, shown from the top. At the moment, the camera was focused on the shell of one of the resonators in the aggregate sector, the precise site of the electrical problems. A few seconds later, the internal pressure increased even more, and then the resonator broke down, producing another shower of sparks and blue flashes. But the pressure in the system remained high.

"A break in the first wall of the diverter," Elia reported.

"OK," Reder answered.

Vernie couldn't control his temper and laughed harshly. He aimed the camera at the reactor, observed it for a minute or two, theatrically rolled up his sleeves, and went to work at the control desk, continually talking to himself.

"Injectors on! Starter. Antiproton wave has been generated. Twist. Oh, the temperature! It's rising—and more. Cooling! First cryopump, quick! No, it didn't hold—poor thing. Influx! Try to change the direction of the stream! Too bad. Attention! Second pump failed too. Cooling system is working at half capacity. Leak is enlarging. Implosions very close to the nucleus! Danger of spontaneous reverse. Now *imminent* danger of spontaneous—" He stopped talking, still glancing at the gauges.

I didn't understand much of his monologue, but the whole time I continued to watch how the marker never stopped moving down through the bright-red zone on the monitor displaying the schedule. Now it was close to the black line.

"Two hundred meters," Elia announced.

"Two hundred," Vernie confirmed and entered his next command.

"Complex switch to the doubling contour," she read from the display monitor.

"Vernie!" Reder's voice interfered. "Vernie?"

"Don't worry!" Vernie responded. "Everything is under control."

In fact, the marker had moved back up again, almost back into the bright-red zone. The thermal parameters were balanced; the diverter and antiproton reactor were still able to contain their supercharged burden, though just barely. The plasma tubes connecting them with the annihilation corpus between them remained in ready mode, with magnetic tracks activated and accelerating boosters charged.

I went to the viewing area. The strange Yusian was still progressing at a slow, steady pace, as he almost always did during his wanderings. None of the other screens registered anything unusual either.

"One hundred meters," reported Elia.

"One hundred," Vernie repeated mechanically, his attention focused on the diagrams with a strange, excessive interest, even with longing, as if he expected them to provide him with an answer to a question that had been troubling him for a long time. He waited like that for almost a whole minute—an agonizing strain on all our nerves—then jumped to his feet.

"Yes, yes—*yes!*" He triumphantly waved his fists above his head. "It worked! My God! This is the refraction coefficient! Now the beam of light will refract again only when *I* want. I can control it completely—"

"Vernie!" Reder interrupted him.

"Go to hell! During all these months while you—but this is a major discovery too. My *own* discovery! Nobody has ever reached this point."

"Phil, fifty meters," Elia said quietly.

"OK. Just let me check these readings once more."

"Everything is being recorded." Reder sounded like he was begging. "You can check them later. Later!"

"Well, OK." Vernie threw himself back into his chair and called up another image on the monitor to his right. He reached over to the main speaker and turned the sound on, activated some other device, lowered his head, and listened intensely to the disturbing sounds coming from the speakers. I turned to the viewing monitors; one of them still showed the interior of the central technology hall, viewed from the top to provide a relatively clear picture of the progress of the tests.

The aggregates in the middle ring were vibrating wildly, the concrete beneath them cracking and breaking up. The cooling system started expelling streams of condensed steam through its safety valves. The hissing grew stronger, mixing with the booming of the generators. A few shakes followed. I turned to the panoramic view of the defractor. Unbelievably, absolutely nothing wrong could be seen from the outside. I relaxed and looked at Vernie with new respect as he continued.

"Twenty meters," Elia said, her voice shaking.

The devices at the desk recorded a surprising decrease in the pressure and the cessation of the vibrations. The monitor displayed the message "PHASE THREE," instantly overriding any previous messages.

Then on the command monitor appeared the annihilator itself, framed to appear as large as possible. It was an incredible human creation, embodying immense power and immense hatred. And *fear.*

CHAPTER 36

The alien slowly climbed the hill. He didn't use the empty strip along the ferns; instead, he plowed straight through them, so the lower part of his body kept appearing and disappearing. These Earth-Yusian plants, as strange as himself, appeared on the monitor to be slicing into his body or devouring it, but it kept regenerating, recreating itself over and over again. The red sun had begun to rise, covering the back of the Yusian with horizontal rays that looked like flowing streams of human blood.

Elia watched him as if hypnotized. I gently shook her shoulder.

"The contact," she murmured and then pulled herself together. "Ehrlich! Contact in thirty seconds. Be ready."

'I'm ready!" Reder said. After a second or two he added, almost to himself, "I've been ready for this for ten years!"

The diaphragms of the plasma tube were fully open; the opposing poles of the buffering zones were activated. The annihilator was prepared for the impulse that would create the ultimate vacuum, the beginning of the *nothing*. And its end at the same time.

Vernie entered the next computer command.

The words "PENDING COMPLEX RETURN TO CONTOUR ONE" appeared on the screen.

All was calm at the Yusian base. They had no cause for alarm—not yet. The strange Yusian was simply enjoying his everyday jaunt. He reached the top of the hill.

"CONTACT!" Elia reported.

In the downstairs gallery, Reder froze.

From his position at the control desk, Vernie reached for a button, the only one covered with a glass membrane. Sweat streamed down his face. His hand was trembling. He jerked it back and then extended it again.

"No—don't do it!" Elia whispered. "We're insane! We can't—no."

I quickly approached him.

"Vernie, Elia! I'm waiting for the signal!" Reder yelled.

Elia didn't move. Vernie looked at me, his eyes as wide open and empty as the eyes of a lunatic.

"What's going on!" Reder yelled again.

"Everything is OK," I answered.

"Simon! For God's sake, how—"

I hit the glass membrane with my fist and pressed the button.

The emergency system produced a deafening clamor. I turned it off. A few more seconds passed when nothing happened, except that the strange Yusian started moving, ready to head down the hill, and continue wandering. But he didn't have a chance. The camouflaged plate beneath him suddenly spun to one side, and he fell onto the descending platform. At this very moment came the first explosion. The plate shifted back in place and the ferns above it quivered and—disappeared. A blinding white wave filled the screen, the camera's last transmission.

We stared intensely at the screen showing Reder. The camera blinked two or three times before the picture stabilized. Reder looked perfectly fine. He even waved at us triumphantly.

"It's over." Elia was stunned.

"Just the opposite," I objected. "Your real work is just beginning."

She regarded me with undisguised, unrelenting hostility.

"Back to work!" I turned to Vernie.

He pulled up the view of the hill from a further camera located on one of the defractor towers. Its panoramic picture included the field where the grass had transformed into ferns just three days ago. Now, of course, there were no ferns. The first annihilation wave, though not as powerful as before passing through the buffer zones, had transformed the entire terrain into something glassy and smooth, a gigantic black mirror reflecting the crimson rays of Shidexa. As the camera zoomed in, the hill looked like a huge reddish-black bubble about to burst.

"That's not enough," I said.

"I know. But we have to wait." Vernie pointed to the other monitor.

The platform carrying the strange Yusian had now descended to the floor of the gallery. He was lying on it, probably still dizzy, and Reder, with remote control in hand, maneuvered the claws of the hoist directly over him. They closed around his body, slowly moved it to the back of the armored truck, and set it down, and the top closed. Reder climbed in front and drove through the gallery. We watched until he was out of range.

His efficiency was admirable: all this was accomplished within forty seconds after the first explosion. There had still been no reaction from the Yusian side—but that wouldn't last much longer.

Vernie now looked very calm, having finally accepted that there was no turning back now. He had obviously calculated every single step: after the explosion, the marker on the display monitor returned back to the black line, indicating that the whole system was stabilized on the very edge of the upcoming disaster. Even that disaster was stabilized, frozen like some impossible hurricane waiting only to be directed by one elite engineer from Earth, Philip Vernie.

"I'm far enough from there now," Reder said on the phone. "Keep going, Phil!"

As Vernie increased the intensity of the plasma stream, the speakers erupted in an uncoordinated chorus of emergency signals. Almost every device in the central technology hall was about to fail.

"Wait!" I exclaimed. "Where are the robots?"

"In the underground storage sector. It's safe for them there."

"Damn it! Why didn't you warn me?"

"About what?"

I broadcast a top-priority message over the direct line to the server. "This is base commander Terence Simon. This is an emergency. All ESSIKO robots are to move immediately to Building B of the defractor!"

"Annihilation wave number two in twenty seconds," Vernie reported.

"Delay it!" I ordered him. "I need at least fifty seconds! I repeat: all ESSIKO robots to Building B! Run!"

"I can't stop the reaction, Simon! Neutralization will only increase the impulse power. The consequences will be—"

On the screen I saw the robots rushing out of the storage sector. "Delay it, Vernie! Hold it—*I order you.*"

He activated the neutralizers.

"Ehrlich!" Elia screamed in panic. "The impulse power will be increased. Be careful!"

The defractor devices looked only slightly compromised; when it passed through the buffer zones, the first wave barely touched them. The robots were running precisely in that direction: more than two hundred of them, maybe three hundred—a huge, compact crowd. I waited until they reached the front line.

"*Now!*" I told Vernie.

He reacted instantly. I saw the second wave hurtling straight toward the robots. When it exited the buffer zone, it opened like a big white fan and launched the whole crowd into the air. As they melted they continued their rhythmical motion, still "running," though now they looked like loosely assembled skeletons. When their energy batteries exploded almost in unison, the wave broke through the buffer zones to the side, slicing off more concrete, ceramic, and metal from the periphery of the devices.

"I'm at depth fifty," Reder reported, out of breath. "The temperature is rising! Things are collapsing around here!"

"Can you keep going?" I asked.

"I'll try. Did you destroy them, Simon?" *All* of them?"

"Yes, I'm sorry I caused you—"

"Oh, don't worry! I would have done the same thing. In fact, the damage isn't that great. It will just slow me down a bit."

"OK. We're waiting for you, Reder."

While I talked to him, I never took my eyes off the monitor displaying the Yusian base. Still no response.

I unblocked the door to the surgery room. "Elia, it's time to finish preparations down there. I want a surgical suit for me too."

She exhaled forcefully but gave me no other answer as she passed me and went downstairs.

The second wave wasn't over yet. Instead of subsiding, the aftershocks suddenly increased in strength. A series of quakes followed, but the key devices were still working. Only two of the mock towers fell, first leaning as if blown by a strong wind and then buckling. Vernie relaxed and turned the speakers off. But we heard other noises—coming from Reder's phone.

I felt my hair stand up. "Reder!"

"Relax," he answered but sounded scared himself. "The road in front of me was just blocked by a boulder. The flexor won't be enough. I'll have to use an explosive."

"No! That could cause new collapses. Wait! Stay in the car! I'll send an REM robot to help you."

"Hurry," Vernie said brusquely, taking my place in front of the monitor displaying the Yusian base. "The situation here is pretty much under control, but those *creatures* are going to show up any minute now. Or at least they should."

The REM robots were situated at equal distances along the gallery where Reder was. After studying the situation, I activated the one closest to him. It took me about ten seconds to adapt to the interactive goggles. The collapse had knocked out the lights, so what I saw was relayed by the REM's infrared receptors. The images were blurred and unclear, as if I were looking through the eyes of a drunk, and like a drunk, the REM staggered forward at a snail's pace. This might be the latest, most improved, Earth model, but it was still very imperfect. As much as I tried to coordinate them, its "hand motions" were irritatingly clumsy, but it was strong enough to toss rocks aside like feather pillows. Still, clearing the way seemed to take forever.

I finally saw the front part of the truck beneath the rocks, blurred but also gleaming luridly because Reder had his helmet light on. He was sitting in the cab, probably listening, his head turned toward the rear of the vehicle. I listened too. Because of the fuzzy radio connection, I could hear nothing but his heavy breathing, which worried me.

"Reder! How's it going with you?"

"With *us*!" He snorted. "Well, it's damned hot for *me*, Simon, but not for the Yusian. *It* has a space suit on and is more—is better adapted. Yes, the Yusian is fine. Just sitting there."

"The REM is six meters away from you," I continued. "There's only one boulder left, but it's too big to pick up. Try to cut it vertically about a meter or meter and thirty centimeters to your left. I can see from here that it's much thinner there."

"Hurry!" Vernie reminded us again.

Reder took out his flexor and managed to cut the rock without leaving the truck. His skill didn't surprise me. I had the REM approach the spot, dislodge the part of the boulder that still weighed at least a ton, and roll it to the side. I repeated the action with the other, lighter, section. Finally I parked the REM next to it.

"Go!" I told Reder, but he was already moving.

"At maximum speed!" Vernie advised him, but Reder didn't need that advice.

The vehicle quickly disappeared from the infrared view of the REM, which made everybody happy. I cut my sensor connection with the REM and concentrated on the sounds coming from Reder.

A minute later Vernie said, "They're coming."

At first I didn't understand, but then I saw them: miniature black dots, growing larger by the second. They expanded into a swarm of black bugs.

"They react slowly, don't they?" Vernie smiled disdainfully. "This 'accident' is probably their first emergency in a hundred years, maybe even a thousand. Reder, where are you?"

"Approaching depth one hundred and twenty," he answered. "Sweep them out, Phil! Don't worry about me. I'll manage."

"Maybe you won't need to, my friend. You keep going, and I…I've prepared for this too!"

From another closer camera, the Yusian "airplanes" already resembled a flock of black, ungainly birds. Vernie waited for them a little longer and then lowered the containment barriers around the annihilator and, from its protected position, deployed its awesome force. He winked at me mischievously as his hands started dancing across the keyboard, a brilliant performance that produced a devastating silent movie on the screens.

The towers still standing rocketed off the ground as if shot out of cannons, carved short parabolas in the air and collapsed back down in clouds of dust. The coordination center burst into flames, its windows exploding and the glass shattering into millions of sparkling red particles. The biostation exploded too, as if it were filled with dynamite. Panels, concrete, metal, machine parts, and even whole machines flew into the air.

The black flock turned left and started moving in the opposite direction but not as quickly as before. There was obvious confusion in the already disordered squadron, a lack of comprehension, as if they were asking each other, "What's going on?" I couldn't help smiling.

"I passed depth one hundred and thirty," Reder informed us. "How's it going with you?"

"Perfect!" answered Vernie. "I'll give you a copy for your birthday."

"How far does he need to go to be safe?" I asked in a low voice.

"At least to depth two hundred. Otherwise it's going to get—much hotter."

"*Too* hot," Elia added behind my back.

I hadn't noticed her return. She was looking at me accusingly, and not without reason.

"I hope you understand that everything up there is *evidence*," Vernie explained calmly. "The last wave has been planned to destroy absolutely anything incriminating."

"What about Larsen and the dog?"

"Don't worry about them, Simon. The command complex is at the base of the second hill, so they're safe there. The wave won't reach there because it's well beyond the buffer zones. But if you left anything of value in the lodge, forget it."

"We had an agreement with Larsen not to leave you there," Elia said quickly. "I was going to contact you too. I would have warned you! Definitely, do you hear!"

"OK, OK. I believe you."

I did believe her. After all, neither she nor Vernie were murderers—yet. But they would be soon.

Meanwhile the Yusian "airplanes" had stopped in the midflight. They now resembled flattened spirals drilled into the sky. After a while they regrouped and flew back. It's worth noting that the "airplanes" had nothing in common with the shuttles they had given us: these were clearly more powerful and adaptable.

"Listen, Phil," Elia started, "what if they decide to help us? To suppress somehow—"

"Oh, they've already made their decision, you can be sure, but they won't have the opportunity to carry it out. Just watch and listen!" Vernie switched on the speakers with a theatrical flourish and leaned over the keyboard like a musician called back for an encore. We heard popping, rasping, hissing, crackling, and crashing sounds—a cannonade straight from hell. Elia nervously reached out and turned down the sound. Everything that was still standing—devices, real and fake buildings, energy blocks, peripheral generators—now rocked back and forth like a flotilla in a choppy sea. Welded joints cracked like matchsticks—shredding like paper. Huge fissures opened on the ceramic shields of the aggregates. Then came new explosions as the already useless diverter collapsed as well.

This time, however, the Yusians didn't retreat. Instead, they sped toward the defractor.

"Depth one hundred and sixty," Reder announced.

And *they* started to descend.

Vernie met them with fire. The flames erupted from the inside, stuck out their long blue tongues at the sky, doubling and tripling in size as they emerged, multiplying and turning from blue to orange. As the "airplanes" kept coming, I sensed something very strange about them, but I couldn't figure it out. Maybe something important—or dangerous—for us.

As the flock cut into the flames, circling through them above the defractor, I suddenly realized what it was: their surfaces didn't reflect the light. Or, to be more precise, they absorbed it, greedily and completely. Yes, they were pitch black, despite the red beams of Shidexa, and remained black even in the center of the orange firestorm. They looked like holes in it, and the cosmic darkness was peeking out of them. Unfortunately, they were not holes. They grouped and merged into a flat construction resembling a roof that abruptly telescoped to a gigantic size and then became flat again, a monstrous bellows expelling—I don't know what. But whatever it was put out the fire.

"Well, it doesn't matter." Vernie broke the long silence. "The annihilation is our queen, and they won't be able to take her over! Reder?"

"Depth one hundred and eighty. The road is—difficult. I'm moving slowly."

"My God!" Elia whispered, indicating images on the screen in front of us with surprise.

Actually, it wasn't surprising at all: after the successful "rescue" mission, the airborne formation was dividing. Half stayed to guard the defractor from new disasters, while the other half moved toward the hill, transforming itself back into a flock as it went.

"Ehrlich!" Elia called. "They're returning to the contact point. Looks like they'll try to land there."

"*End it!*" he yelled.

Vernie accumulated the finishing impulse but didn't release it. The devices at the control desk went absolutely crazy, updating information at astonishing speed, while the display monitor, of course, offered only gibberish.

"Vernie," I warned him, squeezing the back of his neck, "I won't allow more *accidents.*"

"I know—I know." He pushed my hand away. "Let me go!"

The Yusians were already circling just above the crest of the hill, but Vernie continued to postpone the final wave. Sweat poured down his forehead again, and he was practically sprawled across the control desk, trying his damnedest to gain more time for Reder. The commands he entered were totally incomprehensible to me; they might as well have been sign language for the deaf. At least I didn't think any of the systems he was trying to control could still be online after the hellish eruptions he had conjured. I felt the sweat run down my face too, and my nerves were about to snap. But I didn't react. I waited silently with Elia, who was as white as a corpse and looked like she was about to faint. I instinctively put my hand on her waist to hold her up.

The flock began to descend.

Instantly Vernie activated the final annihilation impulse. The wave surged forward, just under the Yusian "airplanes." It didn't touch them, but its incomparable impact spread them around and blew them sky high as if they were ugly black toys. Little toy planes.

The space beneath the wave seemed to shrink, crushed in the white fist of the annihilation. More cameras went dead; even those beyond the range of the impulse were transmitting only painfully sharp black-and-white images. Through their fearfully blinking lenses, we witnessed everything melting like candle wax. Evaporating. The entire defractor complex, that cosmic trap, the most expensive project in human history, was gone. And that hill the others called with hideous irony "the point of contact," surrounded by something that was a field before, was now boiling and bubbling and fizzing, its white crests disappearing into deep black caverns. The cones that had once been five-trunked trees were swept away by the wave, and our lodge, that absurd and ridiculously quaint Eyrenean "home" the Yusians had built for us, evaporated as well.

"Reder, how are you?" Vernie's voice sounded confident.

"Not bad. Thank God! I'm coming in. The load is safe too."

Then Philip Vernie rolled down his sleeves, put his hands behind his neck, and relaxed. He had orchestrated a series of "accidents" culminating in an apocalyptic cadenza and had perfectly concluded his performance. His annihilation defractor was no more. A black crater had replaced it—a giant maw poised in an endless scream, a petrified beast roaring into the lurid Eyrenean sky.

I punched in the code that unblocked the control-room doors.

CHAPTER 37

Dressed in identical surgical gowns, Reder and I stood across from each other at opposite sides of the operating table. The strange Yusian lay between us, strapped to the table. His height demanded an additional smaller table, also on wheels, under his lower limbs. While he was slighter than his fellow Yusians, he still far exceeded the size of any human in the world. Of course, size wasn't his strangest trait, nor was I concerned with his appearance at present.

Until now he hadn't put up any resistance. His eyes, as far as he was using them, didn't even produce the usual psychosensor blocking in any of us. The communication zones of his torso remained completely closed, although, as I already knew, his space suit didn't prevent their emergence or the release of electrical shocks similar to the one that hit me during our chase at the biostation.

"I'm in touch with Vernie," Elia's voice blasted from the intercom. "He's finished the preparation of the base. The montage of the accident is recorded, based on the highlight zones in real time, and has been stored both in the server and in the secure databases in the system. We drafted an official apology about the unfortunate incident and transmitted it to the Yusians. So far, they haven't responded."

"And Larsen?" I asked.

"He's calm. Even offered to cooperate with us. Vernie agreed to let him serve as standby operator at the control desk."

"Good," I said. "Good. Initiate the facility's generators and let's get started!"

The generators overrode the external power source so smoothly and silently that we hardly noticed. The lights in the room flickered only briefly, and the monotonous hum of the insulators ceased for a second or two and then returned. With the flick of a switch, we had walled ourselves in, completely isolated more than two hundred meters underground.

Reder was again regarding me with seething hostility, but I ignored it because I had relieved him of his flexor as soon as he arrived with his precious Yusian cargo. Now his face, thickly coated with burn ointment, was a sickly brick red, his eyebrows and lashes kinky black, and his eyes still bloodshot from the scorching heat in the gallery. I didn't even want to imagine how he would have looked, or even if he would have been recognizable, if Vernie hadn't gained him those few vital seconds.

Soon Elia joined us in the surgery room. Without wasting time, she and Reder precisely adjusted the cameras, microphones, and other recording devices, set the arc lamps at full intensity, and turned on specific monitors, equipment, and measuring devices among those situated in a semicircle around the operating table. Then Elia pulled the surgical cart toward her, where she had arranged, besides the various instruments, numerous test tubes, beakers, pans, and vials, all painstakingly labeled.

We stood in silence for a while, just looking at each other, and then put on the masks and surgical gloves. We had reached the point of no return—a point exactly the opposite of those moments in science fiction movies when evil aliens prepare to perform heinous experiments on helpless humans they've abducted.

The nonhumanoid lay motionless on the table, a living laboratory specimen for us to examine and "understand." We had only one purpose: to learn through him how his fellow Yusians could be killed—many of them at a time, from a safe distance and by means harmless to humans.

Just above him, Elia placed a panel of thermoreceptors specifically adapted to his size. The thermogram on the monitor indicated amazing variations in his torso temperatures: from close to zero up to sixty and more degrees centigrade. Apparently his organs were isolated from each other by vacuum-filled cavities, hindering the heat exchange among them, as if each were contained in a thermos.

"Capable of floating freely. But only reactive and only some of the organs," Reder announced for the record. He took one of the scalpels and slowly, obviously enjoying himself, pointed it at the shapeless "chest" of the Yusian. I knew that, for now, he only intended to cut the space suit and to study the process of its regeneration, but in this case, it was much more important to me whether or not the Yusian knew that as well, if he was intelligent enough to realize that he was not going to be killed this quickly? Or was it possible that he didn't have any suspicion that eventually he *was* going to be killed!

The Yusian didn't react at all to Reder's first cut, but the response of the space suit was almost immediate: both edges of the cut liquefied and then flowed together like quicksilver. During this process, the thermograph recorded a general cooling of the rest of the torso, while the section around the disappearing cut became a "hot spot." Seconds later, the space suit was whole again, and the thermograph reverted to its previous readings.

Reder made a new, longer cut, with the same effect. Then he and Elia removed a piece of the space suit and placed it in a glass pan specifically prepared for the purpose. There it began to shrink, looking like a membrane with expanding holes until it finally disappeared. I checked the measuring devices reflecting the parameters of the room and noted that the air control indicators recorded no variations. Meanwhile, the Yusian's space suit had again repaired itself, leaving no evidence of our intervention.

"I was right!" Reder noted. "This material is somehow connected with the creature's protective mechanisms, and they control its structural changes."

"Yes," Elia said. "We have to find some way to paralyze those mechanisms."

"Or to mislead them by sending false impulses." Reder skillfully attached electrodes to the torso of the Yusian from some device unfamiliar to me, turned it on, and cut the space suit once more. This time the cut remained open about ten seconds longer but finally healed completely.

"So it's not simply reactive; the bastards can control it consciously as well!" Reder stated, turning off the device. "The connections are much more complicated than we supposed."

"Well? What now?" Elia asked him.

"I've programmed a range of impulses in various combinations. We'll try all of them at once when"—Reder glared at me from under his scorched eyebrows—"when the time comes."

"Stop stalling!" I warned him in an intentionally domineering tone. "Your idea of stripping the Yusians of their space suits by misleading them through long-distance impulses sounds juvenile, if not actually primitive. Superficial at best."

"Well, suggest something more profound then," he added sardonically.

"You bet I will! That's why I'm here. But first you need to finish *your* job."

As I expected, Reder wasn't stupid enough to argue with me. However, since he needed to vent his anger anyway, he naturally directed it completely at the tightly bound object on the table. He grabbed one of the syringes and tried to insert its needle into the creature's limb through the space suit. He didn't succeed. He cursed, again turned on the electrode device, and used the scalpel once more, quickly inserting the needle through the cut but unable to draw anything into the syringe.

"Look!" Elia drew his attention to the thermogram.

The section where the needle entered had become a "cold spot," obviously enough to freeze that area completely. Meanwhile the space suit was again repairing itself, and the needle was literally shot out of the creature, probably by a muscle spasm beneath its point. Reder followed its long flight with his eyes, looked down at his now empty hands, and spread them in a momentary expression of confusion.

"Looks like we're losing the games we're playing with the creature's temperature, doesn't it?" His lame attempt at humor did little to ease the tension.

Then the Yusian—the Yusian started to get up. Elia screamed, and Reder reached for his flexor. Realizing that I had it, he gestured at me idiotically, grabbed Elia by the elbow, and dragged her backward with him.

I approached the Yusian: he had almost assumed a sitting position, and the strong silicon ropes that had bound him were limply hanging around his torso, seemingly having been eaten away by acid.

"Watch out!" Elia whimpered.

"Pull yourselves together, both of you!" I ordered without taking my eyes off the Yusian. *His* eyes still remained covered by the forehead membrane, but his communication zones were already blinking under the space suit, flickering somehow feebly—was he begging?—and all of them gradually becoming pale green. Then he lay back, very slowly, returning to the horizontal position he was in before, although no longer tied down.

"He wants to cooperate with you," I said.

"Nonsense!" Reder hissed.

"And why not?" Elia replied sharply. "This is a very intelligent creature! We forget that fact and treat him like a dumb beast, just because he doesn't look like us—and because he was tied to the table, seemingly helpless, like a laboratory animal."

"Elia, you"—Reder was choking with disgust—"well, go ahead; hug him, if that's what you think!"

"Maybe even that would be easier for me than—"

"Keep working," I interrupted them dryly.

"All right, all right," Reder murmured, "but at least point the flexor at it!"

"Don't worry. My reactions are fast enough."

"And make sure not to hit it in those frontal zones. We need them the most. Target its eyes. Yes, Simon! If the creature makes any dangerous moves, blind it!"

The three of us maintained a strained silence. Elia's face above the half mask was as pale as before, but I sensed that the tension draining her of color was now from disgust rather than fear, which in this case was *not* directed at the strange Yusian. She approached him and removed the straps from beneath his torso. He shifted his weight to make it easier for her and then resumed his former position on the operating table.

Next Reder approached him, picked up the electrodes, and placed them beside that ineffective device. "Let's see how manageable you are now," Reder said softly, picking up a second syringe and preparing to puncture the creature. He moved very slowly, giving the Yusian plenty of time to counter its instinct for self-preservation. And it did just that! The only way we had of measuring its reactions was the thermograph, and the creature's body temperature didn't vary in the slightest when the needle pierced the space suit, nor when it penetrated internally. Soon a bluish fluid rose through the needle into the barrel of the syringe, where the fluid looked more like a fog than a liquid.

"It's similar to that substance they use to charge their materials in the warehouses," Elia observed gloomily.

"That's even worse!" Reder snorted.

"Why?" I asked.

"Because, Simon, we've already spent much time and effort studying that substance."

"Well?"

"Its composition is partly material and partly pure energy," Elia added. "It seems to be a mixture of something—"

"And nothing," Reder finished her thought. "Yes, yes, that's exactly the absurd conclusion we reached. But if the blue substance resembles anything recognizable, it would be *blood*. Yusian blood. Damn it! What if it *is* the same?"

"It would mean," Elia began, stunned, "that the Yusians feed their materials blood! And that those materials are either very close to, or identical with, their *flesh*—"

"What about their machines?" I interrupted her. "Are they fueled with the same—substance?"

She shook her head. "No, unless it is used in the manufacturing process. The machines are completely self-contained and self-sustaining. They take their energy from sunlight and the matter around them, just as the plants on Eyrena do!"

"Just as the Yusians do themselves," Reder added. "Which implies that the Yusians not only construct their machines out of materials resembling their own flesh but also build into them a structure that can duplicate their own anatomical functions!"

Nervously trembling, Elia took the container of "blood" to one of the refrigerators, placed it carefully inside, and slowly returned to the table.

"I don't understand," I began, "why you find this so shocking? Very often we base our ideas for our machines on the animals and plants around us. Why shouldn't the Yusians do the same? The difference is that they seem to be limited to ideas based only on themselves."

"Yes, you're right!" Elia rubbed her forehead. "They *were* the only creatures on their planet, weren't they? And later, when they started to travel to other planets, they apparently never encountered any considerably more developed organisms that they could use for new, principally different, models."

"Fortunately for them, that situation changed ten years ago," Reder reminded us, viciously narrowing his eyes as he stared at the Yusian on the table. "They have found any number of organisms on Earth that can serve their purposes—not just as models. Even we serve them!"

The force and truth of Reder's words reduced us both to silence. We also narrowed our eyes as we looked at the creature, and just then he readjusted himself, his torso clefts slowly opening. Obviously he finally intended to break his long silence.

Reder quickly focused the ultrasound on him and activated its scanner. The monitors displayed a number of complex color diagrams that I couldn't identify, and these became much more complicated when the Yusian emitted a prolonged rumbling sound.

"Just as I suspected!" Reder announced abruptly. "They have nothing that resembles our voice box or larynx. They have 'produced' these in some of their representatives specifically so that they can communicate with us!"

"Wait; wait." Elia reached across and focused the diagrams. Then she looked closely at them with growing astonishment. "Why, they have no skeletal system! Only hollow cavities and undifferentiated tissue that reflects the waves at the same degree—"

The Yusian interrupted her by repeating his previous rumble, and this time, I'm sure, trying to "pronounce" it more accurately. Then he rose to the awkward, half-upright position on the table he had attempted earlier, similar to our concept of sitting up. The diagrams immediately changed again, and I realized what was actually happening. His body had responded to the need for inner support and had created it—had transformed tissue into "bones" where they were needed for this precise position. When he lay back down again, the "bones" also relaxed, decreasing their density and expanding their volume into the surrounding empty space.

The Yusian's next movements completely assured me of his fully conscious efforts to show us his body potentials. Yes, he understood that we were interested in them and was trying to prove his willingness to demonstrate them voluntarily for us, to be... *obedient* is the word that occurred to me for a moment and disappeared, leaving me vaguely worried. But that unease also disappeared soon as I was fully captured by the ultrasound reflections accompanying each progressive change in the strange Yusian's position.

Undoubtedly his "tissue" selectively regulated its density in response to the constantly changing movements of his organism. Logic told me that it could then react in corresponding ways to other needs as well—because the tissue was universally adaptable! It could function differently depending on the current need—as bones, muscles, organs—fluids. Perhaps it had the potential to convert itself into a gas as well—or even into plasma?

"This just goes to show that Stein was far from the truth!" Reder's remark, clearly aimed at me, rang with completely inappropriate triumph. "These creatures don't have anything in common with plants—or, actually, with anything earthborn. Nor can their tissue be compared with any substance known to us!"

"*This* Yusian doesn't have, at least not at this particular *moment*," I specified, "but he might have had at other times. When he needed it. Besides, Stein didn't mention any substantial similarities; he only discussed certain analogies on the basis of the life forms he knew."

Elia turned her head to the Yusian and sighed. She gave me a look that was sad and conspiratorial at the same time, a look I couldn't quite fathom. "He is completely sane!" She sounded exhausted. "In fact his brain, and heart, are right where they should be."

"Wherever that might be!" Reder waved his hand in frustration. "Hopefully the X-ray will show us what they think with. At least their brain tissue should be recognizably different, shouldn't it? Unless they have no brain at all."

"Maybe it's all brain tissue," I speculated.

Reder laughed, assuming I had been joking. But had I been? I don't know.

"So now what?" Reder turned his attention to Elia. "I don't see any reasons for your dejection. Our chances of finding what we're looking for are much better than Larsen's ever were. The Yusians may, in fact, have put *too* much of themselves into technology and machines. Consequently, they haven't managed to advance their own bodies nearly as far. Otherwise, they wouldn't still need to wear space suits—"

Reder's remarks were interrupted by the strange Yusian, who suddenly froze on the table in a shapeless heap. He hissed quietly as his surface fringe gradually settled down. Elia pushed the surgical cart aside nervously, while Reder removed a remote control from the pocket of his laboratory coat and pressed one of its buttons. The table began to rise; Reder had engaged the hydraulic lifters attached to the table's wheels. Whether from fear or surprise—probably from both—the Yusian quickly splayed his upper limbs. I had the feeling that he wanted to thrust them forward, but instead he tucked them clumsily into the side clefts of his torso.

Watching him intensely, Reder squatted next to the smaller table and fumblingly unblocked its wheels. He stood up and waved impatiently at Elia, who cleared the way by moving aside some of the surrounding equipment. Then Reder aimed the remote control at the operating table again. It began moving, followed by the smaller table. The scene almost appeared comic, although "incongruous" would be a better description. With two or three maneuvers, Reder managed to direct the tables bearing the Yusian into the X-ray room and position them directly under the X-ray without ever entering the room and then to close the gate before walking toward us.

Elia looked at one of the monitors to confirm that the Yusian was in one of its "normal" positions, which is to say that it was still relatively calm. Then she entered some commands on the neighboring keyboard, but no pictures appeared on its monitor. I didn't know what was going on, but by Elia's and Reder's expression, I easily guessed that it wasn't what they had expected.

Almost a whole minute passed as we waited in a silence broken only by the barely audible hum of the cameras, indifferently capturing something that in fact *hadn't happened*, evidence of yet another failed experiment.

"Noooo!" Elia broke our silence with a groan. "It's not possible. This is absurd!"

As if to confirm her words with his actions, the Yusian started to expand, losing even the poorly defined shape he held before.

"What is he doing, for God's sake?" Elia cried.

"It's *swallowing*," Reder responded tensely.

"What!"

"He is feeding. Consuming, gorging. How can I say it more clearly?"

"He's swallowing the X-rays? All of them? Is that what you're trying to—"

"Yes, that's exactly what I'm saying. Don't you understand? He's expanding, increasing his surface so he can absorb everything we 'offer' him."

"My God! He must think that what we need from him is—to eat! That this is why we put him there!"

"Stop the radiation," I advised her, "or he will x-ray himself to death before you have time to finish 'studying' him."

"Shut up!" Elia snapped at me but immediately turned off the equipment.

"Stop interfering, Simon!" Reder upbraided me too. "You understand nothing about what we're trying to do."

"You're mistaken," I said, growling. "I know *exactly* what my role is here. And that's why I'm calling a halt to your futile round of routine experiments."

"What!" Elia responded, startled.

"That's right. We are starting the vivisection, right now."

CHAPTER 38

From the air, the southern settlement held no surprises for me: houses, stores, parks, public buildings, all built in typically eclectic and gaudy Yusian style, and an abundance of decorative landscape consisting, of course, only of the five modified stages of the original *Sedum* herb.

I made a few low passes over the city to orient myself better before setting the shuttle down next to one of the houses and then walked toward the main town square.

Standing exactly at its center, I crossed my arms over my chest so I could see my watch and remained silent for three minutes—time enough for an enemy's half-formed conjectures and welter of conflicting possibilities to thicken into edgy tension.

When I finished with that part of my performance, I stood with my legs slightly spread, put my hands on my hips, and roared, "Listen, you *pitiful, misshapen nonhumanoids! Cosmic decrepit* old men! I came to show you what it *really means to be human!*"

There was no answer of course.

I waited even longer this time and then used some of Chuks's phrases: "If you are 'in jolt because of our new condition,' the answer is *yes*—you really are 'facing necessity' to communicate with me. 'Should exploit readiness,' because I can explain some things to you. And if you can't understand them, I'll drive you *crazy*! I'll *destroy* you!"

My challenge again went unanswered.

I took a deep breath and continued, "A colossus with feet of clay—that's all your polyplanetary system is. And you, all of you, are its groveling servants. You sense that; you know it's 'rebellion for your instincts too.' Only your cowardice prevents you from doing anything about this. That's why you cling to us. Just as when you implanted eyes in yourselves, you are hoping that, through what you call 'equalized generosity' and a 'contact' with us, you will implant an additional soul. *A human soul*. And that's exactly what you need. Otherwise you will wither completely away. *You will rot!*"

This time the absence of any reaction worried me a little. I started wondering how many more insults and threats they could take.

"Well, fine!" I spoke with arrogant disdain. "Don't answer, but if you continue to play your game with me, *you* will lose! A *person* stands here! Come on, try your idiotic attempts at 'contact' with my *soul*. 'Implant' it into yourselves! Then you will begin to understand what I mean. Or are you afraid even to *try*?"

I threw back my head and laughed raucously.

To no avail. Everything remained as passive as before, frozen in a grotesque imitation of a small provincial town, which was designed supposedly to make the colonists very, very happy. So happy that they wouldn't realize how this very town is gradually sucking out their very souls and replacing them with another, nonhuman, identity. The goal was to make them "mutual" by turning them into deformed psychohybrids—into *subject-mediators*, whose chronal relations with both Earth and the Yusian polyplanet system would enable all kinds of instantaneous interactions between our two civilizations. In the end, however, all of us—both humans and Yusians—will become, similar to the hybrid *Sedum*, mere human-Yusian hybrids, more *subject-mediators* to be made use of by the system. That is what is *really* meant by establishing "contact."

I decided to change my tactics. "By the way, that strange Yusian didn't die in the accident," I announced. "He wasn't annihilated! If you want to know his fate, you're going to have to activate this whole pseudolandscape around me."

I knew that bombshell would have consequences—once the implications penetrated those Yusian thick "skulls." But how this would all play out not even the Yusians could determine. I assumed an arrogantly self-confident expression and started waiting.

In the end, nothing unusual or new occurred. However, in the park across from the square, the five-trunk trees started rocking, although there was no wind. Then they shook their crowns until little clouds of crystals, pink under Shidexa rays, formed around them and started floating gracefully into the air—in my direction.

I looked around and for a moment began to imagine people already sitting at the colorful little tables of the nearby coffee shop. They were smiling, chatting about unimportant but very pleasant trivia, joking, flirting with women, enjoying, and so on.

What? Some illusions created by nonhumanoids.

"I'm sick of you!" I exploded into the crystal clouds gathering above my head. "The same game, over and over again. No, you will never be worthy partners for us if, even in this critical moment, you can't even overcome your *own* stereotypes."

The crystal rain continued to fall, and through my senses, the same familiar feelings began crawling: joy, compassionate concern, ecstatic love, that sense of universal harmony. I tossed them all away like dirty rags.

"But what have you done on this planet so far, damn it? And what have you accomplished on Earth? All you've done is watch people, for ten long years, in every way possible. Yet you still understand *nothing*! Why is that? *Are you stupid?*"

I let the question hang in the air along with their euphoria clouding crystals.

"No, you are *not* stupid," I answered the hanging question after a while. "Even worse: you are *faceless*. Thousands of years ago you decided that your system was perfect, and that's when it began robbing you. It deprived you of stimuli for personal performance and took away your sense of personal significance. As you tell us, you seek 'necessary *impersonal* understanding,' which simply doesn't exist. So what are you now? Creatures that are clearly distinct only in your bodies, not in your minds. That's exactly why you don't understand us. You think we are just like you—an anonymous herd. Well, we do *not* share a herd mentality!"

I shook the crystals from my hair and clothes to make my point. Then I laughed, but—take note—not intentionally. It welled up spontaneously, from a deep spring of joy, deeper and more complicated than any manufactured response. I concentrated and laughed again, now in a different way.

"Do you think your euphoria is euphoric? Nonsense. Exactly during its peak, one of us killed two people, didn't he? He killed his friend: stood before an innocent blue-eyed man with a boyish face, took out his flexor, and shot him point-blank in the head! Well? Is that what you intended with this blindman's bluff game you're playing with something as unpredictable as human beings? *Any human being!*"

I stood defiantly silent. But *their* silence was so palpable, so filled with manufactured compassion, that I lost my temper.

"Check what the word 'vivisection' means!" I shouted, shaking my fist at the empty square. "And then accelerate the 'contact,' because only then can I show you what happened to that wretch of yours."

But could I really show him to them? Well, yes, since they learned long ago how to read the "memories" incorporated in material objects by reanimating the energy processes performed in that material's past. But I had come here to impart something infinitely more complicated and important: *my own conscious memories.* That unique mixture of perceptions, thoughts, and feelings the Yusians couldn't just "read." They had to *experience them with me*, which was exactly my goal.

"A vivisection!" I repeated. "And accelerate the 'contact'! Now!"

But no. Instead, sounds of a lullaby came from somewhere. For a few seconds, I stood overwhelmed, numb with helplessness and fury. But then I understood the delicate hint and crossed the square, following the sounds down the closest street. I passed three or four houses with pseudostately courtyards and finally stopped at the house from which the music was coming. Opening the gate, I walked down a fern-fringed path and passed a glistening oval pool, lined with lounge chairs and boasting a diving board at the deep end. Reaching the front door, I climbed the stairs and jerked it open. The lullaby ceased abruptly, though I sensed that the house was sighing and detected a pungent odor, though not the rank smell of decay.

I walked through the foyer straight to the stairs. I didn't need to look around to know that the furnishings everywhere were luxurious and, so far, relatively normal. After reaching the second floor and checking here and there, I found the bedroom. I approached the bed, pulled aside the silk comforter, and ran my hand over the pale-blue sheet, also silk. But the material was slightly warm and very flexible. I took my flexor from its holster, put on the safety, and placed it on the nightstand. I took the detonator from under my shirt, attached it to the palm of my left hand with the surgical tape Elia had given me, and began to undress.

> *They have achieved a level of development incomparably high-er than ours. But their intellectual capacity, in the strictest sense, if we discount the knowledge they possess, is similar to that of humans. Where they surpass us, then, is in spiritual-ity—the united spirit of their civilization.*

Yes, even Stein, like everybody else, considered the superior-ity of the Yusians an indisputable fact. But he was wrong. So what does it mean for a civilization to have a united spirit? Does it mean that each individual gains billions of times more spiri-tual profundity? The answer is obviously no. Spirituality can't be measured in quantities. It is qualitative and personal. Even if an arbitrary number of individuals with this quality unite, the achievement is still not collective. It remains singular, an indi-vidual quality.

Unification, depersonalization, regimentation, or commu-nism—it doesn't matter what we call it. Nor was it likely that the Yusians achieved this on purpose; more likely, it befell them, insid-iously and gradually, the typical pattern for social disasters. There it is. They have paid an exuberant price for their carefree, untrou-bled, safe life, and they will pay yet again, in this unique duel.

"I'm ready," I announced clearly. "My spirit against the united spirit of all your civilization. *One* on *one*."

Their reaction was banal and predictable: the window shutters automatically closed, and a dark fog surrounded me. I lay on the bed. It didn't squeak; the sheet didn't rustle but did fit itself to my body and then stopped moving. I felt nothing else, except for barely detectable, preprogrammed sleep-inducing impulses. I crossed my arms on my chest and closed my eyes. At first it seemed hellishly complicated: the last thing I wanted was to fall asleep, but I did want to enter a state *like* sleep, to be fully susceptible to the Yusian influence. Unless I could achieve that state, the contact wouldn't take place, or worse, it would take place on their terms. I needed to hold a thought that was sufficiently pleasant to relax me but at the same time disturbing enough to keep me awake, a thought precisely balanced between pleasure and pain. It turned out to be not about some*thing* but some*one*. I thought about Elia.

If I achieved the exact balance, it must have been for only a few seconds. Yet that was time enough for the substances to have received their needed stimulus so they could switch to their next phase. Or maybe the Yusians had finally found the strength to overcome their stereotypes and had really accelerated the contact? I don't know. But when I opened my eyes, although the fog was still as thick as before, my own reflection could clearly be seen about three meters above me.

I looked at it with annoyance; *another optical illusion*, I told myself. Soon, however, I realized that was too simple an answer. Actually, the ceiling was not like a mirror, nor was that figure my reflection. Its eyes were closed, its proportions volumetric. A hologram? Lying horizontally in the air, its face was looking down, its arms crossed on its chest, and it was radiating an inner light—a light that logically should animate it but instead made it appear stiff, deathlike. Its prone position contributed to this impression, as if I were looking at my own corpse, carefully embalmed and arranged and slowly sinking down toward me through the dark fog.

I raised myself on my elbows and looked down. Thousands of phosphorescent lines were crawling over my body, back and forth, left and right, seemingly searching for each other. As soon as they located suitable "partners," they arranged themselves in perfect rows. They continued to move in formation, rows constantly joining other rows, ever more precise. Just as Odesta's figures at the deserted Yusian base had been, I was now completely covered with these dotted lines. Like swarming insects, they were studying me, learning me, and remembering me. I couldn't feel their touch—obviously they were without substance—but I was still absolutely convinced that they were wandering *inside* as well as all over me. Inside my body, inside my brain, and so on. Maybe even in my soul, wherever it is located? They swarmed everywhere.

Resisting an urge to leap up, I lay back down, and what had been a bed with a sheet clumsily splashed with a greasy gurgle. Yet if the substances under me had turned into liquid, why didn't I feel that? Then I realized that I had no bodily sensations at all. I looked up at the form floating above me. It no longer appeared deathlike—just asleep. And it was beginning to wake up slowly, very slowly, as shown by a tightening of its facial muscles, a slight frown, and a pursing of the lips. Not simply a hologram, it might better be described as a plasma robot. Now it was receiving information from the swarming "insects." That was exactly their function: to make him into an exact copy of me.

Realizing this, I carefully reviewed my present condition. My thoughts were clear, and my senses suitably numb considering the situation. This would be a good moment for them to be copied as well.

The plasma robot came closer and closer until his body gradually sank, somehow seeped, into my body, and then suddenly jumped out—or, more precisely, bounced up again about three meters above me. He opened his eyes widely, writhed convulsively, and became *me*. *Me* staring at myself with unseeing eyes. Yes, but I was also here, looking up at *myself*. If I could manage to hold this position, I would be able to witness my transformations from afar.

This presence of mine—this duplicate—was not what the Yusians wanted, of course. Immediately my will started bending under the pressure of blatantly intense forces. No more Mr. Nice Yusian: the game was getting rough. I was nearly unconsciousness, caught in the swampy trap of what had been a bed, not even able to free my fingers to pinch myself awake again.

But I came back to my senses despite their efforts—through another kind of pain, the memory of somebody's oncoming end. My thoughts became clear again, not completely, but enough to realize that I had to act before the next attack.

"No. You can't eliminate me." My husky voice was unrecognizable even to me. "I'm not some colonist! Nor will I *give* myself to you as did the woman I killed. I'll still be here! I *will exist* even when my mind flows with yours, even when you appropriate my emotions. Even if you assimilate my mind completely, *I* will still remain. Because I'm more than thoughts and emotions. And *way more* than any of you worthless creatures!"

After ten years of Zung-style diplomacy, my attitude must have definitely shocked them. When I concentrated, my face above me took on a ferocious smile that contrasted sharply with those empty glass-like eyes.

"You want me asleep or unconscious! You're afraid to stand face to face with even a single human being! You can only 'be in contact' with objects and corpses! Right?"

About a minute passed—apparently the time they needed to interpret and understand my words—before thin bluish bands emerged from the darkness, flexing like snakes, surrounding my new body, tightening their rings around it, and disappearing. Then new ones appeared and kept repeating the process. Some time passed before I figured out what was happening, and only then it became clear because I had watched Reder draw a similar, maybe exactly the same, bluish fluid from the body of the strange Yusian just hours ago. Yusian blood. And no, it wasn't disappearing. It was flowing—into me.

When this most unnatural blood transfusion was over, I already knew what came next—was even impatiently expecting it. They expected it too. I felt their impatience mixing with mine, growing and sharpening—like a hunger. A hunger for change.

My body above seemed to take a breath: my chest expanded enormously and began to sparkle in many animated colors. My huge eyes blinked above me. Heavy shining wrinkles layered themselves around my neck and on my face; my lower limbs thickened and joined together.

A strange creature, neither human nor Yusian, slowly moved down; slowly I landed on the floor. The dark fog drew aside before me like a curtain, opening to reveal those who would meet me here. As I walked toward them, energy waves surged through my body. I closed my eyes; I didn't need them anymore. Now the world burst into me through other, more superior, senses. My senses—I, my own self, going away.

I drifted far from myself, but still a human being was *here*, even though what made me human could not be seen. That bedrock faith in my *self* gave me the strength to offer my *soul* voluntarily for a vivisection.

CHAPTER 39

Garrote—a medieval device for torture by strangulation. An invention of the Holy Inquisition, a metal semiring that can be tightened using a screw until the free ends meet. Or until the victim in question is able to stand the torture without dying. Of course, in this case there is no danger of strangulation, because the victim is a creature that breathes and eats through its entire "skin" surface. The purpose of these two garrotes is to prevent it from moving during the surgical interventions and to register some of its reactions, using the electronics built into them.

———

Now Elia and Reder are tightening the garrotes: she directly above the chest narrowing, and he around the lower limbs. The tissues there are shrinking and thickening, their volume decreasing. When it's clear they have reached the limit of their density, Elia stops her actions. Reder, however, keeps tightening until the Yusian quietly indicates its pain. Then the three of us go into the sterile prep room. We throw the gloves and masks into the disposal shaft, scrub our hands with a disinfecting detergent, and put on new gloves and new sterile masks. We cover our gowns with long silicon coats with elastic hoods. We return to the other room.

While Elia rubs the torso of the Yusian with formalin, Reder and I make sure we have enough receptacles, cylinders, and other containers close at hand to preserve whatever we might remove during the process of dismembering the body, including as well a supply of large, Plasticine pouches for the preservation of bodily organs, just in case we encounter any.

Meanwhile Elia turns to adjusting the surgical saw. I pass behind her to take my place next to the Yusian. In this completely helpless condition, he looks even more feeble and undeveloped than he did before. He desperately tries to free himself from the garrotes, but their grip allows him only unsuccessful spasmodic efforts. His eyes are still closed, and the zones on his chest are no longer visible; the substance over them is now impenetrable. Heat rising from his body is saturated with drops of condensed steam. His surface fringe alternately settles down and bristles up in hopeless attempts to move, to escape. He radiates strong tension, panic, and fear—has finally understood what he is facing.

Elia turns on the operating lamps and begins to outline prospective incisions on his torso with a special marker. The white lines contrast sharply with the brown space suit. As soon as she has finished, Reder attaches electrodes to the Yusian; when activated, these will temporarily paralyze his regenerative processes. Reder then removes a small pump with a rubberized catheter from a box and prepares intubation equipment for deepening the incisions. The presence of a space suit will complicate the task significantly, but it will also keep the object alive as long as possible and, even more importantly, help us determine exactly which procedure causes its death.

Reder turns the electrodes' power to maximum, causing the creature to convulse violently, but Elia is still able to cut his space suit very precisely. Reder grabs one end of the cut with his forceps and peels off a piece of the space suit, exposing the flesh under it. We attach the retractors and stretch the edges of the opening. Elia records the exact time, while Reder is eagerly reaching for the surgical saw. I signal him that I will make the first cut, and he reluctantly lowers his hand.

———

Just as I planned, I ceased remembering exactly at this moment. It turned out to be much easier than I expected. Disturbingly easy. The fog surrounding me was even darker than before. I couldn't decide if my eyes were open or not, even wondered if I were now blind. I had no senses, neither human nor Yusian. Nor did I have any idea where I was—or whether I was in my body or in the plasma robot that had become my double.

But I already had a memory that wasn't mine. Yes, an exchange of perceptions, thoughts, and feelings had taken place. Now I *knew* that not only do the Yusians have control over time and over matter in all its states but at one time, very long ago, they also reached even further, even deeper. They had touched a wellspring deep within themselves, and from that revelation came their ability to make use of their own substance to construct their machines and build their world. In the most profound sense, they were entirely self-reliant. This is why our scientists have been unable to uncover their secrets. The Yusians' power came from deep within their own psyches, as was also true of their polyplanetary system: *the psychic energy of the Yusians constantly courses through it*! The entire system is "ordered" by their collective consciousness. In times of crisis, however, it responds instead to their instincts, as would any living being. That's why I have been able to stay out of its reach so easily. My plan to remain apart from my double conveniently coincided with its impulse to throw me out in order to save its inhabitants from the further, already unbearable, sharing—coexperiencing—of my memory about the strange Yusian.

I smiled in my mind: it did throw me out but not fully and completely. My physical condition, and especially my absence of feelings, proved that I was again at the threshold of the contact. I was still *here*, but did the system successfully eject me? No. The darkness and silence that surrounded me at the moment revealed some hesitation, painful to the point of numbness; this feeling, or any other *feeling*, couldn't belong to any system. Even if the Yusians can order it with everything that animates them, no system can acquire a soul. Despite the energy provided by their collective mind, it would always be simply a colossal robot, spread out at a radius of thousands of light-years—in principle, not very different, actually, from my double, the plasma robot.

So I had begun to establish an unprecedented contradiction between the Yusians and their system: a conflict between their instinct, which was stopping the system from renewing contact with me, and their hope that the unfortunate Yusian garotted on the operating table might still be saved. That hope also led them to prolong this already abominable contact with me.

I didn't intend simply to wait for the outcome of this conflict. Just the opposite: I had to act before that happened, to take advantage of their hesitation and renew the contact myself. But how? Using the plasma robot, of course! It's my only vehicle for accessing the system, and since I'm still here, the connection between us must still be operative. I concentrated on my concept of my double, on drawing him toward me.

He appeared as if out of nowhere, just popped up in the darkness—now unrecognizable, a huge, shining blue lump. But the closer he came, the more clearly this human-Yusian hybrid resembled me. Good! But then he stopped. He too was struggling with some painful indecision.

Well, yes, because the system is guarding the Yusians too closely, protecting them from everything—mostly from themselves. It forbids them to risk—forbids them to hope. They provide it with the highest energy, the energy of their collective spirit, which it accepts while, in the process, discarding their feelings like useless trash, actually lowering them to the level of their instincts. Those instincts thus predetermine how the system will react—always efficient, always pragmatic—based on two principles as ancient as the system itself. Namely, to guarantee complete safety for its inhabitants and to expand its borders, assimilating everything that stands in one of its numerous ways into space.

Safety and assimilation. That was it until one of those ways carried the Yusians to Earth. To humankind. Ultimately to me in particular.

I concentrated my attention again on the plasma robot. A machine. Extremely eccentric, unique, or a unique double at least, but in the final analysis, just a machine. Whose purpose was to serve as a conduit, allowing the Yusians to pour their collective "soul" into me and thus make me fit for assimilation, now known as *contact*.

My laughter echoed, heavy with anger, and at the same time, I saw the plasma robot rock toward me as if I had pulled him by an invisible string. I continued pulling him, now silently, and he continued coming, though very slowly. Through him, somehow, I was approaching too. I could hear my heart pounding in the thick silence like the shattering of a brittle vase. My own inhuman eyes were almost upon me, gazing down at me. My other body started bending, leaning over me. When I concentrated on moving, my body above me started vibrating, and its huge chest exploded against my face into colorful flames. O yes! Even without any help I had started this—body that was mine again. My chest, that other chest, one heart. I gained command over it and moved forward with it. More and more forward, until nobody's instincts could throw me out again.

———

I take the saw and, without turning it on, bend over the Yusian and slowly run its serrated edge across his trembling flesh. He abruptly opens his eyes, and I gaze into them, absorbing both their humiliating plea for mercy and a horror of dying that flows from their depths. I pull away. His horror and humiliation are already in my mind. I can now leave with them and use them as my weapons. I throw off the mask, lay aside the surgical saw, and rip off the gloves.

"Excellent decision!" Reder sardonically pats my shoulder and moves forward to take my place.

"I'm glad we agree." I reply. "There's no sick person here to operate on."

"What—what are you talking about?"

Instead of answering, I casually push Reder aside and switch off his paralyzer device. Elia says nothing, but I turn toward her in time to see her impulsively toss her mask next to mine. I know she has not yet made her choice.

"I'm aborting the entire procedure," I state for the recording device.

Now red blotches appear on Reder's face, visible even under the burn cream. The shock of my words and actions has reignited his hatred of me. I watch it flare to full power and absorb that look of pure hatred. I need it as a reminder.

"Damn you!" he shouts hysterically. "Traitor! No, you have no right and no authority to abort the procedure!"

"Why can't I?"

"We are at war, Simon!"

"Not declared by anybody."

"It doesn't matter! If you stand in the way now, you *will* be sentenced as a traitor! A contemptible traitor of humankind!"

I shrug my shoulders and approach the Yusian again. Despite the retractors, his space suit has completely closed since I turned off the device.

"Summary execution! You will be condemned to death!"

"Yes," I said, nodding at him, "that's possible."

"No, not possible. It's certain. And more than that, if we let the creature live, then what? We can't let it go! The Yusians are hardly going to believe that we *saved* it!"

"We won't claim such a thing."

"And what are we going to tell them? What?"

"The truth."

This fateful word renders Reder as silent as the grave. I begin cautiously to loosen the garrote around the chest of the Yusian.

"Listen, Simon." Reder is trying to address me more calmly and soberly. "We have to continue—"

"With what?" I purposely interrupt him. "With the vivisection?"

"Yes. Yes! This is our only chance. Because as soon as we return to Earth, Zung is going to get the colonization under way. The colonists are ready and waiting. And while the Yusians are transporting them, the Yusian bases on Earth will be destroyed. Which, Simon, will actually mean the declaration of the war."

I stop loosening the garrote and wave my hand, dismissing his comments. "Well, Reder, before the military operations start, we will have at our disposal as much as two hundred years, won't we?"

"Yes, but what if we find a way to kill them, right here, right now? That would change everything! Zung can spit on their agreement! We will immediately capture all the Yusians on Earth and take over their embassies and their starships! Their chronal centers—when we persuade the captives to cooperate. Do you realize it? Those centers will enable us to strike crushing blows against them! We might even take over their whole system, liquidate every last one of the stinking creatures, and then, then—"

He is choking. His own *daydreams* have strangled the speech out of him. He throws off his mask and gasps for air. The light of reason in his eyes has been snuffed out, and in its place burns the lurid flames of rabid Yusophobia.

Elia looks at him with distaste but also with understanding, which doesn't surprise me. Her feelings are not far from his, though not yet maniacal. She tries to reason with him: "Ehrlich, we have failed from the beginning of these experiments. We have no reason to hope that the vivisection will lead to immediate results. On the contrary, it's more likely that we won't be able to determine exactly when and how—we have murdered him."

Reder senses her hesitation, and his look is quickly becoming clear. With so many surgical instruments around us, she would be an important ally in any forthcoming conflict. "But still we have to try, Elia! At the very least, we will gain an invaluable store of anatomic material."

I move to the Yusian again, finish removing the first garotte, and then turn my attention to the second. I am still wearing the silicon operating coat, and my flexor is hidden under it. No doubt Reder will do whatever he can to keep me from removing the second garotte, and I have no time to lose. I watch his every move out of the corner of my eye.

Meanwhile, Elia takes a few steps back and slips her hands into her pockets, showing that she is not ready to take either side. For now, I have no intention of removing the second garrote. My purpose is to provoke Reder, who is slow to react. I recall that he hadn't been as panicked as I thought he would be when the Yusian had broken free of the restraining straps. Anxious at first, but then—as if he realized that this particular Yusian posed no threat to us. That he was manageable. "His world almost vague as yours through our perceptions," Chuks had described him.

I reach to remove the electrodes attached to his body but, at that exact moment, am struck with an insight so stunning, so obviously true, that for just an instant, I take my eyes off Reder. That is all the time he needs. He leaps to his feet, and while one gloved hand turns on the current, the other grabs my hand and forces it onto the node. The shock throws me back against the surgical cart, overturning it, but as bottles crash to the floor, I use my body momentum to make a clumsy backward somersault. I clear the cart but slip on the shards and splinters of glass, lose my balance, and fall to the floor. A falling receptacle slams against my head, and the stench of spilled physiological solutions further disorients me.

Reder has put his mask back on and is all over me. Holding a garotte in his hand, he swings at my forehead, but I twist away so that it hits me on the shoulder. Its metal tightening screw hammers into my right arm, which is becoming numb. He takes another swing at me, this time hitting me in the temple, and then drags me toward the X-ray chamber by my legs. He has decided to lock me in there. I, however, have decided to do the same, but to him.

I relax and try to appear even more disoriented than I am, which is not hard to do. Reder is puffing, trying to muster his energy to maneuver my body. Finally he reaches the chamber gate, drops my legs, and is about to push the button to open it when Elia intervenes.

"No!" she shouts, blocking the gate from the central control panel.

Reder frowns at her and then at me. He makes a few quick mental calculations, abruptly turns his back on me, and runs toward the operating table, where the Yusian is still immobilized by the other garotte. I spring up, my left hand feeling for the flexor under my coat, and rush after him.

As soon as Reader reaches the operating table, he grabs the electrical saw. If he kills the Yusian, I would have no alternative but to play by *his* rules. Even injuring him seriously would be enough to overturn my plans.

"He's a *child*!" I shout to Elia.

When I reach Reder, he aims the saw at me, its serrated edge spinning and glimmering under the bright operating lamps. I jump as high as I can and land a kick right on his jaw. He collapses, but *I* don't have the strength to stay upright either. As we stare at each other almost face to face, the saw skitters under the operating table, continuing to drone. We both dive for it, but Reder is closer. He brandishes it at me as he totters to his feet. When he turns toward the Yusian, I catch his ankle and pull him back, forcing him to his knees. But the hand with the saw is still poised over the table, trying to reach the—child. As I pull him, the saw whines through the table's thick rubberized covering. It's still moving.

Grabbing his other ankle and marshaling all my strength, I jerk him as hard as I can, much harder than before. Howling with pain, Reder stumbles, but his hand remains over the table in an unnatural position. I haul myself up—and see why: his palm is nailed to the table by a scalpel. I look at Elia, her open palm resting on the Yusian's chest. She must have needed that extra leverage to drive the scalpel deep into the operating table from the opposite side. She glares darkly at Reder and doesn't move when he reaches up with his good hand and pulls the scalpel out, his face wrenched with pain.

"You knew," she whispers fiercely. "You knew the whole time that…he…that it—" She looks down and only now realizes what she has been leaning on. She jumps back as if her hand has been scalded.

"No, I didn't know!" Reder snarls at her. "Nobody knew how their kids looked. None of the video materials they gave us contained a kid. But I did *guess* and thought you guessed too and that none of us were talking about it just because—"

"Because it was easier that way?" I interrupt, once again shutting off the saw and that diabolic paralyzer device.

Without paying the least attention to his wound, Reder waves his hands angrily, spattering blood in all directions. "It's high time we ask ourselves *why* they hide their kids from us!"

"They don't hide them at all," Elia objects, nodding toward the poor, still terrified, "strange"—no, simply young—Yusian.

"Anyway, what difference does it make?" Reder again attempts a reasonable tone. "While we may not have planned it this way, this is still our best possible option. If we can find out how to kill their young, our battle will be won! Just think about it—consider the implications."

I dismiss his ravings with an unambiguous warning gesture and turn to Elia. "Give him a tranquilizer and knock him out. Then you can see to his hand."

CHAPTER 40

The Yusians' relief gushed toward me as if a dam had burst its gates. Had their responses been material, I would definitely have drowned in their relief and then been crushed by their approval, as if their entire civilization had collectively patted me on the back and said, "Bravo, bravo! We are pleased with you."

I was also feeling pretty happy with myself but for completely different reasons. I had penetrated a considerable distance into their system and could comprehend it much more fully with my enhanced senses than I ever could have on my previous entering. It was gradually calming down, regaining its balance because the danger had dissipated. My memory revealed its happy ending—like a Yusian fairy tale—and now the inhabitants of the system were jubilant. That prepared them for the moment of sterling, true, ultimate contact with me, and I too was ready.

My situation during this transitional stage hadn't been bad at all. I had managed to retain complete human consciousness, even though that consciousness now resided in a plasma robot and that robot was—the devil knows where. For now I wasn't allowed to see through his eyes or follow his movements. It was as if I were suspended, so to say, halfway between. Apparently the system had only admitted me far enough into its structures to allow my memory to be shared and was now making final checks. But those didn't threaten my further plans either, because I had already determined that, even at this "spiritual" level, Yusians had no telepathic abilities.

More precisely, they can't just read *anyone's* memory, be the individual human or Yusian. To do so, they always need the active cooperation of the subject. Thus their "spiritual union" is primarily expressed through sharing identical opinions, opinions resulting from the uniformity forced upon them by the system. So they *are* individuals with free will, but their wills haven't been stimulated to act individually for a long time. For a very long time—but no longer!

So enough with the delaying checks. It was high time for me to break in this plasma double-image machine again and to ride it down the chronal tracks of their polyplanet system. I had something else to show them, but it wouldn't be a memory. It would happen in the present and, instead of a fairy tale, was going to have all the attributes of a thriller.

"My *patience* is coming to an end," I pronounced. My voice echoed and reverberated as if coming from the abyss—or just from that pseudobed where my physical body lay. "I'm *ready to terminate* the contact!"

My threat had the desired effect: suddenly I could see through the eyes of the plasma robot. But that proved to be of almost no use, just convincing me that, even after this second exchange of perceptions, thoughts, and feelings, I still lacked adequate knowledge to comprehend what I was seeing. Totally alien to me, a chaotic profusion of fiber pipes connected in three-dimensional configurations spread in every direction. Or maybe fiber shaped like pipes? Their gauge varied from a few centimeters to a meter or even more, and all of them were swaying, as if moved by a gentle breeze, and constantly vibrating. Their varying colors were shadowy, as if covered with ash, and their connecting knots loosened at one moment and then tightened the next, as if in reaction to their contents.

I shook off my bewilderment and tried to determine the position of the plasma robot—and thus myself as well—but I can only describe it as being *suspended* somewhere, with no ground under my lower limbs and nothing concrete either around or above me. I was just there, floating in a Yusian nowhere like some grotesquely enlarged fly trapped in one of the wide hollows between the fiber pipes.

But I hadn't come this far just to dangle, a nowhere man going nowhere. I had to move on, to find the *center* of the system and deliver the crucial psychological blow. "To the center. To the center!" I multiplied this command in my mind as if using a stamp and also programmed it into my plasma robot: "to the *center*!"

I heard a sharp, rending sound, perhaps imaginary, but then I realized that it came from all the resolve in the depths of my being. Nothing would stop me. I was firing my *self*, launching myself like a torpedo, heading right for my target. Cutting the knots and breaking the pipes until everything around began quaking. Blue geysers shot out, leaving gaping chasms of blackness. Energy streams stormed and swooped at me, but I swooped back at them. White sparks surrounded me—my own aura—and then were transformed into striking lightning by my incredible speed. As the lightning tore through the upcoming currents, I overtook them one after another, going forward and up—and up.

But they kept repeating endlessly, seemingly chaotic and heterogeneous but actually frighteningly alike. These were the components of the system, united by unbreakable chronal connections—interacting through them instantly and automatically. Without will that could be broken. Without emotions that could be kindled. Without spirit that could stand against mine, yet they were overcoming my élan with their united monotony, snuffing out my diminishing white sparks.

My flight against the currents was over. Now they carried me at dizzying speeds through absolute time. I clenched my teeth to resist screaming, but even my teeth seemed to be melting. Then the next current whirled me straight downward. I painlessly crashed into blackness and continued to fall until a dim light penetrated the dark, as bleak as ashes. I had returned to the nowhere I started from. Yes, the same place—because it must always be the same. No journey can change it. No élan. No target, because there is no *center* here. I smiled bitterly: so this was the sum total of their "united spirituality" and what it was like to be its first human colonist.

I stretched an upper limb, a padded, shapeless semblance of an arm, and touched one of the fiber pipes. Gradually increasing the pressure, I tried to shake it. Nothing changed. It continued to vibrate and sway gently exactly as it had before I approached it. I let go and stepped on it instead, thinking that at least my vibrations would have some effect on it. Not visibly at least, but although it looked as soft and yielding as before, as accepting, it was actually hardening after each contact with me. This was, in fact, the reactive *function* of these psychoplasma fiber pipes. I placed my robot self next to its closest knot and lay down, pressing my communication zones against it. Although they were still in a rudimental stage of development, they were able to begin transforming the vibrations into homogenous sensations of stability, security, and steadiness. Of safety. The fiber pipes were conduits for defense, for universal reassurance—coziness.

I felt that flow of unmediated, unmitigated well-being and hurried to pull back, although I knew it would be to no avail. The zones would continue to merge and expand no matter what I wanted. Before long they would fill me with these sensations, and who knows what else, in any position, nonstop, whether I was in my plasma robot or my physical body. On Eyrena or on Earth—it wouldn't matter because from now on I would always be here as well, in this alien dimension from which nothing and nobody can ever escape. It has no exits—a closed defense cycle designed to reduce even the most powerful sensations of its collective components, myself included, to safe uniformity.

I began to wander through the ancient deceitfulness of its seeming diversity, moving without direction, some psycho-plasma hybrid from which the Yusian collective consciousness would indifferently suck out *my* spiritual energy—*my* feelings, thoughts, hopes—and canalize them. So what's new about this story? Isn't it as human as it is Yusian?

CHAPTER 41

As I stood, not even throwing a shadow in that ashy dimension but gathering my anger, I was not alone in this initiative. Many people were helping me, known and unknown, far from me and from each other, as far away as Earth. I thought about the hundreds of terminally ill people, torn between hope and despair at their upcoming journey to mythical Eyrena; the prisoners with life sentences; and the incurably insane people—all future colonists, elected and prepared so that they could be sacrificed on the altar of Zungian diplomacy to propitiate an alien civilization.

I yearned to avenge Genetti as well, a highly respected scientist who had been belittled into a confused, frightened old man. I evoked him in my mind together with his executioner: Vey A. Zung, who because of his undeniable talents had become Earth's most powerful leader. For ten years, Zung had bowed and scraped before Yusians, listening to their pretensions and pretending to agree while choking on his own helpless hatred— exactly like mine now.

Others came to my aid from even further away. Fowler, Stein, and Odesta had sacrificed their lives for a cause they couldn't really understand but that they knew to be *human*—three corpses that left behind two killers. I thought about those two: one had lost his moral courage, while the other, severed from himself, was now both lying on a Yusian "bed" and wandering here in the shape of a psychoplasma idiot. I reopened even my freshest psychic wounds, returning in my mind to the bunker just after I aborted the vivisection.

I load the delirious Reder onto the truck, his hand probably permanently crippled. "Come on!" I urge Elia, but she has already made the most difficult decision of her life. She has chosen to stay behind with that huge, incomprehensible Yusian child. She knows that this is the only way she can support me. It is a fateful decision, but I accept it. She smiles reassuringly as the armored gates slowly close, cutting her off from my range of vision. In the end, I disable them from the outside; she will be unable to leave. Nor does she, or I, know whether I will come back to free her—or be forced to destroy her.

I still didn't know, mired in this spectral limbo. I tried to marshal as much negative energy as I could, to concentrate it into a force strong enough to attack the all-leveling system, no matter where. The important thing was to make a break in it. I chose the knot across from me as a target, aimed my "chest" at it, and accelerated myself.

"Chuks! Chuks!" A sudden scream echoed. "Settled me as first! The contact going to be in me. In us! It's before happening!"

I staggered, unable to believe my eyes—either pair! Chuks in a psychoplasmic incarnation—the only possibility here—but also transformed into an unrecognizable hybrid, Yusian inside but on the outside bearing *my* body, *my* face, although enlarged, asymmetrically stretched, semitransparent, and also somehow layered. In that monstrous shape, Chuks floated proudly toward me and stopped in front of me, on the same fiber pipe, greeting me with maddening, unearthly enthusiasm—with joy—with serene, even tender, fondness! There could be no doubt that it was sincere. My God! Out of habit I tried to hold my temper, but this time I didn't succeed. Training and self-control—all drowned in the immense absurdity of the situation.

"But *why*? *Why* do you like me, you cretin? I didn't save your little freak! I'm holding him as a hostage. I can destroy him right now! On Earth I broke up terrorist groups, even *ultra*terrorist groups. I learned a lot from them, and I'm here to put that knowledge to work. Against you. Can't you understand that, after all I've said and done?"

"Don't return those 'all,'" he said in his singsong voice. "They are now nothing, Chuks."

"*Chuks*? I'm not one of your *Chuks*! Do you think I stopped the vivisection so that I could give you the object with a tender embrace of love and friendship? Ha! Do you realize how extremely exorbitant the *price* of that object was for us? We also created an annihilation that even you couldn't manage yet! And we destroyed our defractor."

"But you leaned on a chance."

"*You* didn't keep the little Yusian at home and let him shuffle back and forth and look around. That's what gave us our chance! But if you hadn't, we would have lured somebody else—most likely you! I could have done that myself. Staging that 'accident' in order to provide living material for their examinations was the real *mission* of the people here. Their bosses on Earth decided that they would be able to deceive you, but your stupidity exceeded even their most optimistic expectations—exceeded them and turned this into a nightmare!"

"Leave roads of past, Chuks—*Ter*." The psychohybrid Chuks smiled softly with my lips. "Us unite *contact* of ourselves!" he screamed exultantly and skillfully scooted toward me, spreading my "arms" to hug me.

When I pushed him back, he pressed again with maddening persistence. I lost my temper; my last inhibition collapsed. I twisted my limbs around him, lifted him up, and threw him down with all the strength I had. Sprawled on his back, he dangled in that position two or three meters below me. He didn't get up, just kept spreading his arms and bringing them together again as if practicing for the inevitable, though postponed, hug.

"You filthy, damned creature! All those zones, folds, crinkles, and who knows what on your bodies make me sick. *All* that is yours makes me sick! I don't want it!"

I bent down and, with uncontrollable fierceness, bit into the folds around my "chest." I gripped them with the determination of a bulldog bearing down. I could sense and even hear the splitting and cracking, and I used all my force to widen the wound. I tore one fold after another to shreds, ripping the flesh that was a part of me here. I hurled the pieces far from me, and they landed, as if drawn by unknown forces, on the fiber pipes. As they melted, the fibrous surfaces quickly absorbed them. I finally managed to expose my own human form, to remove the last traces of the grotesquely pliant Yusian layers. I found it strange that I had felt no pain, but beneath me Chuks was writhing, apparently in mortal agony.

I stared at him. Now he looked like me much more than before. My image had condensed on his image so that I actually saw an indescribably deformed representation of myself. The eyes, however, were my own, somehow unchanged, which made them looked even more—more alien, as if they were pinned onto his barely visible forehead membrane. They were frantic with fear—somebody else's fear—and still burned with that alien "love," obtrusively soft, ravenous "love."

"I want nothing to do with your so-called feelings! More than anything else, I despise *them*. And who gave you the right to counterfeit *my face*?"

I jumped on him, sank up to my ankles in the plasma that had copied even my heart. I felt it there inside, under my feet, pounding futilely. I stepped aside into the allegedly empty space, gritted my teeth to withstand the pain, and thrust my nails into *my* eyes pinned to *his* forehead.

It wasn't merely pain but the very fires of *hell*. Still, it was intoxicating! I tore the eyes from the head and threw them into the abyss. I tore at the creature's "skin" and ripped out its "organs" and chunks of its "flesh," scattering the pieces and roaring the whole time. I had become the animal that rips off its own paw to free itself from the trap.

The Yusian didn't resist, just lay there, staring at me from under the last remnants of my face. He seemed to radiate suffering, overwhelming disappointment, and despair at the destruction of his broken dreams. The pathetic creature simply endured my savage attempts to reduce him to nothing, to destroy him both here and there, whether in this realm or some other, more material one. I would kill him wherever I found him!

I knelt on his naked, annoyingly limp, torso and drove my hands deep into his center zone, which instantly turned red. I got ready again and…

After a noticeable delay, the system finally reacted. I was stopped just centimeters short of my goal. A force field surrounded us both and enclosed us in separate capsules. A few seconds later, accompanied by a loud sucking sound and an ultraviolet light, the capsule that had wrapped itself tightly around my skin disengaged itself and floated upward, disappearing into a newly formed opening in the fiber above. I heard another, much louder, sucking sound, and the opening also disappeared.

I slowly unclenched my fists, having rid myself of my negative energies, and turned my attention to Chuks. He was still in his capsule, which obviously had functions very different from what mine had already performed. The Yusian was submersed in a dusky-blue substance, the now familiar Yusian blood, but for as long as I watched him, he didn't regain his senses. His entire torso continued to writhe in agony, and his frontal zones were so dark that they resembled huge holes. Rotary jets of the substance periodically sprayed them, but Chuks's body rejected the fluid each time. For some reason, the "transfusion" wasn't working.

I approached his capsule, bent, and extended my arm. It felt as if I were submerging it into electrical jelly. When I pressed my palm against the zones that had gone dark, they felt ice cold, maybe because my hand was so hot. Somehow my touch seemed to effect a heat exchange, and through the material of the capsule, I could feel the torso gradually relax, and the dark zones regained some of their color, though they were still a sickly yellow.

"Hey you, Yusian!" I shook him. "Get up!"

Chuks clambered to an upright position with the sticky blue substance still clinging to him and seeping into his body. I waited patiently for the process to end—a procedure just like the one I was exposed to before I entered this spectral dimension. It suddenly occurred to me that, while I was ripping off my Yusian layers, not a drop of Yusian blood had escaped. In other words, I was still charged with it. That was a fact.

"I was going to kill you," I informed Chuks, just in case he hadn't even understood that.

'But *contact* is still before happening," he responded.

Damn! When I resolved to attempt this impossible confrontation, I knew perfectly well I would be risking my life, but I never considered the danger to my sanity!

"A *contact*? This is your spiritual union? *The two species becoming one*? When will you come to your senses, for God's sake? If you try to apply this "spiritual union" to us, you will actually be digging the first of your own grave. Only the first one, yes, because the rest will be dug by us."

I waited for some reply, fully aware that most likely all Yusians were witnessing this crucial exchange, from one side of their polyplanetary system to the other, without the delay of so much as a nanosecond, through the atemporal channels that connected them. But I was still worried that they wouldn't understand me, so I decided to use simpler language.

"Listen! For ten years we have searched for your vulnerabilities—for a weapon to use against you. Now I've found not one weapon but two. Two! You know the first one: our categorical, final refusal to accept the *contact*! That unresolved problem is enough by itself to cause your entire civilization to stagnate and wither. Now I know that there's another, incomparably more dangerous weapon: exactly the *contact* you are seeking. Such a *contact*, according to your rules, will result in our conquest of your whole system and your total destruction!"

Again I waited for some response, but none came. The complacency of these creatures was itself monstrous. Paradoxically, it grew out of that impersonal, complete lack of individuality that shielded them from any troubling thought or disturbing truth. I tried to be even more direct.

"That's exactly what will happen! We will erase you once and for all from the infinite face of the universe. What do you plan to contribute to this merging? This human Yusian hybrid you want to create will be filled with *our* individualism, *our* egotism, and *our* sense of *self*. You have evolved without ever confronting any other life form but your own. What could you possibly know about the struggle for survival, about survival of the fittest? Absolutely nothing! What's more, you evolved from *plants. We* are *predators*."

"Ter, Ter." Chuks repeated my name almost tenderly. "Why stay lost from fact that our *contact* happens where nobody recognizes self but already knows other? So nobody then has only own origin—"

"Nonsense!" I interrupted him impatiently. "We are going toward a conflict, not a contact—a conflict that is going to take place here, in this dimension, and will be really crucial. For you! Well, yes, this abomination—I mean your collective mind, your system—will immediately start to reprocess and channel our negative energies, but there is no way it can change our instincts. In contrast to our thoughts and feelings, instincts can't be reprocessed. Do you understand?"

No, obviously he didn't understand me, nor was I sure he was even *trying* to understand me. So I switched to the *socratic* method of question and answer, which usually captures the attention of any audience.

"And what will happen when human instincts start spreading through your system, Chuks? Your collective consciousness will undergo transformation because the system itself will stop reprocessing our negative energies. It will no longer consider them something negative to be guarded against or sublimated. You will naturalize our feelings as if they were your own. Then we must remember that the system itself is not a consciousness, just a universal automaton, a psychoconstruction that governs everything, including all of you, through your own instincts—the instincts you share with everything in your system. *Now* the instincts that you completely rely upon will be *our instincts.* That's what this *contact* really means!"

Unfortunately, there was more. The Eyrena colony that had been planned as the first phase of the contact could also prove fatal to us, to humans on Earth. It was a horror to imagine the only "product" that could come from it: insane criminals in Yusian bodies, armed with the colossal power of this advanced civilization, and *very angry* at the race that had abandoned them in the name of its "redemption."

Chuks stood in front of me as silent and motionless as a plasma statue. I knew perfectly well, however, that he wasn't troubling himself over such human truths or even taking them into account. He was simply preparing himself again to complete his mission, to establish our Yusian-human *contact.*

"Don't ignore what I say. Most probably I won't have the time for you again. Very soon your 'mind' will try to destroy me."

"Make a major mistake," he objected calmly. "Destroy incompatible with system."

"It was incompatible until minutes ago, but now it has swallowed my impulse to kill you. My aggressive impulse, my survival instinct, is now in its structures. Before its only choice was to assimilate everything that stands in its way; now it has another one: to destroy all that is not pliable enough for absorption."

"Your pliability sure, Ter. At end *contact*, Ter not need aggressive. Have system protection."

"We'll see. Perhaps I'll be a fire that's been extinguished, or perhaps it is you who will go up in flames. After all is said and done, however, you still have to ask yourself why I am here?

Why did I feel the need to accept this *contact* you had forced on me, even though I was entirely opposed to it?"

"For us details chaotic human nature." The Yusian's voice again sounded maddeningly tender and solicitous. "Going to insert our help into you."

"Enough! Follow your program. I'll even endure your help."

These words seemed to let the genie out of the bottle. It appeared in the form of a cloud hovering above us, shot through with many multicolored striations like a thick rainbow. Chuks quickly moved out of its way, but I stayed where I was. The cloud descended before me and began to change its shape. In the end it looked like a Yusian torso cut at both ends but at least three times larger. Its communication zones pulsed abnormally bright, and it repeatedly activated them, perhaps the cause of the ominous rumbling sounds that began coming from inside the torso. I knew I wasn't going to be destroyed yet, but just to be safe, I decided to step back—and found that I couldn't. The space behind me hardened so that I was literally "up against the wall." Then I realized that, in fact, I was being pressed from the sides as well; panic gripped me, so much so that I was tempted to play my last trump right then and there. But of course I didn't. Now that I had breached the system, I had to stay there and play my part almost to the end, though I had no idea when the end would come.

Now the cloud stood silent, which was no less threatening than the thunder before. All I could do was wait, and the longer it delayed its attack or whatever it had in store for me, the more tightly panic gripped me—but in the opposite direction. Against all reason, even against my will, I feared now that the cloud might draw back—abandon me!

I felt the Yusian blood suddenly bursting through my absurd psychoplasma body. Rushing into my brain, it filled me with incomprehensible—but even more incomprehensibly attractive—images and feelings.

As fast as butterflies fluttering into the bottom of a damp hollow, a whirlwind of sharp crystal flakes thrusts deeply into me and I take them in. A slippery hump fills me with delight, and I cling to it. I sink into a sea of miniscule black grains, flooding my eyes and turning them black, changing them somehow—usefully. I pull down my forehead membrane so they don't escape.

A forehead membrane? Again! I shook my head and stretched my eyes to see if I still at least looked human. Yes, I did, but the cloud was pulsating in front of me, and my heart was echoing its rhythm, every beat and pulsation becoming faster. My blood started pounding in my chest, boiling and bursting out, covering my body with foam. I scooped it up with my hands and then extended my arms and drew the sharp arcs of—the detention. I couldn't stop; I didn't know what this *detention* was, but I felt it was something important. Then the "interdict" split lengthwise, and I felt that the time had come. But for what?

The cloud's glaring communication zones enveloped me, filled my whole field of vision. But no, there would be no communication. They only functioned now as mutual aid organs, I realized the moment before they took me into their cloudy tissues, and when they crushed me in a suddenly stiff embrace, I realized something else too: Yusian aid is also viciously aggressive, in no way "vegetable." I absorbed its radiation ravenously, desperately, although my still-human consciousness strongly objected. It was so well intentioned, saturated with somebody else's belief, that it was necessary for my survival. It worked on me like a drug, like painless euthanasia, providing me passage to another, distant world.

They made me look through the prism of their senses, maybe even their feelings. The world grew ever more distant and expansive, filled to overflowing with radiantly bright spirits, ethereal figures of various live and "nonlive" creatures. Yet they weren't really crowded together, not in the least. Somehow there was plenty of room for all of them; the space was unlimited—infinite. In spite of that, I could still discern each and every one in sharp detail. Distance was no obstacle; here everything was immediate and accessible, simply by meditation. All I needed to do was direct my attention toward something, and I was right next to it. There was no trace of the spectral psychic construct that held me earlier, and no trace of Chuks either.

The figures were not static, but neither were they moving. The movement was in them. I felt it as life spiritual to the point of—perfection. In my meditation floated the oval ghosts of whole planets, an astonishing number! I also saw the wavy silhouettes of oceans and seas, long chains of ancient mountains, mouths of volcanoes, ephemeral winding rivers, and narrow creeks. I even recognized that strange Yusian river despite the fact that its "spirit" wasn't black and grainy. Here it wasn't flowing; instead, suffused with light, it looked almost white.

Where are the spirits from our Earth? I asked myself, and they immediately appeared, very few thus far in this radiant space. Here were the mushrooms, as big as oak trees, silver reflections of those at the Yusian base. I found also the seashells, seaweeds, and moss, each species larger and flourishing here. Even the colossal eyes of insects—all part of this great harmony. A harmony without any human spirit—mine was the first!

But without any Yusian spirit either. Their place, obviously, was higher, I sensed, which gave me a weary feeling of humiliation. After all, I found it repulsive to be placed at the same level as mosses and seashells, even with oceans, mountains, or even planets. It offended my human nature. Besides, I no longer found all this inner life captured statically in frames attractive at all. It seemed to me that the "spirits" of rivers must also flow as oceans need to swell, volcanoes to erupt. Yes, I was ready now to return, leave this *perpetuum immobile*. Only in the spectral dimension of the collective Yusian "mind" would I be able to defend everything that's human, alive, and struggling to the end.

I realized my error a minute later as if someone had shouted at me, *Though now invisible, this* mind *is still here!* Of course! The system itself was the exact outside force that had paralyzed everything here—even me. Unfortunately, metaphorically "to capture the spirit of things" had taken on literal meanings here. I had finally reached the *real* Yusian *control center,* and it turned out to be an entire, but immaterial, cosmic world! A perfect reflection of the visible polyplanet system so that those living worlds could be watched and controlled from here and, if necessary, restrained when disaster threatened: quakes, restraining hurricanes, floods, volcanic eruptions—maybe even people.

The agonizing tension I had felt abruptly subsided and disappeared. Why struggle, since there was no escape? Without the slightest hope of success, why waste my energy? There was no need, no point. So I began to relax. Or perhaps I was *extinguished?* It didn't matter. I had been given incredible, imperishable senses. The need to grow and develop, the categorical imperative to evolve in some material way, no longer applied to me. I felt that I had become a part of something eternal, harmonious, stable, and whole. Deep inside, I knew I never wanted to leave. How could I, just like that, force myself to go back somewhere and stand up for—what?

Those insane, fatal passions? The destroying, even ravenous, aggression? The cruelty, killings, terrorism, wars, mass graves, mass suicides, and in general, the dreadful, eternal *insecurity* of human life—is that what I was defending! Is this what my consciousness was telling me? Isn't our place really here? Aren't we potential disasters that need to be constantly checked and controlled? Yes. That was exactly the kind of help we needed, to be fiercely protected—against our will, our instincts, our being—until in the end, all the demons in us have been crushed forever. So that we can survive—although it wouldn't be "us" anymore. Along with those demons, other things will also be crushed forever: our spontaneity, courage, faith, self-sacrifice—our *human* compassion. Our capacity for love.

Oh, no, no, Yusians! The price is too high, so exorbitant that no matter where I am and how you paralyze me and try to extinguish this fire in my soul, *I'll always* answer you with a single syllable: No!

———

"No!" the *man* repeated, who in spite of everything had stayed there too, in the dimension of Eyrenean reality. "No, no, no" was his every breath, even as the invisible psychoconstruct began to absorb and grind away his negation.

But the hand holding the detonator had already moved. The fingers found the little buttons under the tape, pressed them with slow, mechanical consistency. When each level of protection had been removed, this very hand squeezed the detonator hard—and its thumb activated the program.

The man there started to get up: I, with my weak, vulnerable, real body, was rising out of the "bed" gurgling greasily like slime in a swamp, its substances again radiating the lullaby impulses programmed into them. To no avail, of course. Now Elia's life depended on me. And I knew what I had to do. My human spirit and masculine instincts were becoming inaccessible to them. All future attempts to extinguish or absorb me would be unsuccessful. I stood upright, raised the hand holding the detonator, holding hidden death, and prepared myself for a formal declaration.

"I have activated the detonator sequence for an eight-kiloton Adler explosive device, located in the underground clinic and research facility on the Eyrena base, where a young member of the Yusian race is now being held hostage. The neutrino remote detonator and the device operate on a closed circuit that you cannot interrupt or override. Program number nine, *Autocontrol*, is running: an automatic control sequence keyed exclusively to the registered operator who has activated it. That means that it will detonate automatically the instant the device is no longer in direct contact with my hand, and it will detonate at any abnormality in my brain activity and my neurological reactions due to death, loss of consciousness, hypnotic or medication dependence, or other similar conditions.

It is under these circumstances that I offer you the following ultimatum. I will release the young Yusian hostage *only* if it is fully and irrevocably accepted and fulfilled.

You must for all time accept a final refusal of contact through convergence of human and Yusian civilizations. That acceptance must be evidenced immediately by fulfilling the following concrete measures:

First, you will deactivate the four settlements for the colonists, including pseudo-Earth substances, hybrid plants, and Earth organisms under Yusian management.

Second, you will destroy all ESSIKO robots on Earth, as well as all subsidiary holdings of ESSIKO located there.

Third, you will establish a direct hypercommunication link between Eyrena base and Earth, by means of which we can and will confirm that all terms have been obeyed, before the Yusian hostage will be released.

Warning: the explosive devices can only be neutralized by me and only after personal bodily identification has been confirmed. Moreover, any attempt to breach the underground facility will automatically detonate the explosives.

This is the end of the ultimatum."

I dropped my arm and, smiling maliciously, couldn't help adding a few more words beyond my official demands, "For all the Chuks that might be listening, you can be sure that this little machine of *ours* functions faultlessly. There is nothing you can do to stop it. So obey the ultimatum. And hurry!"

CHAPTER 42

The Eyrenean "night" gave way to the yellow glare of Ridon pouring through the windows. The whole house heaved spasmodically, but the windows didn't even rattle. The pseudo-Earth materials still preserved the illusion of daily human life with all its seeming solidity. The empty bed gaped at me like some underfed animal and then finally gave something like a sigh and settled primly under a light-blue sheet without a hint of a wrinkle.

Obviously my ultimatum hadn't been accepted. I wasn't surprised. I knew the outcome was going to be difficult and also very uncertain—not only for me. I slowly lowered my eyes to the detonator in my hand. I had hoped that I would be able to end all this without resorting to the explosives, to reach my goals by only bluffing. But that hadn't happened. So Elia really had supported me in her possibly fatal decision. The thought of her trapped there had given me the strength to return here unchanged, although the contact was already established and I was losing touch with my human self. Now the radical actions we had both taken proved worth the risk, for another reason we hadn't considered. Instead of being put under control there, I had in fact ensured myself free access to the Yusian control center.

I closed my eyes. I only had to choose an object of meditation and that immaterial cosmic world would lower its barriers for me. Open and vulnerable. The balance of that world now depended to a significant degree on my own consciousness. And my psychic energy, unlike the energy of the Yusians, *remained* my own, unchanneled. That meant I could be very dangerous—very destructive.

I smiled to myself. I had kept my promise and shown them what it really meant to be *human*. But it would be good to make an even greater impression on them. I concentrated on the "spirit" of one of their volcanoes, sure that I could easily disrupt its balance and the volcano would no doubt erupt in the real, material world, perhaps somewhere near a Yusian dwelling or other structures. Otherwise they wouldn't have kept this volcano under control, would they?

As these thoughts crossed my mind, I felt my lips spread in a vicious smile and quickly opened my eyes.

"Damn it!" I whispered to myself, shocked. I had often thought that we should complete the colonization but by sending colonists with superior training and education rather than the criminals, terminally ill, and insane. Now, judging by my own behavior, I understood that other qualities would be equally crucial. "Your pliability sure, Ter." Chuks turned out to be right, at least indirectly. I was pliable, yes, but to the temptations that my victory offered me—yet another proof that the demons in us can be only temporarily and ostensibly crushed.

I moved around a little to test the condition of my body after its long torpor. I had grown numb and was almost lame. I shouldn't stay here any longer. It would be good for me to be outside anyway when this—nobody knows what—begins. I went to one of the windows and looked out. I didn't notice anything that had changed or aroused worry. I went back to the bed and, after making sure the tape still held the detonator securely to my palm, started to dress. Before leaving the room, I reached for the flexor on the nightstand, hesitated, and then decided not to take it.

I began to make my way up the street and with every step grew more steady on my feet. I never realized before how good it felt to be in my own body but was also aware it could be turned into a corpse at any moment. That thought also made me anxious for Elia's safety.

I heard a slight noise behind me and turned around cautiously. A Yusian shuttle was landing in front of the house that I had just left, near the garden gate. A slit opened in the usual way and out hopped Chuks. *He's coming to negotiate!* I thought hopefully, moving back in his direction. He moved too, but in a very strange way, tripping and zigzagging. If he were human, I would have assumed he was either drunk or stoned. His forehead membrane was closed, and his space suit absolutely opaque, so I couldn't guess his condition or mood by either his eyes or the colors of his communication zones. Vaguely suspicious, I stopped. Then to see how he would respond, I took a few steps back.

The creature gave a kind of shriek and without any staggering charged me at full speed. I didn't try to get out of the way at first, thinking that this was like the other times and he would come to a screeching halt just in front of me. That didn't happen this time. Luckily I was fully alert, so I just jumped to the side. Otherwise he would have crashed into me, crushing me beneath that massive body weighing nearly a ton.

I quickly recovered from my shock when I realized that the "contactor" must have a new mission now. As a killer—no doubt the first and only one of its kind among the Yusians. Formed *there*, in that other contact zone, out of my own murderous impulses, and this impulse was now coming back to me as a boomerang.

"Come back to your senses!" I yelled at him. "At the moment you are nothing more than a clumsy, remote-controlled weapon launched by a pitiful collective mechanism that has as its primary and overriding directive its own self-preservation. It wouldn't be stopped by the fact that, with me, you will also be killing the young Yusian. Is that what you want?"

He again started weaving drunkenly. "Have nothing, have nothing can want," he managed to reply before rushing toward me again, prepared to use his weight to crush me. I dodged him. Then, after making sure that the detonator was still firmly taped in place, I put my right hand on the wall next to me and hauled myself over into the front yard of the house next door to where I had just "spent the night." I considered returning there for the flexor and—and ruining everything I had achieved so far.

The alien charged the front gate leading to the yard where I was, crashing through it as if it were made of candy canes. Damn it! It would take the patience of an ox to endure the perverse, grotesque twists and turns of this never-ending game of hide-and-seek.

"At-ten-tion!" I said very slowly and loudly, as if trying to communicate with someone hard of hearing. "If you come near me, I will remove the detonator and throw it away! Then that unlucky little Yusian will scatter on the ground in so many pieces you won't be able to see them even under a microscope!"

I could see that he hadn't known about my hostage, Elia, because my threat froze him in midcharge, halfway through the shattered gate. He struggled with his conflicting impulses, unable to find a way out of the impasse. I was quick to press my advantage.

"Yusians! All of you who are observing this *spectacle*! Don't you understand that you are now accomplices to it? Your impersonal idleness is over. Make your own decision! My psychic connection with your *control center* can be cut off either by killing me or by changing the way you manage your system. Killing me means that *you choose* to sacrifice the young Yusian we are holding. *Or* you can choose to destroy a psychoconstruction that has petrified your *souls*. Those are your options. Bring an end to this all-consuming *collectivism*. It is nothing more than the blind instincts of a herd! *Each one* of you has to decide, on your own. It is time to make *your own choices*!"

"Contact is…still before…happening," murmured the creature like a broken record. "You are…extraordinary element. But colonists…will be in frames."

I was stunned. The *contact*? The Yusians had never found the strength of will to question even the *contact*, and here I was, urging them to give up their collective "mind" after thousands of years of dependency. That was absurd!

But Chuks wasn't entirely beyond hope. He was struggling against his new mission. He didn't want to be the first Yusian killer in history. I decided to give him as much time and moral support as I could. Moreover, I completely stopped hesitating about the flexor.

"Chuks, you are *nonhumanoids*. You are alien to us. That's exactly why you couldn't possibly keep *any* of us in your frames. Humans, whether crazy, normal, or brilliant, always try to gain the upper hand. That's just human nature. Do you understand?"

"No," he replied, "not in understanding."

He stopped "restraining" himself and entered the yard, leaving behind the broken remnants sticking out of the bottom and sides of the huge hole he had made in the fence. Chuks slowly approached me, and just as slowly I backed away.

"What's not clear, Chuks?" I kept repeating his name on purpose. If human beings suffer a shock or some other trauma, they often respond to the sound of their names. It helps them to identify with themselves again. But so far it hadn't helped him. On the contrary, his pace was accelerating little by little.

"Tell me, Chuks!" I repeated insistently, authoritatively, "What is not clear to you?"

"Your ultra...ulti—"

"My ultimatum?"

"Yes!" He accompanied his scream with a sharp turn to the left and an abrupt stop.

"Good, good." I stopped just as abruptly.

"If Ter among truths," he continued, "why resist ESSIKO? Have been describing that it gives you big interest against us."

"I have been describing to you, Chuks." I raised my voice, "I have been describing, showing you and proving to you the same thing over and over, ever since I arrived in this ridiculous parody of a normal human town. That thing is that, the way you have planned it, the *contact* will inevitably destroy your civilization because everything you excel us in, we will then be able to turn against you—even in this initial phase, *whichever* humans become your 'contactors!'"

Chuks threw himself on his back on the modified grass lawn and bit open his forehead membrane. Unintentionally, I looked into his nonhuman eyes, dark and glowing, reflecting the brightness of the nonterrestrial sun.

"You, Ter," he began quietly, "envelope yourself in assertion of saving for us."

"Well, yes, yes," I murmured, naturally not admitting that what I was really trying to do was to save humans from themselves. Anyone with any desire for power would want to control the awesome Yusian technology. Earth could not survive another Napoleon, Hitler, or Stalin with such mind-boggling means at his disposal.

"Until now, Chuks, you could have conquered us or destroyed us physically thousands of times, but you didn't, because you understand that you too would have lost by such needless destruction. Well, it would be the same with us. The *contact* now has vital importance for our civilization too—but as equals! Humans too have dreamed of a "meeting of the minds" with other life forms, Chuks, of universal understanding."

I had the feeling that, flake by flake and layer by layer, I was chipping away at his fossilized soul.

"Run," he said weakly and then suddenly rose, as if he were jerked up like a puppet on an invisible string. I gathered my strength and pushed him with my shoulder before he could reclaim his balance. He fell on his back again. Jumping over him, I moved to a tree next to the fence, caught the lowest branch, and tried to break it. With two hands I might have succeeded, but because of the taped detonator, I couldn't try that. The Yusian was back on his feet again and coming at me.

I dropped the branch, climbed over the fence, and walked down the street at my normal pace, looking back from time to time. The Yusian followed at about twenty meters behind me, trying not to shorten the distance. I could see and also hear how this effort was straining his strength. His surface fringe had become longer and began wriggling like green worms. Deep asymmetrical cracks were, maybe neurotically, opening on his body more and more often, each accompanied by a loud hissing. In the end I didn't even have to turn: the now-continuous hissing revealed his exact location.

I reached the square, intending to cross it and enter the park. Just then, however, the power directing the Yusian broke his resistance, completely overcame him, and forced him toward me. He rushed down the street in a blur. I waited for him a few seconds and then jumped to the side. His body zoomed forward, managed to overcome the accelerated momentum, and stopped in the middle of the square. This attack, as artificial as it was brainless, demonstrated once again that these creatures, whether collectively or separately, had no real clue how to conduct a "battle between the species"!

The Yusian was coming back, although at a considerably slower speed. Turning into the coffee shop with outside tables, I grabbed one of the "plastic" chairs and threw it at him. It stuck to his torso, melted, and flopped down like dough. Then the Yusian vigorously swept away the tables and other chairs between us, but his momentum saved me again. He stopped centimeters after he had passed me, so I took advantage of the opportunity to give him additional acceleration and pushed him from the back toward the nearest window, which even turned out to be useful for him. Without a sound, his body literally flew inside because the "glass" had opened before him and then quickly resumed its wholeness. The chair I threw had "recovered" as well.

Behind the window the Yusian again struggled to right himself. I pulled one of the tables to the tree nearby, stepped on it, and grabbed a suitable, not too thick, branch with my right hand. I jumped from the table, snapping the branch off just in time to confront the Yusian as he came back through the window. This branch wouldn't melt easily even in direct contact with him, which made him hesitate awhile. I had hoped for this reaction because hesitation encourages thinking and would help him come back to his senses.

I returned to the center of the square and threw away the useless branch. I was ready to play my last trump, to make my last stand. I undid the tape that held the detonator in place on my palm and raised my hand high, brandishing the detonator.

"I'm setting a ten-minute term!" I roared. "Ten minutes! *You decide!*"

I crossed my hands over my chest so that I could look at my watch ticking the seconds away. The detonator waited as well in its own heartless way. The Yusian was still standing in front of the coffee shop, surrounded by tables and chairs. The "Welcome" sign hung above him, and to the side, I could clearly see a commercial billboard picturing a Coca-Cola and a plate of fruit-filled wafers—all parts of the general insanity.

My watch kept ticking. We had four more minutes to go when the Yusian started plodding across the square. Against the background of white "marble" blocks, he looked fatally discolored. Doomed. He came closer, towering above me. Although heat radiated from him as if from a furnace, he was trembling, freezing—just like the young Yusian before I freed him from the garrotes. Even his eyes had the same look: begging for mercy, terrified of the close breath of death—which in this case was his own breathing.

"Run—Ter!"

I shook my head. "No."

"No," he repeated like an echo. His upper limbs alternately extended and shortened, at one point becoming so round that they looked like bombs attached to his torso. I stood in front of him without moving. His forehead had split in two: through the space suit, I could see both parts jerking back and forth as if trying frantically to escape. For the first time, I felt no disgust—only pity and compassion. This creature was struggling to fight for his own soul. He desperately needed help but wasn't getting any—despite the specialized organs for mutual aid, despite the thousand-year history of taking precautions, and unshakeable vegetable goodness. Nobody was willing to support him. He was a totally solitary, infinitely lonely alien.

His limb flew toward my chest, knocked me down, and held me there. Then his body phlegmatically flopped on top of me, threatening to suffocate me with his weight: a huge mass of flesh—no "bones" right now just because he didn't need them. He was relaxing his muscles—a soft weapon directed by some psychoconstruction in some other dimension.

Wretches! That's what all of you are. Oh, and I was wrong: your place is not above us. I alone, a single human being, rose above you.

The body completely covered me now with suffocating, impenetrable darkness. The detonator burned in my palm like a live coal—like Elia's burning, beating heart. I longed to fly to her now on the wings of meditation, and tell her—what?

I love you. My spirit overcame a whole cosmic world because your life was in my hand. Now I'm losing my strength under this monstrously spread body. I can't save you. But I would never, never have let the detonator if I had any other choice. Only death can loosen my fingers. This will be our retribution, because the explosion that you will hear for just a split second will echo endlessly in the mind of every Yusian. None of them will ever be the same again.

"No." The sound coming out of the Yusian chest was almost human. "No!"

———

We lay for a long time next to each other, Chuks gripping my hand in his alien extremities, gripping the hand that continued to hold the detonator. Around us was something flat and fruitless: exuberant, immeasurable quantities of deactivated pseudo-terrestrial substances that resembled dried mud. The square was gone. The entire settlement had disappeared.

We looked at each other and started pulling each other up.

"Damn it! You, rotten cosmic blackmailer!" Chuks cursed me.

Well, now we could communicate normally.

"Come on, don't effort yourself!" I replied enthusiastically. "Since no result is meeting you."

THE END